THERE MUST BE A[...]
A WITNESS TO TH[...]
WILL BE COMMIT[...]
GREAT MOTHER I[...]
THE LIFE-DENYING GODS, A CHILD TO
HEAR US AND WORK FOR OUR GOOD
MISTRESS, TO BEAR HER NAME AND
LOVE AND JUSTICE THROUGH ALL
DENIAL, ALL OPPRESSION, ALL
ABOMINATION.

Yes, thought Eirian, yes. Each of those ancient women *is* the Goddess . . . and so am I.

But since Luke's death, she felt the certainty of her childhood slipping away, the doubts of adulthood creeping in. She had the power to heal and to kill. So much responsibility . . .

She lay for a while watching dawn bloom in the window. Just as she drifted back to sleep, she woke abruptly with the sensation of flesh filling her mouth, soft like chicken skin, choking her.

In panic, Eirian sat up. The choking feeling vanished, but there was something hot in her mouth. She seized a tissue, and spat a mouthful of blood into it.

That had not been a dream.

Freda Warrington was born in Leicestershire and grew up in the beautiful Charnwood Forest area, which inspired a feeling for atmosphere, nature and fantasy. After training at Loughborough College of Art and Design, she worked in medical art, graphic design and illustration, while writing in her spare time. Her first novel, *A Blackbird in Silver*, was published in 1986, and she is also the bestselling author of the vampire series *A Taste of Blood Wine*, *A Dance in Blood Velvet* and *The Dark Blood of Poppies*. Her eleventh novel, *Dark Cathedral*, is also published in Signet and *Pagan Moon* is its sequel. She now lives in Derbyshire and, although writing takes up most of her time, she also enjoys music, reading, photography, art, tapestry, psychology, mythology, conventions and travel.

FREDA WARRINGTON

Pagan Moon

A SIGNET BOOK

SIGNET

Published by the Penguin Group
Penguin Books Ltd, 27 Wrights Lane, London w8 5tz, England
Penguin Books USA Inc., 375 Hudson Street, New York, New York 10014, USA
Penguin Books Australia Ltd, Ringwood, Victoria, Australia
Penguin Books Canada Ltd, 10 Alcorn Avenue, Toronto, Ontario, Canada m4v 3b2
Penguin Books (NZ) Ltd, 182–190 Wairau Road, Auckland 10, New Zealand

Penguin Books Ltd, Registered Offices: Harmondsworth, Middlesex, England

First published 1997
1 3 5 7 9 10 8 6 4 2

Set in 9½/11½ pt Monotype Baskerville by
Rowland Phototypesetting Ltd,
Bury St Edmunds, Suffolk
Printed in England by Clays Ltd, St Ives plc

With thanks for their help and encouragement, this book is for Mike, Freda, Jane, Storm, Alan, Luigi, John, Justina, Lynn and Pauline. With special thanks and best wishes to Anne and Stan.

Prologue

THEY nailed him to the cross in the late afternoon. There was nothing left of his tribe but circles of black ash, tent-poles lying criss-crossed like scorched bones, bodies blown apart by cannon-fire and bullets. Every man, every woman and child, dead.

The cross was an X-shape supported by a central post. The shaman hung on it like a five-pointed star, high up so that even through the blossoms of pain that coloured his vision, he could see for miles across the plain. It meant a lot to the invaders, men being nailed to crosses.

No one could claim to own the land that was his mother. Yet the invaders made that claim. They had come talking of some God who'd commanded them to make heaven on earth by seizing all the land and peoples in their way. They came with crosses, black books and guns.

Charged with the wisdom of the tribe, the shaman had known they lied. When the elders sought his advice he had told them; we must never compromise, never surrender.

His people had taken many of the invaders into death with them before they were finished. Dying bravely was better than living with the lies. But still he wept.

Now the invaders said there were devils in him, because he dreamed and prophesied. They'd mocked and spat on him as he lay bound, the last of his tribe. But it was only to hide their terror of his long face, of his wolfishly sinuous form adorned with feathers, pigments and bones. They'd nailed him up to make an example, a warning.

The nails were spikes of iron through his wrists and feet. The alien metal had split bone and nerve, shooting fire along his limbs. His chest was being crushed under its own weight, sweat dripped down the runnels of his weather-lined face, his heart laboured like a huge, deafening drum. His prick stood proud with the pressure of blood. But he refused to die with them watching him. He used his powers to drive back the pain for as long as he could bear. He urinated on them, shook his sweat on to their upturned faces and cursed them in his own language.

So they climbed up ladders and silenced him.

His flesh shrank and he screamed as the cold edge of the knife rasped softly into the hair between his thighs. There was a sawing motion, then his whole abdomen turned to a whirlpool of scalding agony. He stared down at the raw red wound where his genitals had been. He saw a ragged flesh-mouth pulsing around a river of blood. Then a spider's nest of cruel fingers came up, forced his jaw wide, and thrust the sacs of warm, bleeding flesh into his mouth.

He retched and choked around the foul sacs, but couldn't dislodge them. Between blood-loss and exhaustion his struggles soon ceased. He hung mute, dying.

When the sun sank, his executioners grew restless and left. They feared his friend, the night. Now he was alone, he could die.

As the dusk flowed in across the plain he watched the sky. His last ever sunset was a banner of garish pain. A sea of lemon-gold, acid as heartbreak. Streamers of violet and purple, the outflow of his agony. And at the centre, a boiling red wound.

As darkness closed in, the shaman felt others gathering around him. The souls of the dead. Not his tribe – they were long gone to other hunting grounds – but the older dead, the ones who still restlessly haunted the dream-realm. Tattered and forlorn, they came on paws, on hooves, on wings. They limped on broken bones, flesh flapping from their skeletal forms. Their eyes were lamps of demanding hunger. They streamed in across the vast sweep of the plain and huddled around him in the darkness, waiting.

When he'd been the tribe's dreamer he had communed with them. But now he was to join them, they became terrifying.

He tried to scream, but he only choked and gagged around

the soft flesh that filled his mouth. In dumb terror he cleaved to life, even in his bodily torment, knowing that when he died they would claim him.

No use. He was too near the edge to pull back.

He felt their hunger. They were thirsting to absorb his essence. All he had to do was stretch out his arms and float down and he'd be one with them. One with their anguish and rage. Memories would vanish, merging into a dark pool with all the others. Their rage and their eternal restless agony were his. They would all be one. A soundlessly groaning, weeping entity in the wilderness.

All he had to do was to let the pain go and fall towards them. All he had to do . . .

He stretched out his arms like a hawk. His wrists came easily away from the nails; the fiery pain faded like the light. He looked down into the darkness.

He fell –

And Eirian woke, shivering and sweating, her throat convulsing round a scream that wouldn't come.

The afternoon sun slanted through her window, shining on floorboards, the bedside rug, her school uniform folded over the back of a chair against a rough whitewashed wall, a teddy bear gleaming softly gold and benign on the seat. She'd been sitting up on her bed, reading a book for school, when she'd fallen asleep.

Her breath came in shallow gasps. She tried to swallow away the sensation of warm, fleshy sacs in her mouth. Choking.

It had been different from her previous visions, worse. Horribly, vividly real, full of ghastly meaning. There had been nothing good in it, nothing.

Eirian grabbed her teddy bear from the chair and huddled on the bed, resting her chin on its furry head. She listened for the rattle of a fly against her window pane. The window was a square of blue sky, mocking her fear. There was no fly, no nasty little enemy to taunt her – but there was something else. A pressure. A demand.

'Dear Goddess, what do you want now?' she whispered. 'Good Mother, please – I've done so much for you. Make this thing leave me alone!'

No answer from the Goddess. Eirian was alone. She felt the air around her thickening, sucking the rough walls, low ceiling and bare floorboards inwards. Eirian's skin was cold gooseflesh. She sensed icy air moving around her as if disturbed by some huge, famished predator . . .

She needed a weapon, not a comfort object. She put the bear aside and reached out to grasp the long ivory horn that stood propped against the wall beside her headboard.

The horn was four feet in length, a spike of ivory decorated with spiralling bands of gold-leaf and tiny carved figures. The Horn of Rebirth, a sacred medieval object of which she'd enigmatically become guardian. Its power was symbolic, a focus for the hands that held it. A wand of healing, fertility or destruction.

Downstairs in the cottage, Eirian could hear her mother, Beth, singing as she prepared their tea. But she might as well have been a thousand miles away.

The sunlight turned gelid, leaving images on Eirian's retinas of a five-pointed figure hanging against a vast prairie sky. She heard the tick of claws round her bed. Something unseen was pacing back and forth. Seeking revenge . . . That was all she could think of. Revenge for what she'd done to the Goddess's enemies.

Eirian sat cross-legged on the quilt, the Horn bone-hard in her palms. Sometimes she felt strong, filled with a milky moon-white power as softly irresistible as gravity pulling the tides. But at this moment she felt very much a child of eleven.

She sat frozen, breath held tight. She sensed the presence trying to break through into her reality; rearing up, its claws pricking and distorting the separating membrane like the skin of a balloon. She must keep it out.

The scrabbling grew louder. Then a head rose over the end of the bed. A black lupine skull, with green lamps for eyes.

Eirian screamed silently, breath rasping through her throat.

The apparition stared at her. It was transparent, like the ghost-animals in the vision. Flies circled it, like tiny evil souls.

'In the name of the Goddess, go!' she whispered.

She knelt up with the Horn held vertically, sandwiched between the blue denim of her jeans. The pressure against her loins sent a sensual thrill through her body. She visualized a shield of light protecting her. Then she gripped the Horn and lowered it to point at the haunting.

She imagined she was aiming it at all enemies of the Goddess; at priests, witch-finders, inquisitors, judges. Aiming it at Luke, the rapist and torturer of children, who would have killed her if she had not vanquished him. She visualized white light searing along the Horn from root to tip and all those powerful, cruel men falling away, screaming, their bodies imploding in blood and fire.

She felt the membrane shudder. The glowing eyes in the skull went dead. The head seemed to waver in a heat-haze, breaking up, dissolving to nothing.

'Go,' she said. 'You can't touch me!'

The Horn was inert in her hands, all the power in her mind, yet she felt the presence retreating. It went with painfully slow reluctance and she had to force it every step of the way.

It was gone. The rift was sealed. The world was back to normal. For now.

Then she heard her mother calling up the stairs, 'Eirian, how are you getting on with your homework? Tea's ready!'

She exhaled, her tension draining out to leave her shaken and heavy-limbed. Now she would have to go down and smile and pretend nothing had happened. So Beth wouldn't worry and ask questions.

All right.

Eirian slipped off the bed, propping the Horn against the wall. The moment she let it go, her head filled with a ghastly, echoing whisper. For the space of four breaths she felt she was no longer in her room but standing on a great stone in a forest. The stone was translucent, flickering with chaotic, eerie shadows, like a lens transmitting images from the ancient past.

And Eirian too felt translucent, a helpless channel for a thousand rushing voices.

'You are going to be punished. You can't escape vengeance. For what you have done and for what you are, you are going to suffer, and all those around you will suffer too. But don't turn to them for comfort, for those you love may be the ones who undo you.'

Chapter One

BETH knelt on the floor and lit a red candle on her altar. The floorboards dug into her knees through the worn rug. Creamy light washed the crooked walls of her bedroom, sending shadows to haunt the corners. She'd made the altar by covering a low table with a white cloth and decking it with the tools of her craft: incense burner, athame, pestle and mortar, water chalice, herbs.

Her daughter was asleep in her own room. Outside their cottage, Beth heard rain falling and a breeze stirring the woods; no other sound.

With trembling hands, Beth lit the incense. The fragrant smoke soothed her and she began to call softly on the names of the Goddess and the Horned God. A chant to concentrate her mind as she crushed dried petals in her mortar; acacia and myrtle, rose, jasmine and lavender. Carefully she tipped the fragments on to a disc of silk and added appropriate talismans, a red felt heart and a copper coin. The silk was blood-red to represent passionate sexual love. A love charm. For inner power, she added bay leaf, rosemary, oak and holly leaves. Then she gathered the silk circle into a pouch and tied the top with a thin blue ribbon, making seven knots.

As she worked she imagined her lover's face. Loveliest male face she'd ever seen. Elusive – but for a few seconds she captured him clearly and looked into tender green eyes that were shadowed seductively by long eyelashes and thick, dark eyebrows. She could almost have stroked his cheekbones and the perfect mouth on which a mischievous smile hovered. Could have pushed her fingers into his softly shining brown-black hair and pulled him to her . . .

Beth breathed on the charm, passed it through the candle flame and sprinkled it with water. She touched it to the pentagram she wore round her neck, filling it with all the energy she could raise. Charging it with air, fire, water and earth. A spell to bind her lover and bring him home.

A letter lay unopened on the rug in front of her. It was a long blue envelope, not flimsy airmail but good-quality paper, with a Canadian stamp and Newfoundland postmark. The first letter Morgan had ever sent her – and Beth daren't open it.

Instead she breathed deeply and tried to concentrate on her working. As if witchcraft could miraculously change what she feared the letter might say. That Morgan had decided to stay in Canada with his wife after all. That he'd thought he could leave, then realized he couldn't. That his work and his whole life were there, or that his wife was suddenly pregnant so he couldn't break her heart and he was sorry, he never meant to hurt Beth but it was all a mistake . . .

Beth's imagination went on weaving the worst possible things the letter could say as she worked. She tried to shut it out but couldn't.

She held the pouch to her heart. Now it was finished, it wouldn't matter what the letter said. The spell must draw Morgan home to her. It wasn't supernatural. The charm simply represented the focus of her will, her intent.

The door creaked open and Beth's eleven-year-old daughter, Eirian, stood in the doorway against the lamp-glow from her own room. There was no electricity in the cottage. Eirian was in pyjamas, with her long brown hair loose on her shoulders.

'Mum, what are you doing?'

'You're meant to be in bed,' said Beth.

'I could smell the incense.' Eirian came barefoot into the room, surveying the altar and the silk pouch in Beth's hands. Then she picked up the letter and examined it by candlelight. 'This is from Dad!' she said. 'Why haven't you opened it?'

'I don't know,' said Beth. 'It's the first letter he's ever sent me. I'm afraid to read it.'

Eirian understood. She raised her green eyes at the ceiling. 'Honestly, Mum, I don't know what you're scared of.' She shook Beth's shoulders, absolutely convinced of what she was saying. 'Dad will come back.'

Since she'd been tiny, Eirian had seemed wiser and stronger than Beth. So certain of everything. Beth said, 'I'm being stupid, I know, but . . .'

'Love charms won't make any difference. You know what real power is,' Eirian said intensely. She tapped the pouch. 'And it's not in here.'

'I know,' said Beth. She'd felt the true powers of the Goddess within herself – enigmatic, capricious and terrible – and she'd seen them working to devastating effect through her daughter. Biting her lip, she forced herself to dismantle the charm. She shook the contents into a wastepaper basket and dropped the cloth after them, saying softly, 'I don't need to do this. Morgan has to come back because he wants to, not because I've cast a spell.'

'That's better,' said Eirian, pushing the envelope at her. 'Now read it.'

Swallowing, Beth opened the letter and unfolded it, reading aloud while Eirian followed the words over her shoulder. Morgan had written in black ink on the pale blue wove. His handwriting was slanting, curly and somewhat hard to read; distinctive and sensual. In character.

' "Dearest Bethie," ' she read, ' "I only said goodbye to you a few hours ago and I miss you like hell already. I'm writing this on the plane. I wish you were here beside me. Instead I've got a flying phobic who thinks the plane will crash if he closes his eyes. I hope you can read my writing, only he actually grabbed my hand when we took off and I think he's broken a couple of fingers. My attempts to comfort him with safety statistics have been rebuffed so my only course of action now is to stare out of the window and leap up screaming, 'Oh, my God, the engines are on fire! We're all going to die!' As if I would . . ." ' Beth gave a quiet laugh. 'Knowing Morgan, he probably would,' she said. The letter was five pages long, chatty and full of his acid humour. Beth felt both relieved and foolish. ' "I know I'm rambling on about nothing, but it's the next best thing to talking to you so I don't want to stop . . . Well, I'm in the apartment now, having a coffee before I unpack. Had a good flight. It's sunny here but there's a bloody cold wind. Marian isn't back from the research trip yet; I've rung work and apparently the boat isn't expected back in harbour until next week. Seems a lifetime since I was last here, I can't believe it was only a fortnight. All I want is to be back in England with you. Can't even break the news to Glen (our boss), because he's on the trip too. At least I can go into work and sort things out to make life easier for my successor . . . It's hard waiting for Marian to come home, though. I just want to get it over with."'

Beth stopped, her heart sinking. So he hadn't seen her when he wrote this, she thought, but he must have seen her by now . . . damn, if only we had a phone! But then I'd be leaping out of my skin every time it rang. '"Must finish now so I can post this today. I'll write again tomorrow. I love you, can't wait to see you again. I hope you aren't having second thoughts, Bethie. All my love and kisses to you and Eirian, Love, Morgan."'

'There,' said Eirian. 'I told you everything's all right.'

'He hasn't told –' Beth stopped herself, thinking, no, I mustn't unload my fears on to Eirian. I should be reassuring her, not the other way round.

'He loves *us*,' Eirian said emphatically. She kissed Beth on the forehead. 'He's coming home, Mum. Now I'm going back to bed.'

Beth watched Eirian walking away, a slim graceful figure haloed by candlelight. Morgan's daughter. The Devil's daughter, according to Beth's mother.

I want to believe you, sweetheart, Beth thought. You always tell me the truth, don't you, Eirian? When you say Morgan is leaving his wife and coming to live with us . . .

She pressed the heel of her hand to her eyes to ease a familiar stab of pain.

. . . and when you tell me that with nothing but your will-power and your tender young hands, you killed my brother Luke.

*

The brilliant July sunshine came and went, tempered by small clouds. Beth watched swathes of golden light and cloud-shadows processing across the landscaped grounds of Wood-bourne Hall. There was a major show today, so the stately home and its grounds – about eight miles north of the Stafford-shire village in which Beth lived – were swarming with visitors. Beth watched Eirian and her ten-year-old friend Sam throwing bread to the ducks at the edge of a lake. For a pleasant few minutes she felt tranquil.

'Used to come here with Katy, before she went weird on me,' said her companion, Steve. 'Sam's always loved it.' Steve was Sam's father; he had been Beth's lover, until Morgan had re-entered her life. He was still her friend, for which Beth felt grateful and a bit guilty. They'd met after Steve's wife, Katy, had left him to join Luke's religious sect. Beth and Steve had both been alone with their children and in need of companion-ship. She still found him attractive, with his gentle temperament and unconventional appearance. His uncombed blond hair was half-way down his back and today he was wearing shredded jeans and an embroidered waistcoat over a purple Indian shirt. Beth, too, refused to conform. In a medieval-style dress of bottle-green velvet, her hair a jet-black veil that reached her waist, she sensed people looking at her. She was quite tall, very slender and striking, but the way she chose to dress – Pre-Raphaelite, witchy and gothic in style – was not so much an affectation as her armour against the world.

'I think my parents brought Luke and me here when we were very small,' said Beth, 'but I hardly remember it.'

'Oh, there's everything here now,' said Steve. 'Craft work-shops, tea-rooms, garden centre . . . The show's always good, they have a battle re-enactment, the Red Arrows and all sorts.' He trailed off. 'You don't regret coming, do you? You seem a bit preoccupied.'

'Sorry,' said Beth. 'All the shit that happened to us keeps going through my head and I can't get over it in a day.'

'Neither can I,' he said gently, 'but we can take a break from it for one afternoon, surely? It's for the children's sake, really. I want Sam and Eirian to have all the good times we can possibly give them, don't you?'

Beth couldn't argue with that. Luke had put them all through hell a very short time ago. The fact that Luke was now dead didn't help. She felt grief for him that she couldn't express, because of the terrible things he'd done; grief, too, for her mother, Olivia, who was now in a psychiatric ward, suspected of Luke's murder. Such a mess.

'I'm glad we came. The children are enjoying it, that's the main thing.'

Steve placed a hesitant hand on the small of her back. 'Have you, erm, heard from Morgan at all?'

'I had a letter yesterday. He hasn't seen his wife to tell her yet.'

'You know, if he doesn't come back –'

Beth folded her arms, turning away from him. Steve sighed, as if mentally kicking himself. 'Sorry, Beth. Why do I always put my foot in it? Of course he's coming back . . .' He cleared his throat and added uneasily, 'By the way, I'm sorry about the other night. I made a right fool of myself.'

'No, you didn't,' she said. 'I hate to see you upset, that's all.'

A few days ago Beth had gone to Steve's house. He'd had too much to drink and cried on her shoulder, telling her he missed her and wanted her back and he was so lonely . . . Feeling terrible, Beth had done her best to comfort him. She felt a lot for Steve and it would have been all too easy to go to bed with him out of affection and sympathy. But she'd stopped herself. It wouldn't have been fair, on Steve or on Morgan.

'But I want you to be happy with Morgan, I don't want you to think I'm going to be a prat about it.'

'Steve, it's all right,' Beth said firmly, wondering if it would be easier on him not to see her at all than to stay friends. As the children, in jeans and T-shirts, came running towards them, she made an effort to be cheerful. 'What haven't we looked at yet?'

'The craft workshops,' said Eirian. Beth was pleased to see

them both looking carefree, Sam's round, freckled face flushed with excitement. Impossible to understand how Luke could have treated a ten-year-old boy so brutally . . .

'Come on, then.' Beth took Eirian's hand and the four of them walked across the grass. Woodbourne Hall itself was an ornate mansion of wheat-coloured stone. On the vast lawn that spread between its gardens and the lake, crowds of visitors shuffled between clusters of tents and stalls, forming queues for ice-cream, candy-floss and hot dogs. Children shouted and screamed. In the centre, the roped-off arena was empty, while a disembodied metallic voice announced that events would begin in half an hour. The stink of fried onions mingled with the odours of crushed grass, of dogs and horses. Wasps pestered.

The mass of people made Beth feel hemmed-in and vaguely distressed. All these people, she thought, and not one of them is Morgan . . .

A pine-shaded drive led to the workshops, which were in an old stable block behind the Hall, with a courtyard and tea-rooms. Inside, an aisle along the left-hand side ran past a row of stalls that had been converted for craftspeople to make and display their goods. Beth drifted through the crowd, past counters of jewellery, patchwork bedspreads and lace pillows, herb sachets, dolls, embossed leather wallets and wood carvings. She was doing quite well at not thinking. Occasionally a single image would flicker into her mind – perhaps her mother's face, contorted as she spat curses at Beth – but she could dismiss it with only a slight shiver.

Eirian, Sam and Steve stopped to talk to a man who made vintage cars out of wood. Morgan would like those, thought Beth. I should buy him one as a welcome-home present . . . oh, God, that would be tempting fate.

She stopped to admire a display of teddy bears. One of them, a honey-coloured, sad-looking creature, appealed to her. 'Feel free to give them a hug,' said the woman who sat sewing behind the counter. She had a round, attractive face, with a mass of long, dark auburn hair and a friendly, almost mischievous expression. In her thirties, Beth guessed.

7

'I'd love to buy this for my daughter,' said Beth, testing the soft weight of the bear. 'How much is he?'

The woman told her. Beth nearly fainted. 'Oh, I didn't realize. She'll have to wait for Christmas.' She hurriedly put the bear down.

'I know, they do seem expensive if you're not a collector,' the woman said apologetically. 'They're not toys as such. They're all limited editions, you see, and there's an awful lot of work in them.'

'Yes, I can see that. They are beautiful. Thank you.' Beth moved on hurriedly.

A scent of old hay, manure and saddle soap was ingrained in the stables and the light was dingy. But as she moved to the last stall in the row, sudden colours blazed into her eyes, so unexpectedly lovely that she halted and caught her breath. A shining array of stained glass transfixed her; a melting rainbow of art nouveau designs, colours delicious enough to eat. The panel that hung against the window in the back wall was a coral-reef scene, with bright turquoise water, tropical fish like jewels caught between the waving stems of seaweed. In the side window was a design of a peacock, its tail a blue-green blaze.

An elderly man was standing at a work-bench in the centre of the stall, assembling glass shapes on a paper template. Panels and light catchers hung gleaming above his head. The counter that ran along the front was a forest of glowing lamps with intricate leaded-glass shades.

Beth was captivated. She had always loved stained glass but she'd never seen so much of it in one place, never such achingly clear, crystalline colours. They seemed to soothe a raw spot in her soul.

'How do,' said the man, reaching round to take a tool from a shelf on the back wall. He was thin, bald and slightly hunch-backed. His hands, mapped with blue veins and liver spots, shook a little as he worked. A plaque on the counter was engraved with the words, *Tom Jefferies. Custom-made stained glass and Tiffany lamps. Commissions taken.*

'Do you mind if I watch you working for a while?' Beth asked.

'That's what we're here for.' He picked up a soldering iron and began to run lines of leading between the glass pieces. It was a design of poppies, scarlet and deep green.

'What are you making?'

'Panels for a pub. Y'know, to go in the wooden partitions between the tables, like. Got twenty of these buggers to make, a big window for the door and some bar signs.'

'Is it difficult?'

'Not when you know how. Ask an original question, y'get a gold star.'

'Sorry,' said Beth. 'You must get fed up with hearing the same questions all day.'

Beth watched the solder running silver between the glass pieces as the old man drew the heated tip across it. She felt rooted here, almost excited in a strange way. As if he'd sensed her emotions, the old man looked up and said, 'Look, if you're that interested, why don't you have a go? D'you know how to cut glass?'

'No, but I'd love to try.'

'Let me finish this and I'll show you. You can practise on some scraps on the corner of the bench. Keep you out of my hair.' The man scratched his bald head and grinned, showing perfect white dentures.

The children had reached the stall next door. While they talked to the teddy bear lady, Steve came and leaned over Beth's shoulder. 'Sam wants to watch the displays in the arena. Are you coming?'

'Sam?' Beth called. 'What is there to see?'

With his glasses and gingery hair, Sam had an air of bewildered innocence. He still clung too tightly to Eirian's side for Beth's liking. 'Motorcycle display team, police dogs, Battle of Agincourt, birds of prey, the Red Arrows,' said Sam, counting them off on his fingers. 'And camel racing.'

'Camel racing?' Beth exclaimed. She smiled apologetically at Steve. 'I think I'll give it a miss. You take the children out to watch. This gentleman's offered to show me how he makes these wonderful windows and things. You don't mind, do you?'

'Course not,' Steve said, looking mildly disappointed. 'We'll come back for you later, okay?'

Beth watched them walk away down the aisle. It still gave her a pang to let Eirian out of her sight, even though she knew her daughter was safe with Steve. Must stop being over-protective, she told herself firmly. I can't keep her handcuffed to me.

'Come on, then, gel,' said the old man, beckoning her to one corner of the work-bench. 'What's yer name?'

'Beth.'

'I'm Tom. This here's a glass-cutter. Easy when y'know how. We'll start wi' straight lines; glass always wants to break in a straight line so curves are tricky, have to coax 'em. So, hold the cutter like this . . .'

He showed her how to score and break the glass, how to edge it with copper foil to take the solder. Beth's initial efforts were poor; first her glass wouldn't break, then it fractured in the wrong place and she cut herself. Soon, though, she began to get the feel of it. 'It obviously takes a lot of skill to get it right.'

Tom shrugged. 'Just practise. Don't worry too much if the pieces don't fit perfect, y'can fill the gaps wi' solder. Got a book here wi' some patterns in, but choose an easy one, eh? Don't get too ambitious. And just use these scraps here, don't touch the stuff at the back, all right?'

'Great, thanks.'

'Now y'can watch the stall while I go for a cuppa.' Tom rinsed his hands at a sink in the corner, wiped them on his apron, and walked off.

'The bugger, he just wanted someone to mind his stall!' Beth said under her breath. She found a template in Tom's book that she liked, even if it was too ambitious. Leaning over the bench, she began carefully to cut sections of crimson, deep blue and opalescent white glass. She was absorbed; no painful thoughts entered her mind.

While Tom was absent, the teddy bear woman appeared with a Thermos flask and stood watching Beth work. There were no customers; the workshops had emptied out when the displays began. Beth smiled at her and went on trying to cut a fiddly crescent of glass. The shape nearly came, then broke across the middle. 'This isn't as easy as it looks,' said Beth in exasperation.

'Tom does make it look easy, doesn't he? Mind you don't cut yourself.' The woman came to the work-bench and seated herself on a high stool. 'I'm Cordelia, by the way.' She was about five feet seven, the same height as Beth, but considerably more voluptuous. She had a lush hour-glass figure in maroon velvet. 'Dee for short.'

'Hello, Dee. I'm Beth. I won't shake hands, I've got glass dust all over them.'

'Don't get it on your dress, then. That is a beautiful dress.'

'Thank you. So's yours.'

'Another velvet addict,' Dee said with a smile. Her voice, too, was velvety with a slight lisp. She had a chirpy manner, warm brown eyes and full red lips. Beth liked her at once. 'Would you like a cup of tea?' Dee unscrewed two plastic cups from the top of the flask. 'You look like you need it.'

'Oh dear, is it that obvious?' Beth sighed.

'I don't want to seem nosy, but if you need someone to talk to . . . well, I've been told I'm a good listener, like my bears.'

Normally Beth would have politely evaded the offer, but she had the eerie yet pleasant feeling that they'd known each other for years. It might help to tell a stranger the anxieties she couldn't confide in Eirian or Steve.

She sat down on another stool, cradling the plastic cup between her hands and facing Cordelia across the work-bench. 'It'll sound awful,' Beth began. 'My lover is meant to be leaving his wife for me. He's gone to tell her. They live in Canada, you see, so he's had to go all the way back there and I don't know when he's coming back and I just have to sit and wait . . .'

Dee's bright, long-lashed eyes opened wide. 'Oh! What a dreadful situation. You must feel awful.'

'I'm so scared he'll decide to stay with her after all. I can't concentrate, can't sit still, can't sleep. And I feel so bad about his wife. I'd hate her to feel like I'm feeling, but I can't give him up. And I have tried.'

'Do you really not trust him?' Dee said darkly.

'I do, in my heart. It's just that so much has gone wrong in my life I can't believe anything can go right. And I think Morgan's . . . well, too easily persuaded, sometimes.'

'Do he and his wife have any children?'

'No, fortunately.'

'That's something. My husband buggered off and left me with two small boys; oh, I'm over it now but it was hard at the time. Married men!' Dee shook her head, bitterly sympathetic. 'I suppose you didn't find out until it was too late.'

'No, no, it's not what it sounds like,' Beth said hurriedly. 'We were kind of childhood sweethearts, Morgan and me. I was eleven and he was thirteen when we met. I used to stay with my grandparents in the summer holidays and Morgan lived in the same village. I made friends with his mother, Rhianwen, first. I had to visit them in secret because my family absolutely hated Rhianwen.'

'Oh dear, why?'

'Long story, but partly because Rhianwen's a witch and my parents were fanatical Christians. So I deceived them. Morgan and I got on really well.' Beth cleared her throat before making the confession. 'Only when I was fourteen, we got on a bit too well and I, um, had a baby.'

Dee's eyes opened wide. She looked scandalized, yet thrilled. 'Was that the little girl who was talking to me?'

'Yes, that's Eirian.'

'So that interesting-looking chap who's with you isn't your hubby or anything?'

'Ex-boyfriend,' said Beth. 'We're still friends. He's been terribly understanding.'

'He sounds nice,' Dee said thoughtfully. 'So, I bet your parents weren't too pleased when they found out you were pregnant.'

'Oh, God, they went crazy and so did Rhianwen. They stopped us seeing each other. They even stopped us writing. I didn't see Morgan for nearly twelve years. I thought he didn't love me, that I was just one of his adventures – maybe that's why I get this awful feeling every time he's out of my sight. However, Rhianwen had told him I didn't want to see *him* either. He went to university, came out with a degree in zoology, got married and went to work at a sea-mammal research centre in Newfoundland. Meanwhile I ran away from home, a few days after my fifteenth birthday, with a newborn baby in my arms.'

Dee's cheerful expression turned serious. 'My God, how awful.'

'It was.' Beth shuddered. 'My parents couldn't forgive me; they were making my life hell. But when I ran away to Rhianwen and Morgan, they'd left the area, so I had no one.'

'That's terrible. I mean, if I had a daughter who did that – well, I'd be annoyed, but I'd soon get used to the idea. It's nature, not a crime.'

'Mine didn't see it like that. They thought I'd gone to the Devil. *Literally*. I ended up living in a caravan for five years; a family of travelling farm-workers took us in and looked after us. Later I got this job as a housekeeper on a farm and a cottage to live in, and we were doing okay, just my daughter and me . . . until I met Morgan again.'

Beth couldn't bring herself to explain the events that had led to the meeting. They had already been plastered over the newspapers, '*Mystery death of cult leader in child kidnap*,' and all that. She hoped Dee wouldn't associate her with the story, if she'd seen it. She went on, 'I thought Morgan would have forgotten me, but when we saw each other it was like we'd never been apart. We were still in love. Within about two hours we knew we had to leave our partners and stay together.'

'Oh, my God, that's incredible.' Dee added conspiratorially, 'Is he good-looking?'

'Gorgeous.' A warm rush of memories made Beth smile.

'Beautiful. That was what got me into trouble in the first place. But it wasn't just that; looks don't mean anything without personality, do they? He has this real sweetness about him; the charm of the Devil, according to my mother, which just made him more attractive. He wasn't gauche like teenage boys usually are. He was intelligent, very sure of himself, kind of mysterious and knowing. God, I was so infatuated with him, I can't tell you. Okay, I know it was wrong of him to seduce me so young, but he was irresistible. I was innocent, ignorant really, and it could have been a ghastly experience – but Morgan made it wonderful. We used to make love in the woods and fields. Couldn't leave each other alone. He was so loving. It was unbearable, having his child but not being able to see him for all those years.'

'So when did he reappear?'

'All of three weeks ago.' Beth gave a hollow laugh. 'That's why I'm so scared it's all a mistake. We haven't got past the stage of sexual infatuation and I'm not sure that's enough to compete with a wife. Or we could just be totally incompatible.'

To herself, Beth added, *and one of us might decide our relationship is too incestuous after all.* To shock Dee with that revelation, however, might be too much.

'You should have more confidence in yourself,' said Dee. 'You're beautiful, Beth, and I can tell you're a nice person; I feel like I've known you ages. You've obviously been a wonderful mother to his child. So, you should be asking yourself if *he's* good enough for *you*! Believe in yourself.'

'I do, most of the time,' said Beth. 'It's just that where Morgan's concerned, I fall apart. I try to act cool but I can't bear to think of him with his wife, I'm so jealous. In a way it would be less traumatic if he stayed in Canada and I could just carry on as normal. So I'm scared he will come back, scared he won't –'

'He can't win, can he?'

Beth laughed, mocking herself. 'I'm afraid I might do something to ruin everything. So much has happened to me lately, and my friends think I'm this unshakeable earth mother who copes with everything ... I just don't seem to be doing very well at the moment.' She drained her cup and handed it back. 'I think you have a customer. Thank you for the tea.'

'You're welcome.' Cordelia moved away, looking back over her shoulder. 'You will come back and let me know what happens, won't you, Beth? And any time you feel a bit fed up, come and keep me company, eh?'

Beth nodded, smiling. She liked Dee. Beth found it easy to attract friends and she loved them ... but no one could take her heart and tie it in knots, except Morgan.

Beth heard jet planes roaring overhead, but she went on edging her glass pieces in copper foil, brushing them with flux as Tom had shown her, then running solder between the joints. While she was working she didn't notice that two hours had passed; she didn't think about Luke, or her mother, or even Morgan. Two minutes after the noise of jets faded, visitors began to flow in and Tom reappeared.

'Enjoy the Red Arrows?' Beth asked wryly.

'Grand,' said Tom, misty-eyed. 'I were in the RAF. Let's see what you've done.' Peering at her handiwork, he looked pleasantly surprised. 'That's good, lass. That's very good. You'll put me out of business.'

Beth laughed. 'I don't think so. May I keep this, if I pay you for the materials I've used?'

He waved his hand impatiently. 'Don't be daft, take it. Y'need to black and polish the leading, first though.'

'It's really kind of you to show me –'

Tom looked straight into her eyes, and his grey irises were as brilliant as glass-drops. Beth felt a current pass from him to her, an unseen jolt of energy, recognition, fear; she couldn't define it. But it made her break out in gooseflesh from head to foot. 'Know an artist when I see one,' he said. 'I'm going to need you, some time soon. I were being canny, gel, not kind.'

He turned away to his own work and Beth, stunned, didn't reply. Then Eirian and Sam came running in to tell Beth excitedly about all they'd seen. Eirian, for once, seemed an ordinary child, merry, uncomplicated and wholly caught up in the moment. Beth wished she would stay that way.

Steve didn't reappear at once. Beth could hear him talking to Dee. Oh yeah, she thought, since when has Steve been so interested in needlework? After a few minutes they came round the partition together, both bright-eyed and laughing.

'Hi, how's it going?' Steve said to Beth. 'What are you making?'

'A light catcher,' said Beth. 'It's a bit wonky.'

As Steve and Dee bent to look at Beth's creation, they stood very close for strangers and Beth perceived the chemistry between them. She wasn't exactly jealous; Beth didn't want Steve to spend his life pining after her. It would be wonderful for him to meet someone as nice as Dee. Yet she suddenly found it a little scary to realize that if Morgan didn't come back, Steve might not be there to pick up the pieces. Serves me right for taking him for granted, Beth thought ruefully. So many changes in three weeks! I knew it was a risk, letting Morgan back into my life . . . but I'll never regret what happened between us.

'Let's see it properly,' said Steve. 'Hold it up to the window.'

Beth cautiously lifted the panel of soldered glass. To her relief it stayed in one piece. The light shone through and it was beautiful.

'Oh, Beth, that's weird!' Dee exclaimed. The unease in her voice made Beth shiver.

'What do you mean?'

'Don't get me wrong,' Dee said quickly. 'It's lovely but I can see a pattern in it that's not meant to be there. It looks like a face with lightning hitting it, and drops of blood coming out.'

'Oh,' said Beth, dismayed. 'It's meant to be flowers.'

'I know, I can see that. The colours are gorgeous, but . . . Oh, drat, now I've seen that weird face in it, I can't make it go away.'

Beth looked harder, and suddenly she, too, could see something. Glaring eyes, a long face neither human nor animal, a mouth stretched round what seemed a clot of blood – but it wasn't in the glass. It was in her mind. Something ancient flying towards her across a dark ocean –

A child's shrill scream nearly sent her through the roof in shock. It was Sam, screaming and screaming, pointing along the aisle at something Beth couldn't see.

Steve was already with him. Trembling violently, Beth put down the light catcher and rushed out of the stall to help comfort the boy.

Sam went on screaming even while the adults held him, his face scarlet, tears running down behind the thick lenses. He couldn't speak to tell them what he'd seen. Visitors were staring at him, some crowding round, others pretending not to notice. Just a kid having a tantrum – but Beth knew it was something worse.

'What is it, Sam? What?' Steve was saying desperately. And Beth thought, I knew Sam wasn't better. I knew Luke had done some terrible, permanent damage to him.

Eirian was at Beth's shoulder. 'Let me talk to him,' she said. Beth ignored her, but Eirian forced herself between Beth and Steve and said angrily, 'Mum! Leave him with me!'

Shaken, Beth and Steve gave Sam up to Eirian. 'He was doing so well,' said Steve, almost in tears. Beth said nothing, only held on to his arm.

They watched as Eirian took Sam into the corner of the stable and whispered to him. Gradually Sam's cries sank to whimpers, then to snuffles. Eirian gave him a tissue and went on talking softly, intently, to his bowed head.

'Is he all right?' asked Dee.

Five minutes went by, then Sam, seeming much calmer, raised his head and wiped his nose. Beth felt Steve breathe out with relief.

'He's okay,' said Eirian, bringing Sam towards them. 'He thought he saw someone who looked like Luke.'

'Jesus,' sighed Steve.

'Give him this,' said Dee, pressing something into Steve's hand. Beth saw that it was a small bear. 'If he thinks he's too old for it, tell him it's an investment.'

'He's not too old at times like this,' Steve said, smiling at her. 'Thanks, that's really kind. Say thank you, Sam.'

'I think we should go home,' Beth said quietly. 'Sam's tired.'

As they walked back across the grounds towards the car park, Steve tightly holding his son's hand, Beth asked Eirian, 'What did you say to him?'

'I just told him that Luke was a stupid, nasty man who hurt children because he was too weak to pick on adults,' Eirian replied, 'and that Luke couldn't hurt him any more so it's all right to stop being frightened. Sam is going to get over it, Mum. I'll make sure he does.'

As she looked at Beth with steady, clear eyes, Eirian seemed ageless. And Beth knew it was not just Eirian's words but her power of will that had reached Sam. Her daughter's strength seemed awesome, because it was not that of a child.

Eirian's going away from me as she grows older, Beth thought with a sensation like falling. I can see it happening. I used to share all her visions but now she's closed to me, I don't know what she's seeing or thinking ... She's mine and not mine.

And this strange child's father would soon be winging his way across the ocean towards Beth, like the sinister face she'd seen in the glass. A sensation of thrilling terror went through her, the rush of air over ancient wings. Whether the darkness was Morgan himself, or something he would bring with him, Beth could not tell.

Chapter Two

'Dɪᴅ you fuck her?'

'Marian.' Morgan pushed one hand into his hair, resting his elbow on the table. 'I wish you'd let me finish explaining.'

'No, we need to establish that most basic fact. No lies, no qualifications. Tick one answer only. *Did you fuck her?*'

Marian, his interrogator, was sitting opposite him at the round dining table in their apartment. Sunlight made a blazing crescent round her sleek, short blonde hair. Through the window behind her, Morgan could see rows of painted wooden houses stepping down the hill, and beyond them the ice-blue ocean, no colder than the expression on his wife's face.

To pass the time until Marian returned from the voyage, Morgan had spent the morning in the laboratory, reorganizing – for the benefit of whoever replaced him – the information he'd collected on whale populations over the past five years. Then he had gone down to the tanks to check on the marine animals which would be released when they'd recovered from illness or injuries. Afterwards, he'd walked along the harbour and looked at the cold, wild ocean that lay between him and Beth. He was quietly saying goodbye to his life in Newfoundland. Letting go.

He recalled a nightmare of the waves turning crimson with blood; a ghastly premonition that had driven him back to England. A vision sent by Eirian, calling him to come home and help her. But how the hell could he explain that to the utterly sceptical Marian?

He'd stood there for a long time, thinking about Eirian. Throughout the years when he and Beth had been apart, the idea that they had a daughter seemed unreal, a dull, abstract pain that he'd done his best to ignore. But then to meet Eirian and find she was not an ordinary child but a striking creature with her own powerful personality and outlook on the world . . .

To hear her coolly admit that she had killed Luke . . .

Morgan hadn't seen the body but he'd heard a report of Luke's injuries. Torso slit from throat to groin, eyes staring as if he'd seen a vision of hell . . . and his beautiful daughter claimed to have done that.

He was shocked, yet he wasn't horrified. He knew that Eirian had only done to Luke what Luke was about to do to her and Sam. It had been his life or theirs. In effect, Luke had designed his own fate. Eirian was like a goddess of justice, turning cruelty back on the perpetrator so that they suffered exactly the degree of suffering they'd tried to inflict on others; no more, no less.

So, she'd killed an evil man to save Sam's life; that was all Morgan needed to know. He loved her unconditionally. But how eerie to know he'd fathered her, to be in awe of his own daughter!

In the afternoon he'd returned to the apartment to wait restlessly for Marian. He turned on the television and found a new American channel, called the True Light Network, devoted to evangelizing. Morgan's heart sank. A sweaty preacher was exhorting the viewers to live by the Bible, to shun sex and abortion and sin if they wanted to be saved and if the holy spirit inspired them to spread the word, call this toll-free number and have their credit cards ready . . .

Shades of Luke. Morgan's finger hovered on the remote but he watched in morbid fascination. This preacher was more charismatic than most, dark-haired and deep-voiced, grossly overweight but with an immensely commanding presence. Luke was gone but there was always another to replace him. Eirian said they had the souls of flies; however many you destroyed, there were always more.

'Millions of poor saps are probably watching this and believing every word,' he murmured, flicking the preacher out of existence. That was when he heard the door opening, footsteps and the sound of bags being dropped in the hallway. Faintly he heard Marian saying, 'Doesn't look like he's back – yeah, okay, that'll be great.' But when he went through to the kitchen-dining area to meet her, she was alone.

She'd thrown her jacket on a chair and was taking a beer from the fridge. It was a small, open-plan apartment; they'd never meant to stay here permanently. In jeans and a cream cable sweater, Marian looked slender, athletic and wind-tanned, tired but still exuding the sexual radiance that had first drawn him to her.

Morgan usually went to kiss her but this time he didn't. Marian didn't comment on this, only looked at him with a kind of guarded surprise, as if she knew something was wrong.

'Hi, I didn't realize you were home,' she said brightly. Her Canadian accent was soft, verging charmingly on Irish on some syllables. 'Want a beer?'

'Er – yes, please. Look, if you're still angry with me for walking out on the trip –'

'I'm not.' She opened the beers. 'Don't give it a thought. How long've you been back?'

'About a week.' Morgan stood with his hands pushed into the pockets of his jeans, and he knew he couldn't stand here chatting as if nothing were wrong. The longer he left it, the harder it would be to tell her. He had to do it now.

'Things okay at home?'

'More or less, but –'

'So it was a false alarm, the terrible premonition?' She gave him an ironic look, eyebrows lifted in admonishment.

'Not exactly. Marian, something's happened. I have to go back to England. Permanently.'

She stared at him. With the two bottles in one hand she walked to the table and sat down, her blue eyes fixed on him, expressionless. 'What is it? Is your mom ill?'

Morgan pulled out a chair and sat opposite. 'No, she's fine. Oh, shit, this is really hard. I've met someone.'

'Met someone,' Marian echoed. 'As in, another woman? Not as in, "I sat next to this great guy called Larry on the plane," eh? Hey, you're only twenty-eight, kid. You're not meant to go menopausal until you hit fifty.'

'Sorry.' His mouth was so dry it was all he could say. He took a mouthful of icy, bitter beer.

'Christ, you were only gone two weeks!' she snapped. 'How could you have met anyone that serious?'

'It's someone I knew before. You remember the girl I told you about, the one who had my baby? It's her. Beth.'

'As in, "Oh, my God, Beth?"' Marian said acidly. 'Go on.'

Marian sat twisting the bottle between her fingertips as he tried to explain. Her healthily glowing face became a hostile mask, a fortress against him. She listened for a minute or two before she broke in, flinging the question like a knife.

'Yes, okay, I fucked her,' Morgan sighed. 'She fucked me, we fucked each other. We were in bed within about an hour of me turning up on her doorstep, if you must know.'

'You never did waste any time.'

'It might have been an hour and a half. I wasn't watching the clock.'

'Am I following this? You haven't seen this female since you were sixteen and on the basis of screwing her for two weeks, you want to go and live with her?'

'No.' Morgan sounded calm, but inside he felt like death. This was exactly as bad as he'd known it would be. 'Because we love each other.'

Marian looked incredulous, then devastated, then furious. 'This isn't supposed to happen. I always told you, if you have an affair, I don't want to hear about it. You don't have to make a drama out of it and *leave*, for God's sake!'

'I've never been unfaithful to you,' he said, looking hard at her. 'This is not an "affair". I should never have left Beth in the first place.'

Her eyes glittered, but the tears didn't fall. 'You can't do this! What about work? You can't walk out on the project, it's another five years' work at least!'

'Glen will have to replace me,' he said quietly.

'What the hell will you do in England?'

'We have zoologists there, believe it or not. I've written to universities around the Midlands –'

'Got everything worked out? And you just came back to let me know? Thanks. You could've phoned and saved the air fare – or is it supposed to ease your conscience, telling me to my face?'

That, Morgan felt, was uncomfortably close to the truth. 'I didn't want you to think I don't care. Marian, I'm really sorry. If I hadn't met Beth again I would have been happy with you, but . . .'

'You fucking bastard!' she yelled. 'No one does this to me!' Her face incandescent, she snatched up her bottle and for a moment Morgan thought she was going to throw it at his head. Instead she banged it down on the table, leaped up and stalked to the window, arms wrapped tightly round herself. He left her for a few minutes, watching her pass through anger, rejection, shock. Slowly the tension in her arms loosened and her head came up. She was in control again.

Morgan went to her, put an arm round her shoulders and said, 'It's not your fault, you've done nothing wrong. But I have to be with Beth and Eirian.' He expected to be pushed away, but instead she turned into his embrace.

'So, are you planning to stay here until you leave?' she murmured, pressing against him. She smelled of the sea, damp wool, fragrant shampoo. 'Sleep with me a few last times. You know, for old times' sake. You might remember what you liked about me . . . Then you can go back and tell Beth, "Sorry, but I'm staying with my wife."' She gave a short laugh. 'So, you staying?'

Morgan felt a flicker of desire, despite himself. The warm curves of Marian's body were more familiar to him than Beth's and that familiarity would have made it so easy . . . 'I can't. I'll go to a hotel,' he said. 'I never cheated on you, whatever you think. And I won't cheat on Beth.'

'Oh, you can't be unfaithful to *her* with your own wife?' She shoved herself away from him. 'You passed the hypocrisy test, so get the hell off me!'

Morgan opened his hands in defeat. 'Do you want another drink?' he asked.

'Open the Glenfiddich,' she said sardonically. 'Let's celebrate.'

'Jesus, you're weird,' Morgan said softly. He took the bottle from a kitchen cupboard and poured two Scotches. 'Why can't you just cry?'

'What, throw myself round your ankles and beg you to stay? You know I hate all that sentimental shit. And you're the same, so don't call me weird. I hope *she* knows that.'

'She's not sure about me,' said Morgan, leaning back against a kitchen counter. Marian came and leaned next to him, a foot of tension-charged space between them. 'After all, I wasn't there for her when she was pregnant, and for all she knew I didn't give a toss. Worst mistake I ever made in my life. I wanted to see her but I let myself be terrorized out of it by other people. I should have found her, even if it meant missing university and her family prosecuting me.'

'Get real. You'd have gone crazy.' Marian took a mouthful of whisky and stood cradling her glass, biting her lower lip. 'The second or third time we made love, remember? You said, "Wow, that was wonderful," and I said, "Sure, but who the fuck is Beth?" The fact that it took you about a year to stop calling me Beth shoulda given me a hint.'

Morgan winced, embarrassed at the memory. 'At least I told you about her. I never kept it a secret.'

'Sure, you made a fourteen-year-old girl pregnant. Great going, kid.'

'I know, I was arrogant, I thought I could have all the fun I wanted and never pay. But I loved Beth, I really loved her. I didn't realize how much at the time. I closed my mind to what I'd done, I suppose. I want to make it up to them.' He smiled. 'You should see Eirian. She's wonderful. I'm not missing out on any more of her life.'

'And what if we'd had a kid, eh?'

'Well, we haven't. You said you didn't want any yet.'

'Lucky for you.'

Morgan tasted his Scotch then put the glass down. He didn't want the cotton-wool feeling it could give him. Once, after a

24

party, too much alcohol had led him to tell Marian secrets she didn't want to hear; they'd nearly split up over it and he had regarded drink with distrust ever since. Still, he had to touch on those matters again, if only to explain. 'The reason I walked off the boat and flew to England – it was a genuine pre-monition.'

'Oh, please!'

'Listen, will you? Beth had a brother called Luke. He led one of these evangelical Christian sects and he decided that Beth's daughter had the Devil in her. So he kidnapped Eirian and another child, thinking he could save their souls. Beth was frantic when I arrived. I helped get the children back. I didn't do it on my own but I helped. Luke was crazy. He starved the children, beat them, tried to brainwash them . . .'

Marian was staring at him now, shocked disbelief etched over her hostility. 'What?'

'He raped the little boy. He might have done the same to Eirian. He would have killed them if she hadn't – I mean, if we hadn't got them out in time.'

Morgan stopped, his throat tight. Marian said, 'Jesus,' but didn't ask for details.

'I know how you feel about that "supernatural crap",' he said, 'but you tell me how I *knew* something was wrong. Eirian says *she* called me. She needed help, so she called me.'

'I don't want to hear this.' Marian spoke quickly, shaking her head. Flat denial. 'I've warned you before about laying this stuff on me. I always said your mother was nuts, but you're just as bad!'

He was galled by her long-standing dismissal of his and Rhianwen's beliefs. 'But if you'd experienced the things I have –'

'Stop, Morgan.' Her eyes met his, a brief glacial flash. 'Stick to the stuff I understand, like adultery. I mean it.'

'Fine. I wanted you to know the whole story, that's all.'

She breathed out heavily, tilting her head back. 'Maybe I could compete with the woman. Not with the beloved daughter,

I guess. You sure you're not going back for the child's sake? Guilt?'

'I'm going back because I love Beth. There's something magical about her. We just looked at each other and that was it. I'm sorry.'

'Of course you're sorry. Don't state the obvious.'

Silence. Morgan could sense Marian withdrawing, severing the links between them, protecting herself. That she could be so strong and calculating shocked him. He'd known that once he told her, there would be no going back; she didn't give second chances.

Marian composed her mouth into a bitter smile. 'Beth must be pretty amazing, eh? Let me guess. Does she live in a cottage? Keep lots of cats? Have long auburn hair?'

'Used to be brown,' he murmured. 'Now she colours it black. Three out of four.'

Marian responded with a vindictiveness that shook him. 'Why don't you just marry your mother and have done with it?'

'You should have married your father,' he retorted.

'Yeah. Listen, I adore my dad but I know he cheats on my mom. She told me never to look on marriage as anything but a business arrangement. That way you don't get hurt.'

Morgan stared at her. 'Is that all it was to you?'

'C'mon, we both knew the score. You had to have me because the guys on campus were all over me like a rash – and vice versa. Trophy wife, trophy husband. Didn't the wedding pictures look great? And we both wanted the same things from work. "Husband and wife team" – that's a great angle for getting where you want to be.'

The light was changing. As the sun moved along its arc, the apartment suddenly seemed grey, empty. A deception. And Morgan experienced a chilling feeling he had not had for years; the sensation of being watched, haunted by a shadow with a long thin face and famished eyes.

'Didn't our marriage mean *anything* to you?' he said hoarsely.

'Oh, the sex was great. You were the first good-looking guy

I met who was actually good in bed too. But if you mean "love" – oh, spare me. You know something? I always knew this would happen. I knew you'd go back to your mom one day. I knew you hadn't forgotten that girl. And I sure as hell know you never loved me, but that's okay, because I never loved you either. I don't actually think I can "love" anyone like that.'

'It must have been more than that! You make it sound like we were just using each other!'

'Weren't we?'

'Marian!'

'Oh, you're not going to come over grief-stricken, are you? You're the one who's leaving me, remember?' Her voice was a scornful weapon; there was no softness in it to which he could appeal. 'And I'd like you to do it now. Go. Fuck off.'

'I don't want us to part like this. If we could talk –'

'You wanna stay friends? How sweet. I'd hate you to lose any sleep feeling guilty. Get a fuckin' solicitor and I'll talk to him!'

'Don't be like this.' As Morgan spoke, there was a knock at the door. 'Oh, shit, who the hell's that?'

Marian didn't answer. Her expression was closed. She turned away and poured herself another Scotch.

Morgan opened the door and found a tall, well-built man in jeans and a khaki jacket outside on the landing. Their boss. Glen's face was reddish from the sea-winds, but his grey hair and white-streaked beard looked freshly groomed. He was holding a pizza carton in one hand and a bottle of Californian white grenache in the other. Seeing Morgan, his face fell, then lifted again too quickly.

'Hi, Morgan, didn't realize you were home.'

'Obviously.'

Glen frowned, suddenly wary. 'I'm interrupting, aren't I?'

Marian called out, 'No, you're not. Come in, Glen.'

Glen waved the pizza box vaguely. 'Plenty here for three.'

'Don't worry about it,' Morgan said sourly. 'I'm leaving.' He grabbed his leather jacket from the chair. 'How long's this been going on?'

'What?' said Glen indignantly. He tried to look dumbfounded, but his cheeks flushed a deeper red. Marian only glared at Morgan over the rim of her glass, as if to say, *'Wouldn't you like to know?'*

'Well, you've got something in common with my mother after all,' Morgan told her, suddenly bitter. 'You both like older men.'

He pulled on his jacket and made for the door. He tried to ignore the feeling, or at least to attribute it to stress, but it seemed something dark slipped after him like a wolfhound at his heels.

'You've got a lot to learn about her,' Morgan remarked as he passed his boss – his ex-boss, very soon. 'She hates white grenache.'

When the nightmares came, Eirian fought to seize and control them.

She saw Luke through a strange greyish lacquer that made the bare room unreal and menacing. The fluorescent light burned into Eirian's eyes like a migraine. There were no sounds, only silent images and terror. She saw Sam, bent double and crying bitterly as Luke plunged himself grotesquely into the little boy's body. She saw the mean little scalpel glinting in Luke's hand. And knew she must stop him, stop him before he stuck the blade into Sam's thin white stomach and gutted him in pursuit of his sick fulfilment . . .

Now Luke was coming for her instead. He was so big and powerful in his dark suit, his eyes cold with rage, one hand encased in a thick spiked glove. A warrior, bristling with spikes and whips, even his erection a cruel, penetrating weapon . . . and Eirian was only a child, trapped in the dimensions of her slender, defenceless body.

Her strength lay inside her. Eirian thrust the power of her will into his mind, bending his vile urges back on themselves.

Impossible reversal, witch turning on witch-hunter. With the red laser of her will-power, she gutted him.

Ichor, membranes and slippery intestines slid out as he screamed.

But Luke wouldn't die. He was coming for her again, eyes mad in his white face, blood spilling from the vertical rip down the length of his stomach. Blood spattered from his lips as he raised a shaking finger to point at her. '*Witch. Satan-loving witch!*'

Eirian felt the Horn of Power bone-hard in her palms. She aimed it at Luke, at all religious bigots who persecuted others in the name of God. The Horn blazed and crackled with lightning. Luke spiralled away, screaming, his body carbonizing in a sheet of flame –

Eirian woke, exhausted and shivering violently. The room was black, the window a square of brownish-silver light.

'That was only a dream,' she told herself firmly, 'not a vision.'

Her visions were something else. From birth, Eirian had been pulled into physically real experiences of the past and forced to bear witness to the hysteria of the witch-hunts. She'd seen ludicrous beliefs about the Devil used to gather all land and authority to the Church. She'd seen old, harmless women tortured, hanged, burned. Eirian herself had narrowly escaped death. She'd saved one life, rescued the Horn from desecration, and in the process seen enough horror to turn her mad.

Yet she hadn't asked why. She knew the Goddess had chosen her to be a witness, an avenging force – because *someone* had to do it. So, thought Eirian, why *not* me?

Those journeys were over now, but Eirian knew the Goddess hadn't finished with her. She recalled her vision of the dying shaman – a warning? – and the malevolent little head staring at her from the foot of her bed, and voices whispering. The Goddess's enemies wanted revenge on her, but the threat wasn't clear-cut. Sometimes her head ached from trying to perceive it clearly.

She also remembered an older vision. A swirling grey image, shrouded in white noise like a picture transmitted across a vast gulf of time; a group of wise women chanting.

The end of the Goddess times is coming when men will hate us and turn against us and deny their own Mother but men can never destroy her. She will endure through all and there must be a child, a warrior, a witness to the crimes that will be committed against the Great Mother in the names of the life-denying gods, a child to hear us and work for our Good Mistress, to bear her name and love and justice through all denial, all oppression, all abomination.

Yes, thought Eirian, yes. Each of those ancient women *is* the Goddess . . . and so am I.

But since Luke's death, she felt the certainty of her childhood slipping away, the doubts of adulthood creeping in. She had the power to heal and to kill. So much responsibility.

Eirian was brave; she wouldn't give in to nightmares or threats. On the contrary, she felt it was her duty to protect her family from them. She could use her persuasive powers to heal Sam; she could hide her fears from Beth and Rhianwen. But that meant she must absorb all the darkness herself, and be strong for them while feeling there was no one to be strong for her.

One thing she knew. Everything would change when her father came back.

She lay for a while watching dawn bloom in the window. Just as she drifted back to sleep, she woke abruptly with the sensation of flesh filling her mouth, soft like chicken skin, choking her.

In panic, Eirian sat up. The choking feeling vanished, but there was something hot in her mouth. She seized a tissue, and spat a mouthful of blood into it.

That had not been a dream.

When he left Marian, and in the subsequent few days while he sorted things out at work, Morgan kept feeling that something was following him.

He couldn't have described it precisely. It wasn't visible; it was a feeling. A darkness the size of a wolf, lurking behind him. Inexplicably he sensed it as something very fragile and hungry, which was struggling to come closer and feed on his strength. It was something connected with his decision to go home. Connected with the image of his mother practising her gentle witchcraft, grinding herbs by candlelight, stroking a sick cat with her healing hands. And with Beth, too. Morgan and Beth making love on the Hellstone, twelve years ago, while the shadowy spirits of the woods moved around them . . .

And with another experience he preferred to forget.

He didn't have to go back into it. He could change his mind, ride out Marian's wrath and stay in Canada . . .

At times the shadow was absent, as if its hunger had worn it to nothing. But at others, it seemed huge, as if it had risen up from all fours and swelled in size. Morgan experienced it as a blunt dark bulk, tall and swathed in animal skins, something feral that was neither human nor beast. It had a long, razor-boned skull for a head, with spiralling horns. It danced, swaying slowly in some primeval rite, its gaze burning fixedly into his back. Sometimes the sensation was so fierce that his skin crawled. But when he turned round, there was never anything there.

Chapter Three

Bᴇᴛʜ haunted her cottage like a premature ghost, unable to rest. She had found a blood-soaked tissue in Eirian's room. Eirian confessed to a nosebleed, but insisted she felt fine. So Beth took her to school, did her morning chores at the farmhouse, then came home and tried to occupy herself – but in Morgan's absence, nothing seemed real.

She'd visited Tom and Dee at Woodbourne Hall a few times, which helped. Although she didn't like imposing on Steve for lifts, he was glad of any excuse to see Dee. Beth was pleased to see them getting on so well, Steve looking happy again. They never made Beth feel excluded; rather, they were cosseting her, trying to take her mind off the waiting.

The Cleave family at the farm, too, were being very understanding, stressing that they'd somehow manage without her if she left, but if not – if Morgan didn't come back – she would always have a home and work here. Everyone was so kind. It was almost more than she could bear.

The cottage, which had come with the job, was semi-derelict, requiring nineteenth-century drudgery to keep herself and Eirian warm and fed. But it was home; Beth loved the fields and the woods all around. I never planned to live like this or be a housekeeper for ever, she thought . . . but where will we live, what will I do without a qualification to my name? The future was grey and evanescent. Morgan's letters, seven in all, lay on the kitchen table where she'd reread them – but this morning's was a week old and none of them said, 'I've told Marian, I'm on my way.'

At least she had letters now, and photographs of herself, Morgan and Eirian together, hugging and laughing in Rhianwen's garden. Beth smiled at the photos. They were like sacred icons, because for years she had had nothing.

Beth climbed the steep stairs to her bedroom and changed out of her work jeans. Her cats came too; slate-blue Bast, white Cerridwen and creamy ginger Eostre. Aware of their huge eyes following her, she put on a black velvet bodice and a long burgundy skirt of Indian cotton. These were old, comfortable clothes but they still looked good, flattering the curves of her breasts and her slim waist without revealing any flesh.

She turned in front of a full-length mirror, posing satirically. Her hair was striking. Satin-black and full of rippling waves, it slid sensuously over her shoulders as she moved. Beth had dyed it ever since she'd run away from home, a symbol of the death of her old self. She liked the witchy look it gave her. I look okay, thought Beth. I can see myself as pretty, even sexy, if Morgan can . . . but then, would he love me if I were short, fat and plain?

'Stupid question,' Beth said aloud, pulling a face at herself. 'But if *he'd* been ugly or just ordinary, he wouldn't have cast this spell over me, either. Would he, Bast?' Bast miaowed. She was a sleek, cobby cat, barely showing her fifteen years. Rhianwen had given her to Beth the very day she'd met Morgan. She'd always felt the cat to be a link between them, more subtle and mystical than Eirian. 'If it's shallow to love beauty, why is it so incredibly powerful?'

Beth glanced at her bed, where she and Morgan had made love all night, the first time he came back. It had been magical, more than sex . . . How unreal it seemed now.

Taking some clean laundry to Eirian's room, Beth noticed the Horn propped by the bed. Usually they kept it hidden, but sometimes Eirian liked to have it near her. Morgan said it was the tusk of a whale, the narwhal, but in medieval times they'd believed it to be a unicorn's horn, a sacred pagan symbol of fertility and healing until the Church stole it and sanitized its meaning. During her strange visions of those times, Eirian had physically rescued the Horn and brought it back for safekeeping . . . how, Beth would never understand.

She touched it. The shaft felt warm. The tiny figures carved along its spiralled ridges imprinted her fingertips like Braille and she had a vision. She saw two figures struggling for possession of the Horn, as if connected by a bolt of creamy lightning; a young girl confronting a patriarch in holy robes. The image encoded a timeless world beneath the surface of everyday life; the weight of God-given authority warring against the bewitching, feminine powers of night.

That touch contained everything. The ecstasy of sex, the terror of nearly losing Eirian, the horror of Luke's death . . . everything.

Beth shuddered and took her hand away. She felt shaken, but strangely aroused. Did it presage anything? 'I'm paranoid,' Beth told the cats. 'But after what happened to us, why the hell *shouldn't* I be paranoid? Come on, girls.'

She went downstairs to the shabby kitchen, sat at the table and opened her sketch pad. She had begun drawing her own stained-glass designs, discovering an artistic talent she hadn't known she possessed. She'd made a couple of them, with Tom's guidance; her favourite, a panel of dolphins leaping through blue waves, was propped in the kitchen window. She'd made it for Morgan. Tom was showing her other techniques, traditional leading and glass painting. Something wonderful happened when she worked with glass; she forgot everything else.

Almost like being possessed, Beth thought. She picked up a panel she'd made the previous day and held it to the light. It was about ten inches across, an abstract she'd thrown together from off-cuts. The colours were stormy: dark violets, greys, bronzes, spikes of dark red. It resembled a ragged flower with thick stamens protruding, like some poisonous, exotic bloom from an H.P. Lovecraft tale . . . Beth wondered if it looked any better upside-down.

She gasped. Now it looked like a semi-human figure; a wild tribal dancer adorned in a savage outburst of feathers. For no rational reason, the image filled her with dread. It was the darkness hurtling towards her . . .

She lost the image and it was a jumble of colours again. She tried to get it back, so absorbed that a knock at the front door nearly launched her through the ceiling.

Beth found Rhianwen on her doorstep, dressed in jeans, green Indian velvet jacket and a floppy hat. Rhianwen made no concession to being fifty; her face retained its strong beauty and no grey was allowed to show through the deep hennaed auburn of her hair.

Beth's heart quickened, but she tried to sound nonchalant. 'Hi, this is a nice surprise.' She saw Rhianwen's white VW Beetle parked in the rough lane that ran between the cottage and the meadow opposite. Sunlight glimmered through misty drizzle.

'Morning, love,' said Rhianwen. Years of living in England had not muted her melodic Welsh accent. She flourished her car keys. 'Are you busy?'

'Not particularly. Why?'

'Morgan's phoned from Heathrow. He's getting a coach to Birmingham and he wants me to pick him up from the coach station, about half eleven. Thought you'd like to come along for the ride.'

Beth experienced a near orgasmic rush of elation and terror. She'd psyched herself up to wait for weeks; this news seemed indecently sudden. 'Oh,' she gasped, looking at her watch. Ten past ten. 'Let me put my shoes on. Have I got time to change? Damn, I wish I'd washed my hair!'

'You look fine.' Rhianwen smiled, conveying several shades of pleasure and regret. 'Come on.'

Rhianwen had owned the Beetle as long as Beth had known her. It seemed a matter of pride for her to keep it running. The engine made a throaty drone as Rhianwen pushed it to sixty along the motorway.

Beth was still getting used to the idea that her grandfather and Rhianwen would soon be living together, that they'd been lovers almost thirty years ago and never fallen out of love. It was only after Beth's grandmother had died a couple of weeks ago that the affair had come to light – and the real reason Rhianwen had kept Morgan and Beth apart.

'Thanks for bringing me,' said Beth. 'I didn't think you'd want to.'

'Can't fight the inevitable,' Rhianwen said cryptically. 'Are you okay? I thought you'd be excited, but you look as white as a sheet.'

Beth tried to laugh it off. 'I'm really nervous,' she said, pressing her clammy hands together in her lap. 'Worse than the first time he came back.'

'Don't be daft,' Rhianwen said gently. 'It's only Morgan, not royalty.'

'You can take him for granted, he's your son, but I still wonder if he'll vanish for twelve years every time he's out of my sight! I can't believe this is for real. I'm so wound up I don't know what to do with myself.'

Rhianwen made an uneasy movement of her shoulders, the shifting of suppressed guilt. 'This is what you want, isn't it? I know how much Steve meant to you.'

'Well, I suppose it would have been easier for everyone if I'd loved Steve more,' Beth said quietly. 'Steve's sweet, he deserves a break. He took it too well when I broke up with him, as if he expects life to kick him in the teeth and just goes, "Okay." I expect he'll be working at the garden centre until he retires.'

'Probably thinks he's lucky to have a job, the way things are,' Rhianwen put in. 'Goddess knows what Morgan's going to do.'

'Oh, he'll find something,' said Beth. 'Always lands on his feet, you said. Maybe that's what worries me. His looks and charm will always get him what he wants. He talks about being a university lecturer; imagine the effect he'd have on all those eager eighteen-year-old females . . .'

Rhianwen gave a grim smile and shook her head. 'It's natural to have doubts.'

'Are you having doubts about my grandfather?'

'Happens to us all, love. I'm used to living on my own; I don't know how I'll feel, suddenly having Randolph about the place.'

'I don't want Morgan to rush into this, then find out it's not what he wants,' said Beth. 'You've been very kind and understanding, but I know you'd prefer it if we didn't get back together.'

Rhianwen started to protest, then sighed, 'Well, all right, I can't deny I'd rather it hadn't happened. I've nothing against *you*, Beth. I love you, I can't imagine anyone better for Morgan – if only you hadn't been Randolph's granddaughter. As a pagan I should be perfectly open-minded and tolerant, but in real life I don't always live up to my own ideals. I'm a solitary, hedgerow witch; I've never been into Wicca, with its covens and hierarchy. But I wanted a daughter, someone I could pass the knowledge on to. If I could have had a daughter with Randolph, that would have been wonderful. But I didn't, so you became my daughter instead. I still think of you as Morgan's sister. And I was very pissed off with him for not behaving like a brother. For taking you away from me.'

This admission startled Beth. 'But he hasn't! We'll all be together. That's all I want.'

Rhianwen paused; traffic noise saturated the silence. 'Look, Morgan's all right. Okay, I'm biased; he has bad as well as good in him, and I can't make promises on his behalf. But I do know he adores you. Goddess knows, I fought against it for long enough. I waved the white flag, you got your own way – so what are you scared of?'

Now Beth was quiet, while the world ribboned past her as if she would travel for ever and never arrive. An image of winged darkness hung in the back of her mind, elusive and disturbing. She said, 'I'm scared of the power he has over me.'

The coach was late.

'Traffic on the M25,' a passing employee of the coach company told them in a rich Brummie accent. 'Gets worse every day.' He walked on, shaking his head at the craziness of the world.

'If he'd phoned last night, we could have picked him up from Heathrow,' said Rhianwen.

'Then we'd all be stuck on the M25,' Beth said brightly.

The coach station was concrete, wire fences, and patches of diesel. Bleak. When Rhianwen took off her hat and shook down her hair, the dash of auburn warmth plunged Beth back into the summer days of her adolescence. The lush woods, the Goddess's presence in every trembling leaf, and the carnal thrill of Morgan's body pressed hard against hers in a bed of grass and moss . . .

Beth went to the ladies' room and pressed cold tap-water on to her face to steady herself. When she emerged, a tall beige coach had pulled in with 'Gatwick–Heathrow–Luton–Birmingham' signed on the windscreen. Travel-worn passengers were leaking out, gathering round the sides of the coach to collect their luggage from the holds underneath.

Beth's heart gave a double jolt. Was this Morgan's coach? She couldn't see him . . . couldn't see Rhianwen either. Shadows moved inside the coach behind tinted windows. Pallid travellers, loaded with suitcases, barged past her. A mass of people, none of them Morgan . . .

Then a pair of black leather-clad arms embraced her from behind, nearly causing her to leap out of her skin.

'Hello,' he said into her ear, his hands folded over her waist. 'Did I make you jump? Mum said you'd gone to the loo, I thought you'd climbed out of the window and made a run for it.'

'Oh, my God,' said Beth, turning round in his arms. 'Where were you?'

'Round the other side, getting my bags,' said Morgan, tilting his head at the coach. 'We've loaded the car; trouble is, I think you and I will have to walk. I didn't realize I'd got so much stuff; had to leave a load behind, as well. Oh, God, it's good to see you.'

He hugged her. Beth was enclosed against the firm, slender body which she'd never been allowed to know often enough or long enough; held by strong, lean arms and warm hands. Her pulse throbbed frantically. She breathed in the good scent of Morgan's body, felt his lips moving passionately over her face. She couldn't look at him, she was dazzled.

'You know, I wasn't sure you'd be here,' he said. 'I'm so glad. Eirian at school?'

'Yes. I'll fetch her about half three.'

'I can't wait to see her. Oh, Beth.' Morgan rested his head on hers and she sensed his profound fatigue.

'Are you all right?' she asked softly, looking into his tired green eyes, stroking the stubbly line of his jaw.

'Just knackered. I couldn't sleep on the plane or the coach.' But what she saw in his eyes was weariness of spirit, even regret. It must have been harder than he'd realized to leave his wife; perhaps too hard. He added, 'I'm fine, now you're here.' He kissed her mouth then slipped one arm round her shoulders. As the coach pulled away, Beth saw Rhianwen by the Beetle, waiting for them. 'Come on, let's go home.'

Rhianwen's house, Blackthorn Cottage, stood at the edge of Lullingford, the beautiful village where Beth's grandfather also lived. Her stone and brick cottage was surrounded by farmland, gained by a rural lane and fronted by tall hedges, within which the garden was an idyll of laburnham and buddleia, honeysuckle, roses and fragrant herbs. Rhianwen had run a cat sanctuary here for thirty years; the villagers knew her as a healer of animals, a friendly witch. To Beth's mother Olivia, locked in her extreme Christian standpoint, Rhianwen had been a literal acolyte of Satan; to Beth's grandmother, a treacherous husband-stealing bitch.

And to Beth – a child stumbling by accident into this enchanted domain – Rhianwen had been mother and sister, teacher and friend; even an enemy for a while but now, tentatively, a friend again.

The one thing Beth could never feel towards Rhianwen was indifferent.

After lunch they all went in the Beetle to pick up Eirian from school. The school was five miles away in the next village, Barton-in-the-Elms, where Beth lived. It was Eirian's last term there.

Beth felt unreal. Her anxieties seemed ridiculous now, but

the reality of Morgan's presence was, in a strange way, harder to handle. How weird it seemed, to have him beside her at last, this beautiful, affectionate stranger; for even though they'd rescued Eirian from Luke together, and made love feverishly as they tried to catch up on twelve lost years, Morgan still seemed a stranger.

Long separation had given him a gloss of unattainability in Beth's eyes; he was like some mischievous angel or demon, whose purpose was to seduce her and cruelly vanish – and then, just when she was over it, to come back and do it all again.

Beth was desperate to ask what had happened in Newfoundland; Morgan showed no inclination to tell her. But as Eirian came across the school playground and saw him, the expression on her face made all Beth's turmoil worthwhile. Pure delight. Eirian flung herself on to him and he lifted her up, hugging her, laughing.

'Marvellous, isn't it?' Beth said drily into Rhianwen's ear. 'They've only known each other two weeks and they're in love.'

Rhianwen said nothing. It suddenly struck Beth that she was trying not to cry. Realizing, perhaps, how misguided she'd been to keep Morgan away from Beth and Eirian for all those years.

When Eirian saw her father at the school gates – a tall, extremely handsome man with longish, thick hair as dark as his leather jacket – she felt a thrilling wave of happiness. She'd known he was coming but not so soon! She ran to him; he picked her up and clasped her hard against him, and they were both in heaven.

Then she saw the entity behind him. It was like smoke. Tall and horned; a hint of wings. Incomplete. But within the swirling smoke she saw glittering black specks, like hot motes of coal leaping out of a fire to burn her mind.

She clung to Morgan, burying her head on his shoulder. He probably had no idea it was there. Only latching on to him to find *her* . . .

I won't let it spoil things, she thought fiercely.

When she looked up again, the shape had gone.

Beth was pleased when Rhianwen invited her and Eirian to stay that night. They dropped in at Beth's for her to pick up some clothes, then returned to Blackthorn Cottage for a celebratory meal. Beth loved the friendly atmosphere of Rhianwen's house; the big kitchen, with its scrubbed pine furniture, quarry tiles and brick fireplace, the living room with its tasselled floor cushions, ivory walls adorned with Goddess images. Scents of incense, herbs and flowers pervaded the rooms. As a girl she'd felt so at home here that it was like bereavement when she had to leave. Even Rhianwen's oldest cats – slender grey Ankaret, big black-and-white Llew – were still curled up by the cooker, as in the old days.

Morgan seemed preoccupied. When Rhianwen dropped in questions about Marian, he evaded them. Over dinner they talked about his flight, the cats, village gossip; nothing that really mattered. Beth joined in gaily, but she was anxious. *Now it's real, us being together, is he thinking it's a mistake and not a romantic dream after all?*

After coffee, Morgan stood up and touched Beth's shoulder. 'Will you excuse us for a while? I want to talk to Beth alone.'

Leaving Eirian with Rhianwen, they went upstairs to Morgan's room. It was as Beth remembered, with a sloping ceiling and dormer window on one side, a soft green carpet, shelves full of books. The creamy walls had been freshly painted and the posters replaced by framed prints, but the single bed still had the same patchwork cover on which they'd made love, the last time the fourteen-year-old Beth had seen him.

The memories rose up whispering around her. Passion, darkness, fears. Morgan moved wearily, as if about to tell her something he could hardly bear to say. *I'm going back to Marian after all . . .*

'I brought you a present,' he said. Fishing in a suitcase, he drew out a long coat of the softest, finest black figured velvet she'd ever seen.

'Oh, my God, it's beautiful,' she gasped, stroking the fabric. 'Thank you. It must have cost a fortune.'

'Not really. S' only money. Try it on . . . Oh yes, you look great in it. I knew you would. I got Eirian cowboy boots. I'll give them to her tomorrow, when I'm something like awake.' As he helped her out of the coat and hung it on a chair, their tension was mutual. Then Morgan lay down on the bed and said, 'Come here, Bethie.'

She lay down beside him, her arm over his waist and her head cradled against his shoulder. He was wearing pale blue jeans and a black T-shirt under a soft denim shirt, tucked into a belt with a heavy silver buckle. He looked, felt, smelled so gorgeous that Beth could have ravished him there and then, but he only hugged her and looked at the ceiling.

'Sorry I'm so tired. Are you all right? You've seemed a bit distant all day.'

'*I've* been distant?' Beth exclaimed.

'Yes, you know; determinedly bright and cheerful, like you were thinking, "Damn, I wish the bastard had stayed in Canada!"'

Beth gave a dismayed laugh. 'You were thinking that? Oh, my God, no, it's just – well, you obviously had a lot on your mind and I didn't want to push you about it so I was just trying to – you know, give you time.'

'I'm tired, that's all. It's not just the travelling, I haven't slept properly for days.'

She slid her hand under his collar to rest on the warm skin of his neck; his hand came up to clasp her wrist. 'Was it awful with Marian?' she whispered. 'I wish you'd tell me.'

Morgan exhaled slowly. Finally he said, 'Yes, it was about as bad as it could be. I suppose it could have been different, but not worse.'

Beth experienced a pang of sympathetic guilt. 'Was she very upset?'

'I'm not sure. Shocked, definitely. Then furious. It was as if I'd wounded her pride more than her heart. She said, "No one does this to me." And made out she'd never loved me, anyway. We were just using each other, according to her.'

He sounded so bereft that Beth's heart twisted in pain. 'Of course she loved you. She was hurt, so she was trying to hurt you back.'

'I don't know. I thought it was a good marriage; now she tells me it was a cynical exercise in convenience.'

Now Morgan's body felt inert and unresponsive to Beth's touch; she wanted to seize him, drag him back to her. To have him lying beside her, but agonizing about Marian, was unbearable.

'Did she try to persuade you to stay?'

'No. She told me to fuck off. It gets better. I found out she's been planning to screw our boss; he turned up with a bottle of wine, obviously expecting her to be alone. Nearly had a heart attack when he saw me. They didn't deny or admit anything, but I think it started on the research trip because I wasn't there. It wasn't revenge, it was before I told her. Maybe they've fancied each other for ages and I just didn't notice. That's how much I meant to her. Jesus, Beth.'

He pressed his face into her neck and she felt his tears running on to her skin. She held him tight, feeling hollow, torn open. After a while she said, 'Do you want Marian back, now you can't have her? Because I can't live with that. I won't live with it.'

Morgan raised his head and looked at her, as if her tone had really shaken him. 'No, Beth, I want you. But I can't just cut myself off, any more than you can cut off your feelings for Steve. I'd have to be made of stone, and then how could I care about you?'

'I know,' she said, kissing him. 'We knew this wouldn't be easy.'

Hugging her, he went on pensively, 'Maybe Marian's right, I never loved her. I married her because she made me feel safe; you know, she was good company, self-sufficient, and didn't demand constant affection I couldn't give her. And she wanted a decent-looking partner she could work with. And, okay, it was nice to have a regular sex life, because contrary to what everyone seems to think of me, I've never been into screwing around. Even if it was safe these days, I wouldn't do it.' Beth said nothing; it still tortured her, to think of him with anyone else. 'Anyway, she was always pissed off at me for not shaking off my attachment to England, and my mother, and paganism. And you. I never went on about it, but she knew. Said she half expected me to go home one day.'

'Perceptive woman.' Paradoxically, knowing Morgan was hurt – human – made Beth feel more confident of herself. She began to relax. 'I hope she'll be okay.'

'Kind-hearted Beth,' he murmured. 'Well, I hope Marian and Glen will be very happy. If she's doing it for career advancement, good luck to her. I thought of wiping all my work off the computer to get my own back, but that would only have hurt the whales, not them.' He lay back, one hand behind his head, and smiled. 'I got one good thing out of it. Glen's given me the most amazing reference.'

'Grovelling git,' said Beth. Morgan burst out laughing.

'Thanks.'

'What for?'

'Making me laugh. Let's not talk about it any more. How are you, Bethie? What have you been up to?'

Apart from going crazy? she thought. Then she smiled, thinking about her stained-glass efforts. 'I'll show you tomorrow.'

'Sounds intriguing.'

'As for the stuff with Luke and my mother . . . I know it has to be faced, but I don't want to think about it now.'

'You won't be facing it alone. I'm here.' Then he asked off-handedly, 'Have you seen Steve?'

'Yes, I've *seen* Steve. I haven't slept with him, if that's what you mean.'

'I didn't sleep with Marian either,' Morgan said gently. They looked at each other; Beth lowered her eyes and nodded, not wanting to give away how relieved she was. His fingers moved over her cheek and into her hair. 'Bethie, I can't wait to make love to you. Unfortunately I can hardly raise my eyelids, let alone anything else. We'll wait till tomorrow night, eh? Make it special.'

'It was always special,' she said, smiling, a little disappointed though she could see he was exhausted. 'Well, I don't want to leave you, but you'd better get some rest. I suppose your Mum wants me in the spare room with Eirian.'

'Yes, like she hasn't realized how Eirian got here in the first place,' Morgan said sleepily. 'I'll tell Mum where babies come from in the morning.'

'Shut up,' said Beth, climbing off the bed and leaning over to kiss him. 'Go to sleep.'

In the night, Rhianwen was woken by the sound of her bedroom door creaking open. A figure padded across the carpet, lifted the duvet and slid into bed beside her.

'Grandma?' said Eirian. 'I can't sleep.'

'Come on, then.' Rhianwen put her arms around the slender, pyjama-clad form. Strands of Eirian's hair got in her mouth; she disentangled them and smoothed the long, thick hair. 'Nothing wrong, is there?'

'No, but it's a bit like Christmas Eve, my Dad coming home. I wish he hadn't gone to bed early.'

'You'll see him tomorrow,' said Rhianwen. 'You can see him every day now.'

'And you won't stop us any more, will you? You can't.' The words were quiet but barbed. Rhianwen paused, her fingers playing gently with Eirian's hair.

'Love, when you said you'd never forgive me, you didn't really mean it, did you?'

'I meant it,' answered Eirian. 'It's not that I don't love you, Grandma. But you broke Mum's heart, keeping my father away. If I hadn't called him home we'd still be apart now – and that's what you wanted. How can I forgive you?'

Rhianwen's heart sank. 'Darling, I've explained why. Didn't you understand?'

'Because it was incest,' Eirian said bluntly, counting on her fingers. 'Because Mum was fourteen and her parents threatened

45

to report Morgan to the police. Because Granddad Cross would have been angry. And so they didn't have any more children in case they had two heads. What didn't I understand?'

Rhianwen gave a deep sigh. Holding Eirian was like embracing a small vampire; an intransigent child-goddess with the bite of a snake. Rhianwen saw herself as embodying the Goddess's gentle, healing aspect, but there was something of the darker side in Eirian; the Crone. Goddess of death and transformation, wisdom and judgement. Harsh, sometimes, but scrupulously fair.

No, Rhianwen thought, there's Maiden, Mother and Crone in us all. We'd be incomplete otherwise. 'All right,' she said, 'but I have said I'm sorry.'

'No one asked me what I thought!'

'I never meant to hurt you. I honestly did what I thought was best. I know I seemed cruel, refusing to take you and Beth home with me, but I knew you were safe with the travellers. It might not have crossed your mind, but it hurt me too. I wish I *could* have given you a home and seen you grow up! It's in the past, anyway. Perhaps if I'd let them live together, they would have split up long ago. Had you thought of that? Or perhaps I made a mistake.'

'We aren't meant to make mistakes!' Eirian said fiercely.

'Who's "we"?'

'Witches. Followers of the Goddess. Wise women. We're supposed to *know*.'

'Yes, well, if you go around thinking you're infallible, young lady, you're going to be in for a few nasty shocks. Is that what you can't forgive me for – not being perfect?'

Eirian's breathing was like the darkness itself breathing in and out. 'No,' she said at last. 'But can't I love you and be angry with you at the same time?'

Rhianwen gasped at her relentless logic. 'Well, I suppose so. If that's how you feel. I won't be angry back. You can always cuddle up and talk to me like this.'

'I know,' Eirian whispered, softening a little. 'And I will. But sometimes you annoy me, Grandma. You just *exist*.'

'I what?'

'You just live. You don't act. You love the Goddess but you don't tell anyone!'

'Exactly. I did tell Beth, but only so she could make her own choice. Pagans work life out for themselves, they don't go out evangelizing. I hate that kind of thing, I've seen it destroy people! Like your poor grandma, Olivia.'

'I don't mean to evangelize, just tell the truth,' Eirian whispered. 'If I could explain what I went through, with Luke and the witch-hunts, other people could make a choice too.'

As she spoke, Rhianwen became chillingly aware of a presence in the room with them. She sensed a shadow, cut from the nothingness of space, rearing over the bed. A great head seemed to nod above them, sniffing, questing. Rhianwen caught her breath, felt Eirian's fingers tighten on her arm.

Then the moment was over. The room slipped back to its normal dimensions. Rhianwen didn't ask Eirian if she'd sensed anything. If she hadn't, it was unwise to put ideas into her head.

'I wish I could tell people,' Eirian went on evenly, 'so it doesn't happen again.'

Rhianwen released her breath. 'I understand how you feel, but we must keep ourselves to ourselves. You *can't* overcome the prejudice out there.'

'Can't I?' Her voice was dark and determined.

'You're still too young, love. Don't try to take too much on. Be a child for a few years. Be one for Beth's sake, at least.'

'I can't be what I'm not,' said Eirian.

Chapter Four

THE shaman fell forward off the cross. Echoes of bodily pain came with him. Nails ripping through wrists and ankles. Fire burning in his groin. Blood dribbling from his lips and the choking foulness of his genitals packed between his tongue and throat.

Fleshly pain faded, but the torture inflicted by the invaders reached into the other-world. The psychic torment of injustice, which would never allow him to rest.

The shaman felt dead souls flowing around him in the darkness. They came to him like dying animals going to ground, as if they'd been waiting for him, their guide and saviour. They came on broken limbs, fur flapping from eyeless skulls, brains dried in hollow craniums. Their ghost-bodies were pierced by arrows and bullets, blackened by fire. They formed a blanket to catch his falling soul. He sank into them. They poured in upon him until he could no longer separate himself from them.

They all became one and rolled like tumbleweed across the bleak plain, a groaning, sobbing phantom. Human awareness faded. All that remained of the shaman was anguish and need; that of his animal tribe overlaying his own. They were all pain, all hunger, no love.

It was for their sake he must find release. Not only for himself. So they searched desperately without knowing what they sought, but needing *something*, a fount of power in which to quench their craving. Blindly they roamed the dream-realm, hunting psychic scents, as instinctive as a ravenous, wounded wolf . . .

Eirian writhed in her sleep, fighting to escape. She was being tossed on a dark ocean of souls, drowning in their unutterable distress. Nothing to cling to, no ground beneath her, no up or down or past or future. She cried soundlessly. No sense to anything, only anguish. Centuries rolled painfully over her . . .

There was a thread pulling her, black and gold twisted together.

Now she saw a great, rounded stone beside a river. Pine trees and walls of rock towered all around. She – or the shaman-entity – knew that this was a sacred place. They were being drawn here by energies concentrated in the stone. Formless, tingling vibrations. And she sensed also that this rock existed in two places at once. The second place had softer trees, no river and no mountains, yet it was the same. It seemed quite rational that in the dream-realm, two places could be one. A site of pagan worship, where no invasion, no Church exorcism could ever drive out the throbbing powers of nature. Yes, this was where the entity needed to be.

Generations had come here to call on the spirits of nature. Eirian saw ghosts on its weathered surface. A man alone, watching the sky. A couple making urgent love by moonlight. A child sitting on its centre in baking sunshine, squashing a fly.

The shaman-entity reached out, but the power only spilled through fingers, claws, paws. Useless. It hurled itself at the rock, breaking apart and reforming like a wave. Weeping for release. The energy in the stone wasn't enough, there had to be a focus, a living being through which . . .

But Eirian saw humans around the stone, wielding crosses and Bibles. They had the hard faces of the God-fearing invaders, who believed their God sanctioned atrocities against devilish animals and heathens. Luke was gone but his essence – that of all fanatics who saw the Devil in anything alien – lived on. They grinned coldly at her and whispered, *You will die as the shaman died, for what you did. For what you are.*

Eirian was waking up, separating herself from the hideous vision. A pang of defiance went through her. 'Leave me alone! You don't scare me. I won't give in to you!'

Waking fully, she realized she hadn't spoken aloud after all. Early light glowed behind the curtains; the clock said five past seven and her mother was sound asleep in the next bed. The

49

birds sang, the sun shone, and there was no sense of the entity in the room. In retrospect the vision seemed a muddled dream, a nightmare. She didn't understand it yet. But something was different . . . now that her father was home.

Although it was Saturday, she was too alert to sleep in. It was only as she moved that she felt a stinging soreness on the insides of her wrists. Stretching out her forearms, Eirian saw, in disbelief, dark bruises crusted with blood and oozing plasma.

That was where the invaders had hammered the nails when they hung the shaman on the X-shaped cross. His wrists.

Tears came to her eyes. She'd had the blood of his severed genitals in her mouth and now his wounds on her arms. 'I don't want this,' Eirian whispered, swallowing a sob. 'Don't want it.'

For a few seconds she sat with her arms stretched stiffly on her duvet, willing her mother to wake up. But Beth slept on, long enough for Eirian to take control of herself and wipe the tears away.

She probed at the wounds. They were only on the skin, not through to the bone. Slipping softly out of bed, she swapped her pyjamas for a long-sleeved shirt and jeans, then tiptoed quickly to the bathroom to rub in some ointment.

No one must know about this, Eirian thought. Not Rhianwen, and especially not Beth. But Morgan . . . dare she confide in him?

When Beth went into Morgan's room, she found it empty; his bed hadn't been slept in, his bags were gone, and there was a curious blue light in the room, a static distillation of all her terrors . . .

Beth woke, gasping. She sat up then fell back in relief. Christ, what a dream!

She was shocked to find it was nearly nine o'clock. Used to rising at six, she rarely slept so late. The emotions of the previous weeks had exhausted her. She looked over at the other bed but it was empty. Eirian must have got up early.

And Morgan is home, Beth thought with a thrill. Really.

She put on her blue towelling robe and went downstairs. Through the kitchen window she could see Rhianwen and Eirian over by the cages in the right-hand corner of the garden, feeding the rescued cats. Beth made herself a cup of tea and drank it slowly, watching the clock. I suppose Morgan wants a lie-in, she thought. How long before I dare disturb him?

Beth couldn't wait any longer. She made a mug of tea for Morgan and went up to his room. Yes, thank the Goddess, he was there. He stirred as she approached the bed and opened a pair of sleepy, jade-green eyes.

'Is it too early?' she said. 'I didn't mean to wake you.'

'No, I'm awake, honest.' Morgan stretched, his lean arms a pale golden-ivory against the white pillow. Beth loved the texture of his skin with its shading of fine dark hairs, the way the slender muscles moved underneath, loved the shape of his wrists and his long, flexuous fingers. 'I missed you,' he said.

'While you were asleep?' she said teasingly.

'While I was in Canada, and last night.' Leaning up on one elbow, he accepted the mug from her and drank several mouthfuls. 'That's better. You make wonderful tea, Beth.'

She smiled as she sat down on the edge of the bed. 'I think you might be a little bit biased.'

'I'm very biased,' he said, resting his hand on her thigh. They looked at each other and they couldn't stop smiling.

'Did you sleep okay?' she asked.

'Wonderfully. I feel much better. Anyone else about?'

'They're outside, seeing to the cats.' Beth gazed openly at Morgan while he drank his tea. His hair – soft, thick and brownish-black – was hanging in his eyes, tousled from sleep. Her gaze moved over his dark eyebrows and long black lashes, along the exquisite structure of his nose, cheekbones and jaw to his mouth; the expressive, sensual mouth that had given her so much pleasure. She tried to see him as ordinary – to become used to him – but she couldn't. He was beautiful, and she was hopelessly infatuated.

No, it was more than beauty. There was a real sweetness in his face, expressing affection, love of life, intelligence, wicked humour. All the bewitching vitality of his soul gleamed there, changing subtly from bright and friendly to dark and not-quite-safe – but always full of life. That was what had made her fall in love with him.

Morgan slipped one hand inside her robe at waist level. 'H'm, nothing underneath,' he remarked, his palm moving up over her ribs to cup her left breast. Beth arched against his touch, closing her eyes in pleasure.

She reached out and stroked his bare shoulder. His flesh was close-textured silk under her fingers. As her hand travelled on to his chest, Morgan pulled her down to him so her lips fastened on his, and his tongue came questing deliciously between her parted teeth. The kiss was hot, consuming and electric, amazing them both.

'Come on,' he said, putting his empty mug aside and lifting the bedcovers. 'Get in.'

He was naked. His body, too, was beautiful; lean, hard and enticing, like creamy amber. At the age of sixteen his chest had been smooth but now there were dark hairs there; not too many, just enough to be madly sexy. Beth let her robe drop to the floor and slid in beside him, catching a glimpse of the darker hair between his thighs and a curve of semi-engorged, tender flesh before he flipped the quilt over her.

Their arms slid round each other. His body felt as wonderfully firm and silken as it looked, so good against hers that she could hardly breathe for the wonder of it.

'Should we be doing this?' she asked.

'Doing what?' His mouth was nearly touching hers. The warmth of his body was spiced with the delicious fragrance of the talc, shampoo and cologne he'd used the night before, blended with his natural scent. 'We're just talking, aren't we?'

'Just talking. Right.'

'Did you get my letters?'

'Yes. Thank you. They were lovely. Only . . .'

Morgan slid one thigh between hers. 'Only what?'

'Well, you wrote them all before you'd spoken to Marian.

52

And I was worried that when you did see her, you might change your mind.'

'Oh, Beth.' He shook her gently. 'I never came close to changing my mind, not once. By the time I saw her, there was no point in writing, because I would have been home before the letter.'

'I know. I'm an idiot.'

'You're a nice idiot.' Beth felt the heavy, rounded shaft of his erect penis easing its way between her thighs, sliding back and forth along her vulva, igniting whorls of fire in its wake. She caught her breath. Meanwhile Morgan went on talking as if he were simply caressing her. 'You're not the only one either.'

'How d'you mean?'

'I was afraid you might not have waited for me when I got back. That you might have gone off with those travellers again, or just vanished . . .'

Beth was astonished. 'Why did you think that?'

'You made a determined effort to finish it once, didn't you? All the reasons you gave why it couldn't possibly work . . . I was worried you might have decided they were right, after all.'

'So you were scared too?' Beth moistened her lips, trying to control her breathing. She'd been pent up for two weeks, and the gliding pressure was bringing her dangerously close to orgasm.

'You seem to think I take you for granted, Bethie,' he said quietly, 'but I don't. Of course I was scared. But you waited and I came back . . . so we can comfort each other now, can't we? Especially tonight.'

'If you keep doing that it's all going to be over in about two minutes,' Beth gasped.

'Is it? Oh, dear.' Morgan's eyes glinted with a smile so affectionate and wicked that she couldn't resist. Never had been able to resist.

'You'd better stop.'

'I will.' He rolled towards her so his body was covering hers, and in the same movement he slid seamlessly deep inside her. 'Eventually.'

Her breath rushed out in a groan of desire. 'What happened to waiting until tonight?'

'Hang waiting,' he said, his breath warm in her ear as his voice trailed into a passionate whisper. 'We might get run over by a bus at lunchtime. Abducted by aliens. Savaged by feral hamsters. Anything could happen.'

Beth pushed her hands into his hair, her arms hooked around his shoulders, her head tipping back in ecstasy as he kissed her neck. She wanted to touch him everywhere at once, to assimilate him completely. Her nails raked feverishly down his back, then clutched his buttocks.

'Oh, why have I only got two hands?' she whispered. His soft laugh against her throat made her shiver and burn.

She felt his taut muscles bunching as he thrust into her, tantalizingly slow but just hard and deep enough to electrify all her nerves. She was melting, turning to musky oil, the oil running and igniting into liquid red fire.

Their mouths met. As Morgan's tongue came writhing feverishly against hers, the kiss broke her open. Beth came, her frantic urgency cresting into hard waves of ecstatic release, one running into the next, overwhelming her utterly. She cried out, couldn't help it. 'Morgan. Oh, God, *Morgan.*'

Through the cages of her half-closed eyes she saw his face rise over her, his expression one of poignant agony as he let go. She felt him shudder, felt his penis throbbing inside her flesh like a red stamen bursting with the pressure of its seed.

Beth clutched him, laughing and crying. Tears ran down her face. She couldn't speak. He was holding her so tight she couldn't even breathe.

Eventually he said with fervour, 'Oh, my God, it's good to be home.'

He wasn't thinking of Marian now. He was completely with Beth, his hands tangled in her hair and his eyes locked with hers, gleaming with joy and sadness.

'I've been dreaming about this,' she said.

'So've I. It was so cold without you.' A tear fell from his

lashes and landed on her cheek; he laughed and brushed it away with his thumb. 'I don't know why we're crying.'

To herself, Beth added, *I've been dreaming about this for twelve years* but she didn't say it. Didn't want to make him feel guilty about the separation, not now, even though the gulf still burned inside her – more than ever now she'd had a taste of what they'd missed.

'Well, we have a lot of plans to make,' Morgan said, settling back on the pillows with Beth cradled against him. 'Once I find a job we can look for a house of our own. Until then, do you and Eirian want to come and live here or shall I move into your place? We'll be all right for a while, I've got some money saved up . . . Beth? Say something.'

She said quietly, 'Are you sure we're not rushing into things, moving in together? Maybe we ought to get to know each other better first.'

Morgan looked dismayed. 'We do know each other.'

'We've been together for barely a fortnight.'

'What about the other four years?'

'We were just kids! Even then, we only saw each other in the summer holidays, maybe two or three times a week. It's not enough. There might be all sorts of things about each other that we find out we can't stand –'

'I know what you mean,' he sighed. 'Slouching in front of the football with fifteen cans of lager. All that belching, farting, snoring, forgetting to shave, leaving socks all over the floor – but don't change, Beth, I'm sure I'll get used to you.'

'You sod!' she cried, pouncing on him. 'Can't you take anything seriously?'

'Not really, no.' They fought playfully, laughing. 'Come on, Beth, you know me. I'm arrogant, callous, bitchy, sex-mad and completely evil. But I can cook. I even know what vacuum cleaners are for. What more do you need?'

As he teased her, there was a soft knock at the door and the sound of the handle turning. Beth jumped guiltily, and would have sprung across to the far side of the room if Morgan hadn't held her in bed. Rhianwen's face appeared in the gap. 'Morgan – oh, sorry.' She withdrew hurriedly.

'Mum!' he called. 'It's all right, come in. We're only talking.'

She paused. 'Are you sure?'

'Yes. We finished shagging about five minutes ago.'

Rhianwen came into the room and sat on the end of the bed, glowering at him. 'Honestly, Morgan, has it occurred to you that Beth might be embarrassed?'

He looked at Beth. 'Am I embarrassing you?'

Resolving not to feel guilty, Beth met Rhianwen's gaze and said, 'Not at all. I was just helping Morgan to get over his jet-lag.'

'So I see,' Rhianwen said abruptly. 'What if it had been Eirian who came in instead of me?'

'So?' said Morgan, looking hard at his mother. 'She's not naïve. Don't you think it's healthier for her to see Beth and me in bed together than to have witnessed what Luke did to Sam? I want her to grow up knowing sex is a normal sign of affection, not some vicious perversion. I want her to tell her grandchildren, "My parents really loved each other." Don't you?'

'Of course.' Rhianwen folded her arms and looked down, her hair falling over her face. She looked very youthful, in a loose white shirt and jeans. 'I suppose you think I'm a hypocrite.'

'You said it. Sex is wonderful, sex is sacred to the Goddess – but only as long as I don't do it with Beth, eh?'

Rhianwen looked defeated. 'I told you, it's your decision. It's not illegal, it's none of my business. Look, I only came in to ask what your plans are for today, but I'll talk to you when you come downstairs.'

She stood up rather brusquely and walked out. Beth could feel the tension in Morgan's body. 'Don't be angry with her,' said Beth.

'Why not?' He pushed his hair out of his eyes. 'I love her but she really pisses me off sometimes.'

'You should've had my mother,' Beth said acidly. 'You know

what it is, don't you? Rhianwen has to go on disapproving in order to justify keeping you away from me and Eirian for all that time. She can't suddenly be thrilled, it would make her position ridiculous.'

'It was fucking ridiculous.' Then she felt him relax under her hands. He kissed her. 'We're not going to let it spoil things, Bethie.'

'No.'

'I suppose we can't lie here all day. Go and have your shower, madam.' He ran his hand down her spine and between her thighs as she climbed out of bed, caressing her wet, secret flesh. 'I'll join you in a while.'

Putting on her robe, Beth went to the bathroom, then found she'd forgotten her shampoo. She went downstairs to ask Rhianwen if she could borrow hers, but as she crossed the living room she heard Rhianwen's and Morgan's voices in the kitchen. She knew it was wrong to eavesdrop but she couldn't help it; she leaned back against the wall by the open door, where they wouldn't see her, and listened. Their voices were mild, exasperated rather than rancorous.

'I wish you'd be happy for us,' Morgan was saying.

There was a clattering of china, as Rhianwen prepared breakfast. 'It would be nice if you'd stay friends for Eirian's sake, of course, but –'

'Friends. Sure. We'll be back to, "Treat Beth like a sister," at this rate. She's not my sodding sister, Mum!'

'No. She's your niece.'

'Half-niece,' Morgan said thinly. He sounded as Welsh as his mother when he argued with her. 'Courtesy of you having it off with her grandfather. And the one thing that bothered you most was upsetting Dr Cross, wasn't it? He'd have taken a pretty dim view if you'd let his son shack up with his grand-daughter. All you cared about was what he thought of *you*.'

'Randolph took a fairly dim view of you getting Beth pregnant in the first place.'

'So you were punishing us for making you look bad.'

'As Randolph's family had such a low opinion of me, the

57

least I could do was prove I'd brought my son up to behave properly! Thanks a lot.' Rhianwen gave a deep sigh. 'Honestly, I don't know to this day why you couldn't have obeyed me in one simple request and left Beth alone.'

'Nobody had the honesty to tell us we were related.'

'No, but you knew she was far too young, you knew damn well it was wrong, yet you just blithely went ahead – for heaven's sake, Morgan, what got into you?'

'Same thing that got you running into the doctor's surgery with imaginary illnesses and throwing all your clothes off, Mother.'

'Oh, shut up. It wasn't like that. I wish I hadn't told you! And if you ever say anything like that when Randolph's around –'

'I'm working on the wedding speech right now,' Morgan said, ironically threatening.

'Put the cereal boxes out. Please,' Rhianwen snapped. 'You know, I think I should have let Beth come to live with us after all. Two teenagers with a baby; it wouldn't have lasted six months.'

'That's how much you think of me, is it?' Morgan said sarcastically. 'Great.'

'On the other hand, it might at least have made you face the consequences of your actions. It was no fun, seeing Beth suffer while you virtually got away with murder.'

'I wanted to see her. You're the one who stopped me.'

'Since when has anyone stopped you doing what you want?'

There was a pause, the sound of cupboard doors being opened and closed. Then Morgan said, 'Maybe you're justified in feeling uncomfortable about it, but please try to get used to the idea, Mum. Like you said, what we're doing isn't illegal.'

'No, but you can't legally marry and you shouldn't have children. I adore Eirian and, all right, there's nothing genetically wrong with her – as far as we know – but you might not be so lucky another time.'

'There won't be another time. Beth's on the pill.'

'There's always a risk. I'm glad *you're* happy to keep risking it; I only hope Beth is.'

Beth could hardly bear to listen but she couldn't seem to move. A young tabby cat came weaving round her legs, mewing. Beth gathered it in her arms to quiet it.

Morgan retorted, 'That's not what really bothers you, though, is it? It's what people might think.'

'For Eirian's sake, not for mine or Randolph's.'

'But who's going to know? My birth certificate names my father as Owen Rhys, not Randolph Cross!'

'People have a way of finding things out,' Rhianwen said flatly. 'I'm trying to make you think about the consequences, that's all. For all the good it's ever done.'

'We sleep together,' said Morgan, suddenly intense. 'So what? We're not harming anyone. We give each other incredible pleasure and we always did; why do you *think* we couldn't leave each other alone? Now it's no one's business but ours. Why should we stop, just to satisfy other people's ideas of what we should or shouldn't do?'

'I agree with you,' Rhianwen said, almost sharply. 'And I wish we lived in a pagan paradise in which everyone could love everyone else without hurting each other or having inappropriate offspring. But we don't. I love you and Beth, I'm glad you're happy; just don't expect me to leap up and down celebrating, okay? I don't condemn you, love. Goddess knows, I'm as guilty as anyone. Now go and get dressed while I make breakfast, because I'm fed up of arguing with you.'

'Suits me,' Morgan said lightly. 'I won't mention it again, if you don't.'

He came out of the kitchen, wearing a black dressing gown, too fast for Beth to make it to the stairs. She let the cat down on to the floor and tried, unconvincingly, to look as if she'd just come down. Seeing her, Morgan stopped dead, looking embarrassed.

Beth explained about the shampoo.

'You don't have to ask, you daft thing,' he said, putting his arm round her shoulders. 'Just use whatever you need.' As they climbed the stairs together, he added, 'You didn't, erm, hear any of that, did you?'

'I did, actually,' she confessed. 'All of it, I think.'

'Oh, shit. Sorry.'

'Where was Eirian?'

'On the back lawn, playing with the kittens.'

'You hope,' said Beth. 'She picks things up like a radar.'

'I don't think we said anything that Eirian doesn't already know . . . did we?'

'No, but that's not the point. I don't ever want her to over-hear arguments implying her parents are perverts and she shouldn't exist! Do you understand?'

'Yes, of course,' Morgan said contritely. 'It wasn't an argument, Mum and I have always told each other what we think.'

Beth gave him a hard look. 'Well, we can't live here, if you and Rhianwen are going to keep bickering like that.'

'We're not. It won't happen again, believe me.'

As they stood in the shower together, hot water coursing over their bodies, Morgan asked, 'Is this what you meant?'

'About what?'

'Me not knowing you. I don't remember you being this assertive, all those years ago.'

'I've changed,' said Beth. 'I've had to, to protect Eirian – and myself. I'm not a wide-eyed, gullible fourteen-year-old any more. If that's who you were expecting, you're going to be very disappointed.'

'Of course I don't expect that.' He looked chidingly at her, his dark eyelashes and hair sparkling with water. 'Credit me with some intelligence. I'm not an opinionated sixteen-year-old brat either –' As Beth began to smile, he put his finger to her lips. 'All right, don't say it. I want you exactly the way you are, Beth. You were always special. That hasn't changed.'

He moved closer as he spoke, working the soap between his hands then massaging the lather over her back. Clouds of steam enveloped them. Lifting the dripping weight of her hair so he could wash her shoulders, he said, 'Is this what they mean by holding a black mass?'

Beth grinned, her hands working over his lean ribcage and

flanks. She loved the feel of his muscles moving silkily under his skin. 'Do you mind my hair this colour?'

'No, it's lovely. I'm not going to tell you how to look. Dye it green with pink spots, if it's what you want . . . only not blonde, eh?'

'Definitely not blonde,' Beth agreed.

His touch felt wonderful, firm and long-fingered, sensually warm and soothing. Her breasts were flattened against his chest as his hands slid down her spine and over the neat globes of her buttocks. She felt the tender flesh of his genitals cupped against her pelvis. Their thighs were pressed together, feet and ankles dove-tailed. Hot soapy water rivered over their bodies. Beth could have died with pleasure.

'Do you think we should give this up?' he asked softly. He sounded serious. 'Give up sex, and act like brother and sister. Could you do it?'

'Could you?'

'I don't think so,' he said. 'No.'

'No,' Beth echoed. 'I'd rather die.'

'Would you let me do something, Bethie?' he whispered, his breath cool on her moisture-dewed neck.

A dark thrill went through her, a replay of the first time he'd seduced her. She felt the insistent, mischievous pressure of his will, always drawing her deeper than she really ought to go. The Devil in him, her mother would have said. A reminder that however good-natured and compliant Morgan seemed, he would always get his own way. 'What?' she asked nervously.

'Let me comb your hair.'

Later that morning, Morgan walked along the path that led through the herb garden to the back lawn, basking in the warmth. The air was a golden ether glittering with pollen and insects. He wasn't aware of the shadow-shape following him; he hoped it had gone for good. Shrubs and trees were in full leaf, heavy with their own lushness; flowers spilled over borders, cascaded from tubs and hanging baskets. There were unkempt corners with long grass and weeds, caverns of moist shadow.

The garden was beautiful, rampant and full of life, just as it had always been in his youth.

Morgan wasn't sentimental; occupied with university and work, he'd rarely been back. Yet, now he was home for good, he was pleasantly amazed at how right it felt. Yesterday he'd been depressed, worn down by lack of sleep and the memory of hostile encounters with Marian. Today he felt tranquil. Beth had healed him.

He smiled, thinking of Beth. She was so warm. To lie with her for ever, feeding from the nectar of her mouth, drowning inside her . . . there was nothing else he really wanted. He couldn't believe the depths of her forgiveness, after the way he'd abandoned her. Couldn't believe his own stupidity at so nearly losing her.

Morgan found Eirian sitting on a low dry-stone wall at the edge of the herb garden. She was wearing the cowboy boots he'd given her, leaning forward to admire them with her legs stretched out and her heels planted on the lawn. Behind her, a great bank of lavender, rosemary and catmint released its scent.

'Do you like them?' he asked, sitting down next to her.

She looked up and smiled, hooking her hair behind her ear. He had noticed she didn't smile often, but when she did, she meant it. 'Yes, they're great. A bit loose, though.' She was also honest.

'I chose them on the big side, so you won't outgrow them too quickly. You can always wear socks with them.'

'I hadn't thought of that. It's too hot to wear them, really, but I don't want to take them off. They're brilliant. Thank you . . . Dad.'

Eirian was still hesitant to call him that. She looked down at the boots again, uncharacteristically shy. Morgan always knew what to say to Beth, but not to this mysterious child. After a few moments he said, 'I suppose you're too old to sit on my knee . . . are you?'

In response, she gave a slight smile – so like Beth – and slid on to his knee, placing her arms round his neck. She was slim but her weight was warm and substantial. He felt the silkiness of her hair against his cheek, caught the fragrances of fabric conditioner on her shirt, of sun-warmed skin and the faint dustiness of cat-fur.

They sat there and hugged each other. There was no need to say anything, after all.

Morgan found it incredible that Eirian was his, that without him she wouldn't exist. She'd come fully formed into his life, perfect and enigmatic as an angel – and he envied Beth, really envied her for spending all the time with Eirian that he'd missed.

She drew back and looked at him. Morgan thought, she seems so mature for her age; almost too mature. Her hair was rich, deep brown, half-way between Beth's original colour and his own. Her eyes were green, like theirs and Rhianwen's; apple-green, shiny-translucent as jade, deep as forests. Her face, a pale oval, was open, direct and calm. And she was not merely pretty in a child-like way but hauntingly, heart-stoppingly beautiful. Like Beth.

Eirian asked straight out, very softly, 'Why weren't you there when I was a child?'

Morgan rested his forehead on hers, to avoid her gaze. 'Your mother's told you that, hasn't she?'

'Mum's told me. Rhianwen's told me. But you haven't.'

'It's complicated,' he said lamely.

'Grown-ups always say that when they don't want to tell the truth,' said Eirian.

'All right.' Morgan held her face and looked into her eyes. 'I made a mistake, that's all. A terrible mistake.'

'But why didn't you know it was a mistake?' she said fiercely. 'How could you not *know*?'

The burning simplicity of her questions floored him. 'Sometimes you just can't see it until it's too late.'

'Well, I'll never make a mistake like that!' She spoke with utter conviction. '*Never*.'

'I hope you're right,' Morgan said gently. 'I never had a father when I was growing up, either. I only found out who he was a month ago. I know it hurts, Eirian; I should have known better. But I've always loved Beth. I'm staying with you now.'

'I wish I'd called you before,' she said pensively, 'but I didn't think of it. And I only had the power to do it when I was in danger.' Although she was so similar to her mother, Eirian's face wasn't shadowed by self-doubt and wariness as Beth's had been at that age. Weird that she could be so affectionate, yet still seem self-contained. Analytical, but in an adult way . . . 'Dad,' she asked suddenly, frowning, 'you would have killed Luke to protect Sam and me, wouldn't you?'

'I hate violence, I'm not aggressive unless I'm seriously provoked – but for you, yes, I would happily have killed Luke.'

'So you don't think I did the wrong thing.'

Morgan felt a chill pass through him. 'No,' he said firmly. 'You did the right thing. You had to do it.'

'The inquest is next month. I'm going to give evidence. Sam doesn't have to, but they decided I could.'

Morgan was uneasy. 'Do you want to?'

She nodded. 'I don't mind, as long as Sam isn't upset any more. They made us see psychologists, did you know? Said we had to have counselling.' Eirian spat the word, sounding so disgusted that Morgan nearly laughed. 'The psychologist is a nice lady but I don't need it!'

'I know it's a pain,' said Morgan, 'but if we stop you going they'll think we're being obstructive. They're trying to help.'

'It's okay.' The corners of her mouth turned up conspiratorially. 'I know how to say the right things, to get it over with quicker.'

'Good for you.' He wondered where this strange, too-knowing child had come from.

'At the inquest,' she said softly, 'I must tell the truth about Luke's death.'

Morgan was taken aback. He held her shoulders. 'No. Just tell them you don't know what happened, like we agreed.'

'But if I lie, they'll blame Olivia. I don't like her, but I don't want her convicted when she's innocent! It would be unjust.'

'They may not believe you anyway.'

She bit her lip. 'If they do, will they lock me away?'

'Of course not!' Horrified, he held her tight, 'They might make you keep seeing those stupid psychologists, though.'

'I don't care. If I tell lies now, how will anyone believe me in the future?'

As she spoke, Morgan turned cold. Time paused, and the sinister presence he'd sensed in Canada reared up, stretching out cruel claws to pull Eirian away from him and Beth –

He nearly cried out in dread. The menace swelled, trying to force its way through an elastic barrier. Then it vanished.

Morgan let out a breath of relief. He was shaken. Not the first time he'd sensed such things . . . He'd never known whether it was a blessing or a burden, being able to dip under the skin of reality to the inky depths beneath. In his way Morgan was part of the darkness – but Eirian was a wavering light-beam, already far deeper in than he had ever been.

Eirian showed no sign of having sensed anything. She only looked sideways at him, as if wondering why he was suddenly holding her so tight. He relaxed his grip.

She swallowed, seeming hesitant. 'Dad? Can I tell you something, without you telling Mum?'

'Eirian, I don't know about that –'

'Promise!' she said fiercely. 'She'd only worry.' He acquiesced reluctantly. Then she unbuttoned her left sleeve and rolled it back, revealing her forearm. 'Dad . . .' Frowning, she quickly unfastened the other sleeve, then rubbed at the flawless inner skin of her wrists. She seemed shocked, puzzled.

'What's wrong?' he asked.

'Nothing,' she said sharply. 'I'm just rolling up my sleeves because it's hot.'

'You should change into a T-shirt, then. What did you want to tell me?'

She sighed. It was so hard to infer anything from her fugitive emotions, Morgan wondered how many months or years it would take to fathom her. 'Just that I still have nightmares about Luke.'

'Oh, God, Eirian –'

'No, it's all right. I won't give in to them. If I do, Luke will have won.'

Morgan had promised not to tell Beth what Eirian had said to him. When Beth asked cautiously, 'How are you two getting on?' he could only smile and hope she didn't think he was hiding anything.

'Fine, I think. She's absolutely lovely, Beth. And I think she likes me.'

'Of course she does,' Beth said affectionately. 'Who wouldn't?'

In the afternoon, they sat together on the sofa and Beth showed him photographs of Eirian at various ages. Rhianwen had taken many of them but had never shown them to Morgan. She must have known that if he ever saw them, the image of the child would have plagued him until he insisted on seeing Beth.

Beth and Morgan both cried over the photos. He wondered if he would ever be able fully to forgive his mother – or himself.

In the evening, Morgan borrowed Rhianwen's car and drove Beth to her own cottage to fetch her cats. Although the farmer, Gordon, had agreed to feed them, Beth couldn't bear to leave them any longer.

Eirian had stayed behind with Rhianwen. A blue, summer-scented dusk was folding down as Morgan steered the Beetle past the farmhouse, along the rough lane to the dilapidated cottage where Beth and Eirian lived, witches in the woods. Being slightly short-sighted, Morgan wore glasses to drive; he rarely bothered with them otherwise, though Beth insisted, teasingly, that they made him look even sexier.

'I'll go and look at cars on Monday,' he said.

'You can afford to go out and buy a car, just like that?' said Beth, rather astringently. 'Wow.'

'Only a second-hand one. I'll teach you to drive, if you like.'

'Oh, my God, no! That's the fastest way to end up hating each other, so I've heard.'

Morgan laughed. 'Maybe you're right.'

'I can kind of drive,' said Beth. 'I drove all sorts of vehicles on the farms.'

'Well, apply for a provisional licence, then you can take proper lessons.'

Beth cleared her throat. 'I'd like to, but I can't afford it.'

'I'll pay for them,' Morgan said easily, then wondered why Beth didn't reply.

Inside the cottage, the three cats came winding around their legs, mewing indignantly at being left for so long. Beth lit an oil-lamp, carried it into the living room and went round lighting candles on every surface. In the flamy glow the room was of another time, with its low ceiling, crooked walls and cavernous mouth of a fireplace. Yet Beth had made the most of her mismatched furniture, transforming it with shawls of lace and Indian cotton into her own unique, mystical domain. Morgan watched her moving round the room. She moved with straight-backed grace, like a dancer, her hips swaying under the crushed velvet of her long, burgundy dress. The fabric clung enticingly to her breasts and waist. Under the sleeveless bodice she wore a top of black fishnet, revealing glimpses of her pale arms and shoulders as her hair flowed and divided. As she turned towards him, a rope of jet beads and a silver amulet at her throat caught the light. Amid the utter blackness of her hair, her face glowed white, haunted; her eyes were strikingly outlined with kohl, her lips deep plum as if he'd just kissed and bitten them.

She could hardly have been less like Marian. Beth's loveliness left him breathless. He could see in her the child he remembered, but changed and deeply layered by experience; the dark, gothic beauty overlaid on the fresh, innocent girl. The curves of her body were slim and firm, inspiring him with the same thrilling desire that had dazzled him to the consequences in the past.

Blowing out the last match, Beth leaned on the back of a sofa and picked at the dead matchstick. She looked pensive.

'You said you had something to show me,' said Morgan.

'Yes, how could I forget?' She hurried into the kitchen and came back with a stained-glass panel, about twelve by eighteen inches. When she held it up to the candle-light, he saw silvery dolphins surging through waves of marbled white and azure glass. The design was subtle, watery and crystalline, lovely as a Tiffany window. 'It's for you.'

'Beth, that's beautiful,' he gasped, taking it from her. 'Where did you get it?'

'I made it.' Her lips curved in pleasure.

'You didn't tell me you could do this!'

'I didn't know I could, until a couple of weeks ago. Long story. Ever visited Woodbourne Hall?' As Beth began to explain how she had met her new friends, Tom and Dee, Morgan watched the light fluctuating through the coloured glass. Suddenly, through an odd play of shadow, certain shapes seemed to resolve into a face; a dolphin became an eye, a strip of leading a hawkish nose, the waves a ragged spray of feathers . . . and he felt a chill, as if his haunting entity had swooped through the room.

He wasn't aware that he'd reacted openly, but Beth asked, 'What is it? Not seeing faces in it, are you?'

'Erm – well, sort of,' he said, surprised. 'Look . . .' As he moved the panel, though, the shadows dissolved. 'No, it's gone. Trick of the light.'

'Not you too.' She sounded distressed.

'How d'you mean?'

'People keep seeing things in my designs that aren't there.' Leaning on the sofa-back again, she laughed uneasily. 'Really, I can do without any more weirdness in my life.'

Morgan carefully placed the panel on a sideboard and went to her. 'What's wrong? Come on, tell me.'

'Just worried about the inquest, among other things.' She pushed her hair back over her shoulder, an echo of Eirian's gesture earlier. 'Oh, Morgan. I really can't see you living here.'

'Why not?' For a moment he feared she was trying to end their affair again.

'Well, look at it; no electricity, rust coming out of the taps,

68

wet-rot in the floorboards and a pick-your-own mushroom farm in the bathroom. It's not really your style, is it?'

'That's right,' he said, sardonic with relief, 'I expect satellite TV in my Ferrari, so how you expect me to tolerate this I've no idea. For heaven's sake, Bethie, I don't mind! I spent enough time here before I went to Canada; did I complain? If you and Eirian have stuck it for five years, I'm sure I can bear it until we find somewhere else.'

'We've been happy here.' She spoke softly, but there was a defiant gleam in her eye. 'I've worked bloody hard to make a life here and I'm not ashamed of that.'

'I should think not.' Morgan stroked her arm. 'You're proud of it, I hope.'

'Except that I can't offer you a decent home,' she sighed. 'You must be thinking, is this the best she could do for Eirian?'

'No, I'm *not* thinking that,' he said firmly. 'But to be honest, I'd rather you came and stayed at Mum's for the time being. This place can't be healthy for Eirian. Tell Gordon you're leaving and I'll help you move out. You don't owe those farmers a thing. Working you like a skivvy in return for a damp, derelict wreck? If you ask me, they've exploited you.'

Beth was indignant. 'That's not fair! They've been as kind as anything! At least they gave me work and a place to live.'

'Well, okay, I don't know them that well. Sorry.' He hadn't meant to upset her, even if it was the truth.

Her voice fell. 'The point is, I've never asked anyone to support me. I don't see why you should, either.'

Morgan wasn't sure how to respond. How could he tell her that none of it mattered – that he just wanted to look after her – without wounding her pride? Finally he said, 'Well, do you mind supporting me? I've got no bleeding job.'

Beth turned into his arms. Her shoulders shook. Lifting her chin, he found she was laughing and crying at once, tears soaking her lashes. 'Don't,' he said gently, hugging her. 'You'll get panda eyes. Do you think I'm bullying you into leaving?'

'Of course not,' said Beth, calming down. 'I have a mind of my own.'

'So tell me what you want.'

Her arms slipped under his jacket and rested firmly round his back. 'I want you.'

'What a lucky coincidence.' Morgan pressed her warmly to him, feeling her breasts swell against his ribs with her breathing. Echoes of their earlier, delicious encounter trickled hotly through him.

'If I get spiky, it's not you.' She rested her forehead on his collarbone. 'It's everything. Gran dying, my mother in hospital, and Luke . . .'

'Beth. I know.' He caressed her head, her shiny, ebony hair slipping over his fingers. 'It's one of my lesser talents, being tactlessly cheerful when other people are upset. But I'm with you, I'll look after you now.'

'And it's this house,' she went on faintly. 'I don't want to stay here any more. It's a closed episode. It would always remind me of the past, and since Luke came here it feels tainted.'

'We can untaint it, Bethie. So you don't have bad memories.' Morgan pressed harder against her, feeling the electric ache of desire again; he'd been home a day, they'd only made love once and it wasn't enough, a thousand times would not be enough . . . He kissed her neck and felt her responding, the blood rushing through her. 'D'you remember when I first came here? Only a month ago.'

'It feels like a lifetime ago.'

'We made love all night and we felt the Goddess with us; we captured the energy of ecstasy, magic to drive out the demons. The power of sex.'

'Yes,' Beth breathed, moving against him. 'I need that.' She smiled and gasped as he undid her zip and trailed his fingers down her spine. 'Exorcism. Rebirth.'

Beth's pale complexion flushed, her lips parted and her eyes shone, as if this were the most exciting thing in the world . . . oh, and it was. Always had been. Unbearably, bewitchingly exciting. As they slipped down on to the thick hearthrug, the room with its smoking candles seemed an incense-perfumed chapel, their mutual lust a baptism.

And Morgan knew.

With Marian, the world had been glittering, busy, practical, intense – all on the surface. But the world he sank into with Beth was watery darkness, velvet night pricked with stars, moonlight and ocean-deep shadows . . . and it was where he belonged.

The shaman-animal spirit watched. He perceived nothing clearly. His was a world of shape and scent, of urgent instinctual need.

There was flesh moving on flesh, glistening with sweat and candle-light. The heavy scents of sex drew him powerfully. He fell to all fours, becoming a wolfish creature that prowled back and forth around the copulating humans. Parts of him split off into the shadow-forms of stag, boar and hawk, circled and reformed again. He was drawn to the lovers' sexual energy like a hart to a hind, but like an animal he didn't know why. A primal need for the release of his anguish. Centuries old. Desperate now.

The female sat astride the male. The shaman-wolf thrust his muzzle beneath her buttocks to sniff at their joined, swollen genitals. Rich aromas enveloped him; delicate, musky, salty, hot. His tongue slid out to lick their fluids; evocative tastes flowed on to his tongue. In their rapture they were oblivious to him.

But it was their rapture that would feed him. He was wounded, strengthless. Every time he hunted down one of those rare humans who were attuned to the dream-realm, they reacted with terror or indifference. They turned their backs, drove him out, refused to understand. They'd lost the gift of shamanism. He had no power to break through their barriers. He haunted them but he couldn't make them *see* . . .

These beings had been apart too long. They were meant to be together. This gave the shaman-entity a sense of completion, of hope. Their love-making was nature's most elemental force. *Life*. The entity drew in everything; their cries, their fluids, their emotions. When their passion crested it was a wave of colour, rose and crimson and honey, painfully sweet on his tongue. The shaman-wolf drank it in. Felt the cold fire of his multiple soul burn a little brighter.

Every time the humans coupled he would drink again. And each time would make him a little stronger, until at last he could unleash his rage.

Chapter Five

W HEN Beth was a child, her grandparents' house had been
a realm of vibrant promise, the one place she was free
of her parents' restrictions. She recalled the bustling presence
of dogs, the smells of saddle soap and horses, her grandmother's
brisk and powerful personality. But now that her grandmother
Heather was gone, the house was cavernous and silent.

Beth was alone with her grandfather, Randolph. They stood
side by side at the kitchen window, looking out at the garden.
The grass needed cutting. Beyond the hedge, the stables were
empty, her grandmother's horses retired to the quiet fields of
a rest home.

Everywhere Beth looked, she imagined her grandmother;
bathing a Labrador, polishing tack, cleaning her shotgun,
making jam. And she knew that her grandfather, too, must see
those images and feel the silence of Heather's death.

Three weeks ago – just before Morgan made his trip to
Canada – Beth had accompanied her grandfather to Heather's
funeral. Rhianwen and Morgan stayed away because Heather
had hated them: Rhianwen for seducing her husband and
Morgan for being the walking evidence of the affair. Beth was
in the middle, understanding both Heather's and Rhianwen's
pain. How would Gran have felt, Beth thought guiltily, knowing
we're leaving her graveside to go to the arms of the very people
she loathed?

All through the funeral, Beth had talked silently to Heather.
'I'm sorry, Gran. I'm so sorry.'

'Thank you for coming round, Beth,' said her grandfather.

'It's nice to see you,' she said gently. 'How are you,
Granddad?'

'Oh, bearing up.' He was subdued and more confiding than
usual. 'But I didn't realize how empty the house would feel . . .'

'I know. I feel it too.'

His voice sounded hoarse. 'I miss her, Beth.'

'At least you've got Rhianwen now.'

'Yes, but I still miss Heather. I loved them both, you know. It wasn't easy, having to make the choice, but I didn't stay with Heather under sufferance. It was so difficult, having to keep the whole thing hushed up for Heather's and Olivia's sake, not being able to tell Morgan he was mine . . . Seeing as I was Rhianwen's GP at the time, I suppose I should be grateful I wasn't reported and struck off.'

Randolph had used to seem distant and authoritarian, but Beth felt closer to him now than she ever had to her own parents. At seventy-one he was still working and had kept his distinguished looks. He was handsome, tall and slim with charcoal-grey hair and intense grey-green eyes. She could see where Morgan's beauty had come from. Beth wasn't sure she liked the calculation with which he'd forsaken Rhianwen rather than sacrifice his position in the community – but she'd forgiven him. Perhaps that was more than Morgan ever could.

Beth placed her hand on his, where it rested on the draining board, and stroked the fine hairs on the back of his hand. 'Rhianwen told me you have healing powers, like her. That's why Eirian's like she is. Two lots of your blood. Plenty of witches in the family tree . . . I suppose doctors aren't meant to admit to that sort of thing.'

His lips tightened, but he seemed amused. 'Rhianwen can be rather fanciful; I'm a sceptic. If some of my patients have made remarkable recoveries, it could be a testament to my medical skills or simply that I diagnosed them wrongly in the first place.'

'But Eirian can –' Beth stopped, knowing she would get nowhere. 'Okay, never mind. Let's have a coffee.'

Beth made a pot of coffee on the Aga and they sat down at the kitchen table, comfortable together. On the table between them sat Heather's vanity case, an antique box of highly polished walnut. Her grandfather rested his hand on the lid and said, 'Are you sure this is all you want of Heather's?'

'This case is what reminds me most of Gran. It intrigued me when I was a child, all the cut-glass bottles, and the little compartments and drawers. It has her scent and personality in it. This is all I want.' She lifted the lid and traced the blue, silk-padded interior with her fingertips.

'Very well.' Randolph cleared his throat. 'By the way, I'll probably retire next year. Then Rhianwen and I will get married.'

'Do you mind if anyone guesses?' Beth asked. 'About Morgan, I mean?'

'If people want to gossip, let them. I'm too old to care any more. Now it can't hurt Heather, I'd be very proud for people to know he's mine. I only wish Morgan felt the same about me. However.'

'People in this village have long memories. Most of them were Gran's friends. They'll look at you in a different light. You know, thinking you're not quite the saint they thought you were.'

'Wonderful,' Randolph said sardonically. 'Old ladies will snub me at committee meetings. Worse things could happen.'

As he spoke, Beth idly explored the case. She discovered that the mirror in the lid hinged down and had a photograph tucked behind it. 'What's this?' In the flat, faded greys of the 1930s, a young man sat on the edge of a large flat rock that protruded about three feet from the grass. Beth laughed in amazement. 'This is you, Granddad, isn't it?' She passed it to him. 'Sitting on the Hellstone. How old were you?'

'Good grief, had no idea Heather kept that tucked away.' He laughed gruffly. 'I'd be about twenty. My father took it. I didn't realize you knew about the Hellstone. Often used to walk up there with my father.' Randolph became thoughtful. 'Odd place. Very atmospheric. Site of pagan worship, centuries ago, so Rhianwen says. I take it you know the place, then?'

Beth felt herself colouring. 'It's quite special to Morgan and me, actually.' Randolph raised his eyebrows at her, as if he knew exactly what she meant. Fighting an embarrassed smile,

75

Beth replaced the photo and closed the case. 'By the way, does Mum –' the word stuck in her throat. 'Does Mum know about Gran?'

He breathed in and out wearily. 'I told her, yes, but I'm not sure she took it in. I decided to keep the news about Rhianwen and me for another visit.'

Beth could hardly bear to talk about her mother, but her conscience compelled her. 'How is she?'

'Not good.' Randolph spoke of his daughter with a strange detachment, as if she were a patient; to control his pain, Beth assumed. 'The consultant informed me that Olivia is suffering paranoid delusions. These episodes can last weeks or years. Apparently she's lucid enough to give evidence at the inquest, though.'

'They say she confessed to killing Luke.' Beth spoke hesitantly. 'Do you think she did it?'

'God knows. Someone killed him and it can't have been Eirian or the little boy. Apparently Olivia was the only other one there. In her state of mind she might have done anything.'

'What if it *was* Eirian?'

Randolph looked steadily at her. 'I would say she did the only thing she could in the circumstances. I know Luke was my grandson but . . . how he and Olivia turned out like they did, I'll never know. I can't help asking myself, if I hadn't been too wrapped up in work to notice what was happening, could it all have been averted?'

'Don't blame yourself,' said Beth. 'People are born with their personalities; I've found that out from Eirian. I know Mum's ill, but where does her personality end and the illness start? After the way she treated me, Luke and Eirian, I'm not sure I can ever forgive her.'

Randolph held her hand across the table. 'Would you feel better if you could?'

'I'd feel better if I could just *understand* her.'

'I think you should go and see her.'

An intense wave of terror transfixed her. 'I don't think so.

The last time I saw her –' She shuddered. 'She cursed and yelled at me. God, it was horrible.'

'She's calmer now. She's on medication.'

'I don't want to see her like a zombie either.'

'She isn't.' He looked into her eyes, his gaze firm. 'I think it would help you both.'

'All right, I'll go.' She swallowed hard, trying to make light of her fears. 'I'm sure she'll be thrilled to know that I'm living with Morgan.'

'Mmm.' Randolph sounded non-committal. 'About that . . .'

Beth couldn't face any more disapproval, however kindly it was meant. She went on talking, to avoid listening. 'I've left the farm. I didn't think I could but when I did it was such a relief. I said goodbye to Margaret and Gordon, thanked them for all their kindness, packed my stuff – and when I closed the front door on the cottage I felt as if the world had fallen off my shoulders. It was so strange. I'll miss all the woods and trees but it's just as nice at Rhianwen's . . . Of course, Morgan and I want a place of our own but property prices are so ridiculous, I couldn't believe it when we looked in the estate agents'. It depends where he can find work, as well. He's got a couple of interviews today. God knows what I'm going to do; I'm qualified to do precisely nothing, but I can't, I won't let Morgan keep me –'

'But are you happy with him?' Randolph broke in.

The question startled her. She smiled shakily. 'Too happy. He's wonderful, he's everything I ever hoped for.'

'Takes after me, obviously.'

'I'm glad you're his father,' Beth said with feeling. 'It makes us all seem so close, really a family. I hope you don't still disapprove.'

'Well, the taboos, the genetic thing – I'm sure you've heard it all. As I said, it's your decision.'

'That's what Rhianwen said. Then she and Morgan had a massive row about it.'

She saw complex thoughts moving behind her grandfather's eyes. 'Beth, this is what I wanted to talk about. You know I'm moving in with Rhianwen – not too soon after the funeral, obviously. Well, when I do, I'm giving you and Morgan this house.'

She was stunned. 'Granddad – you can't!'

'Why not? I've no more use for it.'

She recovered herself and explained. 'We can't live here. How would Grandma feel, the way she hated Morgan, knowing he was living here with me? She'd feel you'd totally betrayed her. And there would be too many memories. And it's miles too big. Thank you so much, but we couldn't.'

She saw from the downward flicker of his eyes that he was crestfallen. 'I had a feeling you might say that. In which case I'll sell it, and give you some of the proceeds.'

'But wouldn't you have to pay capital transfer tax, or something?' Beth still couldn't believe he meant it. Having an almost phobic loathing of accepting money she hadn't earned, she was trying to find a way to refuse that was not merely stubborn.

'There are ways round it. Let me do this one thing for you and Morgan, please. It is the very least I can do to make up for . . . for everything.'

It was the strangest time of Beth's life, bitter and sweet by turns. Walking hand in hand with Morgan through the woods behind Blackthorn Cottage, she told him of her grandfather's offer. Morgan said, very faintly, 'Bloody hell.'

'Well, what do you think?'

The sun glowed green through the leaves. This was where they'd come as teenagers, to make delicious, forbidden love in the undergrowth. Beth felt euphoric with nostalgia. After a minute, Morgan said, 'It would depend why he's offering. When he says, "make up for everything", does he mean for hurting my mother, ignoring me, and failing to protect you and Eirian from your crazy parents? Does he think he can put all that right by throwing a load of money at us?'

His hand felt taut in hers. 'No, I don't think so,' she said. 'He's genuinely sorry. Come on, if he's still in love with Rhianwen after thirty years, he can't be all bad, can he? I think he simply feels it's the least he can do, to give us some security.'

Morgan looked sideways at her, troubled. 'Are you sure?'

'Positive. I didn't want to accept the money, but . . .'

'We'd be bloody stupid not to.'

'Yes,' said Beth. 'Exactly.'

'We could buy a house of our own, really make it ours. And send Eirian to a good school.'

'Oh, I'd love that,' she said. 'But I'm used to living in abject poverty, dear; having money I didn't earn makes me feel uncomfortable.'

'Well, don't. If we're going to accept the offer, we are not going to agonize over it.' With heartfelt intensity he added, 'I'm sorry we can't get married, Beth. Stupid bloody law.'

'Well, marriages break up, but the excitement of living in truly biblical sin could last for ever.'

He laughed. 'Darling, our diamond sin anniversary! But would you and Eirian take my surname anyway? I'm not being chauvinistic, it's just that I don't fancy being Herne or Cross.'

'Join the club. God, I'd love it!' Beth was thrilled. 'But Rhys was your mum's husband, a man you weren't related to and never even met! That's a bit ironic.'

'Yeah, except Mum's maiden name was Rhys too. Dead common, isn't it?' Morgan pulled her back against the trunk of an oak tree and kissed her passionately. As she surfaced for breath, she realized where they were. The mossy hollow by the oak roots, shaded by bushes and bejewelled with sun-specks.

'Our sacred place,' said Beth. 'Oh, my God, to think I lost my virginity here!'

'Who was he?'

'You, you idiot.'

'Bit careless of you to lose it. Shall we lie down and look for it?'

'You haven't changed a bit, have you?' Beth said joyfully, pressing her body along his. 'Thank the Goddess.' Her arms enclosed his waist and rested on the oak trunk, the bark rough under her palms. The touch connected her with the vibrant energy of sap rising, cells dividing, life throbbing from roots to shimmering leaves.

'Come on. Let's go a bit further,' said Morgan.

'Yes, you were always saying that, too.'

Laughing, Morgan took Beth's hand and led her on to a clearing on top of a rise. In the centre, encircled by oaks, bushes and long tangled grass, rose the Hellstone; a mass of grey rock, like a huge kneecap, three feet high and fifteen across, worn smooth and round-edged by the weather. The word 'Hell', so Morgan said, actually meant 'Holy'. And they'd always felt something disturbingly magical here.

Morgan sat on the edge of the stone and pulled Beth down so she was sitting astride his thighs, facing him. They sat holding each other tight. Beth said, 'I found a photo of Granddad sitting here when he was twenty. He said the atmosphere affected him too.'

'Quite an admission for the rational doctor, eh? Maybe it's hereditary, being drawn here.' Morgan kissed her and whispered into her neck, 'I remember you used to see things. Horned figures and men in black and the Goddess's eyes looking at you . . .'

'You must have thought I was crazy.'

'If you are, I'm crazy too. I always felt energies here. Earth and plants and animals; changing, dying, renewing, mating and bearing young. I've always found nature so sexy. The Goddess at work . . .'

Morgan's voice in her ear and his lithe body against hers were arousing Beth deeply. She felt her juices gathering, her vulva gently swelling and opening. She wanted to make love to him constantly, couldn't bear him not to be inside her. In the woods around them, each leaf was a moist jewel. Wild flowers were unfolding, insects scurrying and fungi bursting out of the earth. This trembling, sensual energy had seduced her away from the Church to paganism.

'My mother saw it as falling into sin,' she said, smiling. 'To me it felt like coming home.'

'Or just like coming.' Morgan slid his hands over her buttocks and moved teasingly against her. He had a wonderful talent for being erotic without ever being crude. 'God, it was exciting, wasn't it?'

'If there is a Horned God, he's definitely you.' Beth knew that, in her mother's eyes, the old Horned God and the Devil were the same being. Morgan grinned, sharing the thought.

'Nah, my legs aren't hairy enough.' He ran the tip of his tongue down her throat and gently bit her. Beth kissed him, her open mouth moving lightly and hungrily over his face. Her loins ached; drenched in heat like honey, she wanted to take him right there on the stone, crude and urgent. In that heightened moment her awareness tipped into another dimension. The woods turned to vibrant crystal, and over Morgan's shoulder she saw a squat animal like a wild pig, dark and grotesque. It wove back and forth on the Hellstone, its muzzle snuffing at the air, as if the scent of their sexuality excited it. And Beth could see through it to the woodland beyond, where other shadow-animals lurked, somehow connected to Morgan . . . His familiars?

The shadows drifted closer, blending together as they came, forming a single writhing entity that towered above them like some terrifying stag-god . . .

'Beth? You okay? You've gone blank.'

The sound of Morgan's voice made the world snap back to normal. 'Yes, sorry.'

He looked concerned. 'You weren't seeing things again, were you? Only I felt something too. Spirits.'

Beth pressed her head into his shoulder. 'This only seems to happen when I'm with you!'

'Does it frighten you?'

'Yes, but . . . Call me weird, but it also gets me very aroused.' They held each other, laughing shakily.

'It's only the faerie folk, Beth, trying to encourage our fertility rites. Maybe we were *meant* to fuck each other too young and have Eirian.'

'Because the Goddess needed her? Oh don't, don't.' However well she came to know Morgan, Beth knew part of him would always remain darkly scary and exciting. 'I'll tell you one thing. I hate to think of Eirian doing the things we used to get up to. And there is no way I'd let her roam around on her own, like I used to. I suppose Gran thought I was safe in those days.'

He grinned, eyebrows tilted in irony. 'You were safe with me. Sort of.' Then he shook his head ruefully. 'But you're right, Bethie. The world's changed. Now I have a daughter, I think I finally understand why your family hated me so much.'

They found the house the next day, simply by noticing it was for sale as they walked through Lullingford on their way for a drink at the Green Man. Morgan rang the estate agent at once. The asking price was far less than Randolph expected for his, because it was smaller and badly run down. But the moment Beth and Morgan saw it, they knew.

The house was just off the village green, separated from the church by a row of stone cottages. White with black timbering and a slate roof, it was set back from the road in a large, overgrown garden with lilac bushes spilling over the front hedge. Although it was neglected and unoccupied, the setting was idyllic. All around, on the green, in the churchyard and the surrounding gardens, mature trees shimmered against the sky; chestnut, birch, copper beech. As a child, Beth had often passed the house, thinking how mysterious it looked standing ghost-like in the overgrown garden. 'But I never dreamed I might have a chance to live in it one day,' she told Morgan.

That evening, they took Eirian, Rhianwen and Randolph to view the house and give their approval. As they reached the front gate, Randolph started laughing.

'What?' said Beth. 'Do you know something ghastly about it?'

'No,' said her grandfather, shaking his head in amusement. 'It's just that my parents lived in that house, until they died in the 1950s. I was born and brought up in it. It's a lovely house, Beth, but Lord, it needs some work. The old boy who's selling it never did a thing to it. Are you sure you want to take it on?'

'Yes,' Eirian broke in. 'It's a good house. It feels right.' And she answered for Beth and Morgan. To Beth, the fact that it had been Randolph's childhood home made it more desirable, as if everything had come full circle.

'Any luck with work?' Steve asked Morgan. Beth was walking between them across the broad lawn that flanked Woodbourne Hall. No show today, only a scattering of visitors. All evidence of the event had vanished and the park was beautiful in its summer foliage, a soft green satin quilt. Beth saw Eirian and Sam in silhouette against the lake, ducks making glass arrows on the bright water. The weather was perfect. Beth felt warm, languid, at peace.

'Had a few good interviews, but it's all lab work,' said Morgan. 'I want to work with animals. There's a whale conservation group I've done consultancy for; I might wangle a full-time job with them but that would mean moving to the coast and it all depends on Eirian's school.'

'What about Twycross or Dudley Zoo?' said Steve. 'I know they don't keep whales, but . . .'

'I've studied other animals, habitats, botany. Maybe, if it was working with endangered species, but I'm not keen on zoos.'

'Picky, aren't you?' Steve said mordantly. 'Have you seen the unemployment figures?'

Morgan didn't take offence. He only laughed. 'Something will turn up, Steve. It always does.'

Beth was pleased that Morgan and Steve got on well. It meant they could all stay friends. Steve had been gracious about losing her – but Morgan had helped to rescue Sam from Luke, and that made up for everything.

She couldn't wait to introduce her lover to Dee and Tom. Morgan was all in black; a T-shirt with a Celtic knot pattern in white, his long legs beautifully contoured in needlecord jeans, a belt with a skull buckle sitting acoss his flat abdomen. His dark hair was glossy and dishevelled, his eyes as green as leaves and he moved with an athletic, sexual grace that Beth found hypnotic. She couldn't stop gazing at him. He took her breath away.

Beth was in a long, transparent skirt of deep jewel-colours, a laced black bodice, black leggings and Victorian-style boots. She knew they made a striking couple. That pleased her immensely.

She called the children, and they all walked along the drive to the old stable block. In the courtyard, people were enjoying tea and scones at tables outside the tea-rooms.

The workshops were crowded with Sunday visitors. With Morgan holding her hand and Steve close behind, it took Beth a while to thread along the narrow aisle. In the last stall but one, behind a mass of teddy bears, Cordelia was sitting on her stool, head bent over her work and her dark auburn hair cascading over her shoulders.

'Hello,' said Steve.

Dee looked up and smiled broadly. 'Steve! Hi!' But when she saw Beth she seemed to freeze, her lips parted. The children had stopped at a stall with wooden toys, a few yards back.

'Hi, Dee, how are you?' said Beth. 'I brought Morgan to say hello.'

Dee's face relaxed into its normal, perky expression. 'Oh, he turned up then?' she said jokily. Standing up, she leaned over the counter and shook Morgan's hand. She looked fascinated, delighted.

'You're kidding, when I had Beth waiting for me?' Morgan said, raising his eyebrows. 'Of course I turned up. It's nice to meet you, Dee.'

'You too. Oh, he's lovely, Beth. You didn't exaggerate.'

Beth smiled, blushing. 'Now come and look at this,' she said, pulling Morgan towards Tom's stall. 'Back in a sec, Dee.'

Dee said quickly. 'Beth, hang on –'

Beth walked two paces and knew why Dee had looked so concerned. Tom's stall was empty, swept clean. Even his sign had gone. In shock, Beth backed up against Morgan. 'Where's Tom?' she cried.

'I'm terribly sorry,' Dee began. 'I only found out what happened this morning. I was going to let you know.'

'Oh, God.' Beth put her hand to her mouth.

'No, it's all right, he's not dead!' Dee said hurriedly. 'Apparently he had some sort of collapse a few days ago and decided to give up work. He is eighty-something. He's gone into a nursing home, I can get the details off his son.'

'Would you mind?' Beth said, still in shock.

'You know, you ought to take over his stall,' Dee said wryly. 'He was always on about how good you were. He left a load of work unfinished; I'm sure his customers would be desperately grateful if you took over. I think it's what he wanted, if you could have come here more often.'

Beth gazed at the empty space. Where there had been a forest of limpid colour there was only red-brick emptiness. 'I wanted to,' she said. 'I've been kind of preoccupied.'

'Mmm, I can imagine,' Dee said cheekily, glancing at Morgan.

'I suppose these stalls are terribly expensive to rent,' Beth said impulsively.

'Depends what you consider expensive,' said Dee. 'You'd have to talk to the estate manager, Harry. And there's all your materials and equipment to buy, of course – but you could get a bank loan. I've got masses of info on setting up small businesses.'

Dee's enthusiasm touched her, but Beth could only see it as an unaffordable dream. Morgan squeezed her shoulders and said softly, 'Would you like to do it, Bethie? You know you've got the talent, and there's your granddad's money . . .'

Before she could answer, she heard a man's voice, calling out from the far end of the workshops, 'Hey, Morgan! Morgan Rhys?'

'Who the hell's that? Hang on.' As he walked past Steve, Morgan dug him in the ribs and said, 'Give her a kiss, Steve. I can't stand the suspense.'

Then he was gone, easing his way through the crowd in the aisle. Steve had gone red. Leaning across the counter to give

Dee a peck on the lips, he knocked several bears off the display and hurriedly put them back. 'I'll, er, take the children for an ice-cream,' he mumbled. 'I'm sure you two want to talk.'

When Steve had left, Beth and Dee burst out laughing. 'Steve's so sweet,' said Dee, pulling Beth behind the counter out of people's way. Impulsively they hugged each other.'Well, you look a lot happier than the first time I saw you. Morgan is definitely a bit of all right! You look positively radiant.'

'Thanks,' said Beth. 'So do you, actually.'

'Steve and I have been seeing quite a bit of each other,' Dee said seriously. 'I hope it's not a problem.'

'Of course not! I couldn't wish for Steve to find anyone nicer than you.'

'Sam gets on well with my boys, Pete and Hugh. And they both like Steve.'

'Sounds as if you could be a perfect family,' Beth said happily.

'I've been on my own for so long, I'd given up hope of meeting someone like Steve.' As Dee went on talking, Beth dared to imagine herself in Tom's place. There's no harm in trying, she thought, her heart beating faster with excitement. It would be something I could do for myself, without anyone's help.

Fifteen minutes went by. 'Where's Morgan got to?' said Beth, stricken by anxiety. 'I'd better go and look for him. Back in a minute.'

She edged her way along the aisle and through the exit. She still couldn't shake off the fear that Morgan might vanish like a ghost and never be seen again.

He wasn't in the courtyard. She stood on the drive between the stable block and the garden centre, looking up and down. No sign of him . . .

Then Morgan appeared round a pine-shaded curve in the drive, walking beside a bearded man in a waxed jacket and flat cap. Relieved, Beth waved. The man patted Morgan on the arm, said a few words, then walked off in another direction. Morgan ran to Beth, picked her up and swung her round in the air, setting her breathless on her feet again. 'Beth!' he exclaimed, grinning so broadly that she couldn't help laughing. 'Something brilliant's happened. That guy I was with, he's an old friend of mine, Harry Campbell. He used to run a bird sanctuary I worked on in the holidays when I was at university. Now he's the estate manager here. He's just been telling me, there's an area of woodland on the edge of the estate they're turning into a nature reserve. There'll be a visitor centre, butterfly farm, stuff like that. They want someone to set it all up and run it; he's only offered me the bloody job! It's exactly what I want to do!'

'That's wonderful!' Beth gasped, hugging him. 'Your mother was right about you.'

'What?'

'You *do* always land on your feet.' She smiled, teasing him. 'You must be a cat, a beautiful black cat with big green eyes.'

'Yeah, someone always takes me in and feeds me.' They laughed, their arms around each other. 'There's something else, Bethie. Harry really wants me so I made a few conditions – one of which is that you get Tom's stall, rent-free for the first six months.'

'Oh.' Beth didn't know what to say. She'd wanted to prove her independence but Morgan had pre-empted her. Her stomach fluttered. A forewarning – there and gone.

'Beth, what's wrong? I thought it was what you wanted. I've seen what you can do and there was such a glow in your eyes when you were talking to Dee about it.'

'Of course I want it! It's just – well, you didn't have to do it for me.'

He paused. 'First I'm in trouble for giving you no help at all, now you're mad at me for giving you too much. Stubborn, aren't you?' he said mildly. 'Bethie, it would be a business agreement. I expect a share in the profits.'

'Profits, eh?' Beth laughed, trying to shake off the feeling. 'I'm sorry. I don't mean to sound ungrateful. I can't get used to your relentless optimism.'

Morgan looked hard into her eyes and said, 'Do you know

what you're telling me? "I can cope if you fuck off." I know you find it hard to trust me, I understand. I don't expect you to get over it in a day. Only give me a break, Beth. I'd do anything for you.'

They stood holding each other, Beth leaning her head on his chest, feeling his warmth. Perhaps she couldn't afford the workshop without Morgan's help; how much did it matter? To be working together in this beautiful place! 'Oh, dear Goddess, we are so lucky,' Beth said fervently. 'This is the best day of my life.'

'That's better,' said Morgan. Steve, Eirian and Sam emerged from the tea-rooms. 'Shall we tell the others?'

'No, it's too soon,' Beth said quickly. 'Let's wait until we've sorted things out.'

'We'll have to tell them something; Harry wants to show us round the nature reserve site. How about giving yourself permission to celebrate for once, madam? There's nothing to stop us being happy now.'

'What's your dad like?' Sam asked Eirian as they trudged along thickly overgrown paths between woods and marshy meadows. The adults were in front; the bearded man, Harry, talking intently to her father, Beth and Steve following, the children trailing at the back.

'My dad's great,' Eirian said pensively. 'Only I wasn't expecting to feel . . . left out.'

'How d'you mean?'

'I always had Mum to myself before. But now she and Dad are more interested in each other than in me. I'm glad they're happy, but . . .' Voicing her thoughts, Eirian felt strangely melancholy. 'I've always been alone, anyway. That's why we have to be strong, Sammy, in case people let us down.'

He looked worried. 'I'll always be your friend,' he said.

'Thanks. And I'll be yours.' Eirian gave a ghostly smile. Sam was still such a child, like a little brother. She needed an adult confidant, but who? She'd tried to tell Morgan about the wounds on her wrists, only to find they'd vanished. After that she'd lost her nerve. She felt isolated. Nothing had happened since her last vision of the shaman but she was waiting. Watching.

'What's through here?' said Sam, climbing a wire fence and pushing through hawthorn. Eirian followed and they found themselves on a lip of rock overlooking a deep bowl of granite with a lake at the bottom. The sides were steep and dark, the water iron-grey. It looked a long way down.

'Don't go too near the edge, Sammy,' Eirian said automatically. Then she went dizzy, and the world became a dark metal web, thrumming. She saw a child's face under the lake surface, turning paler as it rose up from the depths. There was something else down there, a monstrous bulk sinking into the murk. Irrational horror clawed at her. The unseen bulk sank in swirls of turbid water but the child floated up, white as death, eyes staring. The small body came right up out of the lake, cloaked in pond-weed and rivulets of watery blood. It seemed to float along the lake's edge towards the bush-shrouded rock wall. Eirian ached to follow the child but it was vanishing into blackness . . . She heard a plaintive cry, *Come back, don't leave me* . . .

A loud, male voice shocked her out of the vision, so violently that she nearly lost her balance and went over the edge. The summer day crowded in on her senses. She was disorientated.

'Oi, you two!' It was Harry, looking stern. 'I told you to stay on the path! If either of you goes in the quarry, no one wants to be bothered with fishing you out. Now come on, and don't wander off again.'

Eirian, who hated being spoken to like a child, recovered herself. 'You should put some warning signs up,' she said acidly. 'It's dangerous.'

The nursing home was a pleasant, sunny place, nothing institutional about it. Beth had dreaded finding Tom half paralysed by a stroke, but when she and Morgan met him in the communal sitting room he looked as perky as ever. His right wrist, though, was in plaster.

'Took yer time, didn't yer, lass?' he said in greeting. 'Where've you bin?'

'I'm sorry,' said Beth. 'I've no excuse, I was just busy. I only found out you were ill yesterday.'

''Ent ill,' he said brusquely. 'Old is what I am. Had this blasted dizzy spell, fell and broke me wrist. Game's up, I thought. I were glad, really; deserve a rest, I reckon. Just sorry I didn't get all me orders finished . . .'

Beth began, 'Actually, about that . . .'

Morgan wandered off to charm some old ladies in the corner while Beth talked to Tom. She thought he might be offended at the suggestion that she take over his business, but he only shook his head impatiently and interrupted her. 'Took you long enough to catch on, din't it? Shoulda retired five year ago, but I hung on until you showed up.'

'Me?'

'Someone wi' an eye for it. Right person. Knew I'd know 'em when I saw 'em.'

'I won't let you down,' said Beth. His grey eyes burned into hers, glittering marbles in his wrinkled face.

'I know, lass. Now I'm goin' to phone me son. All me stuff's in his garage; equipment, unsold stuff, orders and that. I'll tell 'im it's all to be given to you; he'll take it over to the workshop for you. Y'can pay me for it when y'can afford it. Any time.'

'I will,' she said, glad that he expected payment. 'Thank you, I'm so grateful.'

He leaned forward and clasped Beth's wrist with his good hand; he smelled faintly of camphor, and his eyes had the disturbing glow of prophecy. 'Any time y'want advice, I'm here. A good craft'll never let yer down, lass. It'll be there when you've lost everything else.'

Again the flutter of dread, like missing a step. She shook it off.

Tom's son, a fat car dealer, didn't like Beth. He delivered his father's materials with ill grace, regarding her Indian velvets and witchy black hair with sneering disdain. She didn't care. She was charm itself in response. He was soon gone, and she stood alone in the centre of the stall, looking round at the rough red walls and the worn benches in a wash of dusty sunlight. Soon, she thought with a rush of excitement, it'll be a forest of colour again. Sapphire and amethyst and ruby. My domain.

There was so much to do, and it was all up to her. She was her own master. And she knew she had to be successful, to prove herself to Tom, Morgan, Dee, everyone.

She examined squares of glass, holding them to the light to admire the glowing colours. She felt compelled to make something. Her hands began to move of their own volition, cutting pieces without a template, edging and fluxing and soldering.

For some reason, Beth felt nervous as she worked. *When you've lost everything else.* What did that mean?

Presently she knew the design was finished. She let the solder cool, then lifted the panel up to the light. Nothing sinister after all. The image was of an angry-looking cherub, with a milk-white body, black hair, slips of green glass for eyes. It would make an amusing present for someone who'd had a baby, perhaps. Beth leaned on the work-bench and exhaled, releasing a mass of tension. Laughing at herself.

A good school for Eirian, a house of their own, Steve and Dee together, Morgan working almost alongside her . . . why was everything suddenly going so well? Maybe I should stop looking for the worm in the rose, Beth thought. If I'm not careful, when Morgan says life can change for the better, I might even start to believe him.

Chapter Six

THERE'S nothing to stop us being happy now, Morgan had said. And if this doesn't do it, thought Beth, nothing will.

The hospital was a Victorian edifice of forbidding red walls with row on row of narrow windows. There were flower beds edging the car park, but their cheering effect was overshadowed by the towering wall of a prison next to the hospital. Beth sat staring out of the car windscreen, feeling so cold she could hardly move.

'Let me come in with you,' Morgan said gently, leaning on the steering wheel. The car he'd bought was a sleek sable cabriolet in too high an insurance group for Beth's comfort.

'No, it's all right,' said Beth. 'I don't think my mother would appreciate seeing you, somehow.'

'I don't care what she thinks. It's you I'm concerned about.'

'I'll be okay.' She took a deep breath and opened the passenger door. 'Right, here goes.'

'Hey,' he said, kissing her cheek. 'Don't let her get to you, Bethie.'

As soon as Beth walked into the entrance hall, the smell hit her. Sweet disinfectant, reminding her of her father's dental surgery. The aromas of lino, old paint, stale human breathings. She almost ran out again; instead she found herself sleepwalking along corridors, following the signs to the secure unit.

Secure unit. How sinister that sounded. To think of her mother being locked up in this place tortured Beth. She called up inner power, a shield of psychic light to protect herself.

There was a nurses' station outside a white, heavily reinforced door. VISITORS REPORT HERE, said a sign on the glass panel; Beth looked through and saw a middle-aged nurse sitting at a computer, frowning at the screen. 'Excuse me,' said Beth. 'I've come to see Olivia Herne. I'm her daughter.'

'Wait a moment, Mrs – '

'Miss,' Beth said without thinking.

The nurse lifted a telephone receiver. 'Hold on, I'll get some-one to take you in, Miss Herne.'

It was a shock to hear the name. Beth hadn't called herself Herne for years.

'John? Visitor for Mrs Herne,' said the nurse. She put the phone down and returned to tapping at the keyboard. 'Blasted machine! I'm sure I'm using the right command, but – you don't know anything about computers, do you, dear?'

'Not a thing. Sorry,' said Beth. 'My boyfriend does but he's in the car park.'

'Hmph. Fat lot of use that is.'

The sheer ordinariness of the exchange made Beth relax a little. But the moment she heard the locks on the white door clanking open, her tension closed in harder than ever. Her heart hammered. Her limbs felt like lead.

A young male nurse came out, his face ebony against the white of his uniform. 'Miss Herne? Hello. I'm afraid we have to search you before you go in. Security. You don't object, do you?'

'Er – no.' A stocky, unsmiling woman came out behind him and ran her hands lightly over Beth's sides and legs. 'All right,' she said briskly.

'Sorry about that,' said the male nurse. 'Bit of a nuisance, I know.'

The door slammed shut behind them. The security woman let them through a second door of wire and metal. Beth heard voices. They sounded ordinary, muffled, threaded with laugh-ter. Someone was playing the piano. But it was the same tune over and over again, and in an unseen room a man kept barking out some incoherent phrase.

The nurse, John, led her along a plain, carpeted corridor, round a corner and through an unlocked fire-door into another corridor. The walls were decorated with crude paintings and raffia work. 'Don't look so worried,' he said. 'Your mother's in good hands here. It'll do her good to see you.'

'How is she? Has she said anything about me?' Beth asked anxiously, but John didn't answer.

'Here we are.' Reaching a door about half-way along, he looked through the grille, knocked lightly and entered. It wasn't locked, to Beth's surprise.

Beth had expected it to be like prison visits she'd seen on television; herself and her mother separated by glass in a grim room with iron bars and warders. Or she'd visualized a long ward, peopled by wandering, lost souls in striped pyjamas, her mother isolated and frightened among them. Instead the door opened on to a pleasant, simple room with a single bed and white melamine furniture. It wasn't luxurious but it could have been a student's bedroom, even a hotel room.

Her mother was sitting at the far end, at a dressing table which doubled as a desk, reading with her back to the door. Sunlight shone through the window, feathering Olivia's brown hair with gold. A scene of serenity was the last thing Beth had imagined.

The light dazzled her, and she found her retinas imprinted with the image of bars.

'Someone to see you, Olivia,' said John.

'I don't know how many times I've told you to call me Mrs Herne,' Beth's mother said stiffly.

'I'll leave you to it,' said the nurse. 'I'll be across the corridor, if you need me. Leave the door open.'

He was gone. Beth stood gazing at her mother, not knowing what to say; Olivia gazed back. Her eyes were as intensely blue as ever, her face stiff and expressionless. She was two years younger than Rhianwen but she looked older, her skin mapped with lines. And yet she was still a handsome woman, with her hair cut to shoulder length and in a soft fringe on her forehead. There was a lot of grey in the brown. She was rather too thin, but in her navy blue skirt and flowered blouse, she looked . . . ordinary, normal.

'Hello, Mum,' said Beth.

Apart from one recent, ghastly encounter, Beth hadn't spoken to her for eleven years. Her last memories were of her mother treating her like a pariah for having Morgan's baby. After Beth had fled they'd had no contact. Yet Olivia didn't look surprised to see her. She didn't look shocked, relieved, pleased, anything. All she said was, 'Well, you'll have to sit on the end of the bed. There's only one chair.'

Obediently, Beth went and sat on the end of the bed, a couple of feet from her mother. Olivia turned the plastic chair round and faced her. She studied Beth, taking in her black hair and black clothes. Beth had dressed down, wearing a long, plain dress and no make-up, but she still looked like the very thing her mother had dreaded her becoming. A witch. Beth had only been prepared to compromise so far; she wanted Olivia to face what she was. Still, after all this time, she wanted her mother to accept her.

Although Beth had psyched herself up, her mouth was so dry she could hardly speak. While she was trying to frame a pleasantry, Olivia demanded, 'What have you done to your hair?'

'It's only dye.' Beth's calmness fled. One question from her mother was all it took to pierce the psychic shield and reduce her to a terrified little girl again.

'It looks terrible. I don't know why you've come here. What do you want?'

'To see how you are, that's all.'

'When have you ever cared how I am?' Olivia said thinly. She began to turn away, as if to pick up her book again.

'Don't turn away from me!' said Beth. 'Mum, please. I'm sorry you're not well –'

'There's nothing wrong with me. I don't know why I'm here.'

'Don't you remember the things you said to me, when they first took you to hospital?'

'I don't remember seeing you,' Olivia said brusquely.

Beth, who'd never erased the image of her mother spewing curses, was stunned, but she let it pass. She tried again. 'I'm sorry if I hurt you, running away. I thought you might be pleased to see me . . . or relieved I'm not dead in a ditch, at least.' No answer. 'I thought – well, maybe we could start again, if we could forgive each other.'

That brought a response. '*You* – forgive *me*?' Olivia spat. 'For what? I did everything to give you a decent, godly life and look how you thanked me! What wrong did I ever do you?'

Beth worked hard to keep her tone mild. 'You tried to destroy my child. You let Luke kidnap Eirian. You condoned it.'

'Don't you mention Luke to me! I never want to hear that name on your lips.' Then the name came out as a groan of agony. 'Luke.' Twisting away, Olivia planted her elbows on the dressing table and began to weep bitterly. Beth was overcome with pity. Fighting tears, she tried to put her arm round her mother's shoulders, only to be thrown off with revulsion.

Shaken, Beth backed off and sat down again. 'Mum, don't. I hate to see you like this.'

Olivia grabbed a tissue from a box and blotted her face. Muffled, she said, 'I killed him. My only son.'

'No, you didn't!'

Beth's mother swung round, her face and eyes fierce. 'No, *she* made me do it!' Her voice was low, not loud enough to make the nurse come running.

'Who?' Beth thought she meant Eirian.

'The Crone. The whore your kind worship.'

'What kind is that?' Beth said, beginning to feel angry despite her resolution.

'Witches. Devil-worshippers.'

'We don't worship the Devil!' She steadied her voice. 'Mum, stop this. You've got everything wrong. I think we should drop the subject. This is a nice room, isn't it? Tell me, erm, tell me about your routine –'

'Your whore-goddess,' Olivia went on as if she hadn't heard. 'Eve. I understand now. Eve – evil. It's there in her name!'

It was a vain hope, but Beth seized the chance to open a rational discussion. 'If you're equating the biblical Eve with the Goddess, you're right in a way. Eve was a remnant of the great Goddess. Male religion reduced her to a vessel, like Mary, but –'

Olivia wouldn't listen. 'Eve caused the Fall. She copulates with the Devil. She is all corruption and all betrayal. She's in you, Bethia. She's in that evil daughter of yours. You're corrupt, you betrayed me, you made me kill my son! She's everywhere! She's in your father, that's why he's –' Olivia stopped. She meant, Beth presumed, *That's why he's homosexual* – but Beth wasn't supposed to know that.

'And is she in you?' Beth said, leaning towards her.

White rings blared round her mother's irises. Beth had hit a nerve. 'Is that what you're scared of, Mum? The Crone in you?' Beth tried to touch her, but she jerked away as if her daughter's hand was a scorpion's sting. Her hostility wounded Beth. Olivia reached into the neck of her blouse and clutched her silver cross.

'I could tell you things that would stop you being afraid,' Beth said quietly, 'if you'd listen for five minutes.'

'Don't. I heard all the lies years ago from that whore, the damnable lies that corrupted *you*.'

'Which whore are we talking about now?'

'Rhianwen. The bitch who took you away from me!'

'Right,' Beth sighed. Her palms were soaked with sweat.

'Oh, the Crone's inside her with a vengeance. But she can't enter me while I keep praying.'

'Well, no one can stop you praying. Could I have a drink of water, please?'

Olivia poured water from a plastic jug into a paper cup and gave it to her. Beth swallowed the lukewarm liquid. She sat with her legs crossed and her hands clasped round the cup, trying to hold herself steady. 'I don't think I can say anything you want to hear, can I?' said Beth.

'I'm sure you have nothing to say that I want to hear.'

'Nothing I can do to make you consider forgiving me?'

Olivia thought. 'If you went down on your knees to repent of your evil, cut off your foul hair, disowned that vile daughter of yours, and denounced all your false and satanic beliefs. If you came back to God and truly meant it, then you would have a chance of redemption. But God will be your judge. Not me.'

'There's no chance of me doing any of that,' said Beth. At least she was no longer afraid to tell her mother the truth. After all, Beth thought, how can she hurt us now? 'I have a few more things to tell you that you won't like.'

'I'm not interested.'

'Good. So it won't upset you to know that I'm living with Morgan. My name isn't Bethia Herne, it's Bethan Rhys.'

Olivia didn't react overtly, but Beth saw a wave pass through her, like a breath of despair. 'To throw your life away on that filthy rapist is exactly what I would expect of you.'

'He didn't rape me, Mum. We loved each other. I wanted it, I really wanted to have sex with him and I thoroughly enjoyed it. Don't put your hands over your ears. It's the truth. Everyone wanted to keep us apart but they couldn't. Oh, and I found out that your father is his father.' Olivia winced, but Beth went on. 'The secret's out and I know why you half killed me over it; it's like a serpent's hiss, isn't it? *Incest.* So, which is worse, incest or homosexuality?'

Olivia had gone white. She clutched the cross so hard Beth thought it would pierce her palm. 'The Bible forbids them both.'

'I don't give a fuck what the Bible says,' Beth said softly. 'I love him.'

'He ruined your life!' Olivia broke in, suddenly animated. 'You were such a good girl, Bethia, obedient and spiritual –'

'It was all a sham,' Beth said between her teeth. 'It's been a sham since I was about twelve.'

'Oh, I know it, you treacherous little viper – but before that bitch Rhianwen got her claws into you – you were doing so well at school.' Her sudden bleak pain tugged nerves within Beth, so deep she'd thought they were dead. 'You could have been a perfect teacher, a spiritual guide to others. You had such a bright future, such a wholesome, godly life in front of you. There were several sensible boys at church who would have made a decent, Christian husband, even to a plain girl like you. You might have been married with a nice little family by now, dedicating your lives to the Church. Instead you have to fornicate with that – that lustful, evil witch's spawn and produce a baby that should never have existed! Your father and I did our very best to redeem you – and you show your gratitude by running away! You end up living with *gypsies*, for heaven's sake! And then, God give me strength, you end up in a virtual slum, entertaining degenerates, fornicating, taking drugs, practising witchcraft – '

'It wasn't like that,' Beth said tiredly, knowing it was no use to protest.

'Luke told me all about it! Oh, you belong to Satan, heart and soul, you little slut. You are going to Hell on Judgement Day!' Olivia's passion rose. Foam gathered at the corners of her mouth. 'Luke, Luke died trying to save your daughter's rotten soul! I could see she was beyond redemption but Luke was so good, so forgiving he was still prepared to try. He wouldn't give up and he died for it. *He died for your sins.*'

'Mum, Luke was sick,' Beth said desperately. 'Don't you know what he did to the children? You must know! Why won't you believe it?'

'My son was not sick!' Olivia said fiercely. 'He was possessed by the Holy Spirit. If anyone is sick it's you and that daughter of yours. How could she be anything else, with that bastard as her father?'

Beth retorted thinly, 'Mum, that "bastard" is your brother.'

'He's no relation of mine – and neither are you! Your whoring with him made everything go wrong. If it wasn't for that child, Luke would still be alive. It all went wrong the day you conceived her!' The words rang painfully in Beth's head. 'You're not my daughter. You're some changeling sent to torment me. Do you think I'm going to fall for Satan's wiles and clasp you to my breast?' Olivia rose to her feet, leaning over Beth as she had in the old days, when a beating had been imminent. 'Witch. Serpent. You can get out now and don't come back. I don't want to see you ever again. I don't know you!'

'All we did wrong was to have sex too young.' Beth stood up, confronting her mother as she'd never dared to before. 'So what? You want to make it sound the filthiest thing that ever happened but it wasn't. It was beautiful and loving – but you wouldn't know love if it jumped up and bit you! Grandma and Granddad loved you, even Rhianwen did once. But you pushed us all away. Why? You needed the Church to fill the hole inside you but nothing ever can, the hole's so big it swallows everything! Even God!'

Beth was shaking. Olivia had put her hands over her ears. 'This is the talk of Satan,' she chanted. 'Out, Satan. Out, Satan!'

Beth felt a hand on her arm. She jumped violently; she'd been so involved she hadn't heard the two nurses come in. 'Miss Herne,' said John. 'Would you mind coming outside?'

Beth obeyed. Glancing back, she saw Olivia on her feet, still shouting, a female nurse trying to coax her to the bed. In the corridor, John spoke sternly to her; his smile had vanished. 'You'd better leave, Miss Herne. If you're going to upset your mother you'd better not visit her at all. You're hindering her recovery, disturbing her like this.'

For once Beth was too worked up to apologize. 'She's been disturbing me for years,' she snapped, jerking her arm free and stalking out.

The heavy doors thudded shut behind her, making her shiver. At the nurses' station, Beth tapped on the glass and said urgently, 'I want to talk to a doctor about my mother. Please.'

The harassed computer operator looked up vaguely. 'The duty psychiatrist is very busy. You'll have to wait. Your mother's name is. . . ?'

'Olivia Herne.' Beth leaned back against the wall, pressing her hand to her temples. Her fingers were ice-cold.

The doctor who came was an elegant young Asian woman in a red sari, with glasses perched on her slim nose. 'I need to talk to you about my mother,' said Beth.

'Sit down while I find her notes.' The doctor seemed abrupt and in a hurry. Beth sank on to a seat in the waiting area, her head in her hands. It was a long ten minutes before the doctor came back. 'Now, what did you want to know?'

Beth floundered. Her anger was fading into wretched depression. 'Well, what do you think is wrong with her?'

The doctor looked hard at her, as if this were an unbelievably puerile question. 'We cannot always put a label on these things.'

'Is it schizophrenia?'

'Your mother has not been diagnosed as schizophrenic. Mrs Herne presented with persistent and deep-rooted delusions which are related more closely to obsessive-compulsive disorder than to schizophrenia. She's suffered a massive emotional breakdown but she is responding to treatment. Her case will be reviewed regularly but for now we have to keep her in the secure unit on police advice, because she confessed, rightly or wrongly, to a murder; you do appreciate that?'

Beth nodded wearily. 'Will she recover?'

'These episodes are unpredictable. They may recur all her life. She will certainly not recover if you come in here and upset her.' The doctor seemed hostile and patronizing, as if she thought Beth a time-waster.

'I want to help her. I don't know how.'

'Families are often the last people who can help. You may help her best by staying away.' The doctor tapped her pen on the notes, then looked at her watch. 'Your mother is more fortunate than most. She has her faith to help her through this.'

Beth gasped in disbelief. 'How long have you been out of medical school? It was religion that made her crazy in the first place!' She stood up and left before she said anything else she would regret.

As she got into the car, Morgan turned off the radio and put his arms round her. The thin black rims of his glasses accentuated his beauty, making him look very gentle, intellectual. She buried her head in his shoulder, grateful for his warm, sure embrace.

'Oh, Christ,' she said. 'I fucked that up royally.'

'I'm sure you didn't.'

'I should have remembered she was ill and just listened to her. Instead I had to argue, tell her things I'd always wanted to say. Selfish.' Morgan held her, listening intently as she explained what had happened. She didn't want to cry but he was so loving she couldn't help it.

'Sshh. Bethie, don't. She's not worth it.'

'But she's my mother. I just want her to love me.'

'I know. I know,' Morgan said gently, rocking her. 'But how could anyone not love you? She doesn't deserve you, Beth.'

'Mum clings to this black and white view of the world, as if it makes her feel safe,' said Beth. 'Maybe it's too frightening to admit that she was wrong and you might be a kind, loving person after all. Easier to carry on calling you a lustful, evil, Satan-loving rapist, or whatever.'

She felt sudden tension in Morgan's arms. 'Charming,' he said grimly. 'My mate Satan speaks so highly of her. A rapist, Christ, that is way out of order! She hardly even knows me! Actually, Beth, I'm not convinced your mother is ill. I think it's all ego. She has to convince herself she's beset by enemies on all sides to make her feel significant. A soldier for God.' He shook his head disgustedly.

Beth rubbed her tears away and sat back, taking deep breaths. Her head ached. 'The awful thing is that while she was sitting there criticizing me, I could see myself so clearly from her point of view. She wanted to bring me up a good, clean-living Christian woman. Instead she looks at me and sees all her worst fears come true. An incestuous witch with dyed hair and an illegitimate child. All she sees is her own failure. It doesn't make me feel good, knowing I let her down like that. It just hurts. I must have broken her heart.'

'Assuming she has one,' said Morgan. 'Don't let her torture you like this. If this is how your mother makes you feel, you shouldn't see her any more. Ill or not, she's poison!'

Beth clasped the hand he was resting on her thigh. She had to rebuild some detachment and self-belief. Feeling calmer, she said, 'I think I've been rather naïve, imagining I could change anything today.'

'No,' he said softly. 'You care about people's happiness. Nothing wrong with that. Come on.' He stroked her hair, kissing the path his fingers made. 'You're tired. I'm taking you home. A hot bath, brandy and lots of love. And that's only for the car.'

'A quick rub down in the garage for me,' said Beth.

'Exactly.'

When her daughter had gone, Olivia sat straight-backed at the window. She saw them down in the car park, the witch and the demon cavorting behind the windscreen, laughing at her fate.

The world had turned its face against her. Why had God allowed a saintly man like Luke to die while those satanic wretches lived? Why were they allowed to rampage lasciviously through the world while she was kept locked up?

Olivia knew the Lord was testing her. But, dear God almighty, it was hard.

As they left, she saw the shadow of the Devil following them, a huge horned figure squatting above the black car. She shrank back in horror. She remembered the first time she'd seen that figure, the skull-like head, the horns, the probing fingers . . . Shuddering, she blanked out the memory and began to pray. She'd done that the first time, too – run to church and prayed for dear life.

She'd been fifteen. All her childhood she'd been drawn to Christianity. An only child left to her own devices by busy, professional parents, she'd found solace in flights of imagination, stories of angels, creation and sacrifice, hierarchy and order. But in adolescence she'd begun to have bad feelings. She knew she was sinful, the Bible said so. And then she'd met the Devil, so she knew it was all real, she'd go to Hell if she didn't give her life to God . . .

The village church couldn't answer her needs. Dishwater teaching. Through her teens she tried different churches, until she met the wonderful Pastor Blair who'd changed her life. His church knew, as she did, that Satan was right there at work in the world and you had to fight him with all your soul.

She'd met Philip there. Two good Christians, joined by God. And soon, two perfect children, Beth and Luke. How had it gone so wrong?

Before Olivia married, a young Welsh woman had moved to the village and taken Olivia in with her friendliness. Olivia, sensing a potential convert, had responded. They were friends for a couple of years, arguing religion in a good-natured way, Olivia viewing Rhianwen's stubborn paganism as the ultimate challenge. She hadn't realized, until it was too late, that Rhianwen wasn't simply misguided but hideously evil.

Then came all the horrors of betrayal. Rhianwen seducing her father, having his child, plotting to steal him from her mother with cunning and witchcraft. In her turmoil, Olivia received savage visions of the truth from God. *Rhianwen was in league with the Devil.* Some said Olivia was ill, but Pastor Blair told her she was right, God had chosen her to fight for her father's soul. God won – Randolph stayed with his family – so the Devil waited a few years and took Beth instead.

I did nothing wrong, Olivia thought, pricking her hands with her nails. Everyone betrayed me. I thought Philip was perfect too . . . During the business with Rhianwen, she'd rushed into marriage with him and had two babies very quickly. And then found out that Philip's true inclinations were homosexual. His marriage to her was his penance, ordained by the pastor – so Olivia, in her bitterness, made sure it became one.

I was right to chastise Luke too, she thought fiercely. He was the only one who didn't let me down. I should have beaten Beth more. Then perhaps she wouldn't have let that demon drag her into the mire.

At least Luke was in heaven now, watching over her. She mustn't let him down. Satan was everywhere. No deliverance without pain, blood and sacrifice.

The nurses didn't allow her anything sharp – and she wouldn't use her cross in case they took it away – but she had her teeth. Olivia raised her left arm to her mouth and bit hard into the soft flesh of her inner forearm, among the older bruises and scars. She winced, her eyes streaming, blood bursting metallic into her mouth. But the pain helped. It drove the Crone and the Devil away.

Eirian lay thinking, unable to sleep. All evening, her parents, Rhianwen and Randolph had talked about Olivia. Morgan had been annoyed with Beth for feeling guilty; Randolph stern with Morgan for saying, 'Forget her, leave her to rot!' Rhianwen had struggled to keep the peace. But in the end they'd all agreed that professional help was Olivia's only hope.

Eirian had simply listened. She felt no hatred for Olivia – even though Olivia had wanted her dead – but no pity either. What she felt was a sense of failure. I showed her a vision of the Goddess, Eirian thought, but she still clings to her God. My fault; I only showed her the Crone – and the Crone is terrifying if you don't understand her.

But Olivia deserves to suffer for the way she hurt Mum. She'll never change. There are some people even the Goddess can't reach . . .

Eirian drifted into a doze then woke again, suddenly pierced by terror. The room was dark. She clutched the edge of the duvet and stared at the colours her eyes made on the darkness. She couldn't hear her mother's breathing. She was overwhelmed by the sense of a presence in the house, something hungry and dangerous. She sat up and liquid spilled from her lips, running hot on to her fingers. Blood. Nearly crying with fear, she grabbed a tissue and wiped it away. The image of the shaman haunted her and her wrists ached as if the bones were being forced apart.

'Mum?' Eirian said faintly. 'Mum!' *Please be there . . .*

She was still a child. She needed her mother now. Shaking, she pushed back the bedclothes and fell to her knees on the carpet, but the bed next to hers was smooth and flat under her fingers. Beth had gone to Morgan's room again.

Eirian rested her cheek on the cold duvet cover. She felt

exhausted and nightmare-ridden, as if unseen enemies were draining her strength. She needed to be strong for the inquest but they wouldn't leave her alone.

Trembling, Eirian crept along the landing and softly opened the door to Rhianwen's room, but her grandmother wasn't alone. Randolph had stayed the night. Always in the past she had been able to slide in beside her grandmother for companionship; Eirian even found comfort in being unable to forgive Rhianwen, a power in knowing she could be angry and Rhianwen would still love her.

But not tonight. Lying in Eirian's place, her grandfather was a barrier she couldn't cross. She backed away. A cold blue light spilled along the landing and a powerful sense of foreboding drew her towards Morgan's room. She tiptoed, silent on the thick carpet, to his door. The glow was unreal, a ghost-light, a bad dream.

The door stood ajar and through the narrow gap she could see her parents, bathed in the uncanny-blue light. The duvet was thrown back and she saw their long white limbs moving, her mother's head tipping back, her hair a black waterfall on the pillow, her teeth gleaming in a smile that was half joy and half pain. She saw her father's back and legs as one long palely sculptural line, his slim hips moving between Beth's outflung thighs as if they were welded together in that place by delicious fire. She heard their voices, laughing, murmuring.

Eirian had seen people making love before, in visions. She knew what it meant and yet she didn't; she knew she shouldn't watch but she couldn't stop. The mystery of it disturbed her, stopping her breath and sending trickles of weird electricity through her. And it made her feel . . . excluded.

A psychic flash transfixed her. There was a presence between them, and they didn't know! A mote in Beth's womb, the solid coagulation of their ecstasy. Eirian's mind reeled in dismay. *I'm not part of the trinity any more.*

Then she saw a smoky shape circling the bed. It resembled a wild boar with a domed, ribbed back; a long hungry head, tusks and fangs and glaring colourless eyes. Her parents seemed unaware of it but Eirian watched in horror as it mounted the bed and thrust its head down to sniff and lick at their genitals.

'No!' she cried in her mind. 'Come away. It's me you want, not them.'

It raised its head, muzzle questing at the air, then turned on its haunches and came towards Eirian. Her breathing skimmed the top of her lungs. Its eyes burned into hers. She had to lure it away from her parents, even though they were betraying her . . .

On the bed, Beth and Morgan writhed with convulsive passion. Her mother seemed to sob; her father actually cried out, quite softly, as if in sudden pain. Eirian felt a pang in her loins, fearful confusion. Then her parents stretched out, utterly relaxed and languid now. As their voices fell to whispering and laughing again, Eirian backed away, leading the entity with her. She must take it out of the house. She felt the power of the moon pulling her, a sweet white blossom on the edge of bursting.

The creature brought the weird aura with it. As she backed downstairs, it lunged as if to snout between her thighs; she swung back against the banisters, nearly screaming. Her reaction startled it and it shied back. Never taking her eyes off the beast, she went barefoot across the kitchen, unlocked the back door and slipped into the garden. She sat on the wall by the herb garden in the moonlight while the entity circled her, tongue lolling. It seemed to swell in size and although it was transparent it felt solid in her psyche, a huge weight of bone, muscle and hair. Her heart was beating so hard she could hardly breathe.

'What do you want?' she whispered.

Again the threat. *What you did won't go unpunished.*

'Go away. You don't scare me.'

In response, the entity rose up on to its hind legs. It towered over her in a swathe of cobalt light and burning sparks. Now it was a goat-god, with spiralling horns that pierced the moon. Eirian hugged herself. She tried to scream and couldn't.

Then, through the entity's transparent form, she saw Beth's

three cats sitting in a triangle on the lawn. Sinuous shadows. Messengers of the Goddess, reminding her of her strength. Gathering her willpower she imagined the Horn of Power in her hands, so vividly that it was actually there. She aimed the pale shaft at the demon and, with all her power, charged it to depart.

It transformed again. For a second it was a wild, feathered figure, dancing frantically, pointing long accusing fingers at her. She noticed that it had no penis, no tongue. Then it vanished and she collapsed, shuddering, her head on her knees. The eldritch blue light disappeared with it. The cats came around her, mewing. She caressed their furry heads and wept.

Bast put her front paws on Eirian's knees so they were nose to nose, the cat's eyes glowing into hers. Then the cat seemed to speak. 'You have a choice. You can run away from this, or you can face it and understand it.'

This was the Goddess speaking to her. 'Whose side are you on?' said Eirian.

In response, Bast gave her a vision. The cat's golden eyes merged into one and in the glassy orb Eirian saw a polished wooden box, like her great-grandmother's vanity case. Then she saw some sheets of yellowing paper, a letter, but the words were cryptic squiggles that delivered a frightening image.

She saw her grandfather, Randolph, lying helpless in a strange mist of netting and sinister bluish radiance. Through this fog the entity came dancing and cavorting. It rose over Randolph and straddled his body, writhing, wild. He lay on a bed yet she sensed he also lay on a great stone, lobed as if one image were overlaid on another. The scene was vague and incomprehensible, but it filled her with crawling horror.

This entity has haunted us before. Why?

Bast touched her tongue to Eirian's nose and the vision ended.

'What shall I do?'

'Use your wisdom,' said Bast. Her rough tongue rasped across Eirian's lips. Then she fell to all fours and she was just a cat again, all sensual innocence.

Eirian knew she had been kissed by the Goddess. She flexed her palms and found a textured, warm shaft of ivory in them. The Horn of Power was really there. How? The Horn had been hidden under Beth's bed . . . unless Eirian collected it in her trance, without knowing what she was doing. Whatever, it felt sharp and comforting, like a weapon. A reminder of her strength.

The entity was still out there, prowling, drawn by sexual heat. It was growing more powerful all the time. Eirian shivered. Knowing she was the only one of her family strong enough to confront it made her feel very isolated. They were all in loving couples except her. The Virgin Huntress.

Eirian spent the rest of the night cross-legged on the lawn, the Horn held loosely against her, like a warrior-woman guarding an ancient encampment. She felt threats circling in the darkness, but she held them off.

There was no one else sentient in all the world. There was only Eirian, with the Goddess moving darkly inside her, and the horned moon shining above.

Chapter Seven

THE banal tranquillity of a motorway service station kept Beth anchored to reality. She was grateful for the simple tasks of queuing for sandwiches and coffee, finding a table, sharing out little sachets of sugar and salt. Anything to still her jagged thoughts.

The inquest on Luke's death was over. They were on their way home.

The cafeteria was light and airy, with green-stained wood and floor-to-ceiling windows. Eirian, Morgan, Rhianwen and Steve sat around the table with her, tired and subdued. The inquest had been held in Middlesbrough – a few miles from the premises where Luke had imprisoned the children and met his death – so they'd stayed in a hotel for a few days. Randolph had travelled up separately with Beth's father. They were already in the café, at another table. Beth acknowledged them with a wave.

She was doing her utmost to act normally, but inside she was numb, fragile, confused. Life had been so good . . . until, early this morning, a black storm-cloud had quietly enveloped her. Nothing to do with the inquest, although one anguish magnified the other. The strain of keeping it to herself was flaying her raw, but she couldn't tell Morgan. Then, unfairly, she half hated him for being oblivious.

The previous day, Eirian had been impressively composed as she answered the coroner's questions. Her bald description of her ill-treatment at Luke's hands sent whispers of horror around the courtroom. Then she stated, 'Olivia didn't kill Luke.' *Eirian, no!* Beth thought, rigid. *Oh, God, she's going to admit it!* 'I wanted him to die the same way he was trying to kill Sam and me, with the scalpel and the spiked glove. Then he suddenly seemed afraid, as if he realized what he was doing. He backed out on to the landing and I was willing him to die –'

The coroner interrupted, 'Who had the scalpel at this point, you or Luke?'

Eirian frowned. 'Luke did.'

'Was there anyone else on the landing?'

'No.'

The coroner's gaze seemed hooked on hers. 'So Luke was alone on the landing and he had the scalpel. Did you see how he received the fatal injuries?'

Eirian hesitated. 'I stayed in the room. When I dared to look, Luke was dead. There was blood everywhere. But Olivia couldn't have done it; she only came up the stairs as we ran down.' Beth breathed out. She'd wanted Eirian to act the innocent child; instead, without actually lying, she'd skirted alarmingly close to the truth.

When Olivia gave evidence, flanked by a nurse and a policewoman, she seemed as composed as Eirian. 'The children came running past me down the stairs. I went up and found my son's body at the top. After that – it's confused. I ran down again calling for help, I remember being outside . . . then I went back to my son. I sat down in the blood and picked up the scalpel. I was convinced I'd killed him, it was all my fault. But I don't remember doing it. I loved him!'

Beth shuddered to remember the wintry glare her mother had given her, seeing her in the bosom of her mortal enemies, the Rhyses. No words had been exchanged.

In the end, the coroner – shaking his grey head at the untidiness of the case – had recorded an open verdict. There were no witnesses, insufficient forensic evidence to prove anything beyond reasonable doubt. Luke could well have disembowelled himself in his madness.

Luke. Beth closed her eyes and recalled the vivid dream she'd had last night. A naked boy-child, walking away from her along a white, sea-washed beach. In the dream she'd yearned after him, desperate to enfold him in her arms – but he only drifted further and further away. At first the boy was Luke, her little brother as he'd once been. Yet when he turned and looked sadly over his shoulder, it wasn't Luke any more but a beautiful child with dark hair and eyes green as willows. Her whole body ached and pulled with the love she felt for him. She wept. *Please don't leave me* . . . but he was going away from her and she knew she'd lost him.

The ache had woken her, urged her into the hotel bathroom where she sat on the cold tiles and cried. Now she knew what the dream had meant. But Morgan, to her relief, had slept through her crisis.

'Beth?' The voice shook her back to the present. 'Could I have a word?'

Her father, Philip, was leaning on her chair. He was in a grey suit, every inch the reserved, respectable dentist, his eyes emotionless behind his glasses. They were on tentative speaking terms after twelve years of alienation. One day they might progress to warmth. Or not.

'I've spoken to Olivia's solicitor,' Philip said quietly. 'They're dropping the charges against her. But they're going to keep her sectioned for the foreseeable future.'

'Why?' said Beth, ashamed that she felt relieved.

'Because she's been violent to the staff and patients. And she keeps trying to harm herself. If only they would release her, I'd look after her.'

Was that guilt speaking? Beth knew now that her parents' marriage had never been happy. A few weeks ago, her father had admitted that he was gay and that Olivia had been punishing him for it for years. 'I know, Dad. How are you otherwise? Still, er . . . on your own?'

Philip smiled ruefully. 'I expect I always shall be. That's the legacy of my beliefs, even if I don't hold them any more. Well, we'll be on our way now. Keep in touch, won't you?' He was so formal.

'Eat something, Bethie.' Morgan pushed a plastic-wrapped sandwich at her as her father left. 'You hardly ate any breakfast. I'm not having you passing out.'

Rhianwen leaned over to her and touched her hand. 'Are you all right, Beth?'

'Yes, I think so.' She fiddled with the wrapping.

'And how about you, love?' Rhianwen asked Eirian.

'Fine,' said Eirian, stirring her coke with a straw. She was brooding. 'I tried to tell the truth but I couldn't. I knew they wouldn't believe me.'

'You said exactly the right things,' said Morgan. 'The only things you could have said.'

'I know.' Eirian's self-absorption made Beth feel excluded and annoyed.

'How could you even have thought of admitting it?' Beth snapped. The others looked at her. 'Just be grateful it didn't occur to them that you *could* have killed Luke.'

Steve exclaimed, 'Look, if Eirian did do it, she deserves a fucking medal!' He subsided, his hand resting in the dull-blond tangle of his hair. 'Sorry. But she saved my son's life.'

Silence. As Beth forced down mouthfuls of her sandwich, she noticed Morgan gazing across at another table, where a woman with long tawny hair sat on her own. Great, she thought. This is all I need. He's looking at other women already.

The woman looked up and caught Morgan's eye. 'I'm sure I know her,' he said.

'Really,' said Beth.

'She was at the inquest,' said Steve. 'That's where you saw her. She had a notebook. Probably a reporter.'

'I didn't notice her . . . but if it's who I think, she is a journalist . . . Hang on.'

He was gone, to Beth's chagrin. She saw Morgan leaning on the table beside the woman, the tawny head turning to face him. They talked animatedly for a few seconds. Then the stranger stood up and embraced him. Morgan brought her to their table, his hand guiding her affectionately.

'Mum, it's Suzanne,' he said, his face glowing with pleasure. 'You know, Mark Tate's wife.'

'Hello, dear,' said Rhianwen. 'I didn't recognize you. Grown your hair, haven't you?' She stood up and kissed the woman on the cheek.

'Lovely to see you, Mrs Rhys.' Smart in a beige suit, Suzanne was attractive, about thirty, Beth guessed, with a sharp-featured, tanned face and a friendly, open expression. She looked nice, but Beth felt hostile towards her.

'Suzanne, this is Beth, Eirian, Steve . . . Mark was my best man,' Morgan added by way of explanation. 'I went to school with him. How is he, by the way?'

'Oh, you know Mark,' Suzanne said. 'Still rugby-crazed and driving me up the wall. I can't believe this.' She slipped her hand through Morgan's arm, too friendly. 'We haven't seen Morgan for years. Not since his wedding! How is Marian?'

There was an awkward silence. Suzanne breathed, 'Oh, my God, I've put my foot in it, haven't I? I'm terribly sorry. This is pretty embarrassing all round.'

'No, it's okay,' Morgan sighed. 'I split up with Marian. I'm with Beth now.'

Suzanne looked stunned. 'Oh. Oh, I see. Now it all makes sense . . . I think. Look, I don't know whether you saw me but I was at the inquest. I wanted to ask for an interview, but the fact that I know Morgan makes it rather difficult.'

Beth leaned forward, folding her arms on the table. 'I told all the reporters when we came out of the inquest, we are not giving any interviews.'

There was an awkward pause. Suzanne looked at Morgan. Beth, usually a friendly soul, felt at odds with everyone. Morgan cleared his throat. 'Why don't you sit down and join us, Sue? I'll fetch some more coffee.'

'I'll come and give you a hand,' Suzanne said hurriedly.

'May I have some apple pie, please?' Eirian called after them.

'My God, you're full of surprises, aren't you?' said Suzanne, as Morgan pushed a tray of coffee and cake towards the cash till. 'How did you meet Beth?'

'Have you got all day?'

'Like that, is it? Must be love if you don't mind taking on someone else's child.'

Morgan laughed. He hadn't been called to give evidence

and nothing said at the inquest had made it clear that Eirian was his. 'But Eirian's my daughter.'

'What – biologically yours?'

'Yes. Don't look at me like that.'

'But how –'

'The usual way.' He smiled ruefully. 'Another long story. I never told Mark. Wasn't something to boast about.'

'God, you're a dark horse, Morgan. Aha, did Beth have something to do with you leaving school in a mysterious hurry when you were sixteen?'

'Good grief, Sue, no wonder you're an ace investigative journalist,' said Morgan, gathering a handful of coffee creamers.

'Look, about that . . . I understand how Beth must feel about publicity, but I'm not working for some crappy tabloid. I'd like to talk to you about what I'm doing.'

'That's fine with me.' Morgan trusted Suzanne. She was decent, intelligent, a good friend.

'But Beth doesn't seem to like me.'

Morgan shook his head. 'It's not like her. She's usually so friendly. She's had a rotten time and she's tired; we all are. She'll come round.'

'I can't imagine what she must have been through,' Suzanne said gravely. 'Having her daughter abducted . . . oh, your daughter, too, of course.'

'It wasn't an experience I'd want to repeat,' Morgan said quietly.

'I'm researching a book about religious cults,' Suzanne told them. 'It'll be serialized in a national newspaper, one of the heavyweights. It's a serious study, not sensationalist. If you'd agree to talk to me about your experiences I'd really appreciate it.'

The moment she began to speak, Eirian received one of her Goddess-given flashes of certainty. This is what I'm meant to do, she thought, electrified. Tell the Goddess's story. This is what she wants me to do!

Suzanne looked at Beth as she spoke, her blue eyes sincere and persuasive. Beth appeared unmoved. Eirian knew she had an absolute horror of publicity. The one time Beth's photograph had appeared in a local newspaper, Luke had found her and taken Eirian.

'I'm sorry,' said Beth. 'It's out of the question. I've hated all this, Luke's name being in the paper, Eirian and Sam being "Child A" and "Child B". All I want is for it to die away and be forgotten. I don't want people staring at us in the street.'

'It wouldn't be like that,' said Suzanne. 'Your anonymity would be sacrosanct. All names would be changed. If we used any photographs, they'd be posed by models.'

'I think it would be good,' said Morgan. 'You know, cathartic. Sue's a good writer, she'd tell the truth.'

'I don't mind,' said Steve. 'I can tell you loads about Sam's mother, Katy, leaving me to join Luke's cult.'

'This is just the sort of thing I need,' Suzanne said enthusiastically. 'There could be television as well. I'm in contact with a documentary-maker who is very interested in the subject – yes, Beth, I know that sounds even worse, but they can interview anonymously too.'

'I can't stop Steve,' said Beth, 'but I won't do it. And definitely not Eirian.'

Agitated, Eirian broke in vehemently, 'But I want to do it, Mum. I really want to talk about it.' She couldn't put her passion into words, it was so strong. This was her chance to speak, she couldn't let her mother ruin it. She saw shadows gathering, a smoke-form rearing up behind her father. The goat-demon again, with a hideous lean head, a wolf-hide on its shoulders, fangs dripping saliva and blood. She felt a brief, searing pain through her wrists and ankles. Her enemies, warning her to be silent . . .

I won't, she thought, holding herself steady until the worst of it passed. In the name of the Great Mother, go! I won't be silenced by you!

'Better to talk than bottle it up,' Rhianwen put in.

'No,' Beth said firmly. 'I absolutely will not let my daughter be interrogated by journalists. I want her to have a quiet life and do well at school.'

'But Mum!' Eirian cried. 'I need to tell the truth, I've got to!'

The very intensity of her voice seemed to alarm Beth even more. 'No!' she said fiercely. 'It's out of the question. The answer is no.'

'Mum!' Eirian was outraged. Preternatural enemies couldn't silence her but her mother could.

Suzanne sat back, sighing. The others looked dazed; Beth could be very intimidating when roused. 'Look, I'm really sorry,' said Suzanne. 'I know you're upset and I've picked the worst possible time to approach you.' She glanced at her watch. 'I ought to be on the road. I apologize if I've intruded, but . . .' She fished in her briefcase and gave Morgan a business card. 'Here's my number, in case you change your mind. We're in London.'

As she went, Morgan kissed her cheek and said, 'Give my best to Mark. You'll have to come and visit.'

'Invite them to the wedding,' said Rhianwen.

'Oh, yeah. My mother's getting married, can you believe it?'

When they arrived home, a couple of hours later, Eirian was speaking to no one and no one was speaking to Beth. Beth felt she must be giving out an aura of black spikes to frighten them off, but she couldn't help it.

She took Eirian by the arm, marched her upstairs to the guest bedroom, and closed the door behind them. They sat facing each other on the twin beds.

'Eirian.' Beth took a deep breath and tried to sound gentle, 'I know the inquest was very upsetting for you. But if you want to talk to someone, why can't you talk to me?'

Eirian's face was set with anger. Not a child's expression. 'I'm not upset. But I need people to listen to me.'

'Your Dad and I are here to listen.'

Eirian shook her head, impatient. 'That's not what I mean!

You don't understand, Mum, I've got to speak out about Luke and the witch-finders so people understand how evil they are! The Goddess wants me to do it!'

'Oh, does she?' said Beth. 'I don't care, I am not having you used to make a good story by people like Suzanne. I want you to forget all this, have a good summer holiday, then concentrate on your new school.' To herself she added, I want you to be a normal child, Eirian, *please*.

'You're as bad as the people at the inquest!' Eirian hissed. 'I caused Luke's death by letting him destroy himself – but how could I explain? They'd never understand! But he deserved it, and people need to know why, and I have to tell them!'

'Stop,' said Beth, beginning to tremble. Eirian looked anything but childish. Her face was flushed, her eyes narrow and green-gold with inner light. She was a woman, a goddess. What was this terrifying creature Beth had borne, capable of exacting such terrible revenge?

'You've got no right to be angry with me, Mum.' Eirian's tone was dark, admonishing. 'What's upsetting you isn't just Luke, is it? You have to tell Dad.' She leaned forward and placed her hand on Beth's abdomen. Then her face fell and she gasped, 'Mum – I didn't know – you have to tell him!'

Beth jumped up. How had Eirian known? She couldn't take any more. The blackness was closing in around her, stained with jagged colours, like migraine. She went blindly through the door, ran downstairs to where Morgan, Steve and Rhianwen were quietly having a cup of tea.

'Did you know what Eirian was planning to say at the inquest?' Beth shouted at Morgan. 'Why the fuck didn't you tell me?'

He gaped at her. Not waiting for an answer, Beth rushed through the kitchen, out across the garden, through the little gate into the meadow beyond.

She'd come this way with the newborn Eirian in her arms. Up this grassy slope and into these woods, the trees and undergrowth folding wetly around her. It had been dark then; now there was a sunset, purple sky, thick gold light, blue shadow, but she felt every bit as remote from reality.

Beth staggered through the trees, the pressure swelling to bursting point inside her. Eventually she found herself at the Hellstone. A pagan site, full of resonance. She and Morgan had conceived Eirian here. Beth had nearly died here, alone with her baby. She didn't know whether she loved the place or hated it.

She needed to be alone but Morgan was coming after her.

'Beth, what's wrong?' he called, concerned. As he came out of the trees into the clearing, she suddenly saw him as her mother must see him. A demon. His lean form the stretched torso of a wolf, his arms and legs adorned with spiky black feathers, his face part wolf, part hawk, inhuman. Green cat's eyes with no trace of tenderness in them. Only grinning amorality.

'Have you ever slept with Suzanne?' she said.

'What?' Morgan stopped a couple of feet from her, looking stunned. 'No, I haven't. Surely you didn't think –?'

'What do I know about you? You think it's all right for Eirian to tell the coroner and the whole bloody world that she killed Luke!'

. Morgan lifted his hands helplessly. 'No, but I'm just finding out how stubborn she is! Hasn't it occurred to you that she did something very brave, getting Olivia off the hook?' His tone was conciliatory, but the pressure inside Beth distorted everything. The worm had eaten the soft centre of the rose away and now it was bursting out through the fragile outer petals, monstrous, bristling with poisoned spikes.

'But Eirian –' Beth lunged forward and gripped his arms, her fingers digging into him. 'What is she?' she whispered. 'What have we made, Morgan?'

His green eyes opened wide and his hands came up to hold her off. 'Bethie, don't.'

She took a sobbing breath and spoke quickly. 'Maybe Mum was right. Luke died, Mum's in hospital, Dad's on his own, Gran's dead – all because you seduced me. I mean, did you know?'

Morgan went white. He took a step back from her. 'Jesus, Beth. You thought I had some master plan to destroy your family? Come off it! It was lust, simple as that. I know I behaved badly but for God's sake, how much more guilty do you want me to feel?'

'How could you say you loved me, then get me in trouble and leave me all alone?' Beth wrenched away and struck his chest. She wanted to stab him. 'I nearly bled to death on this stone because you and Rhianwen deserted me! How could you do that to me?'

Morgan turned almost grey. He didn't look demonic now, only human and hurt. 'If I'd known – I never meant to hurt you, I'd do anything to change the past, but I can't. Christ. You once said this would poison us.' His voice was quiet and raw. 'You really hate me for what happened, don't you? I didn't understand, I thought I could put everything right.'

'I don't hate you,' she said bleakly, 'but have you heard of history repeating itself? You made me fall in love, planted a demon baby in my womb, and then you vanished. Now you can do it all over again.'

'What? Beth, you're scaring me. For God's sake tell me what's wrong!'

Beth felt her blood draining away, leaving her pale and cold. She'd tried so hard to keep the secret, failed miserably. She spoke bitterly, knowing she'd ruined everything. 'We're not meant to have another child, are we? "There won't be another time," you said to Rhianwen.'

Morgan breathed in and out softly. He came closer but didn't touch her. 'Are you saying what I think you are? But you're –'

'On the pill, yes, but I forgot one, just one, because there was so much happening. Just my luck. We are so accident-prone, and you have quite a track-record of running away from accidents . . .' Her throat closed up.

He looked devastated. 'Beth, are you upset because you think I'm going to leave you again? How could you think that? I can't stand you not trusting me, it's so unfair! I know we didn't plan another baby, but – oh, God, I don't know what to say.' His hands crept lightly on to her shoulders. 'Beth, if you want it, so do I. I'm staying, whatever happens. Don't look so sad. God, I'm thrilled.'

'Morgan,' she said sharply, to stop him.

'What?'

'I had a miscarriage this morning.' She turned, and she was going to leave him, walking on knives, but he caught hold of her.

'Why the hell didn't you tell me?'

'Don't shout at me!' She tried to break loose, but the woods tilted, and the next she knew he was helping her to sit down on the rounded edge of the Hellstone. The pressure inside her broke, like the ocean bursting through a sea-wall. She wept helplessly. His arms cradled her. He was crying too, his lovely face all shadow and reflected light. No demon. She didn't know how she could ever have seen him like that.

'Don't push me away, don't go back to your mother's side,' he whispered fervently. 'Stay with us, for love.'

After a while she found she could speak, leaning limp and calm against him. 'It happened in the hotel, early this morning, while you were still asleep. I woke up with cramps. I went into the bathroom and lost a load of blood. I wasn't even sure I was pregnant until then, I only suspected. It must have happened just after you came back from Canada, about six weeks.'

He groaned. 'Why the hell didn't you wake me up?'

'It was very undramatic. First I thought, now I don't have to admit I'm pregnant and risk you vanishing again. But then all I felt was . . . heartbroken.' She let out another sob; Morgan held her tight. 'It's like I can't let anything of yours go, I love you so much. I was dreaming about the baby before I woke. He was a beautiful boy and we called him Auryn. He was so like you, this . . . sexy angel.'

'Why Auryn?'

'Eirian and Auryn, silver and gold. Welsh.' She breathed out shakily. 'But he's gone. It's everything; losing Luke, Gran, Mum, being terrified of losing you, and now this . . . I didn't want to be pregnant but the moment I lost Auryn I wanted him, right or wrong. I really wanted him.'

'So did I.' He meant it; she heard his pain. 'Oh, Bethie, why do you think you have to go through everything alone? Don't you ever dare shut me out like that again!'

'Sorry. I've ruined everything.'

'No, no, you haven't. Hush. Did you tell Eirian?'

'No, but she knew,' said Beth. Dusk folded around them as they clung together, mourning. She closed her eyes, aware of the rich dark earth thrumming in empathy around them, the shadowy sexual forces that had drawn them together. There was no division between friendship and physical desire, love, tenderness, infatuation, obsession. It was one seamless spectrum, all colours mixing to white light. Their mouths joined, opening warmly to each other. Morgan tasted sweet and warm, then salt, his tears seeping on to her tongue.

For the loss of Auryn, Beth had consolation; the certainty, at last, of Morgan's love.

I'll never have my mother to myself again, Eirian thought, when her parents came back into the house. They were pale and quiet, but closer than ever. I'll never have my father to myself either.

Eirian had willed Morgan to come home. She didn't regret it. She wanted Beth to be happy. But it had never crossed her mind she would feel so excluded. They wanted that baby, she thought guiltily, but I didn't.

Rhianwen reacted with intense sympathy when they told her, hugging and kissing them both. She did not say, 'I told you so.'

Randolph was gently matter-of-fact. 'Miscarriages are very common, Beth. The foetus may not have been viable for genetic reasons. You must go to your doctor first thing and arrange to see a gynaecologist for a check-up.'

'But tonight we need healing,' said Rhianwen. 'We've all had a rough time. A healing ritual will help us start again.'

Steve had gone home to be with Sam and Dee. Randolph

looked dubious at the prospect of a pagan ritual. 'It's optional,' Rhianwen said brightly. 'But we're not going to summon Beelzebub, or anything.'

'I didn't think you were. No, I may as well join in,' he said, to their surprise. 'If I'm going to live with you, I'd better get used to it.'

Rhianwen cleared a space in the living room, lit candles and incense until the room became a glowing bower, with goddesses looking down from the walls. Several cats flopped in a furry heap on the sofa; the five humans sat cross-legged on the carpet, while Rhianwen – elegant in a russet *djellaba*, her hair a loose auburn mass – began a low, beguiling chant.

She invoked the names of healing goddesses and gods. She burned certain herbs, passed round a chalice of salt water to draw out negative emotions, asking them each to say what they most feared and desired.

Eirian understood that magic lay not in casting spells, but in effecting psychological change. Drifting on the haze of fragrant smoke, seeing the beautiful faces of Beth and Morgan, with their pale skin and dark hair, she knew it was working. The cone of energy they generated was strong, kind and uniting. But . . .

With the soothing warmth of love, Eirian felt a darker presence come in. Swiftly she visualized shields of psychic light, to protect the others and keep the vision tight to herself. This was her battle.

The X-shaped cross reared huge and stark in the centre of the circle. Eirian felt rough hands seizing her, splaying her limbs, driving nails through her wrists and ankles. Her pain was only a shadow of reality but still it congealed in her chest, heavy and suffocating. She felt pain boiling in her pubic bone, bloody sacs filling her mouth. She saw fires burning below and the invaders staring up, faces sweaty in the fire-glow, hands clutching guns and Bibles. Cruel, sneering faces, burning with self-righteous hatred of pagans, heretics and savages. Warning her, *This will happen to you if you dare to speak out!*

Eirian fell forward off the cross. She was a bird flying. A

primeval bird with heavy wings, flapping laboriously towards the violet line of the horizon. Cawing her pain to an indifferent ocean.

Then she became a boar, snouting between the thighs of a copulating couple. Ripe evocative scents filled her head but she couldn't make them aware of her, because she was only a ghost. An amalgam of tortured spirits, wretched and weak . . . but growing stronger each time Morgan and Beth or Randolph and Rhianwen made love. Feeding hungrily on the energy of sex and witchcraft . . .

With a huge effort, Eirian pulled free and found herself back in the circle. The horned and feathered entity towered in the centre, all glittering black sparks, steel-blue radiance. She felt the ice of its breath. It smelled of fire and autumn. I won't let it taint the ritual, she thought fiercely. And she conjured the Horn of Power in her mind like a spear to drive it away.

Its response stunned her. It fragmented into several components, creatures that drifted seperately out of the main body, grotesque with psychic pain. Each chose a different path out of the circle. A furless cat with blistered skin went in Rhianwen's direction, a goat towards Randolph. A stag and a wolf passed right through Morgan's body; Beth attracted the boar and the hawk. But the creature that slithered and dissipated through Eirian was a huge, scaly serpent. She felt a tingling rush of revulsion. Then it was over.

Drained, she opened her eyes to glowing candle-light and serene faces. There was no sense of the entity; they'd been unaware of her struggle. Rhianwen brought the ritual to a close, then they all kissed each other, and shared wine and cake. The healing had worked, ending the sad day in amber warmth . . . so why did she feel this trace of resentment, that she'd had to face it all alone?

This is my purpose, Eirian thought. To protect my family. To speak out for the Goddess. And no one is going to stop me; not the entity, not even my mother.

*

Morgan was where he needed to be, inside Beth, and she surrounded him, loving, receptive, transported. He loved the way she responded blissfully to his touch and soared to orgasm in astonished ecstasy. As her spasms gripped him he began to fall after her, couldn't hold back. The hot moist walls of her vagina round his achingly engorged penis felt too exquisite to bear; how could anything feel so urgent, so *absolute*? The sharp fire gathered, peaked and exploded outwards. Morgan gasped aloud, thrusting, dissolving into the darkness, with Beth's hands warm on his hips.

Some men, he knew, feared losing themselves in sex, feared the power of women to give or withhold. But Morgan was not afraid of the female darkness. He loved it, worshipped it.

Afterwards, they lay on their sides, face to face, her outer thigh over his and their bodies still joined. 'I've never known anyone have orgasms like you,' he said affectionately. 'They seem absolutely devastating. Did Steve do that to you?'

'Honestly, Morgan!' She exhaled. 'Physically, I suppose. Not emotionally. I would never have wanted children with him either. Never with anyone but you.'

That morning, the consultant had confirmed that Beth had lost a baby. Any miscarriage was deeply traumatic, he told them. While it was natural to mourn, it would be unwise to try again, he went on, gently explaining the genetic risks of their too close relationship. They were subdued as they left his office, hands tightly entwined. But tonight Beth had been emotional, passionate.

'We've never talked about it, and we should,' said Morgan. 'Do you actually want any more children? I don't mind either way but we've only been together a few weeks, we need time alone.'

'Yes,' she said. 'Oh yes.' A pause. Then, quietly bereft, 'We know we shouldn't together. That's the point. It's incest, we *mustn't*. They say.'

'Well, we have one perfect daughter. Don't let's tempt fate.'

He felt her heartbeat against him, the pain of her slow, pensive breathing. 'It's not even that I'm maternal. It's these awful psychic dreams, about the gorgeous human he would have been. Auryn wasn't any man's baby, Morgan, he was *yours*. Glorious proof that we had each other, over and over again. And I wanted to relive my pregnancy with Eirian, and do it right this time.'

'Yes.' A spurt of anguish. 'I wanted that too.'

'But he's gone. And the dreams tell me that I'll never conceive again. That's why I feel bereaved. I watch him drifting away and I wake up crying.'

'Only dreams, Bethie.' But he knew the power of her dreams. His own too.

She smiled bleakly. 'Anyway. I wouldn't be without Eirian for anything, but she worries me. I'm not sure I *could* cope with another one like her.'

'I could have a vasectomy. That way we'll be sure. I don't have macho hang-ups about it.'

Beth gave a soft laugh. 'Oh, love, that's unselfish . . . but not yet. Look, every time we use contraception it goes wrong. I think we should let nature have her way instead. If we are meant to have another child, I want it; but if nothing happens – and I'm sure it won't – at least we gave it a chance.'

Her intuition was so heartfelt, he couldn't argue. 'So you're saying we should use nothing?'

'Nothing,' said Beth. 'Just fuck each other senseless.'

'Sounds reasonable.' He drew her thigh up over his hip, stiffening inside her again. 'It wasn't only lust, when we were teenagers,' he said tenderly. 'It was the intimacy. It was you. You were so wary and innocent but so responsive. It was the way you loved being held and caressed. You were like a cat.'

'I was like an addict, actually,' she said, moving sensuously against him. 'Once I'd had a taste of it, I just couldn't stop.'

'It was such a beautiful feeling, wasn't it?' The corners of his mouth curved up. 'And it was forbidden, that made it even sweeter. I've never had feelings like that with anyone else.'

'Grass isn't greener,' Beth said languidly.

'Hell, if I'd realized, I wouldn't have let you go for twelve minutes, never mind twelve years.'

'Steve and I turned up to see Rhianwen three years ago, and we saw you and Marian leaving. I wonder what would have happened if we'd bumped into you? Embarrassing, or what?'

'I know what would've happened,' said Morgan. 'Exactly what happened when we finally did meet. Goodbye Marian and Steve.'

'Oh, God.' Beth pressed her head into his shoulder. 'For being a few minutes late, I missed three years with you. And maybe all the crap with Luke wouldn't have happened then.'

'Well, it's over.'

'But it affects the rest of our lives.'

'So does everything we do. That's why we're going to be happy from now on.'

Morgan heard the door creak softly. As he looked up, he caught the impression of a wolfish shadow dissolving in a bar of light from the landing. Eyes playing tricks. A slender long-haired figure in pyjamas slipped through the doorway and came towards the bed.

'Mum?' said Eirian. 'Are you all right?'

Uncoupling, Beth reached over and switched on the bedside lamp. 'Fine now, love. What is it?'

'I want to ask you something.' To Morgan's surprise, Eirian climbed on to the bed and lay down on the cover. There wasn't much room so she was on top of them rather than between them. They hugged her and there was a moment of blissful unity.

Morgan, looking at Beth, felt a pang of guilt that they'd spent so much time alone, leaving Eirian with Rhianwen. As their hands met around their daughter, he sensed the same tension in Beth's touch.

'I really need to talk to Suzanne.' Eirian's voice was softly persuasive, almost seductive. 'I don't just want to, I *need* to.'

Beth let out a very long, soul-weary sigh. 'All right. I don't know why I'm giving in. You're just like your father, you always get your own way in the end.'

'Thank you,' said Eirian in the same velvet tone. 'So you'll phone Suzanne for me, won't you, Dad? Tomorrow.'

Chapter Eight

E IRIAN appeared in silhouette on the television screen, a faint wash of light outlining her head and the long hair spread on her shoulders. She sat very still and answered the questions articulately, seeming totally composed. Her voice had the lightness of a child but her delivery was an adult's, so self-assured that she was bewitching.

Beth sat beside her daughter on the sofa, Morgan, Rhianwen and Randolph also watching in rapt silence. Eirian's interview formed only a small part of the hour-long documentary. A bishop and a psychologist spoke about the dangers of religious cults; survivors related their experiences. All told compelling stories. But Eirian's appearance in shadow was something more, magnetic and extraordinary.

The unseen interviewer didn't ask about Luke's death, only about Eirian's ordeal at his hands. Then she asked if Eirian knew why Luke had abducted her.

'Because his beliefs made him imagine that I was possessed by the Devil,' said Eirian. 'All his followers suffered from the same delusion. They think the Devil is real.'

'Don't you think they may have had a sincere faith?' asked the interviewer.

'Oh, they were sincere. But their faith was based on lies.'

'What kind of lies?'

'The lies in the Bible,' said Eirian.

There was a brief pause, as if the interviewer were taken aback. 'Don't you believe in God?'

'Not that sort of God. The Bible splits everything in half; spirit and flesh, holy and profane, heaven and hell. But you can't split life up like that. Pagans believe that everything is interconnected, so our bodies are as sacred as our souls; how can you separate them? To teach that we're sinful and need saving is misguided.'

'Would you call yourself a pagan?'

'Yes. My parents are too. That's why Luke thought we were evil. Christians seem to think we're Satanists, but they're judging us by their standards, not our own. I would like everyone to realize they're wrong. We're ordinary people.'

The interviewer's voice was soft, very much in the background, but Beth heard her tone change as if she were treading on unexpected territory. 'But how can anyone have moral standards without a religious code such as the Bible to guide them?'

Eirian replied as if the answer were obvious. 'If you believe that life is sacred, you automatically treat other people with kindness and respect. Pagans believe the Earth is their mother, but Christians see it as a place of banishment – so, which of us is more likely to treat nature with reverence?'

The question was left hanging, while the scene changed and the psychologist brought the documentary to a close. Morgan unfolded himself from the sofa and turned off the television. 'That's over with,' he said.

'Well, I thought it was very good,' said Rhianwen. 'Pretty unbiased, for a change.'

'Unbiased?' Randolph exclaimed. 'Even that bishop was enough to put you off organized religion for life. Very well presented, but I'd hardly call it impartial.'

'What's wrong with that?' said Rhianwen. 'About time we redressed the balance.'

'I thought I sounded pompous,' Eirian said morosely, undazzled by seeing herself on TV. 'And childish.'

'No, you didn't,' said Morgan. 'You sounded incredibly grown-up.'

'They used hardly any of the stuff I said.'

'The BBC people were talking to you for two hours, if you remember,' Morgan pointed out. 'They could hardly fit all that in.'

'I could have said it all better. I was much younger then.'

'All of six months!' Rhianwen exclaimed.

'I'll make a cup of tea,' said Beth, and escaped into the kitchen.

Her own kitchen. All pale golden oak and terracotta tiles, brand-new but warmly old-fashioned in style. Last summer they'd bought the house with which they'd fallen in love, her grandfather's childhood home on the village green. Only ten minutes' walk from Rhianwen's, half an hour's drive from Eirian's new school and twenty minutes from Woodbourne Hall. They'd stayed with Rhianwen until October, when they were able to move in. Now it was March. The kitchen and bathrooms were finished, other renovations in progess, all the decorating still to do. The house was going to be beautiful. Next to the big, warm kitchen there was a dining room with dark rosewood furniture and, across the hallway, a sitting room with beams and huge brick fireplace. Upstairs were four bedrooms with wonderful views of the village. Beth was making stained-glass panels for the front door and some of the windows; images of goddesses and green men, patterns of oak and ivy leaves, holly with red berries like blood-drops. Eirian and Morgan expressed delight at the work she was doing.

Beth switched on the kettle and put mugs on a tray, relieved the documentary was over. I'm so proud of Eirian, she thought, her composure was absolutely stunning. Yet it had been oddly disturbing to see her daughter on the screen, distant, shadowy and compelling . . .

Morgan came in and put his arms round her. 'Well, that was painless, wasn't it?' he said cheerfully. 'The newspaper articles and Suzanne's book don't give a hint of who Eirian actually is, like she promised.'

'It's been okay,' Beth sighed. 'Suzanne's been marvellous, really helpful and responsible about all this. I hope she's forgiven me for being so hostile the first time we met.'

'She understood.'

'Eirian's so articulate. I don't know where she gets it from.'

'Go and tell her how good she was, then.'

'I don't want to encourage her.'

Morgan looked chidingly at her. 'She needs your approval, Beth.'

'Does she?' Beth sighed. 'Yes, okay, I'll tell her.'

'Come on, Bethie, it's all over now.' He kissed her cheek, her mouth. Familiarity never made him any less exciting to her. She was always thrilled by the dark soft fall of his hair, the mischievous green gleam of his eyes.

Beth smiled. 'I only hope Eirian's got this compulsion to talk out of her system. It's so easy to forget she's still a child, but she is. I hope we did the right thing.'

'Look, we know she's not an attention-seeker,' said Morgan. 'So if she really needed to tell her story, we were right to let her.'

'I suppose so,' said Beth. 'If we hadn't, she might never have forgiven us. On the other hand, she might turn round when she's twenty-five and say, "Why didn't you stop me, Mum? Why didn't you protect me?"'

'Do you expect to win, or something?' Morgan said, grinning ironically. 'Nothing more will come of it, so stop worrying. It'll all be forgotten by tomorrow.'

Her miscarriage hit Beth harder than she could admit. To her it was not, as outsiders seemed to think, a late period, a non-event. It was the loss of Morgan's son, another Morgan, the beautiful child of their vibrant ecstasy. As the days and weeks passed, Beth dreamed endlessly about Auryn: an untouchable angel who always left her, though she ached and wept for him to stay.

In reality, she knew, a baby would have come too soon. Morgan was right, they needed time alone to get to know each other, freedom to work and travel and enjoy themselves. But the ache of emptiness lingered. Morgan understood, and was tender to her, so in spite of the loss they were exquisitely happy.

At work, Beth went into a creative frenzy. She made designs of stunning intricacy, soaring windows of glorious rich colour. Sometimes she unconsciously added a white angel to the design;

an elongated figure, nothing like the glass cherub she'd made, the first day she'd taken over the stall. That, she knew too late, had been a foreshadowing of Auryn. Now it seemed all she had left of him.

When Beltane came, the eve of May Day, Beth and Morgan went to the woods with their family and friends. The Hellstone glimmered in the dusk, its rounded bulk as sensual as female curves. They erected the Horn as a symbol of rebirth in the centre, heaped flowers and fruit as gifts for the Goddess and Horned God around it, cast a circle with candles and musky incense. The clearing became an enchanted bower, glowing amber, old gold, velvety green.

Another witch, a friend of Rhianwen, conducted the ritual; the handfasting of Beth and Morgan, a pagan wedding. It had no weight in law but it meant more than conventional marriage to them. It was also a celebration of life, renewal.

A year passed. There were no repercussions from Eirian's documentary appearance, to Beth's relief, and at her new school Eirian seemed settled and content. Beth passed her driving test and bought a small van in which to deliver commissions. Marian divorced Morgan, quite amicably, on the grounds of adultery. Steve and Dee bought a house together in Lullingford, while Sam – with the friendship of Eirian and Dee's two sons – grew into a happy, well-balanced lad.

As Beth had predicted, she did not conceive again. Perhaps medical tests would have revealed scarring, a blockage, but it would only have told her what she already knew. Nature was harsh, punishing the conception of two precious, forbidden children by taking one away and allowing no more; and nature was kind, giving Beth and Morgan their sensual freedom without consequence.

Now it was May again and in a month's time Eirian would be thirteen.

Spring was Beth's favourite time of year. She was spending a pleasant afternoon rearranging the bedroom, with the window open so she could hear the birds singing and Morgan's and Eirian's voices in the garden. Beth had lavished all her care and love on this room. Fresh paint, William Morris wallpaper and fabrics in deep blues and rusts, floral borders, Pre-Raphaelite prints on the walls, A thick autumn brown carpet. All the furniture was dark oak, and she'd made a large stained-glass panel for the main window, Aphrodite under the Tree of Life. Luxury undreamed of in the days of her derelict cottage.

Beth sat on a stool at the dressing table and opened her grandmother's vanity case. She'd been meaning to clean it for months. First she removed the old photograph of her grandfather on the Hellstone and propped it against the mirror. Then she took out the cut-glass bottles one by one, sniffing the residue of old cosmetics and lotions. The case had fascinated her as a child, with its lining of padded blue silk and mysterious compartments.

As she worked, an odd rustling noise seemed to come from inside the case. Beth froze, skin crawling. There was a secret drawer in the base, she remembered . . . Could something alive have got inside?

As her hand found the hidden lever, she saw something from the corner of her eye. A squat dark shape like a pig, vivid for a second, then scuttling across the carpet and vanishing through the wall. Beth gaped. At that moment the drawer sprang out and hit her hand. Violent shock jolted her. Disoriented, she probed into the space behind the drawer, found some folded paper, warily drew it out. The rustling stopped, but the atmosphere remained warped like thick yellowish glass around her.

In her hand was a four-page letter, in black ink on yellowing paper, addressed to her grandmother. Beth recognized her grandfather's writing. It was dated 1944; Randolph would have been twenty-six then. Beth knew he had joined the medical corps in the Far East after qualifying, but she didn't know the details because he never reminisced about the war. How odd that Heather should conceal one particular letter. Beth felt an irrational dread of reading it, yet the eerie pressure compelled her to do so.

My darling Heather,

They tell me I am still fevered and insist on my staying confined to bed, but I am quite well again, only weakened by this heat. I want to take up my duties. The bed oppresses me. I cannot face another night like the last, and my only relief is writing to you. I was visited last night and, forgive me, I must relate the experience or go mad. They say I was delirious but nothing will convince me it was a dream!

I woke to the heavy, still heat of the night, with insects singing outside the thin walls of the hut, the man in the next bed to mine snoring – that convinced me beyond doubt I was awake. It was stifling yet I felt cold. Slowly I became aware of faces all around the bed, staring at me. At first I thought they were medical staff and that I must be dying; I tried to ask what they wanted but they didn't answer. Then in horror I recognized them as all the men I've seen die since I came here. These ghosts had bullet holes in chests, guts spilling out of abdominal wounds, an arm hanging by a thread or a thigh bone shining in a crimson hole. Their faces were terrible, a deathly bluish-white, and their eyes! Dead grey eyes staring at me. As they came towards me a strange paralysis lay on me. I saw them through the gauze of the mosquito net, and I thought, at least the net is between me and them! I cannot describe the utter terror I felt, something beyond earthly terror, a hysterical revulsion – yet I was deadly calm, as if my mind were weighed down by the same ice-cold ropes as my body. These were the men whose lives I failed to save! Brave men who'd cracked jokes through agonizing pain, who'd looked on me as their saviour. It was as if I'd failed them, *I*, not bullets or the jungle parasites that ate them away. Now they wanted something of me. Not vengeance! I felt it was help they demanded. Yet their demand made no sense for what help could I give the dead?

Now I saw their faces very close to me, with the misty folds of the netting *behind* them. My heart faltered and I was drenched in cold sweat. I knew that when they reached me, I would die.

Next it seemed that the ghostly faces began to waver, swelling and becoming featureless, like blurred moons. They all coalesced into one swollen sphere of bluish-white luminescence. Something moved inside this sphere. I cannot sufficiently emphasize the dread it roused in me. I glimpsed green eyes, a long dark head more animal than human, long limbs fringed with feathers like clashing knives. It seemed to be dancing. I felt I was watching a scene that no human should ever see.

It seemed at first very far away, then very close. It was on the bed. As if it were transparent I could no longer see it, only feel its feathers scraping my skin, its breath on my face, its weight like a blanket of darkness covering me. It was inside the net, under the sheets, lying on top of me, right against my skin.

My dear, what happened next will offend you, even repulse you. Don't read on if you can't bear it. I perceived the demon as male but it mounted me like a female, forcing me to enter some unnatural orifice in the front of its body. I tried with all my might to resist, but my will was a match-flame against an iceberg. It stimulated me against my will. It would not be putting it too strongly to say that it raped me. I felt a spasm, an ejaculation, more like the release of terror than pleasure – and with that the entity was gone. I saw the folds of the net stirring sluggishly. Then I slept deeply and woke, soaked in sweat, to daylight.

I shall pray for the ghosts and demons not to come again tonight, but of what worth is a God in whose name men are parted from their families and sent to die wretchedly in this hopeless place? If I survive the night without a second visitation, I shall have hope of coming home to you and our little Olivia.'

The letter ended there, unsigned. Beth sat holding the brittle pages, feeling shaken. It was a side of her grandfather she had never dreamed existed. He obviously wasn't himself when he wrote this, she thought, but – a voice made her start violently. 'Hi, Morgan said it was okay to come up. Sorry, didn't mean to make you jump.'

It was Steve. He hovered in the doorway, grinning, his hands in the pockets of his long patchwork jacket. 'Come in,' said Beth. 'I was miles away.' He came and hugged her; his tangled fair hair smelled of incense. His presence should have dispelled the dark atmosphere, but it didn't. 'Is Dee with you?'

'In the garden with the kids. We just dropped round to say hi. Anything interesting?'

Beth passed him the letter. 'I found this hidden in my Gran's case.'

Steve read it, sitting on an oak blanket-chest at the end of the bed. Then he shrugged and passed it back to her. 'Did your granddad have malaria, or something?'

'He must have done. Gran must have thought he'd gone barking mad when she got this. She couldn't bring herself to throw it away, so she hid it instead.'

'Well, your granddad's still around, so at least you can ask him about it.'

Beth breathed out heavily. 'I don't think so. It's so long ago. He hates talking about the war, I think he'd just be embarrassed.'

'Aren't you even going to show it to Morgan?'

'Can't see much point, really. It's already all he and Granddad can do to get on, I don't want to make things even worse. No, best just to put it back and pretend I never found it.' It was only as she replaced the letter, pushed the drawer back in and closed the case, that the world flickered back to normal. She sat frozen in pure astonishment.

'My lips are sealed,' said Steve, oblivious. 'Bit of all right, this house, isn't it? You've made a beautiful job of it. It's great to see you so happy. Lucky, aren't we? Never thought I'd meet anyone to compare with you, but Dee is wonderful. Sam gets on brilliantly with Pete and Hugh. It's really good for him to have a step-mother and brothers.' He stood up and stroked her shoulder. 'Come on, let's go out in the garden before they think we're up to something. We brought cider . . . Hey, Beth, you all right?'

'Yes,' she said, mentally shaking herself. 'Sorry. I really need a drink, after that.'

They sat on the grass in the spring sunshine, Morgan and Beth, Dee and Steve, sharing a bottle of cider. The edges of the rough lawn blurred into shrubs, so the garden seemed to have no boundaries. Everything shimmered with new green leaves; tulips and hyacinths sprouted promiscuously between the trees. Eirian was with Sam, Peter and Hugh, kicking a ball at the bottom of the garden, half seen through the blossom laden branches of apple and cherry trees. Their voices were exuberant, carefree. The air, scented with earth and flowers, was divinely intoxicating. Beth forgot the letter. Nothing could disturb this idyll.

'You could do wonders with this garden,' said Steve. 'Do you want me to help you? Y'know, call in the professionals, ha ha.'

'That would be brilliant,' said Morgan. 'I seem to spend my whole life digging lately. I always wanted to get close to nature but this is ridiculous.'.

'Was that your doorbell?' asked Dee.

Morgan rose to his feet. 'I'll go.' Beth watched his slim, athletic form disappear into the house through the open french window. A few minutes later he was at the kitchen door, signalling to Beth. She excused herself and went into the kitchen. Suzanne was there, wearing a loose, stylish cream suit, her hair piled casually on her head.

'Hi, Beth.' Suzanne said brightly. She was smiling but Beth perceived an anxious set to her eyes. 'I hope I'm not interrupting.'

'Not at all, it's lovely to see you. Would you like tea, cider, wine?'

'Tea would be lovely.'

'Sit down. I'll do it,' said Morgan.

Beth and Suzanne sat down at the kitchen table. 'I was telling Morgan, I'm on my way back from doing an interview in Nottingham so I dropped by on the off-chance that I'd find you in. Otherwise I would have phoned from London later on, but I really wanted to talk to you both in person.'

'Oh yes?' Beth said non-committally.

Suzanne cleared her throat and interlinked her long fingers on the table-top. Her nails were flawless, coated in clear varnish. 'The documentary Eirian appeared in last year has just been shown in America. People I've spoken to over there have commented on Eirian's poise. You should be very proud of her.'

'Yes, of course we are,' said Beth.

'Did you feel that giving the interviews caused her any problems?'

'None that I'm aware of.'

'Quite the opposite, if anything,' said Morgan. He put three mugs of tea on the table and sat down next to Beth. 'She's been really settled and happy, hasn't she, Bethie? She even likes school.'

'Oh, that's good to hear,' said Suzanne.

'Yes, so it's all behind us now,' Beth said firmly.

'Yes, of course.' A pause. 'The situation is that an American producer contacted me yesterday. He produces a talk-show in New York – similar to Oprah Winfrey, you know the kind of thing? They have a serious theme every week and people discuss their experiences. He's planning a programme about cult survivors. He was so impressed with Eirian he is desperate to get her on the show. I told him I could only ask, it was up to her parents . . .'

Suzanne trailed off. All Beth felt was dismay, denial. Morgan waited for her reaction. Beth said levelly, 'I'm sorry, it's impossible. The school is very strict, they wouldn't let Eirian have time off. We wouldn't want her to miss the work, anyway.'

'That's not a problem,' said Suzanne. 'The show's not until late July. She'd be on holiday then.'

'We can't afford it,' Beth said quickly. 'We've put everything into the house.'

'Actually, the TV station would cover all your expenses. Flights, accommodation, everything.'

Suzanne's persistence was annoying Beth. It made her feel she was being irrational, not wanting Eirian exposed. Beth looked at Morgan, willing him to come to her defence. 'Morgan, you can't think it is a good idea, surely?'

'Well, I said I wanted to take you to America. We could combine it with a holiday.'

'But I don't want Eirian being used to spice up some TV show.'

'I wouldn't let her be used!' Suzanne protested.

Morgan said, 'I don't know, I really don't know if it's right or wrong. But we shouldn't dismiss it out of hand. It could be a great experience for Eirian.'

'It's a respected show, Beth,' Suzanne added. 'She could keep her anonymity, like before. But it's up to you, obviously.' She sat back in her chair. 'I didn't mean to make you feel pressured. I said I'd ask, that's all.'

Beth sipped her tea and straightened her thoughts. Maybe I'm overreacting. Maybe they're right, it would be an enriching experience and she'd make new friends, have a wonderful time . . . She took a deep breath. 'So, we fly to New York, Eirian makes one appearance, then we're free to enjoy a holiday?'

'Yes, exactly,' said Suzanne, relaxing. 'They'll treat you like celebrities, the Americans are marvellous. You'll have a wonderful time. I could even come with you, act as a buffer between you and the TV people if you feel they're being too pushy.'

'I'll think about it,' said Beth.

Morgan squeezed her hand. 'Haven't we forgotten something? We ought to ask Eirian first. She might not want to do it.'

That gave Beth a flash of hope. 'I'll call her.'

Eirian came bouncing into the kitchen, bright-eyed and flushed from running. Between them they explained Suzanne's proposal. By the time they'd finished, the colour had gone from Eirian's face and she was completely still, her green eyes intense and glowing with determination.

She spoke without hesitation, to Beth's dismay. 'Yes, Mum, of course I want to go.'

Now it's beginning properly, Eirian thought. Goddess, I've waited long enough!

She ran out into the garden again, but didn't rejoin the three boys at once. She stood at the edge of the orchard, watching them weaving between the trees with the ball, their raucous voices washing over her.

Eirian had been very patient, supporting Beth after the miscarriage, concentrating on schoolwork. She'd known the Goddess would summon her when she was ready; no point in trying to rush things.

The entity had been quiescent. Still there but at arm's length. Just a shadow at the door of her mind, a wind wailing mournfully in the far distance. Eirian was in control.

Now, though, she felt nervous at the weight of her responsibilities – to say the right things, to make people listen, to do the Goddess justice – but she was also deeply excited. It had been good talking to Suzanne and the BBC interviewer, but it was a long time ago and oddly unsatisfying. Just a toe in the water. Now her chance had come at last and she had so much to say she hardly knew where to begin. But the Goddess would guide her.

It was nothing to do with Luke any more.

She stood looking into the future, only half seeing the blossom-laden trees and the rough grass. Then the world turned brittle, patches of it decaying to leave holes into a darker dimension; inky holes shaped like hawk and boar, serpent, cat and goat. Shivering in dread, she watched the shapes blend into a single towering form. It glared down at her, its eyes boiling pools of violet, yellow, visceral red, its mouth stopped with torn flesh.

Eirian caught her breath, her hand flying to her lips as the eyes burned their message into her brain. *'Don't go. Don't speak out. If you do, like us you will be silenced.'*

'I don't know why I feel so uneasy about this American trip,' said Beth. She was adjusting pieces of glass on a paper template, while Dee leaned on the edge of the work-bench, watching her. It was nearly lunchtime and there was a lull in the flow of visitors.

'Yes, you do. You're afraid of her being exploited,' said Dee. She was wearing a white muslin skirt and a laced black bodice, putting Beth in mind of a voluptuous eighteenth-century milk-maid. 'I'm sure there's nothing to worry about. She was so good on that documentary. She has a wonderful power to make people actually stop and listen.'

'Yes, that's the trouble. Her charisma will draw people's attention to her and I hate that. I'm scared someone will spirit her off, like Luke did.'

'I understand how you feel,' Dee said reassuringly. 'But people go on chat-shows all the time and nothing happens, you never even hear of them again. Now come on, you; let's take a break and talk about what a great time you're going to have. You can work too hard, you know.'

'Thanks,' said Beth, amused. She and Dee had become very close over the past eighteen months.

Beth enjoyed being her own boss. She could work her own hours, completely in love with what she was doing. She loved the glass, clean and brittle and as sensuous as jewels, the pleasure of creation, the delight her customers expressed. Her designs, from simple jewellery boxes to elaborate windows, had a distinctive style; art nouveau sensuality and melting colours.

Those were the artifacts she made consciously. But when the urge came from her subconscious, she'd find herself making a panel as if her hands were possessed. She had quite a collection of them now, showing a stormy landscape and a savage figure like a feathered demon. Sometimes another shape appeared, amorphous and white, angel or ghost. The images disturbed her, but she kept it to herself.

When she'd made one, she would display it for a while, as if to exorcize it. There was one hanging in the side-window now, a goatish-looking thing with tattered wings.

While she and Dee were talking, Morgan appeared, looking wonderful even in ancient jeans and green wellies, with a quilted body-warmer over a black sweater. It was a cold day and his face was glowing from the chill wind.

'Bloody hell, it's freezing out there,' he said, wrapping himself round Beth. 'Help me warm up.'

'You're damp and you smell awful,' she said. 'What have you been doing?'

'Dredging about two foot of silt out of a pond. Trying to create a habitat for our aquatic friends.'

'Aren't students or young offenders meant to do that sort of thing?' said Dee.

'Yes, while I stand over them with a big stick.' Morgan shook his head. 'You just can't get the staff these days. I don't suppose you'd – no.'

He met Beth for lunch every day, and her heart always gave a leap of pleasure when he walked in. If it was raining they'd stay in the workshop, but on fine days they would sit on the lawn in front of the Hall. Sometimes he took her to the nature reserve afterwards, a five-minute walk, to show her how his work was progressing. Beth couldn't believe she was working in such beautiful surroundings, so close to him.

Beth sat Morgan in front of her two-bar electric fire, then hurried to the tea-room to refill the flasks with coffee. When she came back, Dee joined them and they ate sandwiches in pleasant companionship. 'I've been telling Beth what a good time you'll have in New York,' said Dee. 'She's in two minds about it.'

'Oh, that's her birthsign,' said Morgan. 'Gemini.'

'Right,' Beth laughed. 'Half of me is cool and confident, the other half is a wreck.'

Morgan squeezed her knee, his eyes gleaming under long lashes. 'The wrecked part is even better.'

'Shut up,' Beth said affectionately. 'Aries the Ram, very

appropriate. Eirian's birthday is three days after mine and she's the same; half child, half goddess.'

'No, Eirian is what you get if you cross an angel with a demon,' said Morgan. 'And no points for suggesting which is which. I know we're going to have a great time in the States; the thing about Beth is she never believes anything until she has concrete proof.' He gave her a warm, meaningful look. 'Sensible woman. What's your sign, Dee? Must be Cancer, you're very caring and motherly to your friends.'

'Isn't he sweet?' said Dee. 'Virgo, actually.'

'Rats. I won't give up my day job.'

When he'd gone back to work, Dee said, 'It's good to see you both looking so happy. I can see why you fell for him. He's lovely.'

'Most of the time,' Beth grinned. 'Okay, you could cut yourself on his tongue sometimes, but I've only known him lose his temper over major things, like Luke. Never with me. I was so scared it wouldn't last, but he stayed. He's just gorgeous, Dee. He knows he can twist me round his –'

'But you love it.'

'Quite.'

'Of course he stayed.' Dee rolled her eyes. 'He's besotted with you, you silly bugger.'

Beth laughed quietly. 'The truth is, I was so scared when I lost the baby that I tried to wreck everything – to make Morgan prove he was strong enough for me, I suppose. But I learned something. If I *must* have these premonitions, I have to be calm and measured about it, like a true witch. And use the knowledge to protect us. Especially Eirian. I've a feeling she's going to need it.'

Morgan walked past the Hall and down the footpath into the nature reserve, feeling at peace. Birdsong fluted around him, so dense it physically textured the air. The sun came out to ease the chill of the morning. The trees around him were thick with fresh green leaves, glistening with rain, a mass of wild plants sprouting through the earth around their roots.

He saw Harry through the trees, over by the half-built visitor centre. Morgan waved and walked on, deeper through the woods towards the quarry. He was thinking fondly about Beth. When he imagined what might have been if Auryn had lived, and when he touched the depth of Beth's pain, he felt grief-stricken. He'd wanted to run away sometimes, but only from himself, because he would rather have died than put Beth through what she'd endured. Twice, now. Yet somehow, in trying to convince Beth he was better than he really was, he had changed. Learned that there was far more to love than sex and good times, and learned to love the darkness too.

He had Beth to himself, at great cost. But he was content. The trip to New York would be another step into the future.

Yet he wondered what was in her mind, to make her produce jagged images like the one she'd had on display today, a demon in stormy greens and purples ... He'd said nothing, but he had noticed it.

Morgan circuited the top of the disused quarry along a thin footpath. The lake at the bottom would attract wildfowl; his object was to make each habitat as welcoming as possible to the species it could support. Bushes clouded the rim, obscuring the safety fence; could do with replacing the danger signs, he thought. I'll talk to Harry. The water was a grey-green mirror, cupped within the eerie walls.

Beyond the quarry, he pushed through close-set trees to the silted-up pond he was clearing. It was thirty feet across, a green oval in a lush, secluded setting. Morgan waded in to assess progress, his wellingtons squelching, water surging round his calves. The spring day was shimmering, invigorating, perfect.

Suddenly the world changed. The birdsong became mechanically strident. Everything turned stiff, like glass; a perfect but inimical reflection of itself. Morgan looked up and froze. He'd had this feeling before, a long time ago.

The pond surface boiled and arrowed. Transfixed in dread, he stared at the movement. Then, a yard from him, the water exploded.

A shape came rearing up, a gout of dripping mud with legs,

arms and eyes. Mud and water seethed down its sides, cascading back into the pond. Morgan took two frantic steps backwards, lost his footing and fell.

The pond was shallow but he went under the surface. Water clamoured in his ears. The shock of coldness was devastating. As he struggled up into the air, coughing, he found himself lying prone, water to his chest, the entity rising over him. Its long featureless face loomed above his, frilled with silt and weeds. It was the creature that had followed him from Canada and it looked . . . oh God, it looked like the demon in Beth's stained-glass panel . . .

He felt hands exploring his thighs. The grizzled body was lowering itself on to him like a lover. Over its shoulder he saw an arching branch and a lump of mud clinging to a leaf as if to a trembling flake of glass.

Under water, the hand travelled to his groin and closed on the denim-covered bulge of his penis and balls.

'No,' he whispered. 'Not this time.'

In a rush of panic, Morgan twisted on to his front, managed to bend one leg under him and levered himself away. He ran and stumbled, the mire sucking at his boots. Looking over his shoulder, he saw the creature lunging after him, a roaring winged shadow; then it seemed to fragment into a million drops of water that rained loudly back into the pond. The water roiled and was still. Morgan found himself lying on the marshy bank with grasses tickling his face.

The world was tranquil again. Morgan sat up, feeling stupid, shaken, and very cold. He was soaked and black with silt. When Beth asked him what had happened, he would laugh and say, I slipped over in the pond, what an idiot. He couldn't tell her the truth.

Oh, Goddess, he thought, dropping his head on to his hands. Why is this happening again now?

Closing his eyes, he immediately saw an image of the Hellstone. Yes, it had happened near the Hellstone before. For some reason that made him remember something else: breath-taking pictures in a book of a domed mountain against the sky, waterfalls, forests. And as soon as he thought of it, he felt his fear of the apparition receding. As if it had got some message across?

'Fuck,' he said out loud, exhaling heavily. 'Yes, we must go there. I always wanted to. I suppose you knew that, did you, my horned friend?'

Chapter Nine

As the jumbo jet surged off the runway, Beth felt her heart accelerating and her stomach falling away. Eirian was staring out of the window but Beth couldn't look. The plane climbed on buffeting wind-currents and she became horribly aware that there was nothing underneath. Her grip on Morgan's hand tightened.

'Are you all right?' he asked, amused.

'I'm scared stiff,' said Beth. 'This is the first time I've ever flown in my life.'

'I know it feels weird, but it's nothing to worry about. Ask Sue, if you don't believe me.' Suzanne was travelling to New York with them, seated a couple of rows in front.

'It's all right for you, you're used to it!'

'Exactly. If I was sweating heavily and demanding a parachute, you might deduce there was something to worry about. They'll bring drinks round soon; have a couple of whiskies, you'll feel much better.' He leaned across to Eirian, who was in the window seat next to Beth. 'You're not nervous, are you, love?'

'Not at all,' said Eirian. 'It's exciting. Don't worry, Mum.'

'Okay. I'll be fine,' said Beth, taking a deep breath. 'As long as you don't get up to anything.'

'Like what?' Morgan said indignantly.

'Jumping up and screaming that the engines are on fire.'

'If anything like that happens, I won't need to mention it. Believe me, you'll know.' He grinned. 'Bethie, relax! I'm only teasing you.' He leaned closer and whispered in her ear, 'I know how to take your mind off flying. We could nip in the loo and join the mile-high club.'

Beth laughed and began to feel better. 'You would, as well, you sod.'

*

A couple of hours into the flight, as Eirian realized that nothing much was going to happen, she grew bored. When lunch was brought in plastic trays, Beth let her have wine. Afterwards she fell asleep, visions rolling over her like the inescapable drone of the aircraft.

She was a wolf, dying from a gaping bullet-hole in her chest. She looked up, tongue lolling, and saw a man above her, his face crude and sneering under a broad-brimmed hat. A musket smoked in his hands. 'Another of the Devil's servants dead,' he said, poking her with his boot. 'Another victory for God.'

Eirian-as-wolf dragged herself away to die. Her body expired but her shade went on, searching in lonely anguish. She found others, broken ghosts like herself, huddling in the shadow of a gleaming marble cathedral. High on the steps she saw an angel in white. A saviour. Through bright light she glimpsed an impression of hands raised in benediction, pale hair and a serene face. Eirian felt a thrill, a pull. She wanted to go to him, but the feeling was one of unravelling, like losing her beliefs, her free will, her self . . .

In a burst of terror, Eirian woke up.

Her mother was dozing, her father watching the film, leaning out into the aisle so he could see the screen. The cabin lights were dimmed, the atmosphere peaceful.

It's no good threatening me, Eirian told her enemies. When you attack me, it only makes me more determined to speak out. I must be calm now. Good Mother, help me to be very calm.

Eirian glanced at her father. He was intent on the film, his chin resting on his hand, soft dark hair feathering his forehead, his eyelids half-lowered over his jade-green eyes. A misty-dark shape flickered at his shoulder and vanished. Images fleeted through her mind: a pale sacred stone, a flow of black water between banks of snow . . .

Eirian often wanted to ask him if he was aware of the entity, but she thought, how can I possibly mention it when I don't understand it myself? He'd only brought part of the entity into her life, perhaps the human part, like the last piece of a jigsaw.

Enough to let it take a wavering shape then feed on his and Beth's sexual energy . . .

Eirian knew they were travelling towards something; an answer, a confrontation, a life or death battle. A blaze of terror seized her. Goddess, I can't bear this alone but I've bloody well got to . . .

'Are you all right, darling?' said Beth, waking up.

'Fine, thanks,' said Eirian. 'Is it much further?'

A limousine met them at the airport. As the chauffeur took charge of their luggage and led them out of the main concourse, a furnace blast of heat enveloped them. Eirian instantly felt sweat forming on her face, as if they'd entered a steam-bath. Her mother gasped and said, 'My God, the heat!'

'That's New York in July, ma'am,' the chauffeur said apologetically.

Eirian noticed a thick, musty odour that caught in her throat. 'What's that smell?'

'That's humidity,' said Morgan, pulling a face. 'Now you know why Americans go everywhere by car.' As they settled themselves in the spacious, leather-scented interior of the limo, the driver shut the doors, sealing them into an air-conditioned cocoon. Suddenly it was almost too cold.

'This doesn't feel right,' said Beth.

'What?' said Morgan.

'Us, being treated like celebrities.'

The others laughed. 'Well, I did warn you,' Suzanne said, patting her arm. 'Just enjoy it. Jamie – that's the producer – said to call him when we arrive, and he'll take us to dinner. He can't wait to meet you.'

'It's really good of you to come with us, Sue,' said Morgan. 'Hope Mark doesn't mind.'

'Oh, he couldn't care less about travelling,' Suzanne said dismissively. 'He'd much rather be on the rugby field or down the pub.'

Eirian felt excited to be in New York, her anxieties forgotten. The drive into the city, along a tangle of roads swarming with unfamiliar vehicles, seemed endless. She and Beth were looking everywhere as the car inched through the traffic, necks craning at skyscrapers. Morgan pointed out the Empire State Building, the twin towers of the World Trade Center standing mistily white in the distance. He'd been to New York before, he said, with Marian.

At street level, the city looked grey-brown, forbidding, heaving with cars, yellow cabs and pedestrians. To Eirian, used to quiet villages, the energy of the city felt alien but oddly thrilling. 'Well, what do you think?' said Morgan.

'When you see a place on television, it's hard to believe it's real,' said Eirian. 'It's wonderful.'

'I've never seen so many people,' said Beth. 'It's overwhelming. I wasn't expecting it to look . . . so old and brooding. A bit sinister, really.'

Suzanne laughed. 'Well, they say you either love New York, or loathe it.'

The limousine brought them to the canopied entrance of a vast, marble hotel near Central Park. Suzanne dealt efficiently with reception, then they rose nineteen floors in a mirrored lift. Their room was huge and luxurious, with a king-sized bed. They were still gaping at the dimensions when Suzanne opened a connecting door to an identical, adjoining room. 'All yours, boys and girls,' she said.

'Isn't that your room?' asked Beth.

'No, it's for Eirian. I'm on the next floor.' She studied her key card. '2018. Well, I suggest we get a couple of hours' rest. I'll call Jamie, ask him to meet us about seven. Give you a ring at six-thirty, okay?'

When Suzanne had gone, Morgan put his arms round Beth and hugged her, grinning. 'Will this do?'

'I wasn't expecting anything quite so . . . over the top,' she said.

'It isn't. It's a fairly standard American hotel room.'

'You're joking. You could open a pub in here!' Beth crossed half a mile of carpet to the windows. As she opened the curtains, a stunning view of Manhattan was revealed. A thousand towers floating in a heat-haze, beige and silver. 'Oh, wow, look at that.'

Morgan and Eirian came to her and they were silent for a few minutes, hugging each other. 'Now are you glad you came?' said Morgan.

'What do you think?' Beth said softly. 'Look, Eirian, you've got a whole room to yourself! How d'you like that?'

Eirian ran into the adjoining bedroom and bounced on the bed. 'It's brilliant,' she called. 'I'll be able to watch anything I want on telly without having an argument about it.'

'Not for long, you won't,' Beth said sternly. 'You'll be too tired. Come on, let's unpack, then we can have a rest before dinner.'

Eirian obeyed, and was back in her parents' room within ten minutes. Lying on their bed while they unpacked, she found the remote control and turned on the television. 'I can't find anything that isn't adverts,' she said in disgust, flicking through the channels. A religious programme appeared. There was an overweight preacher talking in a deep, commanding voice, a lock of dark hair falling over his sweating face. He was ugly yet almost sexually magnetic. The camera moved over the bright, excited faces of the congregation. Their shouts of assent punctuated every phrase and his delivery was that of a great actor: soft and slow, fast and emphatic. His timing was perfect, utterly manipulative.

'I saw this channel when I was in Canada,' said Morgan. 'The True Light Network. This is what they do. Evangelize and raise dollars.'

'Turn it off,' Beth said sharply. Eirian turned and saw her mother in the bathroom doorway, looking stricken, as if she'd seen a ghost of Luke. 'One of you, turn it off!'

'Okay, sorry,' said Eirian. She pressed a button and the screen blanked to grey.

'Now, why don't you go and have a lie-down on your own bed?' Beth said firmly, her colour returning. 'We don't want to be falling asleep over dinner.'

*

Alone in her room, Eirian stretched out on the bed and turned on her own television. She kept the volume low. This privacy felt luxurious, grown-up.

She found the True Light Network and watched for an hour, horribly fascinated. The preacher was healing the sick, calling people forward and pressing his massive hands to their heads. The service ended with some excitable gospel singing, then a grinning Barbie-doll of a woman announced, 'The phone lines are going crazy here! We've raised another $750,000 towards the Bible college, praise the Lord!' There followed – to Eirian's utter amazement – a series of advertisements for overpriced religious icons. A letter-opener, $250. A tiny stained-glass panel – not even proper leaded glass like her mother made, but a printed design – for $500. A special prayer book-mark was free when you ordered videos of the preacher's inspirational sermons for only $750 the set. A grinning clean-cut man exhorted the viewers to take a Bible course and learn to spread the Word.

The preacher's name was the Reverend Paul Gregory Keay. They called him PGK and had ghastly, insistent slogans like 'Find the Way with PGK.' You could ring up and 'prayer warriors' would pray for you or your loved ones. Then came the preacher, all passionate admonishment, to question your faith, take it apart, humiliate you, then lovingly put it all back together again. So you could feel cleansed and instructed, all at the same time.

It was a soothing, mesmeric brew, comforting as chocolate. Each line was delivered in the conviction that the Bible was the first and last word on everything, that God was the absolute reality. There was no room for doubt or disbelief. Eirian could understand why people needed such certainty in their lives; it seemed almost cruel to take it away.

But necessary, she thought.

PGK was on screen again, in an advertisement for his expensive video tapes. He snarled straight into the camera, as if challenging Eirian herself to give up her wicked ways and turn to God.

'I can do better than that,' she said under her breath, staring into his strong, magnetic face. 'And tomorrow, I will.'

After they'd rested, showered and changed, they met Suzanne in the hotel bar. She introduced them to Jamie Baker: a black, five-foot-six barrel of a man, with grey hair crusted around a shiny brown pate and thick-rimmed glasses. He simmered with energy and rough-edged humour, eager to put his guests at ease. Though he seemed startlingly loud at first, Beth couldn't help liking him.

'It's so great to meet you folks,' he said, clasping Beth's hand. 'First time in the States, Beth?'

'Well, mine and Eirian's. Morgan's been before –'

'How're you liking it?'

'Very exciting but the heat –'

'Yeah, we chose a bad time of year for you folks from England, but you're gonna have a great time. We're so pleased you could make it. Never seen anyone like your little girl on that document-ary, Beth; so poised, and that English accent! And she is real beautiful. You both are. You sure you're not sisters?'

Beth laughed. 'I like this man.'

Jamie took them into the hotel's roof-top restaurant, talking non-stop. A waitress seated them at a table with nothing to separate them from the chasm of sky-scrapers beyond but a thin wall of glass. Lights sparkled through the evening haze. 'It's gonna be an important show. Val – that's our presenter, Val Kantaris, you heard of her? – she's real excited. We got some real sad cases, young men and women sucked into these cults and their lives ruined. We got some parents still struggling to get their kids out.' Beth shuddered with empathic horror and Jamie asked, 'You okay, Beth?'

'Yes. I hate to think of what they must be going through, that's all.'

When Jamie lowered his voice, he became very persuasive. 'If you want to share your feelings, Beth, we'd really like you to appear on the show alongside your daughter.'

'Oh!' said Beth, shocked.

'I'd like that, Mum,' said Eirian, who wasn't visibly excited or even nervous. Morgan and Suzanne smiled challengingly at her. Morgan said, 'Go on, you'll be great.'

'You can come on too, if you think it's so easy!'

'Think about it.' Jamie opened a shiny-white menu. 'Now, what would you folks like to drink?'

'Something strong,' said Beth. 'Suddenly I'm nervous.'

'Don't you worry about a thing. The show is gonna be great.'

With a couple of margaritas inside her, Beth felt more relaxed about the idea. She loved the atmosphere of the restaurant, its soft lighting and art deco luxury. Jamie and Suzanne did most of the talking. Beth instinctively trusted Jamie; beneath his brash manner he was sensitive, self-deprecating and frighteningly intelligent.

'It's a peak-time, evening show, goes out live.' Jamie spoke directly to Eirian as if she were an adult; Beth liked that. 'We'll send the limo for you around six. They'll take you to the hospitality suite and you'll meet Val; she'll put you right at ease. And don't be nervous, honey, because it's all very relaxed. Don't worry if you can't think what to say, 'cos there's always someone ready to jump in, believe me.'

'Oh, I'll know what to say,' Eirian replied.

Jamie chuckled. 'I'm sure you will. Hey, how d'ya like the hotel?'

'It's lovely,' Eirian answered politely. 'I've got my own room and television. I was watching an interesting programme this afternoon. A channel called True Light Network.'

Sometimes Eirian's conversation sounded superficially child-like, while all the time she was winding in the information she needed. Beth and Morgan looked at each other. Jamie laughed. 'Oh, good ol' PGK.'

'You've seen it?'

'Sure, everyone's seen it. You don't get religious broadcasting in England?'

'Not much, thank God,' Morgan said sardonically.

'You're lucky. You can find better things to watch than that, honey, even on American TV.'

'But I'm interested.' Eirian looked steadily into Jamie's eyes. 'Tell me about these television preachers.'

Jamie whistled, shaking his head. 'Where to start, eh, Suzanne? A lot of folks think it's a big laugh but there's just as many take it seriously. There's a whole bunch of these stations now, raising dollars by preaching. Funny, the Bible extols poverty but these preachers all seem to be millionaires . . . You sure you want to hear about this?'

'Yes,' Eirian replied intently. Beth could see him thinking, strange thing for a thirteen-year-old to care about . . . she took a mouthful of her third margarita, tasted the burst of salt, lime and tequila on her tongue.

'I'm not the best guy to ask; I'm a goddamn liberal,' Jamie said drily. 'I tell you, there's some dangerous trends going on here in the US. There's a real nasty backlash against liberalism, feminism, and so on.' He hesitated, looking at Eirian as if unsure that she understood. 'You heard of the Evangelical Right?'

'No.'

'Well, they're people who believe every word of the Bible is true. They're pro-family, anti-feminist, anti-homosexual, anti-abortion, anti-evolution. Intellectual they ain't, but they have a very strong message: the Bible equals American values. If you're against God, you're against America – and vice versa.'

'I understand,' Eirian said, nodding. 'It's about male power.'

Jamie looked startled, then he grinned. 'Yeah, male power. You got it, honey. And they're getting more powerful every day.'

Eirian kept Jamie talking for another hour, squeezing every drop of information out of him. She would have talked all night, if Beth hadn't diplomatically brought the evening to an end.

'You are gonna be incredible, honey,' Jamie assured Eirian, squeezing her hand as they parted. He grinned at Beth and Morgan. 'You have one special child, you guys.'

When they'd said goodnight to Suzanne and returned to their rooms, Morgan asked Beth, 'What did you think of him?'

'Larger than life,' said Beth, 'but very genuine. And on our side.'

He slipped his arms round her waist. 'Are you okay about this?'

Beth nodded. She felt drunk. 'I suppose so. It's exciting, really. Sorry I made a fuss.'

'You didn't,' he said softly. 'You're right to be protective.'

Eirian, in pyjamas, put her head round the connecting door. 'I'm going to bed, Mum.'

'Well, get in and I'll come and give you a goodnight kiss.'

Eirian paused and looked candidly at her parents. 'By the way, if you're going to make love, please do it quietly,' she said imperiously. 'I need my sleep.'

'Eirian!' Beth gasped, but Morgan only laughed.

'I'll try to stop your mother swinging on the light fittings,' he said. As Eirian withdrew, he pulled Beth down on to the huge bed.

'Honestly, you encourage her,' she said, trying unsuccessfully not to laugh.

'She was only joking. These walls are soundproof.' His mouth met hers, warmly erotic, sending a thrill from her tongue to her loins. Beth moaned, interlocking her thighs with his and pressing herself against him. They looked at each other, their breathing feverishly shallow. 'Come on, let's say 'night to our baby, then we can carry on,' Morgan said into her ear. 'If you're not too tired, that is . . .'

'Flick me with wet towels,' said Beth. 'I wouldn't miss our first time in America for anything.'

Eirian had never been inside a television studio before; the BBC people had interviewed her at home. Everything fascinated her; the blazing lights, the cameras, the technical staff rushing about and talking urgently into headsets as they prepared to go live on air. The audience in the tiered rows of seats were a colourful, ever-moving mass; her father and Suzanne were among them, half-way up on the centre aisle. But she observed all the activity through a glaze of cat-like detachment. Beth, sitting beside her, was nervous; although she looked coolly beautiful in a long dress of pale violet cotton, black hair loose on her shoulders and an amethyst at her throat, Eirian sensed her tension. But Eirian herself felt calm and sure. This was what the Goddess wanted. Her enemies couldn't stop her now.

They were seated on a semi-circular couch on a tasteful green set, with two dark-haired sisters sitting alongside them. The other guests would be brought on at intervals, they'd been told.

After talking to Jamie last night – and some of the other guests in the hospitality suite – Eirian felt she'd absorbed the knowledge of several lifetimes. I thought I knew everything, she thought . . . but I've learned so much more in just one day. Thank Goddess I had that talk with Jamie. Now I'm better armed.

Jamie had said Beth and Eirian could appear in silhouette if they wished, but since no one else asked to, Beth agreed to appear on camera. 'I don't want everyone thinking I'm paranoid,' she'd said. 'No one here knows us from Adam anyway.' Eirian was glad. She wanted people to see her eyes.

The floor manager announced that they were going live. Then Val Kantaris herself came bounding down the centre aisle to an explosion of whooping and applause. As she introduced tonight's theme and guests, Beth pressed her hand on Eirian's. Val was six feet tall, generously built with glossy brown hair and vivid make-up. She radiated intelligent warmth. 'And we have Beth Rhys and her daughter Eirian from England, who'll tell us that this kind of experience is not confined to the United States. But first we're talking to Jane and Kitty Jones, who used to laugh at stories about the Moonies and never thought it could happen to them . . .'

The sisters told their painful story, then – after the ubiquitous commercial break – it was Eirian's turn. Beth, despite her nerves, spoke eloquently of her emotions when Luke had taken her daughter; Eirian took up the tale she was now weary of telling, intent on diverting it into something more profound.

Val's questioning was salient but non-judgemental. 'And did you understand why your uncle had abducted you?'

'Oh yes,' said Eirian. 'He wanted to save my soul. He thought we were evil because we're pagans. He was wrong, but he could never see it because he was convinced God was on his side, and that gave him the right to do anything. The phrase "God's will" is used to sanction any atrocity. I was watching a preacher called PGK on TV yesterday; why does having your soul saved involve sending him so much money?'

Laughter. Eirian went on, 'He reminded me of Luke. If he met me, he'd want to burn me too. Most people think that's crazy, but they *still* don't question the image of a witch as evil. But we're not evil, we don't worship the Devil, we just have a different way of looking at things –'

'And I'm sure everyone watching tonight understands that,' Val interrupted firmly. 'We'll be back after this break to speak to a young man about his experience with the Children of God.' As the commercials ran, she went over to Beth and Eirian and patted their arms warmly. 'You were both great. Perfect.'

'Val, I didn't finish what I was saying,' said Eirian.

'I know, honey, but we have to give the other guests a chance. You stay right there, we'll come back to you later if there's time.'

Eirian acquiesced, but her confidence wavered. This wasn't so easy after all.

Morgan became aware of a pressure at his elbow, several seconds before he responded. Suzanne was nudging him. 'Good, weren't they? I can see where Eirian gets her poise.'

'Me?' said Morgan, joking half-heartedly.

'I meant from Beth.'

The show resumed, with new guests in place and the others shunted round the couch. Eirian said nothing while the young man spoke. Then a psychologist was introduced to counsel a middle-aged couple and the thin, hollow-eyed daughter who sat, hunched and defensive, between them.

'Tammy wants to stay with the sect,' Val was saying, 'and she says her parents are breaching her civil liberties by trying to force her to leave. *They* say she is brainwashed and doesn't know her own mind. Let's see if we can sort this out here. Now, Tammy, what is it about this sect that attracted you?'

Tammy began in a dull, sincere voice, 'I believe that our leader is a prophet of Christ. I believe he will fulfil the prophecies in the Book of Revelation and it's my right to follow my beliefs –'

'But look at her!' the mother broke in. 'We don't want to force her to do anything, but you only have to see how skinny she is! She used to be such a healthy girl, full of life. She's just breaking our hearts –'

'Starvation,' said Eirian. She leaned forward, addressing the girl directly. 'That's part of the brainwashing, Tammy. You can't think straight if you're weak with hunger all the time.'

'I am not!' Tammy said indignantly. 'We lead a healthy life in God's love.'

'Yes, in Luke's church they surrounded each other with love and support, promises of eternal life in heaven,' said Eirian. 'But if you deviate and don't repent, they say you'll go to hell. Your peers make you feel an outsider even for questioning God's word, don't they? No one wants to be an outsider. You want approval so you give in and they love you again. It's psychological fascism.'

Someone in the audience spoke. Val rushed to him with a microphone. 'You wanna say what?'

A man, stout and thirty-odd, stood up. 'Jesus didn't teach fascism! He taught love and forgiveness!'

'But why can't we have love and forgiveness without the threat of hell?' said Eirian. 'Can people only be good out of fear, not out of common decency? What kind of God would create mankind, then condemn most of us to an eternity of torture? The Goddess also gives compassion and love, without threats.'

'Can I say something?' said Tammy, glaring at Eirian. 'I am not brainwashed!'

'We all are! We're all trained at school to believe the Bible is true! Even the people who reject it hardly ever find out there's anything deeper.'

'The Bible *is* true,' said Tammy, as if Eirian were a silly little girl. There was a spattering of applause. 'It's the Word of God.'

'Or it's the story of Hebrew patriarchs trying to replace goddess worship with their own jealous, war-like god. That goddess wasn't evil; she was a threat to their power. The Great Mother was the first deity and she was worshipped for hundreds of thousands of years before God was invented.'

The counsellor was shifting uncomfortably, as if he sensed Eirian usurping his role. 'It's really not helpful to replace one type of monotheism with another in this situation –'

'I'm not,' said Eirian, crisp as ice. 'I'm trying to explain to Tammy how her faith is based on a reversal of nature. Of course the first deity was female; everyone has a mother and men can't give birth. Gods are projections of the ultimate divine mother or father; I thought you'd know that.' The counsellor looked startled. Val and the audience were hushed, riveted to the composed figure of Eirian. 'Does your leader make you feel extra-sinful to be a woman, because Eve brought death into the world?'

Tammy nodded. 'Of course. It's our burden. But we can become male in Christ –'

'Who was born without sex to a virgin mother, and whose priests counsel his followers to shun femaleness and sex for ever if they want to reach heaven. That's how the Bible's writers handled their hostility towards women; they completely eliminated the female sex from the creation or the purpose of the world. The Great Mother's power to create and destroy terrified them! They equated the female with death and they set out to escape death. They wanted to deny nature and exist as pure spirit, so to do that they twisted nature and flesh to seem evil. Real life is a circle, Tammy; it's messy, female, and sexual. Religion is a straight line; one life, one death, one sterile unchanging after-life. A fantasy. It's led to half the human race being treated like dirt for four thousand years and we're barely crawling back into the light. Evangelists like PGK and your prophet want to drag us straight back down '

'That's blasphemy,' Tammy said weakly.

'No, the Bible is blasphemy,' Eirian snapped back. 'Against life. If you think Earth is just a testing ground and a place of banishment from Eden, how can you ever really live, Tammy?'

Tammy started crying, fingers pressed to her lips and the bruised skin below her eyes gleaming with tears. Eirian went on, her voice gentle but mesmerically forceful: 'In the Goddess, everyone is sacred, male and female alike. Don't let your leader tell you you're shameful and sinful, just for being born; he's wrong. You have your own power. The Goddess is in you and you are sacred. We love life just for being itself. Women are lovable and acceptable just for existing, because they *are* the fount of life. You don't need "saving", you're fine being yourself. I'm not trying to convert you, only to tell you there's another side. Come back into the circle and don't be afraid.'

The effect of Eirian's words on the young woman was stunning; although she sat still, she seemed physically to change, as if she were emerging from a shattered plaster cast. Morgan saw that it was not so much what Eirian said as her charisma that had reached Tammy; her aura of stillness and conviction. Morgan was spellbound, seeing his daughter as he'd never seen her before. Was this the same child who played football in the garden, who teased the cats and swore over her homework?

Tammy was weeping on her mother's shoulder. Val leaned over to her. 'What did you say, Tammy?'

The girl was barely coherent through her tears. 'Mom, I think I wanna come home for a while.'

The audience detonated into whoops and cheers. Morgan met and held Beth's gaze through a forest of raised, clapping hands. She looked nearly, but not quite, as stunned as he felt.

As the applause subsided, Val was moving through the audience, canvassing opinions. Most comments were favourable, until a big, gingery man stood up and announced angrily,

'We've heard all this feminist witchy claptrap before! This is just more of the same anti-male garbage –'

'You may have heard it, but you didn't *listen*,' Eirian retorted. 'Life is circular and that's what you can't stand; dying to give way to others! You want to take everyone else with you in an apocalypse – and of course you'll be with the Chosen who live for ever in paradise? It won't be me who gets cast in the pit, no sir; doesn't everyone think that? But you're going to die one day, so *face it*.' The man's face lost its colour and he blinked at Eirian, seeming hooked on her eyes. 'But until you do, why not live as if this life is your only one, and sacred? Enjoy it. Feel the rain and the wet leaves on your naked body.' Laughter in the audience. 'Love the world, don't exploit it.' Eirian's voice changed subtly, as if a razor had sprung out of its nectar. 'Stop hitting your wife, because she is the Goddess.'

The man sat down heavily, as if someone had pushed him. He looked dazed, as if Eirian had looked inside him and drawn out his ugly soul like offal.

A smart, middle-aged woman stood up and said, 'If anyone should be burned, it's macho idiots like him. This little girl talks sense. I say, be open-minded and listen to her.' More applause. Val sprinted down the steps to the stage. 'I wanna talk to Beth. Beth, this is your daughter's first appearance on a talk-show and it must be pretty overwhelming; were you expecting her to be so articulate?'

'Erm,' said Beth, looking ironically startled. 'I'm in shock, actually. Well, she's always had powerful ideas of her own without me telling her what to think. I've tried to give her the freedom of thought that my own parents never gave me.'

'Thank you, Beth and Eirian, thank you to all tonight's guests.' Val turned to the camera. 'Well, that's all we have time for but I'm sure we'll be returning to this controversial subject again very soon. Goodnight and God bless – whoever he or she is to you.'

'There,' Suzanne whispered as the closing music rose over the applause. 'You can relax now.'

'Can we?' Morgan said under his breath. 'I've got a horrible feeling it's only just started.'

Eirian was in bed, Beth sitting beside her. It was quiet at last. The telephone in their room had not stopped ringing until Suzanne had the calls diverted to her own room. Every TV station and newspaper in the States, it seemed, wanted to interview Eirian.

'I was okay, Mum, wasn't I?' Eirian asked. She needed her mother's approval. Beth had always fought fiercely to protect her and she was only doing the same now; Eirian understood that.

'You were amazing, we all told you that. But it was meant to be one show, love. Just the one!'

'I know, but –'

'We can say no to everything and go away,' Beth said ardently. 'Just the three of us. I won't let you be bullied into anything you don't want!'

'I know. Mum?' She met her mother's eyes. 'You know I have to speak out for the Goddess, don't you?'

'Why you?' Beth sighed.

'Because someone has to! Because I can make people listen. Isn't it worth it, if I can save just one person like Tammy from falling prey to someone like Luke?'

'Yes, love, and if you were twenty-five I'd say fine, do whatever you want, I'll support you. But you're just so young!'

'Yes, and they listen *because* I'm young! Come on, you know this started before I was born; I have no choice!' Eirian put her arms round Beth's neck. 'Just a few more interviews, Mum. Suzanne and Jamie said they'd advise us which were the best ones to do. Only the best ones, Mum . . .'

'Oh, *shit*,' Beth whispered into her hair. 'You always do this to me. I mean, it's not as if you're being naughty. If you were doing something normal like smoking or going out with the wrong boys, I might know how to handle it! Look, how about a compromise? We let you do the interviews that Suzanne says are okay – but when we say stop, you stop.'

'Yes, that's fine,' said Eirian, who'd got what she wanted. 'I agree.'

'Give me a kiss,' Beth said in relief, cuddling her. 'You know we love you, don't you? I only go on at you because I love you. But be careful what you say. Please be careful.'

'Why?'

'Because you'll upset people.'

'But that's the whole point. To upset them, to make them think! Stop worrying about me, Mum.'

'And for an encore I'll give up breathing,' said Beth.

After her mother had gone back to her own room, Eirian slid under the covers and fell heavily asleep. But deep in the night she woke and sensed someone standing over her.

She opened her eyes and whispered, 'Dad?'

There was a thick blue light in the room, but for some reason she couldn't look straight at the figure beside her. It was a rippling shadow in water. She put out her hands to drive it away as she had so many times in the past.

It grabbed her wrists.

The pain was like ropes burning her skin, nails driven between the two bones of her forearms. The pressure was real and she couldn't move, she was caught fast and being pulled towards the entity. She caught an impression of a thin grey torso, staring ribs, ragged feathers. Not animal, not human, a corpse . . .

It was dragging her right hand up towards its mouth. She fought with all her strength. She tried to scream but her breath wouldn't come.

Her fingers made contact with its mouth. But instead of lips she felt a ragged mass of flesh, an edge of torn skin like a rind surrounding a fruit of bloodied pulp. Her stomach clenched in disgust and she turned her head away, unable to look.

She hung paralysed in its grip. Felt it lowering her right hand from its mouth towards its groin. She knew what it was doing and she resisted desperately, helplessly as it forced her fingers into the warm, pulsing wound between its legs.

All the entity's rage and frustration were transmitted in that violation. *You've gone too far, you've broken the silence. Feel our pain!* it screamed soundlessly. *Listen to us and feel our pain!*

Eirian opened her mouth wide in horror. Tears flowed from her eyes. This time when she tried to jerk her hands away, it let her go so abruptly that she fell back on to the bed and lay sobbing.

The light had gone. There was only the glimmer of Manhattan behind the curtains. But she could still feel the blood, slippery and metal-scented, on her fingers.

Chapter Ten

'I wasn't expecting all this fuss and attention,' said Beth. 'It's too much, but I feel sort of . . . paralysed. I don't know how to stop it.'

She was standing with Suzanne at the rail of a crowded ferry, watching the Statue of Liberty's majestic form drawing steadily nearer. Following the oxide-green figure upwards with her gaze to the serene face and the upheld torch, Beth turned dizzy. Morgan and Eirian were at the front of the ferry, taking photographs.

'I know,' said Suzanne, leaning pensively on the rail. 'I feel responsible, having set up the first show. But she's doing so well. And you can stop it, Beth.'

In the past ten days, Eirian had appeared on five coast-to-coast talk-shows and given numerous press interviews. They'd put her in debate against Church leaders and she'd demolished them. Editorial columns were written about her. 'Child prophet urges return to Goddess-worship.' Clergymen of various faiths had predictably labelled her a 'satanic influence' or just 'misguided'. Every day there was a pile of letters at hotel reception, the majority supportive.

Beth relished the warm breeze in her face. Liberty towered over them, benign and breath-taking. 'Eirian's like a force of nature . . .' Beth pointed up at the statue. 'She's like that; you have to go round her, she won't move for you. I'm really proud of her, but Goddess knows where she came from!'

'She's got something special, Beth,' said Suzanne. 'Charisma. People may have heard her arguments before – I mean, there are plenty of witches and pagans in the US – but she has the power actually to sway people. That's why they're making such a fuss over her.'

'That's what scares me. It's no fun turning on the TV and

seeing some sweaty preacher saying your daughter is possessed by the Devil.'

'Who was that?'

'Oh, that PGK on True Light, or whatever it's called. "She don't speak for no goddess, she speaks for Satan," and all that crap. I suppose good grammar is the Devil's work too.' It wasn't only the thought of Eirian making enemies that alarmed Beth; it was also the fear of what Eirian might do in retaliation.

'Beth, how awful.' Suzanne frowned. 'You haven't had any other . . . problems, have you?'

'No death threats, if that's what you mean,' Beth said sharply. 'A couple of churches wrote, more in sadness than anger, saying they'd pray for her. It's ironic, but the angriest letter came from a witch who said Eirian had no business speaking out against other religions. She said pagans still need to keep their heads down, and Eirian was only stirring up hatred and intolerance. I don't know, I just wanted a quiet life . . .' Beth exhaled, making a decision. 'I'll talk to Morgan later. Eirian can do the show she's booked for tomorrow, then that's it.'

'I don't mean to attack people's faith or convert anyone,' Eirian told the tanned, grey-haired man who was interviewing her against a false backdrop of skyscrapers. He was intelligent, but too flippant for her liking. 'But how can people make an informed choice when they only know one side? I can't explain the Goddess without challenging entrenched ideas. The Bible presents humans as flawed and sinful, living in exile for daring to seek knowledge. The creation story is taken to "prove" that women have a lesser role and that men have dominion over the earth – so it's no sin to enslave women or exploit the earth. Goddess worship teaches the opposite, that the earth is our mother and that women and men are equally sacred.'

'But if you reject the teachings of the Bible, where does your morality come from?' There was a ripple of agreement from the large audience; Eirian looked hard at them.

'It's simple. It comes automatically if you respect life. Do what you will, *as long as you harm no one.*' She smiled at the interviewer. 'Would you respect a woman who slept with you on the first date?'

He looked stunned. 'My wife sure wouldn't.' A roar of laughter, but Eirian didn't let it deflect her.

'Because if you felt it degraded her, you must also have degraded yourself. And if you're still noble, so is she. You can't have it both ways. Christianity has propagated the idea that sex is mostly base and degrading. But if we were taught to regard sex as natural and sacred, pornography would cease to exist.'

There was a loud surge of approval. Eirian waited impassively for it to subside.

'Okay, Eirian, so how do you see Jesus?' He sat back with an expectant look, as if waiting for her to impale herself on this sensitive subject.

'I see him as a sacred figure. In a mythological sense, he was an archetypal sacrificial king; the son of the Goddess, slain so his blood gave life to others. His feminine qualities of kindness and tolerance made him remarkable. Mary's goddess nature is apparent in the way that she's complete in herself, able to give birth without a human consort. But that's been misinterpreted to present her as an impossible ideal; a vessel who gives birth without sex. Mary is only allowed to be holy because she's not a normal woman. Jesus didn't demean women – and yet even he denied his earthly mother in favour of his heavenly father. That denial of biological ties is the most disastrous mistake mankind has ever made.'

'You have some very profound ideas, for someone so young,' said the interviewer.

'They're not *my* ideas. They've been written about for years. But people rarely get to hear them.'

'You don't feel feminism has gone too far, then?'

'It's barely started! We're thirty years in, after several thousand years of mistakes! I'm not against men; witchcraft is the one religion that seeks to reconcile the sexes. Suppressing the sacredness and worth of women demeans men too. And it's still going on, women being told, "This is your role, the holy book says so." Some countries still burn witches; at least they don't here! I'm grateful to be in America, where I can say what I think. There are a lot of places where I couldn't ' Another heartfelt burst of applause. She went on intensely, 'Don't give away your freedom to the Evangelical Right. All organizations like the True Light Network want is power.'

A woman in the audience rose and spoke angrily. She was grey-haired, a shiny-pink mass of scar tissue covering half her face. 'You say they don't burn witches any more? Just look at me!' She pointed at her ruined face. 'A group of biblical fundamentalists did this to me five years ago in Georgia! They heard I was a witch so they tried to drive me out my neighbourhood and when I wouldn't go they fire-bombed my house! These evangelicals are dangerous! I tell you, listen to this little girl before America turns into one of those countries where you *can't* say what you think! Listen to her!'

She sat down to another wave of clapping and whooping. 'Well, we got that message loud and clear,' the interviewer was saying. 'You've been a big hit in the States this summer, Eirian, and you're still only thirteen years old; so, what do you see yourself doing when you leave school?'

'Oh, I'll probably be a vet or a psychologist or something,' she said vaguely. There was laughter at the diffidence of her reply.

'But you'll go on speaking out for your Goddess?'

'Your Goddess too,' she said. 'For as long as it takes.'

'Ladies and gentlemen, *Eirian Rhys*!'

Eirian stood in the foyer of the TV studios with her parents, waiting while Suzanne spoke to a researcher she knew. 'How are you doing, love?' Morgan asked, kissing the top of Eirian's head. It was early evening and the sunlight was heavily golden outside the glass doors.

'Great, thanks. A bit tired and very hungry.'

Beth began, 'Well, we'll go and – oh, my God, look who's coming!'

A huge man in a grey suit was striding towards them between

the pillars and potted ferns. It was the preacher from the True Light Network. 'He was in the audience,' Morgan said grimly.

'We are not going to get into an argument with him,' Beth said firmly.

The preacher arrived in front of them. His presence was overbearing; he was six foot five and at least twenty stone. But it was his personality, not his size, that weighed on Eirian. She received a wash of impressions; he was sincere, powerful and obsessive. He was smiling benevolently but the expression sat badly on his heavy-featured face and lipless mouth. It made his eyes narrow to nothing.

'Hi, hope you don't mind the intrusion. It's a real privilege to meet you folks. You have one exceptional child there,' he began heartily. He held out a hand to Morgan, who didn't take it. 'If I may introduce myself, mah name is Paul Gregory Keay.'

'Er – yes, we recognized you,' said Beth. She clasped Eirian's shoulders protectively and he let his proffered hand fall with no sign of embarrassment.

'Hope you're enjoyin' your stay. How y'all copin' with the weather? You should get out of the city. Come down to mah church in Georgia.' His voice was deep, velvety and sincere. 'You'd be welcome.'

'Why?' said Morgan. 'You must have realized we're not Christians.'

'All the more reason for you to come.'

Morgan began coldly, 'I'm sorry, do you seriously think –' but Beth nudged him. 'Thank you,' he said more diplomatically. 'Another time, maybe.'

'Don't leave it too late,' said the preacher. 'I'll be prayin' for you.'

'Please don't pray for me,' Eirian broke in. 'On your show you said Satan was talking through me. I didn't like that.' She felt Beth's hands tightening on her shoulders.

PGK sighed. 'I'm sorry, darlin', but it's the truth. It's not your fault he's picked on you; you're just a child and he's the

Devil. We hate the sin, child, but we love the sinner.' His voice fell. 'I could help you.'

He reached out a large hand as if to bless her. Eirian backed away, glaring at him. She felt the weight of his will, like Luke's, felt her own power gathering to throw his arrogance back at him ... then Beth gave her a tiny but emphatic shake, as if she guessed. 'My daughter had no intention of offending you personally,' said Beth, 'but people still have the right of free speech in this country, don't they?'

'They surely do, ma'am. But be warned; there's only so far you can go before Satan trips himself right up over his own tongue.' PGK stepped away, nodding politely as he went, fixing Eirian with a look of pity that she found loathsome. 'You're in a sad way, folks, but the Lord's offer is always open.' They watched as he forced his bulk against the inertia of the revolving glass door.

'This is just what I was afraid of,' said Beth. 'You making enemies.'

'He's nothing, Mum,' said Eirian. 'I could take him on with both hands tied behind –'

'I'm sure you could,' Morgan sighed, 'but not this time, eh? Come on, let's go and get something to eat. We need to talk.'

They took a yellow cab to the Hard Rock Café and escaped the stifling heat of the street for the cool interior. Suzanne had diplomatically gone shopping instead. The café was all dark wood and stained glass, walls plastered with guitars and signed photographs of groups. Rock music blared from the sound system. A waitress, nearly falling over her own feet as she saw Morgan, sat them at the bar until there was a table free.

They sat on high stools, Eirian between her parents, and sipped iced tea. Beth and Morgan talked about the show and PGK, but Eirian didn't feel like talking any more. She looked around at rock memorabilia on the walls, people at the bar. She watched a man walk in and sit down next to her mother.

Eirian noticed him because of his hair. It seemed pure white, then she realized it was actually blond, fine and fair as milk.

It was very long, tied back in a pony-tail. He was pale and he wore narrow black sunglasses. She wondered if he was albino. She watched him as he ordered a whisky and ginger, and sat stirring the ice with a straw. He wore white cotton jeans and a cream silk shirt.

'Your Mum and I have been thinking,' said Morgan, breaking into her reverie. 'We've got ten days left before we go home, and you've done quite enough work.'

Beth squeezed her arm. 'We're very proud of you. You've been brilliant, darling. But it's enough. You're tired, aren't you? We all are.'

Morgan went on, 'We want to take you away from the city and have a proper holiday. No more interviews. Just the three of us.'

They'd made up their minds but were being gently persuasive, expecting her to argue. 'Okay,' she said quickly. 'Where are we going?' Her parents looked at each other, stunned she'd agreed so easily. But Eirian knew they were right. She'd done enough for now.

'Somewhere I've always wanted to go,' said Morgan, 'where they don't even have television. But you'll have to wait and see. It's another flight, and it'll still be hot, but less humid. And the scenery . . . you've never seen anything like it.' He smiled, and Eirian was suddenly interested.

'And you haven't been there before with Marian?'

'No,' said Morgan, glancing ironically at Beth. 'It'll be the first time for all of us.'

'Excuse me, ma'am,' said the stranger next to Beth, 'could I trouble you to pass me a menu?' Beth obliged, and he added, 'Do I detect an English accent?'

'I'm afraid so,' she said, smiling.

'Which part of England are you from?' He took off his shades and Eirian saw that he wasn't albino; his eyes were brilliant blue, turning to green at the centre. His eyebrows were white-blond, his lashes gold, and he had a sculptural, intelligent face, like an actor. About thirty, Eirian guessed.

'The middle bit,' said Beth, who'd discovered that most

Americans had only the haziest idea of British geography. 'North of Birmingham.'

'Sure, I know. Beautiful countryside in the Midlands.'

'You've been there?'

'Yeah, spent a lot of time travelling around England and Europe. My favourite place is Amsterdam; that's my Dutch ancestry, I guess. I'm Gabriel, by the way.'

As they talked, Eirian studied him. He was tall, slim and rather beautiful, like the angel she'd seen in her vision on the flight. None of the shocking psychic recognition she'd had with PGK; Gabriel just seemed a pleasant, friendly man. The neck of his shirt was unbuttoned and he was wearing a pentagram; the five-pointed star symbolizing the cycle of life. He's one of us, she thought.

At any moment she expected him to recognize her, but he didn't. Maybe he hadn't watched any TV lately. Eirian was glad. She had no nerves on camera, but, strangely, being recognized embarrassed her.

After ten minutes the waitress – grinning brightly at Morgan – came and said their table was ready. Eirian half hoped her father would ask Gabriel to join them, but he didn't. 'Nice to meet you guys,' said Gabriel, raising his glass to them. 'Enjoy the rest of your stay.'

As the waitress led them into the dining area, Eirian looked back at him until her mother dug her in the ribs. 'Eirian, stop staring!'

'You fancied him, didn't you?' Morgan said teasingly to Beth, as they took their seats.

'Of course not!' exclaimed Beth.

'Come off it, you were flirting like mad.' Eirian realized he was only half joking.

'You're jealous,' said Beth, with satisfaction. 'Anyway, what about you and the waitress? She was practically salivating.'

'It's not my fault she's got good taste,' Morgan retorted. 'Stop changing the subject.'

'I'm going to the loo,' said Eirian. She slipped out of her chair and left her parents to it. The washrooms were down a flight of stairs, along a corridor of treacly wood hung with pub mirrors. As Eirian emerged and made her way back, the stranger, Gabriel, was coming down the stairs towards her. He smiled, and she felt touched by warmth, a kindred spirit. Flashback to her vision of a white-haired angel on marble steps, arms outstretched to welcome her . . .

'Hello again,' he said. He had a nice voice, deep but gentle and confiding.

'Hello,' said Eirian, feeling awkward. And she never normally felt awkward.

'I hope you don't mind me saying this,' he said, smiling but concerned. 'Please don't take offence, but when I look at you . . . I see a shadow following you.'

Her heart speeded up, and shivers prickled her skin. 'What kind of shadow?'

'Oh, don't be alarmed. I often see things like that around people. At first it was like a big cat or a wolf, but now it's more a winged human. A familiar or a guardian angel . . . Were you aware of it?'

Eirian went hot, ice-cold, dizzy. 'No. Yes. But I –'

His voice was very soft now, almost hypnotic. 'I'm so sorry, I didn't mean to alarm you. But if it worries you, I could help you.'

'No,' Eirian gasped. She couldn't discuss the entity with her parents; how could she tell a stranger something so private? 'Thank you.' She ran up the stairs past Gabriel, returned to the table and sat down, shaken. To her relief, her parents didn't seem to notice that anything was wrong. They were too busy teasing each other.

Although they were in the café for another hour, and she constantly watched the bar and exit, she never glimpsed the pale-haired stranger again.

Twenty-four hours later, they were in San Francisco.

Suzanne was staying in New York and they'd meet her there in nine days for the flight home. Until then, to Beth's delight, she had her lover and her daughter all to herself.

They stayed in a hotel near Fisherman's Wharf and spent a day exploring the roller-coaster streets and the handsome, Spanish architecture. Beth took to the city's airiness and friend liness, so different to New York. Then Morgan hired a car and they drove across California to the Sierras. There was an endless road winding round the slopes of green-brown mountains, a pine forest, a tunnel carved in the rock. As they emerged from the tunnel, Morgan pulled off the road and parked on a viewing point by a low stone wall.

'This is what I've always wanted to see,' he said.

They got out of the car and went to the wall. Below them spread a valley, wide and flat and green as the sea. On either side rose sheer walls of rock; to the left, a vast pleated block tinted pale gold, to the right an out-thrust of three peaks one above the next. Behind the peaks, as the valley wall curved into the distance, stood a magnificent half-dome, grey and silver against the azure sky. The vista was so sublime and breath-taking that Beth and Eirian both wept.

Morgan slipped his arms round Beth from behind and stood with his chin on her shoulder. 'Now you know why I wanted to come,' he said softly. 'Worth all the travelling, wasn't it? Yosemite National Park.'

From above, there was no sign of human habitation. But on the valley floor, in the forest, the roads were milling with cars and visitors. There was a campsite and an expensive hotel, but Morgan – lucky to get a cancellation, he said – had booked into a log cabin. Beth expected something primitive, but the cabin – all brown wood and beige décor – had electricity, a well-equipped bathroom, and two double beds.

'But look,' said Morgan as they dumped their bags. 'No television. Signal can't make it over the mountains, I suppose.'

'Thank Goddess for that,' said Beth with feeling. Outside the window, beyond the village of cabins, the valley walls soared to breath-stopping heights, the trees on their upper slopes as tiny as matchsticks. 'Let's get changed quickly and go for a walk, it's so beautiful.'

There were crowds of tourists, backpackers and school-children outside, but after they'd walked for fifteen minutes the crowd thinned to nothing. There were trees, wild flowers and streams. The only sounds were of birds singing, a waterfall skeining hundreds of feet down a rock-face. Beth felt drunk on beauty and even Morgan, for once, was virtually speechless. A huge glacier had carved out this wonder of nature millions of years ago. Now Beth had an awesome feeling of isolation, as if she – and, more importantly, Eirian – were hidden in womb-like safety from the world.

As evening drew in, clouds sank on to the peaks like bridal veils. The valley darkened to blue shadow, but the sun turned the upper slopes to pale, mint-gold.

'I've always felt drawn here,' said Morgan as they strolled back to the village. Eirian was beside them, sometimes running to investigate a plant or insect that had caught her attention. Beth was now feeling quite interested in finding the bar. 'I've wanted to do this for years.'

'I'm glad the first time you came was with me,' Beth said warmly. 'For once.'

In the night, Eirian woke to find ghost-creatures all around her bed. Animal skulls stared at her, weaving, nodding, howling without sound; as if each flickered on its own piece of ancient film. They had once been wolves, stags, cats, birds of prey. Now they were revenants, frozen in hideous injury, their eyes glowing phosphorescent green. She sensed their seething pain and rage.

Eirian was more resigned than afraid. She had no choice but to go with them. *We warned you to be silent but you spoke out. You rejected us. Now you must answer to us.*

She was in pyjamas. It didn't occur to her to put anything on her feet as she opened the cabin door and softly entered the night.

Outside it was winter.

The paths were thick with snow, every twig and pine needle sheathed in glass. Eirian felt the snow crunching under her feet, smelled the icy bite of the air, saw her own breath wreathing out. The moon burned oval and silver, rimmed with darkness. All around her the mountain walls reared bleak and majestic.

Her companions, half seen against the snow, herded her onwards. Eirian knew that she was on a journey to the realm of the dead, like a shaman. That she'd been slowly travelling towards this ever since her father came into her life.

The waterfall was a strand of its summer-self, bearded with white. She heard the thunder of ice breaking up in the mountains. But the forested valley felt hidden and secret between massive walls.

Eirian didn't notice the cold. She felt cocooned.

The animals led her beside a stream. The banks were thick with snow, a tangle of boulders and branches under a thick white quilt, but the water was black. Around her the ghosts rose on their hind-legs; totemic animals, stag-god, goat-god, wolf-god. All unjustly slaughtered, in their time, as Satan's allies. On the far bank she saw their leader. Fear slid into her heart. He was the shaman from her dreams but vividly *present*. He was tall and wiry, his stomach sucked in under a stark ribcage, his bony arms and hands knotted like ancient oak. His face was long and dark, with eyes of bright green glass. There were feathers in his straggling hair, feathers flaring from his shoulders like broken wings. Grotesque, wild beauty.

He'd been a visionary, no gentle priest, but a fierce figure existing on the threshold of life and death. For that, the invaders had killed him.

Although Eirian feared him, she pitied him. He was wounded. His mouth was stopped with torn flesh and a crimson wound gleamed at the juncture of his thighs. She remembered, with a shudder, how he'd forced her fingers into that soft, bloody place . . . Every time he had tried to communicate with her, she'd rejected him.

Now he beckoned. The animals crowded her and she had no choice but to step into the water. Bands of coldness around her ankles made her gasp. The current pushed at her as she waded across. Pebbles impressed her soles. Then Eirian stepped on to the far bank and entered the spirit world.

She was shaking, but she must accept her fate.

The shaman waited for her on a raised area like a wide, shallow boulder. The snow around him was pristine; the only footprints were Eirian's. As she felt the rock tingle with energy beneath her feet, she understood that this was a sacred place from her visions. The Hellstone's twin. The two stones were linked as one in the dream-realm. So this encounter could only take place here, where the inner and outer worlds touched and the shaman had his full power.

This was why Morgan had felt compelled to come here, though Eirian doubted that he knew it.

She stood trembling before the shaman, yet he didn't touch her. He indicated his lips, his groin. He was waiting for her to touch him . . . and Eirian finally knew what he wanted. Hesitantly, holding her breath, she reached up to his mouth. The demanding eyes blazed down at her. Grimacing, she eased her fingers inside the lips, felt hard teeth and loose skin. She gripped an edge of flesh; it was slippery like chicken skin, but she tugged and eased until it slid over the teeth and lay in the palm of her hand. The twin sacs of the testicles and the wrinkled tube of the penis.

The shaman breathed out through his lips, *Ahhhh*, then she heard his tongue moving round the inside of his mouth, loud as the lapping tongue of a dog.

She lowered her hands to his groin. She pressed the organs in place, wound to wound, and held them there. Closing her eyes, Eirian conjured her energies, felt healing power gathering in her diaphragm and flowing out through her fingertips.

Healing. That was all he'd ever wanted from her.

She took her hands away and the organs stayed in place. That was where they belonged, in the triangle of bushy dark hair. And now they looked plump and healthy, as if the mutilation had never happened. The sight of the long, thick penis didn't disturb her. She saw no crudeness in it; only ignorant humans could have seen his nakedness as crude or threatening. To Eirian the shaman was a god of nature.

His hawkish eyes seared into hers. She thought he might speak now his mouth was free, but he didn't. She was aware of animal shapes moving around her, so close she could smell their odours. Their heat steamed in the frost-bound air. In wonder she saw their bodies mutating, becoming sleek and whole again . . .

As she healed the shaman, she had also healed them.

'I have to go back now,' whispered Eirian.

The shaman shook his head. Did that mean, *No* or, *I don't understand*?

'I've healed you,' she said. 'Do you still need to punish me?'

No answer. Reaching out, he rested his fingertips on her shoulders. He seemed to have no way to communicate with her, except through fear and touch. 'I speak out for our kind!' Eirian said angrily. 'I'm on your side! If you punish me, you punish the Goddess!'

She could say no more. A terrifying rhythm caught her, like the throb of drums. Her own heart. The shaman's hands crept slowly over her shoulders, down her collarbones and over her breasts. She realized she was naked too. His touch was feathery; the tough pads of his fingertips like birch-bark, hard yet silky. She wanted to pull away, couldn't move. Then something shoved her from behind. It was the smooth, muscular flank of a stag flowing across her back. She lost her balance and fell.

A dozen hands – or paws, or wings – caught her and bore her backwards. It was like floating. The snow felt like goose-down beneath her. They were all around her and she felt their silky fur, horny hooves, hot breath. Her skin tingled from the shaman's hands moving lightly over her, his hair and feathers brushing her – and long ropes of beads in his hair, nodules of cold glass and clay stroking her stomach.

Eirian was in a dream. They were a multitude and yet they were all one dimensionless, breathing whole, each a different manifestation of the same god. Although she was terrified, she didn't want to stop them. They were caressing her in love, not anger. Love. Hot tongues trailed animal kisses all over her body . . . *They had not been sent by her enemies, they were nothing to do with Luke or the witch-finders. When they said, 'Don't speak out!' they were warning her, not threatening her. Trying to protect her from the attention of her enemies – because they needed her.*

The long shaggy head of a wolf rose over her – or was it still the shaman? Yes, it was him, human in animal guise. They met each other's gaze as equals and she saw that to him she was not a child; she was her ageless, essential self. Eirian: shaman, witch, goddess.

She felt warm as he caressed her, touching his animal tongue to her face. The warmth concentrated in her abdomen. A name came into her mind. *Ictinike.* She said it aloud, naming him. 'Ic-tin-ee-kay.'

She was floating, arching backwards as wings and paws gently set her down in another place. The heat was building into a breathless sweetness. She gasped. The night whirled around her. The sweet warmth exploded between her thighs and she had no idea what had happened, could only give herself up to sublime cosmic ecstasy. As if the Goddess herself had touched her.

Eirian cried aloud, couldn't stop herself. The sensation brought her abruptly out of her trance and she found herself in bed.

A light went on. Her mother bent over her, apparently woken by her cry. Behind her, in the other bed, her father was leaning up on one elbow, his hair tousled. 'Eirian, love, what's the matter?' Beth asked.

Eirian blinked at her, completely disorientated. 'Sorry, Mum. I must have had a weird dream.'

'What about?'

'I don't remember.'

'Have a drink of water.' Beth gave her a glass and stroked her hair. 'It's probably a reaction to all the stress you've been under. Do you want me to get in bed with you?'

Suddenly Eirian wanted exactly that, to be a child again and cling to her mother. But she had a feeling she'd left childhood behind tonight.

'No, it's all right, Mum. You stay with Dad.'

In the morning – the valley simmering lazily in summer again – Eirian walked with her parents down long, flat paths through the pine forests. Despite the heat they all wore long trousers, boots and long-sleeved shirts to protect themselves from ticks. Sometimes she walked behind Beth and Morgan and sometimes in front, but never beside them. She felt too alone.

Her experience the previous night haunted her. Everywhere she looked, she saw the same trees and rocks coated in snow and ice, felt the tidal pull of the moon and saw the shaman's green animal eyes staring into hers. At the same time she was vividly aware of her actual surroundings; each pine needle pricking her mind, mosquitoes whining, wild animals warm in their dens. She walked in a trance between different layers of reality. She imagined that if she took a drug, mescalin or peyote, it might feel like this . . . but Eirian was open to other worlds without hallucinogens.

I think I understand, she thought. I've already encountered the Goddess, so this time I have to encounter the Horned God. The lord of animals . . . He's not the Devil but that doesn't mean he's safe. He can be savage and demanding . . . but he loves me and I don't know whether to be ecstatic or terrified.

All I know is I can't push him away any more. We're bonded together now. For ever. Was last night the end or the beginning?

'Did you read the guide book, Eirian?' Morgan asked, turning round to her. 'There used to be a tribe of native Americans living here. They were driven out by the government claiming the land. Typical.'

'I know, Dad,' she said. She knew without having read the guide book. For a moment the valley crystallized around her and she felt the throbbing of drums through her blood and nerves.

Ictinike. My lover.

*

Morgan and Beth sat on a sun-warmed rock, hot and tired and battling clouds of insects, but happy. Their reward for the long climb to Glacier Point was the view; an endless unfolding of mountains, green and blue and soft purplish-brown. The sun burned from a cyan sky, but it was a dry heat, pleasantly soporific. Morgan had noticed that the light was never the same twice; it changed constantly, revealing the Sierras in fresh new beauty every hour.

They sat close, Morgan's arm wrapped round Beth and his hand firm on her waist. Eirian was a few yards away, scrambling over a pile of rocks. Reaching the summit, she stood with her back to them, hands on hips, staring out over the valley. Although she seemed tranquil enough, Morgan couldn't forget the cry she'd let out in the night.

'Something's happened to her,' said Beth.

'Well, this trip's given her a lot of confidence,' said Morgan.

'I know. I don't mean that. I feel like she's going away from me.'

'She's growing up, Bethie.' He kissed her head and she leaned into him. They were quiet, holding each other. In the silence Morgan felt the ground begin to shake. Not an earthquake; it was a steady *boom-boom-boom*, like a resounding drum, so deep it was heard rather than felt. They looked at each other. 'What the hell –'

The drumming swelled. There wasn't time to reach Eirian. They could only cling together as a vast herd of animals swept over the crest of the peak and came stampeding straight towards them.

Ground and air thundered. Beth gasped, clutching him. These creatures weren't shadowy like the ones they'd seen at the Hellstone; they were clear like glass, distorting the landscape behind them, throwing off white and gold flashes of sunlight. As they reached Beth and Morgan they divided, flowing past on both sides. He caught the impression of antlers and wings, horns and pounding hooves. Chaotic exhilaration.

Other walkers on the mountain, Morgan saw, went strolling

on as if nothing were happening. But Eirian was calmly watching the stampede.

In the centre of the brightness, something dark appeared before him. Time stood still. Morgan was no longer aware of Beth in his arms; he was alone, facing the long dark figure of the entity.

Since that day in the nature reserve he'd tried not to think of it. But now he couldn't turn away. He must know what it wanted.

It looked different. Sleeker, more powerful. Its terrible gaze met his as if in a mirror. It made him feel he'd failed somehow and was being judged.

Morgan said, 'I'm not afraid of you. You got me here, so what do you want? Either tell me or leave me the hell alone!'

Its face was obscure, but Morgan could have sworn it *smiled*. The look seemed to say, *I have what I want*. It raised its arms to the sky, and as it did so he noticed the big male organ stirring in the bush between its legs. Morgan gaped in shock. That was not . . . not how it had been before.

The entity grew taller, transmuting into a goat-god towering on its hind legs. Curling horns sprouted from its head. Its feathered cloak boomed in the wind. Then it leapt. Morgan ducked, but it went clean over his head. Time moved again; he found himself holding Beth, a warm breeze blowing and the drumming of hooves fading into the far distance. The world was peaceful again, basking in sunlight.

'What the hell was that?' Beth gasped. 'Eirian! You okay, love?' Their daughter appeared unharmed. She came running towards them as they rose shakily to their feet, her face flushed. It had all happened in the space of a few seconds.

'I wouldn't like to guess,' said Morgan. 'Are you all right, Bethie?'

'Yes. But you felt it?' she said. 'It wasn't just me. Animals made of light.'

'Did you see them?' Eirian called excitedly. 'Weren't they beautiful?'

'Beautiful,' Morgan echoed. 'That's one word for it.'

She came into their arms, looking reprovingly at him. 'You weren't frightened, were you, Dad?'

'Frightened, me? The very idea. You saw animals, did you? Anything else?'

Eirian frowned. 'Just animals.'

'Me too,' said Morgan. He didn't want to hear that Eirian or Beth had seen the human part of the entity, especially not Eirian. Couldn't contemplate it.

'But no one else saw anything.' Beth looked at other hikers wandering past. 'Just us three. Why us?'

'I don't know, why do we see anything?' Eirian sounded impatient. 'If there are psychic imprints on a place, we're sensitive to them. Do you know what it meant, Mum?'

Beth breathed out. 'I suppose the fair folk are here too, as well as in England.'

'So they showed themselves to us,' said Eirian. 'That's all it meant.'

Morgan said nothing. He hoped that, for once, Eirian genuinely didn't know more than she was letting on. He wished they could talk openly about it, as they talked about most things – but it was unthinkable. The entity was a guilty secret he must keep to himself for ever.

Chapter Eleven

'REWIND the tape, Gil,' said Nathaniel. 'Let's see it again.' Pushing his long milk-blond hair back over his shoulders, he leaned forward on his desk, gravely fascinated.

Nathaniel De Vries's office was dark, the blinds drawn, but the huge television screen cast its glow over the thick carpet and expensive furniture. The slim black man standing beside him pointed the remote and the talk-show sprang to life again.

Close-up of a young girl's face; a creamy oval with vivid green eyes and long, wavy skeins of dark brown hair. A child's light, English-accented voice and the words of an adult. *'The Great Mother was a deity who gave birth to the world, suffering birth pangs to create us – and of course that is the only way life is created, through biology and birth. When they replaced her with a male god we had a ridiculous paradox; a deity making a clay man with his hands. A denial of nature's reality . . .'*

'She's incredible,' Nathaniel breathed. 'She is so beautiful. Wait until she's sixteen, seventeen . . .'

'I think someone's in love,' Gil said waspishly. He was in his twenties, muscular and agile from martial arts training. Although Nathaniel loathed his narcissism, Gilmour Jones was invaluable. He was a psychopath, a super-efficient assassin of Nathaniel's enemies. Their hostility was mutual, but so were the rewards. 'You wanna screw her?'

'Wash your mouth out. Jeez, she's thirteen years old!'

Gil's full lips tightened. 'Hey, I don't do children either.'

'You do anything I damn well tell you,' Nathaniel said softly. 'However, I am not asking you to kill a little girl. No, I want to help her. Make something of her.' Nathaniel toyed with the pentagram he'd been wearing in the Hard Rock Café, the day he'd met Eirian in New York. He'd since replaced it with a cross, as befitted his role. But he would wear a Star of David or a swastika, call himself Gabriel or any other name, if it would get him what he wanted.

'Save her soul?'

'Something like that. Get on the phone.'

'I'm not your goddamn secretary.' But Gil obeyed, making the calls Nathaniel demanded. As far as Nathaniel's colleagues knew, Gil was just a 'personal assistant'.

Nathaniel sat riveted by Eirian. No one else was aware that her charisma was preternatural, but he felt her power like a current. Potentially lethal. But so young and tender...

He remembered the time he'd met her, the shock of that shadow-figure at her shoulder. That was the worst aspect of his power, seeing horrors like that around folk. It was everything he despised, some Pan-like thing, a god of chaos. But at least he was forearmed. *One* of us is going to possess you, Eirian. It or me?

'Nothin' doing, man,' said Gilmour, fifteen minutes later. 'She's left New York, maybe on her way back to England, no one knows. Anyhow, she is not available for any more TV appearances.' Nathaniel's hand tightened on the pentagram. 'Sorry to ruin your day, sir,' Gil added. 'Better get your fun pickin' on someone your own size.'

Nathaniel smiled. 'If we don't stop her while she's this size, she is going to be one dangerous adult. The fact that I can see it when you can't is what makes me your boss.' He looked into the assassin's brown eyes, needling him with the power of his mind. A reminder that he had ways other than money to control people. Gil slapped a hand to his left temple, insolence crumbling as tears of pain and terror spilled down his cheeks. 'Stop it! Hey, I was jokin', I'm sorry! Please!'

'Migraine again?' Nathaniel said, acidly sweet. 'You should see a doctor about that.' Ignoring Gil's moans, Nathaniel turned back to the video of Eirian Rhys. 'Never mind,' he said to himself. 'There's plenty of time. We can afford to be subtle. I wonder how Paul would like a trip to England?'

*

Leaving Yosemite, flying to New York, flying home to England, Eirian had no sense of Ictinike following her. Every time she closed her eyes she saw his face, felt his feathery touch on her body . . . but these were only memories, not visions. She wanted to tell him she was sorry for trying to push him away, for taking so long to understand. But he wasn't there.

It came to her that when she'd healed him she'd somehow diminished his power. The link between them was drawing out thinner and thinner, like wire cutting at her heart and mind.

He'd danced for her, that day the ghost-animals had surged over the mountain. She'd hated lying to Beth and Morgan, but how could she explain? He'd stamped and whirled in their midst, a sort of courting dance, such as a bird might perform for its mate. Their way of thanking her . . . and of saying goodbye?

No, she thought. We haven't finished with each other. Don't desert me, Ictinike, please.

'Was the trip worth while?' Rhianwen wanted to know. She'd taken Eirian on her own into her kitchen, ostensibly to help with the washing-up. Her eyes were gentle but shrewd, demanding an honest answer.

'Yes, of course. I made people listen to me about the Goddess. You should see the letters we got, and the newspaper cuttings!'

'Well, that's great,' Rhianwen said softly, passing her a plate to dry. 'I am glad, love. Would you do it again, though?'

Eirian felt a shadow of tiredness on her heart. 'Yes, I'd do it until I made everybody listen. Mum got a bit fed up with it, though.'

'She says you've been preoccupied. Anything wrong? You know Beth worries about you because of the things that happened to you in the past.'

Eirian was quiet, drying and stacking plates. 'I know Mum would have liked a normal child who wasn't such a nuisance.'

'Don't talk daft,' Rhianwen said sternly. 'She adores you, and you know it. Has anything happened?'

Eirian wanted desperately to explain about Ictinike. Perhaps Rhianwen was the only person she *could* tell, but ... 'Yes, something happened.'

'Come on, you can talk to me.'

'I know,' Eirian said softly, 'but I'm not going to.'

'Why not?' Eirian didn't answer. Rhianwen let out a long, soft breath. 'I see. Still punishing me? Okay, I can take it. I probably deserve it. But don't punish Beth, eh?'

'I wouldn't!' Eirian exclaimed. 'I'm fine, there's nothing for her to worry about!'

'Good.' They went on washing and drying in their usual state of companionable truce. 'So, back to school soon, isn't it? Looking forward to it?'

'I suppose so,' Eirian sighed. 'It's going to seem really dull after America.'

'That's real life, I'm afraid. At least you'll see your friends again. And we've got the wedding to look forward to. Put it off long enough, but the time feels right now. By the way, if you want to invite any schoolfriends, feel free. Your Granddad and I want to make it a really happy day.'

Back at school, Eirian felt restless and out of place. The school, a magnificent old edifice of red brick, was the heart of a small Derbyshire town with Elizabethan buildings and a market cross. The girls wore a uniform of white shirt, black skirt and tie, and there was strict emphasis on discipline and academic success.

Eirian found herself a minor celebrity at the start of term. Her fame in the States stirred interest in the British media; only a brief flurry, since they didn't know quite what to make of her. Beth allowed her to give one newspaper interview, then insisted that was an end to it, she must concentrate on her studies.

Soon Eirian discovered the down side of fame. America had been a different world, but in everyday life the attention embarrassed her. Her schoolmates questioned her; most were friendly, but some seemed jealous, even hostile. She didn't want to be singled out. She would talk about her views to anyone she sensed was genuinely interested, but otherwise she coped by withdrawing into her small circle of friends. Then she found herself with a reputation for being standoffish

Her closest friend was Lisa, a shy mousy-blonde girl. One bright, warm day in late September, as she and Lisa sat under a chestnut tree during the lunchbreak, two other girls approached. Lisa was reading, while Eirian worked in a sketch pad. She'd drawn a picture of the shaman hanging on the cross-poles, and around it she was scribbling tiny, da Vinci-style notes.

'We heard you invited Lisa to a wedding,' said Serena, plonking herself down. She was tall and athletic with short, copper hair and a high opinion of herself. Eirian liked the other girl, Tricia, who was dark, friendly and bespectacled, but Serena was too pushy. 'Why didn't you invite us?'

She sounded hurt, managing to make Eirian feel guilty. 'I'm only meant to take one friend.'

Serena looked unconvinced. 'Whose wedding is it, anyway?'

'My grandmother's.'

'Your *gran*? Come off it, people's grandmothers don't get married! You're full of bullshit, Eirian. I bet your being on American telly was no big deal. It probably never even happened, you just make up stories to draw attention to yourself. Like all that crap about you being brought up by witches in a caravan! My mum says you must be a compulsive liar.'

Eirian bit her lip. 'You can think what you like. I don't have to prove anything.'

'Please yourself. But you've been a right miserable sod this term, Eirian. I thought we were friends.'

Eirian didn't want to make enemies. 'I'm sorry. I would like you and Tricia to come to the wedding, okay? At least you'll see I wasn't lying about my gran. There's a party afterwards.'

'Will there be any boys there?'

'Yes, a few.'

'Great,' said Serena, brightening. 'All right, we'll come.' She craned over Eirian's shoulder and stared at the crude, powerful image of the shaman, red crayon blood pouring from his wrists and ankles, mouth and genitals. 'That's disgusting,' said Serena. 'What's it meant to be?'

'Scripture project,' said Eirian. She hated lying.

Serena was squinting at the tiny, frenetic handwriting. 'What's it say? If he's the mani something of the what? Horned – ?'

' "If he's the manifestation of the Horned God",' Eirian read out quietly, ' "did the men who castrated him realize that shamans used to do the same to themselves, to make themselves female, because they believed that magic can be channelled only through the female? The wound in Christ's side is like the labial wound, through which the life-giving blood is shed. So when the men killed the shaman they made him more powerful. When I healed the shaman I closed the female wound, so although I made him whole I took some of his power away. That's why he can't find me now, but needs me more." '

'That isn't scripture,' said Serena. 'You're weird!'

'That's what it says,' Eirian retorted, flipping the book shut. 'You did ask.'

Rhianwen wore ivy in her hair and a medieval-style dress of pale green silk for the ceremony; Randolph a dark suit. Morgan, acting as best man, experienced a confusing surge of emotions as the registrar joined them. This is so strange, he thought. Mum loved him for thirty years and I didn't know; my father was alive all the time, I'd even met him, and nobody told me. Don't know whether I hate him or love him, the bastard.

Beth and Eirian were in holly-green velvet, with leaves and flowers in their long hair. They looked like beautiful sisters, goddesses of autumn. Morgan wore a black velvet suit that Beth and Dee had made for him. He liked the effect it had on Beth. She expressed a desire to ravish him every time he tried it on.

Some commitment at home had kept Suzanne and Mark from the ceremony, but they were expected at the party later. Morgan hadn't seen Mark for years; they'd been too busy to make the promised visits. Now Morgan was looking forward to seeing the old idiot again.

Photographs taken, the wedding party travelled back to Lullingford for the reception in the village hall. There were a hundred guests, mostly from the village, with a handful of Rhianwen's aunties and cousins from South Wales. Rhianwen had apparently told no one that Randolph was her son's father. As Morgan moved around the hall, showing people to their seats, he heard gossip flowing everywhere.

'This was meant to be a quiet wedding,' said Morgan as he took his seat beside Beth. Eirian was at a separate table with her friends. 'I knew it would be like this. This stupid gossip.'

'Ignore them.' Beth leaned in to him, squeezing his thigh. She looked enchanting, her skin like ivory against the flower-entwined blackness of her hair. The green velvet clung to her body beautifully, and her lips were dark as wine. 'Here, have some champagne. They'll probably short-circuit their brains trying to work it out and go home none the wiser.'

'Yeah, but I'm supposed to make a speech,' said Morgan. 'I'm going to sound like a total hypocrite unless I tell the truth.'

'Morgan,' Beth said warningly. 'Don't do it without asking Rhianwen and Granddad first.'

He kissed her and smiled. 'Don't worry, I'm not totally crass and tactless.'

He expected Rhianwen and Randolph to react with dismay; instead, they assented gladly, as if relieved to have the truth in the open at last. As the meal ended, Morgan stood up somewhat reluctantly and tapped a wine glass for attention. 'Everybody got a drink? Good, you'll need it.' There was a ripple of laughter. 'Well, it's not every day that your mother and father get married,' Morgan began, to louder laughter. 'Better late than never, I say. Better thirty years late than never. You think I'm joking.' He smiled, his gaze moving over an array of amused and startled faces. 'All afternoon I've been hearing suggestions that I've gained less of a step-father than an actual father. Well, I have my parents' permission to tell you that it's true. For those of you who've been dying of curiosity, I hope this has put your minds at rest. It's customary at this point for the best man to tell salacious stories about the groom . . .' More amusement; Randolph looked ironically embarrassed, but Rhianwen started laughing so hard that tears ran down her cheeks. 'Yes, well, I think we'll leave that one. All I want to say is this; my mother has waited a very long time to be with the man she loves, and I wish her and my father all the happiness in the world.'

As the applause and raising of glasses subsided, Morgan went on, 'Just to put the other rumours to rest, my wife Marian and I divorced last year and I'm with Beth now.' He put a hand on Beth's shoulder. 'I should have been with her all the time because we have an embarrassingly grown-up daughter.' He indicated Eirian, who reacted to the attention with complete serenity. 'Many of you will know that Beth is Dr Cross's granddaughter. Please don't give yourselves a headache trying to work it out. We love each other, we're very happy and that's all there is to it.' There was a silence, a sort of generalized gasp, then a scattering of applause. Beth caressed his hand. 'Now I'm going to read out the cards and messages.'

When he'd finished, Randolph stood up and thanked Morgan. 'Well, I hope that's given you all enough to gossip about for the next couple of hours, at least. It's true I've been in love with Rhianwen for over thirty years; as you know, I had a family to think about so nothing could come of it. I thank God, or whoever is out there, that she had the forgiveness, patience and generosity to wait for me.'

Rhianwen was crying now, not laughing. Morgan, sipping his champagne and studying the faces of the guests, knew they'd made the right decision. In telling the truth they'd won people's sympathy, not their condemnation. I don't really give a damn what people think, he thought, but it matters to Mum. She needs people to come to her with their cats and their troubles.

Later, the tables were pushed back and the hall darkened for the dance. Rhianwen and Randolph left in a welter of hugs and kisses for their honeymoon in Italy. Beth slipped home, taking Dee with her, to feed the cats and get changed. Just after they'd gone, Mark and Suzanne arrived, apologizing profusely for being so late. Morgan was pleased to see that Mark hadn't changed, apart from adding a stone to his rugby-player's frame. He was good-looking in a sporty way, with short fair hair, grey eyes, a misshapen nose. Still the same boisterous, jokey personality, none too quick on the uptake but always good-natured. How he'd ended up with Suzanne, Morgan would never know, but they seemed comfortable enough together.

Mark had never met Beth. When she came back to the party, an hour later, the hall was dimly lit, flickering with coloured lights, throbbing with rock music. Eirian and her friends were dancing. The floor was strewn with the debris of the reception, crushed flowers and napkins. Morgan was with Suzanne, Mark and Steve at a corner table, when Beth and Dee reappeared and made their way to the bar. Beth had changed into a dress of wine-red lace, which sheathed her slender body and flared to handkerchief points at her ankles. Her inky hair hung loose and she looked so breath-taking that Morgan stared as if he'd never seen her before. Mark's mouth fell open. 'Wow, that female with the black hair! Back off, Rhys, I saw her first.'

'Er, mate . . .' Morgan was about to tell him it was Beth, but Mark was rising unsteadily to his feet. Wickedly, Morgan let him go. 'Oi, you're married!'

'Bet you five quid I haven't lost my touch.' Mark made his way to Beth, who was leaning on the bar waiting to be served. Amused, Morgan followed and heard him say, 'You're breaking the rules.'

'Pardon?' said Beth.

'No one's allowed in until they give me a kiss.'

Beth looked at Morgan, her eyebrows raised. 'Is this guy safe?'

'Yes, he's a bit of a prat, but harmless. He's Mark and I'm Morgan.' A suppressed laugh flickered over Beth's face. 'You can give him a kiss, but only if you give me one as well.'

'Okay,' she said. 'Hello, Mark.' She hugged him, turning her face so his kiss landed on her cheek.

'My turn,' said Morgan, pushing his friend aside and embracing Beth. 'No tongues.' They shared a passionate, open-mouthed kiss that went on for so long that Mark began to dig him in the back. Finally Morgan pretended to prise Beth off, gasping. 'Gad, woman, I said no tongues! Put me down!'

'You bastard, Rhys!' Mark exclaimed, light finally dawning. Dee was doubled up with laughter.

'She's my girlfriend, you stupid sod! Took you long enough to catch on, didn't it?'

'You bastard,' Mark repeated, shaking his head. 'Well, it's great to meet you, Beth. I'm fed up now.'

'You'd be even more fed up if Suzanne saw that,' Beth said, laughing.

'Nah, she's used to me. How come Morgan gets all these wonderful-looking women? He was always doing this at school.'

'Don't exaggerate,' said Morgan, kicking him in the foot. The last thing he wanted was for Beth to be regaled with stories of what he'd done at school.

'Oh, he'd always dump his mates for a female. Morgan used to be brilliant in the summer holidays; a gang of us'd go camping, cycling, all sorts. Then suddenly he wouldn't come with us any more, boring git. He had to stay home so he could see this girl who used to stay with her granny in the summer. Some girl he was off shagging in the woods. What happened to her?'

'That was me,' Beth said crushingly. 'I was the girl he was off shagging in the woods, as you put it.'

'Oops,' said Mark, turning crimson while the others fell about. 'So you're Little Red Riding Hood!'

'What?' Beth exclaimed.

'Me and his mates had this image of you skipping through the woods to visit your granny. So we called you Little Red Riding Hood.'

Beth looked from him to Morgan, her expression stunned but highly amused. 'And no prizes for guessing who the wolf was,' she said.

They were still laughing about Mark when they arrived home a couple of hours later. Beth felt relaxed and pleasantly drunk.

There had been champagne, wild dancing followed by luscious slow dancing, her body welded to Morgan's and a thousand feelings passing unspoken between them. Thrillingly close to having sex in public. When the reception ended, they invited their friends home. Eirian disappeared to her bedroom with her friends.

The adults spread themselves around the sitting room while Morgan put on music and poured drinks. Steve and Dee were there, Suzanne and a dozen others. Morgan and Mark were a double act, relating anecdotes that made the others howl with laughter. When the doorbell rang, Beth was laughing so much she could hardly stand up to answer it. Probably the parents of Eirian's friends. She composed herself.

A young woman with short golden hair stood on the doorstep, dressed in jeans and a fawn raincoat. She was attractive, with a business-like expression on her tanned, healthy face.

'Hello,' Beth said cheerfully. 'I know Lisa's and Tricia's mothers, so you must be Serena's.'

'No,' said the woman, slightly taken aback. She had an accent, American or Canadian. 'But you must be Beth.' She glanced Beth over appraisingly. 'Sorry if I've come at an awkward time. I'm Marian.'

Beth felt the hallway lurch violently around her. All desire to laugh vanished in a hot-cold rush of sobriety. 'Oh,' she said.

'Morgan's wife. Ex, I mean.'

'Yes, um,' Beth floundered. 'Well, would you like to come in? We're having a party, I'm afraid we're all a bit pissed. Rhianwen got married today. Any excuse, you know.'

'Morgan told me she was getting married, but he didn't say when.' Marian stepped into the hall. She seemed very cool and sure of herself. 'If I'd realized it was today, I would've called round tomorrow instead. Look, I didn't mean to embarrass you, turning up out of the blue like this. It's awkward for me too.'

They stood looking at each other. Marian was a couple of inches shorter than Beth, and nothing like as intimidating as the blonde goddess Beth had envisioned, but she had a very down-to earth allure.

'I'll tell Morgan you're here.'

'Beth, wait a minute,' Marian said quickly. 'While we're on our own. I haven't come to get him back, you know. I'm on my way to a conference in Scotland and I've brought the rest of his stuff from Canada. I just wanted to drop it in, see how you're doing. It's nothing to worry about.'

Beth thought, the arrogance of the woman, assuming that she *could* get him back! She took control of herself. 'It's all right,' she said reassuringly, as if Marian were the nervous one. 'It's nice to meet you.'

Beth went to the doorway of the sitting room and tried to attract Morgan's attention through the music and laughter. Suzanne and Mark were the first to see Marian beside Beth; Mark mouthed, *Oh fuck!* Then Morgan looked up, and shot to his feet.

'Marian's here,' Beth said, pointlessly.

'Erm – hi – erm,' he struggled, putting a hand in his hair. He'd taken his jacket off, and with his waistcoat unbuttoned over a loose white shirt and narrow black trousers, he looked irresistibly dishevelled. 'God, this is a surprise!' he said, coming out into the hall and shutting the door behind him. 'How are you?'

'Great. I brought the stuff you couldn't take when you left.'

'Oh, thank you, that's really thoughtful.'

Morgan leaned towards Marian and kissed her cheek; not the gesture of two people who'd missed each other desperately, but it still made Beth bristle with jealousy. She said, 'Would you like a drink?'

'I'd love one,' said Marian, 'but I've a colleague in the car who wants to get to the hotel.'

'Well, let's unload the car, then he can go and we'll order you a taxi later,' said Morgan. 'You can't just rush off.'

'Thanks,' said Marian, smiling at him. 'You assumed my friend was a he.'

'Isn't he?'

'Y'got me there. Actually, it's Glen.' Their voices faded as they went out of the front door. Beth found it heartrending to see them together, to think of all they must have shared. He'll realize he still loves her, said the demon in her head. She'll tell him some sob-story. Or she'll want a lift to her hotel and they'll go to bed for old times' sake, then he'll come back and say nothing happened but I'll never believe him . . .

No, she thought sternly. I won't let this happen. Morgan chose me.

As he and Marian returned with the bags, and Beth was briefly introduced to Glen, a selection of parents arrived to fetch Eirian's girlfriends. That kept Beth busy for twenty minutes as protests were lodged and reluctant goodbyes said. Morgan disappeared into the kitchen with Marian.

'Who's Dad talking to?' asked Eirian. Dee's sons, Peter and Hugh, were with Sam on the stairs.

'His ex-wife's come round to see him,' said Beth. 'Take the boys back up to your room until Steve and Dee are ready to go home, okay?'

Beth watched the four children – teenagers, now – bounding up the stairs. Then she took a deep breath and entered the kitchen. Morgan and Marian were on opposite sides of the room with the table between them, but they were talking intently about the whale project. As Beth went to Morgan he absently put his arm round her waist, but went on listening to Marian with a glow in his eyes. Each whale had a name, and Marian described their behaviour as if they were members of her family.

'I'll leave you to it,' Beth said, smiling. 'You obviously have a lot of catching up to do.'

'No, don't go,' said Morgan. His arm tightened and Beth realized that, privately, he was embarrassed and trying to reassure her. Feeling more powerful, Beth extricated herself.

'I'd better not neglect our guests.' Beth went back to the party and sat down on the floor, leaning back against a sofa. Steve leaned down and said, 'Everything all right?'

'Fine,' said Beth, moved that he still cared. 'Isn't it wonderful that we can be so civilized?'

Twenty minutes later, to Beth's surprise, Marian came in

and sat down beside her, clutching a fresh bottle of wine and two glasses. She poured the wine and passed Beth a glass. 'I hope I didn't ruin your party,' Marian said ruefully.

'Of course not. Like I said, it's nice to meet you.'

'Morgan just introduced me to your daughter,' she said. Beth was learning to tell the difference between an American and a Canadian accent. 'She is gorgeous.'

'We like her,' Beth said drily.

'He told me you lost a baby. I'm really sorry, Beth.' Marian was sincere; she seemed likeable, not a terrifying ice maiden after all.

'Well, I can talk about it now without bursting into tears. That's progress. We're happy with just Eirian. We really are extremely happy all round.'

'I can see that. Look, I didn't come here to piss you off, or upset you, or to get Morgan back. I was curious, I guess. I needed to see what you were like. I came here wanting to hate you but I can't. You're too nice a person. And the way you look is stunning; Morgan's always had a thing for witchy stuff but I could never get into it. I saw the way he touched you just now; he was never like that with me. Maybe 'cos I don't need it. I don't know. He's such a sweet kid, I don't bear a grudge. I just want him to be happy.'

As she spoke, Morgan came in and sat down by Mark. He glanced at Beth and Marian with trepidation, as if wondering what they were saying. Music covered their soft conversation.

'You're being very understanding,' said Beth. 'I didn't set out to ruin your marriage, I hated it. But I love Morgan so much, I'd die without him.'

'Hey, he's not God, you know. You gotta realize he's not perfect. He's way too close to his mother, for a start.'

'How close is too close? I don't think he was actually sleeping with her.'

Marian gave an explosive laugh. 'No, but he likes to keep it in the family, eh? Sorry, I shouldn't have said that.'

Perhaps Beth ought to have been offended; instead she found herself laughing too. It was the wine, or the way Marian said it, that set her off. From the corner of her eye she saw Morgan give them another nervous look. 'He thinks too much of himself,' Marian went on. 'He's great-looking and charming, and he knows it. He can be cruel. He speaks before he thinks, and he'd rather be witty than kind any day.'

'I know all that,' Beth sighed. 'I've known him an awfully long time, Marian, and I'm not under any illusions. Okay, he has faults, but he's also affectionate, considerate, intelligent and a lot of fun. He's a good person.'

'Yeah, he is. And great in bed.'

'Yes,' Beth agreed, chuckling. 'Fantastic. Even when he was sixteen, which must be pretty rare.'

Marian topped up their glasses. 'Oh yeah? Tell me more.'

'He gave me my first orgasm sitting on a five-bar gate,' said Beth.

'What?' Marian nearly choked on her wine. Shaking with mirth, they began to exchange more intimate confidences as the wine took effect.

'And what about the weird sex, eh?' said Marian, slurring a little. 'Oh, my God.'

'What weird sex?' Beth was puzzled.

'C'mon, he must've told you. One time after a party, a group of us were pretty drunk and we started comparing our strangest sexual experiences. You know, like I said, "Remember that time we did it on a boat on Lake Ontario?" and Morgan said, "That wasn't me, Marian," ha ha ha. Well, Morgan told us about the time he got seduced by a demon in the woods.'

'A what?' Beth was suddenly uneasy, chilled again towards sobriety.

'He said he was walking in the woods when he was about nineteen, and he saw this *thing*, a monster that was half-human, half-animal. Scared the shit out of him. Knocked him down then it got right on top of him and had sex with him. Like a sort of vampire thing, begins with *l* – '

'Lamia?' Beth said faintly. Morgan had never told her anything like this.

'Yeah, that's it. But it was the way he told it, completely

freaked me out. Like, this thing didn't have a proper vagina but a wound? Wow! I thought he was having these sick fantasies about fucking wounds, you know? Either that or he was nuts. Boy, did we ever have an argument about it! He was real pissed off with me for not believing him. Didn't he tell you that one?'

'Er – I tried to forget it,' Beth lied. All at once she was jolted out of her alcoholic haze into some distorted, malevolent dimension.

'Guess I shouldn't've dragged it up. That's the wine talking. But you know something, Beth? He always had that kind of weirdness around him and I couldn't handle it. But you can. That's why he needs you. I hope you'll be real happy together. I'm doing pretty good with Glen; he doesn't screw around on me and he's not flaky like Morgan . . .' She looked at her watch. 'Hey, I ought to be going. It's been great to talk to you but Glen'll wonder where I am. Can I use your phone to order a taxi?'

Beth and Morgan were alone. Eirian was in bed, Mark and Suzanne asleep in the guest room, and everyone else had gone.

Beth sat in bed, watching Morgan undress by the cosy light of the bedside lamp. She wasn't angry with him, only wondering what else he hadn't told her. He sat naked on the edge of the bed and looked at her. 'You're pissed off at me, aren't you?' he said. 'Was it Marian turning up, or Mark acting the prat?'

'I'm not pissed off. Mark was just funny.'

Morgan sighed, and stroked her shoulder. 'I'm really sorry about Marian. I can't tell you how bad I felt. I still like her, but it's you I love; you know that, don't you? So does she.'

'It's not Marian's fault. She was great, I'm glad I met her. It was something she told me.'

'Oh, yeah? What were you two talking about, anyway?'

'What you're like in bed, of course. Don't look so horrified, it was all flattering.'

'So what's the problem? Did she tell you I like to be tied up and covered in salad cream by Chinese boys, or something? I'm over that now.'

Beth could have kicked him, for making her want to laugh when she needed to be serious. 'It was about you being seduced by a demon.' She repeated what Marian had said.

His reaction shocked her. The colour drained from his face and he looked mortified. Groaning, he leaned his head on one hand. 'She told you about that? Oh, Jesus.'

He seemed so distressed that she wanted to comfort him. She put her hand on his bare thigh and asked gently, 'Why didn't you tell me?'

'I couldn't. I only told Marian because I was drunk and we were all trying to outdo each other with ridiculous stories. I wanted to go one better, I suppose. Big mistake.' Morgan lay down, his head on her breasts. 'It was just after Mum had moved back to Blackthorn Cottage, after we'd been away for three years, so I must've been nineteen. I was in the woods, up near the Hellstone. Beautiful day, birds singing, bees buzzing. Then the world suddenly changed; it felt kind of stiff and hostile, like looking through ground glass. It was such a physical shock I thought I was having a stroke or something. Then this dark shape came out of the trees. I was petrified. It was so unreal, like drowning. This thing was very tall, shadowy, human-shaped – except it had wings and horns. It put these huge claws on my shoulders and pushed me down in the grass. It smelled of blood. Christ, I've never been so scared in my life.'

'But you managed to have sex with it?'

'It straddled me and I undid my jeans. I don't know why. I felt desperately excited, like you do in a dream, without any reason for it. I remember its thighs, greyish and sinewy. Male thighs.'

'And it had a wound, not a vagina.'

'Yes, here.' He indicated the stem of his penis. 'Like it wasn't really female but a mutilated male. I remember its pubic hair stuck in the edges of the wound. It was disgusting but I couldn't stop myself. It lowered itself on to me and I didn't try to resist, I penetrated it. I don't understand what happened; I mean, I don't fancy men, human or otherwise, Beth. I never have! It was horrible.'

'But you came, anyway.'

'Yes, I suppose so. Yes, I came, but it wasn't a good feeling. A nightmare. It had its wicked way with me and disappeared. I came round, lying in the grass as if nothing had happened. But there was blood on me. I was so shaken up I didn't even tell Mum.' Beth stroked his hair. She didn't know what to say. Morgan added, 'Bethie, I'm sorry. You must be revolted. Do you blame me for not telling you?'

'I suppose not. But I'd rather we didn't have secrets.'

'Please don't let's have a row. I nearly lost Marian over it.'

'We're not having a row.' Beth spoke softly, and felt him relax. 'I believe you, love; I've seen too much bizarre stuff myself not to. But what the hell was it?'

'One of the not-so-good folk. God knows.'

Beth brooded for a few seconds. 'Was it like some of the stained-glass images I've made?'

'Yes. Exactly like them.'

'Oh, bloody hell,' she murmured. 'Why didn't you say something?'

'How could I? It hasn't touched you, has it, Beth?'

'No. But I must have been picking up images from you telepathically, or something.' She climbed out of bed and retrieved her grandfather's wartime letter from the vanity case. 'I think you should see this,' she said, settling beside him again. She stroked his chest and lean abdomen while he read the letter, her breasts pressed against his ribs.

When he'd finished, his hand dropped and he leaned his head back on the pillow. 'Oh, fucking hellfire,' he breathed. 'Yes, that's what it was like. Sounded worse for him.'

'Granddad doesn't know I found the letter. I can't bring myself to ask him about it. It only happened once, didn't it? And it's so far in the past for both of you.'

'Beth?' Morgan was hesitant, then the words came out in a soft rush. 'I've got a confession to make. The damned thing started haunting me on and off when I left Marian for you – about the time you started your stained-glass work, yes? It was more a creepy feeling than anything. But in the nature reserve, a few weeks before we went to America – it tried to attack me physically.'

'It didn't rape you again, did it?'

'No! No, this time I ran like crazy.' As he described the second encounter she rested against him, disturbed. 'That's when I got it in my head we must go to Yosemite. I wanted to go there anyway, but how come seeing it reminded me? And I saw it in Yosemite too, that time on Glacier Point.'

'I didn't see it, but I remember you saying something odd,' said Beth. '"Tell me what you want or leave me alone," something like that. What was it doing?'

'Nothing, just looking at me. But it had got its prick back.'

'What?' said Beth. As Morgan explained, they both started laughing helplessly. It seemed so ludicrous. 'But what is it?' Beth asked as she recovered. 'What the hell does it want with us?'

'I wonder if Eirian knows anything about it?' said Morgan.

Beth went cold. 'No. I'd know. She would have said something. I am not going to put ideas in her head by mentioning it!'

'I agree.'

'I don't think we should do anything at the moment,' she went on. 'Just keep calm about it. If anything else happens, we could talk to Rhianwen. But if it doesn't, we'll just keep it to ourselves, okay?'

'Yes.' Morgan smiled, green eyes gleaming as he slid his hand between her thighs. 'Love me, Beth. It can't touch us while we're making love.'

In the night, Beth was woken by a gale blowing around the house. She could hear it tearing through the trees, rain sheeting down. Morgan was sound asleep beside her. She felt uneasy, fearful of the dull blue light that glowed outside the curtains.

Then she became aware of a faint tapping at the front door. She knew what it meant. The design of the stained-glass panel in the door was all wrong. She had to go and change it this minute, or something terrible would happen.

Beth left the bed, went naked down the carpeted stairs into the hallway. The hall looked longer than normal, distorted. She saw a blue glow through the crystalline picture of a corn-goddess, shadows of trees fluctuating wildly behind the glass. Beth knew she had to take the picture apart and add a serpent to it. She hadn't time to fetch her tools. She went to the door, felt the thickly textured glass under her fingers, and began to pluck at the leading. She was breathing hard. Panic and night-mare fluttered around her.

Then through the glass she saw a silhouette. Someone out-side, tapping to be let in. Holding her breath, Beth grasped the handle and opened the door. Against a tumultuous back-ground of rain and wind-racked trees, a nice young man stood on the doorstep, holding a bunch of flowers.

'I've come to see Eirian,' he said. But as he came past Beth into the house she saw that only his top half was human. His torso blended into the tail of a serpent, thick and black and scaly, curving away into the darkness behind him. The flowers were white chrysanthemums and they smelled of formalin. He glided past her and the snake-body kept coming and coming, rasping like silk as it undulated along the hall and up the stairs, gleaming faintly and horribly...

Beth screamed.

The next thing she knew, a light snapped on and Morgan was behind her, saying, 'Beth, what on earth are you doing?'

She came back to herself and found that she really was in the hallway. There was no gale, no rain. She couldn't have opened the door because it was locked. But she had been picking so frantically at the leading in the door that there was blood under her fingernails.

'You must have been sleep-walking,' Morgan said worriedly. 'Come back to bed.'

Chapter Twelve

O<small>N</small> Monday, back at school, Eirian avoided Serena. She regretted inviting her to the wedding. Although Serena hadn't spoiled the day, she'd been domineering, having to be the centre of attention but lacking the charm or wit to justify it. She was a manipulator. And she'd flirted with Dee's older son, Peter, to an embarrassing degree. For some reason that had made Eirian look at Peter differently, and feel jealous.

Eirian hoped the connection would die a natural death. But at morning break, Eirian entered the cloakroom and heard Serena's voice. Even at low volume it was brash. Peering round the end of a long coat-rack, Eirian saw her holding forth in a corner to three girls whom Eirian had thought were trustworthy. '... and Eirian's family are all witches, and they've all got green eyes like her. They practise black magic. And I found out something so disgusting about them that you'll puke if I tell you!'

'What is it, what is it?' The other three were wide-eyed, giggling.

'I can't tell you. But it's why Eirian's so weird.'

'Oh, come on, tell us, please!'

'I might if you're very nice to me. You all have to do me a favour before I tell you the secret.'

Eirian stepped into view, folding her arms. 'Oh, go on, tell us now,' she said. 'It sounds fascinating.'

The others squirmed. Serena turned, her face flushing. 'It's rude to eavesdrop!' she snapped.

'Not as rude as telling lies behind people's backs.' Eirian felt furious but ice-calm. 'You had fun at the wedding, I thought you liked me. What have I done to upset you?'

Caught out, Serena covered her embarrassment with aggression. 'You didn't want me there. You hated it when Peter preferred me to you. You make up all this witchy Goddess stuff to look important, because really you're nothing.' She came forward threateningly, eyes glittering and her red face lurid against her copper hair. She was bigger and taller than Eirian. 'It's all crap. You'd better stop telling lies and keep your head down, or I'll tell everyone your nasty little secret.'

Eirian was aware that she was being bullied. Horrible feeling, but she stood her ground. 'If you think you know something, say it. You can't, can you? You just make things up to use people.'

The other girls were listening in taut silence. Eirian hoped Serena would see sense and back down, but she responded viciously, 'No, I'm not! All right, you asked for it. Your mother and father are committing incest. She's his niece. He admitted it! An uncle having sex with his niece is dirty, filthy and illegal, my mother says.' Eirian felt everyone's eyes on her in fascination. 'That's why you're so weird, Eirian. Because you shouldn't have been born. The children of incest are always mentally and physically defective. Your parents are perverts and you're a freak!'

Eirian felt tears springing to her eyes. It was nothing she hadn't known, but to hear the words pouring foully from Serena's mouth made it all seem different, sordid. She could feel the others thinking, freak! Even Luke had never made her feel like this; why did it hurt so much, being attacked by a supposed friend? 'You've no right to talk about my family like that!'

'I can say what I like. You're illegitimate and so is your father. Which makes your grandmother Rhianwen a right slag, doing it with a married doctor. My mother says –'

'Oh, fuck your mother!'

Serena slapped her across the cheek. Eirian's tears spilled. 'Don't you swear at me!' Serena hissed. 'Or I'll tell everyone in school your dirty secrets. So you'd better start doing what I say, hadn't you?'

Eirian rushed beyond anger into the fiery realm of the Goddess. 'Otherwise you'll tell everyone?'

'Yeah.'

'I don't think so.'

'Oh, how're you going to stop –' Serena broke off with a strangled gulp and clutched her throat. She struggled to speak, sticking out her tongue and gagging. Eirian watched calmly as she went purple, clutching the air in panic. The other three clamoured to know what was wrong, but Serena couldn't even whisper.

'What did you do to her?' cried one of them.

'Who says I did anything?' Eirian said, walking away and glancing back with glacial eyes. 'She's lost her voice. Happens to people who talk too much.'

Eirian didn't see her tormentor for several days. Serena stayed off school all week, while the girls who witnessed the incident treated Eirian with wary respect. But on Friday evening, while Eirian was sitting on her bed doing her homework, her mother came in. 'Serena Whitney's here with her mother,' said Beth, standing in the doorway with her arms clasped. 'Mrs Whitney says Serena's got laryngitis, but she's desperate to see you for some reason. What shall I tell them? I don't want you catching it.'

'I won't catch it, Mum,' said Eirian. 'Okay, send her up.'

A minute later, there was a tap at the door and Serena came in, pale and anxious. She stood looking nervously at Eirian as if she daren't come near her.

'So, are you ready to apologize now?' said Eirian.

Serena pointed to her throat and shook her head. Her eyes were defiant but very scared. Eirian got up and gave her a notebook and pen. Serena wrote, 'What have you done to me?'

'Scary, isn't it?' said Eirian with a slight smile. 'Who says I did anything, anyway? You've just got a bad throat, haven't you?'

'I can't even whisper!' Serena wrote. 'Please do something.'

'Why should you have your voice back, when you'll only use it to spread tales about me?'

She wrote emphatically, 'I WON'T!'

'Promise,' said Eirian. 'Write down, "I humbly apologize and retract all the unpleasant things I said about Eirian and her family. I promise and swear on my life never to say anything nasty about them ever again." And sign it.' Serena wrote, her lips compressed, her hand shaking. 'If you ever go back on your promise,' said Eirian, meeting her frightened eyes, 'worse things will happen to you than losing your voice.'

She put her right hand on Serena's throat, her fingertips tingling. Serena flinched. Presently Eirian took her hand away. Serena swallowed hard; then, looking astonished, she cleared her throat and spoke aloud. 'It's gone. That horrible feeling's gone! You *are* a witch!'

'But I'm not a bully,' Eirian said calmly. 'I'll only hurt you if you hurt my family or friends first. Keep the promise and you'll be all right.'

'I will!' Serena rubbed her throat, trembling. 'But you can't go round doing that to people.'

'No, *you* can't go round being a vicious bitch. I wanted to be friends, but you don't like anyone except yourself. You want admirers, not friends. Now, if you don't mind, I need to finish my homework.'

'Look, I'm sorry.' Serena sounded defeated, self-pitying. 'It won't happen again. Ever.'

'No, it won't. See you on Monday,' said Eirian coldly. Five minutes after Serena left, Beth reappeared and stood over Eirian. 'Well, what was all that about?' she asked sternly.

'Nothing, Mum,' said Eirian.

'Serena had laryngitis all week, but after ten minutes with you she can speak again!' Beth sat down on the bed and clasped Eirian's hand. 'Did she know you can heal? Or was it something else? Mrs Whitney was under the impression you'd had a quarrel and she wanted to make it up. Did you do something to her?'

'No!'

Beth picked up the notebook and read what Serena had written. 'So what's this?'

'Mum, for heaven's sake! She was vile. I had to teach her a lesson. I only did it because she was bitching about you and Dad.'

'What about us?'

Eirian told her, her throat tightening as she spoke. 'Oh, my God,' Beth groaned. 'That explains why Mrs Whitney was giving us funny looks downstairs. Ghastly bloody woman, anyway. No wonder her daughter's like she is.'

'I didn't do anything to upset her, Mum. I always tried to be friendly. What did I do wrong?'

'Nothing.' Beth hugged her fiercely. 'She tried to twist our happiness into something dirty because she's jealous of you, love.'

'Why?'

'She probably feels you have something she hasn't.'

'Like a personality,' Eirian said contemptuously.

Beth laughed. 'You shouldn't have done it . . . but I don't blame you. Be careful, though. You have an unfair advantage over people and that might tempt you to go too far.'

'What's too far?' Eirian rested her head on her mother's shoulder. 'Luke? I used to feel so certain of everything. Now I'm not. Why?'

'I think it's called growing older and wiser,' said Beth.

That night, Eirian dreamed of Ictinike.

As she slept she was aware of a dark shape travelling slowly towards her. A pinpoint at first, it swelled slowly in her mind, gliding across vast plains, mountains, a black ocean. Coming nearer, nearer. She *was* the entity, an ever-transmuting mass of need; now wolf, now stag, now shaman. But she was also herself, watching and waiting with breath suspended. No escape. He must find her, wherever she was.

She opened her eyes, entering a trance between dream and consciousness. Her bedroom seemed a cavernous dark chamber that rippled gently around her. There was a warm salty breeze. She felt warm and weirdly excited, her mind and body poised on the edge of something profound.

She caught her breath as he came sliding out of the shadows. He took the form of a huge serpent, but his face was that of a beautiful young man. The sinuous body reared over her and she saw that his eyes were all gold, with a vertical pupil. He scattered white petals over the bed.

Eirian sank back as his long, silky, scaled body slid along the bed beside her. She wanted to touch him. His face was so dark she could barely make it out. A bit like Morgan, a bit like Peter, but somehow wolfish. Beautiful with his gold snake-eyes. His sinewy hands stroked her shoulders and his lips touched hers. Her heart began to beat very hard. Strange ache in her stomach ... She was very aware of her own body changing as an elixir of hormones swelled through her. Still too young for this ... But in the dream-realm she and her lover were both ageless and timeless.

'I've waited so long for you, Ictinike,' she whispered. 'Where have you been?'

Travelling. Always travelling towards you.

Her hand found the organ she had healed. It felt smooth and thick, almost velvety. Not a weapon of violence or selfishness, but a wand of life and ecstasy, as it should be. Eirian caught her breath. Ictinike's hand moved between her thighs, cupping her warm mound with thrilling reverence. His palm pressed an aching, pent-up spot in just the right place. Eirian's head fell back, her mouth opening. She felt the ache contracting into a point of agonizing pleasure, then exploding outwards, fluttering, curling.

The dream dissolved. She fell back loosely, so shaken that she could only lie there, drained and trembling. Her lover was gone. She tried to reach for him but she was too tired, sleep was pulling her down into oblivion.

In the morning she found blood between her legs.

She wanted to tell her mother, but Beth seemed too busy and wrapped up with Morgan to pay attention. In the end – as with other wounds she'd had in the past – Eirian kept it to herself.

*

'It's exactly what I was afraid of,' said Beth. She was at the workshop, drinking coffee while she watched Dee stuff a bear. 'People like Serena starting on at Eirian about incest, being cruel to her.'

'Children can be vile, they'll pick on each other about anything,' said Dee.

'I knew we couldn't keep it secret for ever. Okay, we could move to a different area, but why should we? We don't feel we're doing anything wrong – but what effect is it going to have on Eirian? Other people's dirty minds! I couldn't bear her to get hurt, and end up resenting us.'

'I'm sure that won't happen,' Dee said firmly. 'She's too sensible.'

'I wish I knew what she's thinking,' Beth went on. 'When she was little, we were virtually telepathic. Now she's getting more and more secretive.'

'It's normal teenage behaviour. Believe me.'

'Well, I wish she'd stayed ten!' Beth said vehemently. They laughed.

'My ex-husband reckoned he was psychic,' Dee said thoughtfully. 'It's true, he did pick up odd things about people. But he could annoy the hell out of me and I'd think, if you're psychic, how come you can't tell that you're really pissing me off? Whatever aptitudes you share, it's no guarantee of understanding.'

'You can say that again!' Back in her own stall, Beth studied three panels she'd just made. All showed a wild background, rags of cloud in a stormy sky, and a long dark shadow; winged man or feathered serpent. In the first, it was a mere sliver of smoked glass; in the last, it almost filled the panel, with yellow crescents for eyes. Coming closer.

There's an explanation for this, she told herself. I'm picking it up from Morgan. But does Rhianwen know? Or Eirian? How can I ask? It haunts us but it can't be mentioned, like some embarrassing dark secret in the family.

One afternoon, on her weekly visit to Tom in his nursing home, Beth took the panels to show him. Sitting in the common room, with the big bay window behind him, Tom looked frail, translucent, but serene. 'I make these out of scraps, like I'm in a trance,' she said. 'Did it ever happen to you? What does it mean?'

'Blimey, gel, d'you think I'm a ruddy fortune-teller or summat?' said Tom. He studied the panels, sucking at his dentures. Finally he passed them back and said abruptly, 'Your daughter's growing up.'

Beth made an instant connection. 'These are my subconscious fears surfacing about all the lascivious men who are going to take my daughter away from me? No, no, it's more than that.'

'Mebbe it isn't. You answered yer own question, me duck.' He tutted. 'I could never do owt wi'out a template. But you c'n make stuff like this wi'out even thinking – and all y'can do is complain about it!'

When Beth was leaving, on impulse she went back to Tom and tenderly kissed his bald, blue-veined head. She'd never kissed him before. Tom batted her away as if embarrassed, but he seemed gruffly pleased. 'Go on wi' yer, gel.'

The following day, the nursing home called her to say he'd died peacefully in his sleep.

As the weeks and months passed, Beth forgot her horrible dream of the serpent and sold the panels to a gothic nightclub. She and Morgan were exquisitely happy. Randolph and Rhianwen were enjoying married life, and any gossip they had to endure was teasing rather than malicious.

At the nature reserve, the visitor centre and animal hospital were complete. Morgan had his own office, laboratory and staff. He'd created a butterfly house, an aquarium and a reptile collection of which he was rightly proud. Meanwhile Beth was kept busy with commissions, almost more work than she could manage. Life, as it passed from autumn to winter to spring, couldn't have been better.

Letters still came from America about Eirian's television appearances. Beth vetted them before she let Eirian see them, but most were positive. 'You lifted a whole weight of guilt off me.' 'Your words freed me from the terror of hell, from disgust at my sexuality . . .' 'I felt as if the Goddess were talking right to me, setting me free to live the way I am.' 'Come back, you have to come back and reach more people . . .'

Eirian took the letters in her stride. She hadn't let her brief stardom go to her head. She concentrated on school and friends, to Beth's relief. But one day in winter, Beth came into her room with an armful of clean laundry, and found Eirian gazing out of the window as if in a trance. Opening a drawer to put the clothes away, Beth saw a packet of sanitary towels. 'Eirian, have you started your periods?'

Eirian turned from the window, her face pale, eyes very cold. 'I started months ago, Mum.'

Beth was devastated. 'Why didn't you tell me?'

'Why didn't you notice?' Eirian retorted. 'You were too busy with work, and Dad, and everything. So I sorted myself out.'

Beth sank on to the bed, her hand to her mouth. Yes, I should have noticed, she thought. Yes, I was too preoccupied to watch for my daughter's most basic development! 'I wish you'd told me. There's no need to feel you had to cope on your own. You know we're here!'

'Are you?' Eirian was hurt. So was Beth.

Then something struck Beth. She said quietly, 'When I started mine, my mother made a big fuss about it, like I'd turned into this wicked carnal being overnight. Did you pick up that fear from me?'

Eirian frowned, eyes brooding. 'Maybe.'

'I'm not Olivia. I'm sorry, I should have known – but you should have said something, too. Why didn't you?'

Eirian suddenly came to her, hugged her and burst into tears. 'I don't know, Mum. I don't know.'

The following June, on Eirian's fourteenth birthday, Suzanne phoned. 'There's a big religious convention near Nottingham in a couple of weeks, an inter-faith rally. The organizers called me, they want Eirian to take part. Would she be interested?'

'What do they want her to do?' asked Beth.

'Take part in a panel discussion, I think. One Christian, one Pagan, one Hindu and so on.'

'It sounds okay, I suppose. Hang on, I'll ask her.' As always Beth hoped Eirian would say no, but she inevitably said yes.

'May I give them your number?' Suzanne asked. 'By the way, Jamie Baker sends his regards. He's hinting about Eirian going on his show again, but I suppose you won't be keen . . .'

'We'll have to see,' said Beth.

The young man who called later sounded friendly and genuine. He was called Dave and had a broad Nottingham accent. 'Personally I'm a Christian, but the idea is to get people of different faiths together and find the common ground. We've got people coming from all over the country, even from the States. It'll be a great day out. Parts of it will be televised live, is that all right?'

Two weeks later, Eirian walked with her parents across a flat green park towards a huge marquee. The car park was packed solid, people everywhere. There were smaller tents clustered around the main one, selling food, books, religious trinkets. Eirian saw a couple of big white vans to the left of the marquee, sporting aerials and satellite dishes. That made her feel excited.

'Worked out what you're going to say?' Morgan asked, his hand resting lightly on her back.

Eirian shrugged. 'No, I never do. The Goddess tells me.'

'So you're not nervous?' He grinned teasingly at her.

'Not really.' Over the entrance to the marquee, there was a sign that read MIDLANDS INTER-FAITH RALLY, and underneath, SPONSORED BY TLN ROADSHOW. 'What's TLN Roadshow?'

'Perhaps we should have found out more about this before we came,' said Beth.

'Mum, will you stop worrying? You're so suspicious.'

'I prefer cautious,' Beth said drily.

Inside the marquee, the heat and the smell of crushed grass were overwhelming. A central aisle ran between two blocks of seating to a stage with a red velvet backdrop, a podium, and a large sofa. On the backdrop was a large white cross. There was a man on the stage adjusting a microphone, some of the audience were taking their seats, others milling around. Eirian saw two cameramen guiding their equipment into position on the stage, a familiar sight. Daylight glowed creamily through the canvas, but the stage was bright under glaring television lights.

As Eirian and her parents stood looking round, two men rushed up and greeted them. One was the man who'd phoned, Dave; he was thirty-ish, plump and balding. The other was an American in a suit, with tanned skin the same caramel-brown as his hair. They were both overwhelmingly friendly.

'We're really glad you could come, Miss Rhys,' said Dave. 'There's been a slight change of format with your panel, I hope you don't mind. Not all the speakers could make it, so we had to change things round a bit. Anyway, Aaron'll explain while he takes you to the green room. We've reserved special seats for your parents; Mr and Mrs Rhys, if you'll come this way.'

The caramel man, Aaron, whisked Eirian away and she glanced back to see Beth and Morgan being seated virtually in the back row. They looked uneasy. Eirian already sensed, from the taut, volatile atmosphere in the marquee, that this event was not quite what she'd expected. 'Saw every one of your TV appearances in the States,' Aaron was saying. 'You have a real way with words, and I know the folks back home are going to love seeing you again.'

'This is being broadcast in America?'

'Sure, by satellite. So you gotta bear with us, there'll be a little waiting around to get the timing right; technical stuff, honey.'

'Oh, technical stuff,' said Eirian. She didn't like him. He was over-familiar.

The green room was a smaller tent that led off the marquee behind the stage. She saw a handful of other people hanging around but she had no chance to talk to them; Aaron kept talking at her, keeping her occupied. 'This is what'll happen.

I'll introduce the item, then we have an American TV personality to say a few words. Then he'll get you and the other participants involved; it's gonna be real exciting.' On and on he went, telling her nothing. Eirian began to feel uncomfortable. It was so hot. Oppressive.

After half an hour, she was ushered on to the stage. Against the glaring lights she saw that the marquee was packed, people standing all around the sides. Aaron guided her to the long white sofa and she found herself sitting beside a boy of about sixteen who looked wild-eyed with nerves. They said a quiet hello. Next to him there was a shockingly thin girl, maybe eighteen. Eirian had expected adults, not young people like herself. 'They normally clip microphones on us,' Eirian whispered. 'I wonder why they haven't?' The boy didn't answer. He was thin and rather pretty, with blond hair and grey eyes. 'I'm Eirian, by the way.'

'I'm Alastair.' He had a Scottish accent.

'So, what faith are you?'

'Presbyterian, originally,' he said. 'Although I – I came with some lads from this Christian group in Birmingham.' He could hardly speak for nerves; she sympathized.

'I'm the token pagan. What's TLN stand for?'

He raised his shoulders nervously. 'It's some American TV channel, I think. The preacher's doing a gospel tour. He's meant to be fantastic. That's why we came.'

And Eirian remembered. 'True Light Network,' she said, a roar of noise swamping her words. They were on air; Aaron was shouting into a microphone over a sudden blare of gospel music.

'Here's the man you've all been waiting for, the most influential preacher of our time, now live here in the UK for the very first time to hit you with the holy Word of God – Reverend Paul Gregory Keay. Give him a warm Midlands welcome! Here's PGK to show you the way!'

The preacher came bounding on to the stage, exactly as Eirian remembered: overpowering, vivacious, magnetic. As PGK strode up and down the stage, the roar of applause became deafening. This was more a congregation than an audience. She wondered what Beth and Morgan were thinking.

'We got a real special show here today,' PGK announced, his voice gravelly with passion, a thread of sweat running down his forehead. 'We have a young woman who wants to quit her drug addiction and come back to the Lord. We have a young man' – he indicated Alastair – 'who seeks to be purged of the demons of homosexuality that plague him. And we have one special little girl called Eirian Rhys who sorely needs to repent her misguided ways and see the one and only True Light! Lord, we are goin' to see some healin' here today! Hallelujah!' The crowd roared in response.

By the time Eirian realized she had been betrayed, it was too late to escape. The tent was packed. She refused to run away, in any case. Her heart was pounding, her eyes stinging with anger. If people of other faiths had been invited here it was only to convert or humiliate them. And everyone seemed to be in on the conspiracy except her.

PGK was talking feverishly against a background of swelling music, goading his followers to a state of ecstatic hysteria. They cried out for him to lay healing hands on the poor unfortunates.

He went for the skeletal drug addict first, pulling her to her feet and shouting at God to drive the demons out. She hung limp, eyes closed and head lolling back. PGK touched her head and she toppled back on to the couch as if she'd been electrocuted. Then he swooped on Eirian. 'Kick out Satan, let in the Lord,' he whispered grimly.

Angry and scared, she tried to evade him. 'This isn't why I came,' she began, but no one could hear her. PGK dragged her to her feet, yelling; Eirian wondered painfully what her parents must be thinking as they watched from an impotent distance. He struck her head with his fat hand; it was like being hit by a brick. She fell back on to the couch, shocked and dazed. But as she began to recover, she found she'd picked up a thread from his psyche. PGK had power, but it was not his own; someone else had infused him with it. Perhaps he could heal, but it was a temporary fire.

Eirian sat trembling for a few moments, humiliated but furious. In her rage she felt the Goddess's power stirring inside her. PGK wasn't as evil as Luke, he didn't deserve to die, he was only someone's lumbering puppet – but he had to be stopped, all the same.

As he reached down to clasp Alastair, Eirian met the preacher's eyes and his soul opened up to her. She sensed a mass of inhibitions, rigid walls built against natural inclinations. And with the skill of the Crone, she took the walls away, so softly he didn't even feel them dissolving.

Gripping Alastair, PGK ordered his demons to depart. But after a few words his strident voice trailed off. The boy hung in his grasp, looking up with wild eyes. Sweat ran down the preacher's face, shone greasily in his fringe. There was a lull, a moment of awkwardness as people began to see all was not well.

'*Go on,*' Eirian's mind said to his. '*Do what you want to do. There's nothing to stop you now.*'

PGK's thin-lipped mouth came down on Alastair's. Not a kiss of blessing, the audience quickly saw, but a sexual kiss that went on and on, becoming openly lascivious. But it was only when the preacher pushed the startled youth down on to the couch and unzipped his own flies that Aaron and two others rushed to drag him off. There were no curtains to mask the scene and she guessed that the broadcast – unless it was controlled by TLN – was continuing.

In the midst of the commotion, Eirian rose and went to the microphone. PGK – looking dishevelled and dazed as he was led away – met her eyes as if clearly aware of what she'd done. Oh, yes, he knew!

'I wish to state that I was brought here under false pretences,' said Eirian. Her voice rang out from the loudspeakers. 'I was expecting to take part in a rational discussion, not medieval hysteria. All I can say is, if you paid to get in, I hope you got your money's worth.'

She turned and stalked off the stage. The audience were on their feet and she couldn't see her parents; perhaps if she could force her way out of the nearest exit, they would find her outside. She escaped into cool air, ignoring people's stares, and stood between the guy ropes to get her breath back. She could hear Aaron's voice, trying to restore order. Then she saw movement from the corner of her eye and turned to see Alastair emerging from the marquee. He was deadly white and shaking all over.

At once she was filled with remorse. She'd been so eager to humiliate PGK that she'd completely forgotten the boy's feelings. And he was the one who'd got hurt.

Eirian went to him and said, 'Are you all right? I'm really sorry.'

'Why?' he said, staring round-eyed at her. 'It wasn't your fault.'

'But I –' But no, of course, he had no inkling that Eirian was responsible for PGK's behaviour. 'I mean, I'm sorry it happened.'

As she spoke, three young men in camouflage trousers and white T-shirts, with shaven heads and crosses round their necks, approached and tried to pull Alastair away. 'Come on, brother, come with us, we'll help you.'

He looked even more distressed. 'Sod off, leave him alone!' said Eirian. The brothers regarded her with contempt, but as she glared at them their expressions disintegrated to recognition, doubt, fear. They backed off and left, muttering. She touched Alastair's arm, 'Come on, I'll buy you a cup of tea. My Mum and Dad'll find us eventually.'

She took him to a burger stall a few yards away. He sipped heavily sugared tea from a polystyrene cup and his colour returned. 'So, are you gay?' she asked.

'I think so,' he answered miserably. His Scottish accent was pleasantly soft and he was tall, thin and very attractive with his floppy pale gold hair. 'I've never . . . done anything, but I have these feelings. I'm confused. That's why I came, I thought I might get cured here. That's what those lads from the Christian group told me, anyway. These feelings are wrong, I know they're sinful, everyone says so, but I can't get rid of them. I'm meant to be a Christian, I can't live with the way I feel.'

'Yes, you can,' said Eirian. 'I can help you. Maybe you should stop associating with people who make you hate yourself. I'll tell you what I think; all acts of love and pleasure are sacred to the Goddess. She won't mind if you love other men. As long as you're loving and not nasty, what does it matter? And do all that safe sex stuff, of course.'

Alastair blushed. 'For God's sake, you're embarrassing me.'

'You put your faith in that preacher and he's just an old hypocrite. At least you're honest.' Eirian put her hand through his arm. 'Come on, let's find my parents. Where do you live?'

'Birmingham,' he said as they walked. 'My mum works there. I'm at college. My dad's still in Edinburgh, but they're divorced.'

'I live near Tamworth. Not that far away.'

'I feel I can talk to you,' said Alastair. 'I do like girls, actually. I'm just really confused.'

Eirian found Beth at the front of the marquee, raging at the organizer who'd invited them. There was no sign of Morgan. 'You got us here under false pretences! We were led to believe it was a panel discussion, not this bloody travesty!'

The plump man, Dave, was smiling grimly. 'Mrs Rhys, I'm sorry you feel like this, but we did try to explain the format had been changed and, um, the people from TLN were responsible for the changes –'

'Bullshit!' said Beth. 'You deliberately set out to exploit my daughter!' Seeing Eirian, Beth rushed to her and hugged her. 'Are you all right, love?'

'Yes,' Eirian said into her ear. 'PGK isn't, though.'

Morgan appeared. He gripped Eirian's shoulders from behind and kissed the top of her head. 'I've been looking everywhere for you!'

'I'm all right. This is Alastair.'

'Hello, Alastair,' Morgan murmured, walking past them in pursuit of Dave, who was trying to sidle away. 'I'll be making a complaint about this. Someone deliberately misled us about the nature of the event.'

Dave's eyes hardened. 'Believe me, what we did was with your daughter's best interests at heart.'

Eirian thought her father was going to hit him. 'Dad, leave it. It doesn't matter.'

'Nah.' Morgan gave the man a contemptuous grin. 'Come on, let's go home. He's not worth it.'

Eirian exchanged phone numbers with Alastair, and said goodbye. As she walked back to the car with her parents, Beth asked, 'So what happened with the preacher?'

'I looked him in the eye and suggested he follow his natural inclinations,' said Eirian. 'Whatever he did, he did it to himself.'

They'd been at home for a couple of hours, unwinding and talking over what had happened, when the telephone rang. It was Jamie Baker, calling from New York. Eirian took the call, Beth and Morgan listening on the extension.

'Boy, have you ever caused a stir over here!' Jamie chuckled delightedly.

'How?' said Eirian.

'PGK's rally in Notting-hahm. It was broadcast live by satellite on TLN. The cameras just kept on rolling; they musta been too slow or too stunned to stop the broadcast. They showed it again on the news. I tell you, TV evangelists have been caught out at some stunts in their time, but attempting homosexual rape on air, that has to be a first! They've pulled the plug on his UK tour. He has some music to face when he gets home. And are there ever gonna be some journalists wanting an interview with you, young lady!'

Chapter Thirteen

NATHANIEL De Vries sat behind his desk, his long hands serenely folded, his hair loose in a fall of icy silk around his shoulders. His eyes were gelid with the dispassionate authority of a judge. On the far side, across the mirror-lake of polished walnut, the preacher PGK sat hunched and wretched.

'Dear Lord above,' PGK said in anguish, 'temptation was visited on me and I fell. Oh, Lord, I have sinned.' He squirmed in his seat as he spoke, hands jammed between his fat knees and his big head bowed. To Nathaniel's disgust he began to sob.

'Very good, Paul. But save the performance for the cameras.'

'I ain't performing!' PGK said passionately. 'I have fought so hard to resist sin! I swear I ain't touched a boy in twenty years! Ask my wife!'

'Paul, I don't care if you screw horses. First rule of your job is, don't get caught. When a preacher-man commits homosexual assault in front of millions of devoted viewers, it kinda confuses folk, you know?'

'Lord help me. Lord help me.' Tears ran down PGK's flushed, sweating face. There was one being he feared more than God, and that was Nathaniel.

'I'm sure God forgives you. But have you any idea how much money we lost, having to pull you out of the UK road-show? Have you any idea what you've done to the credibility of the True Light Network? I gave you the simplest of tasks, to knock the bullshit out of that Rhys girl, but you still managed to fuck up. What the hell went wrong?'

The preacher struggled for a moment. 'It was her! The child is a witch. She made me!'

'How?' Nathaniel said coldly. 'I prepared you beforehand, didn't I?' He stretched his intertwined fingers. 'You'd be nothing without me. I'm the one who feeds the charisma and power into you, every time you walk out in front of the cameras. And I programmed you with enough energy to blast that child's blasphemous ideas clean out of her head. A healing of the soul, an exorcism. Why didn't it work?'

PGK blotted his face with a large handkerchief. 'I did it like we planned. But the power didn't touch her. It was like she blasted it back at me, and somethin' snapped. Next thing I knew, I was kissin' the boy. I tell you, she's Satan's child!'

Nathaniel paused, irritated by Paul's nervous fidgeting. 'Since she first appeared last year, contributions to our funds have dropped by twenty per cent. Since she appeared again last week, we've already lost another five per cent. It doesn't take Einstein to work out that if she carries on she is going to ruin us all – like she's ruined you.'

The preacher let out a shuddering breath. 'What'll happen to me?'

'You're finished, Paul. You can do one appearance, the big fallen evangelist confession thing – that'll get great ratings – then you'll disappear. Some log cabin in the mountains, new identity, pension.'

The bulky body slumped. 'Please, Nathaniel, give me another chance. TLN is mah life!'

'No second chances,' Nathaniel said coldly. 'I kept the police away from you, that's the best I can do. You did this to yourself, lost me my best preacher. I guess Aaron'll have to fill in for now but it won't be the same. I'm very disappointed in you. Just thank God you're leaving with your life.' PGK hung his head, broken, but Nathaniel felt no touch of pity. 'Go. Rehearse your number. Don't mention Eirian's name; it's not gonna look too credible if you blame your depravity on a little girl, is it?'

PGK lumbered out, still snivelling. Alone, Nathaniel sat in his darkened office, the chill dry breeze of the air-conditioning blowing over him. He rewound the video tape and watched the marquee scene again, concentrating on Eirian. Although she sat there like innocence incarnate, he saw her inner power rippling out to compromise the hapless preacher. Nathaniel cursed himself for not taking the danger seriously enough.

He'd seen Eirian Rhys as a bewitching young girl whom he could crush with a casual blow. Now he was seeing her as a much darker threat. That entity at her shoulder was the power of chaos on her side ... To be honest, he'd thrown PGK against her to test her strength, see if she was an opponent worthy of Nathaniel's personal attention. He'd been prepared to waste PGK, just to prove a point.

Nathaniel stopped the video but she was on screen again! Being interviewed on some TV show about PGK's fall from grace. He hated to watch, but she was compulsive. He flicked the video on to record as she denounced the True Light Network, describing how they'd tricked her.

'If you send your money to these religious networks,' she said straight to camera, her eyes hypnotic, 'you are sending it into a void. But there are worse things than being ripped off. I've seen the hysteria these preachers whip up at their meetings. I've seen the psychological damage it causes. Don't give them that power over you!'

He'd heard many sceptics in the past speaking out against exploitative broadcasting, only for the money to come flowing in faster than before. Believers were loyal to their stations. But Eirian was different. She had the power to make people believe her. Nathaniel could see the graph line of his profits plummeting even as she spoke.

Another one like me, he thought. If I let her reach adulthood she's going to destroy all I've achieved!

Nathaniel's loathing of her swelled to the very tips of his fingers. Leaning back in his expensive leather chair, he closed his eyes and saw a vision. His ancestors: a noble wave of men with white faces and Puritan garb moving across the continent, taking it for God. Hordes of feathered savages falling to the clean power of guns. Order subduing chaos. Some grotesque witch-doctor dying slowly on a cross-pole while the conquerors, with quiet dignity, read passages from the Bible. Such a perfect image: the triumph of light and law over uncontrolled darkness.

But where had it got them? The States was suffering the encroachments of Native Americans, foreigners, blacks, feminists, pagans and the liberals who let it happen. He felt a visceral loathing, instilled by his upbringing, of the degeneracy they threatened. He needed order, power, control. Must fortify his empire against the pit of witchy chaos, Eirian's domain. Women, he thought with bitter irony, are dangerous if they think they're anything but vessels for divine male seed. Uncontrolled, all females are treacherous.

As a child, he'd discovered that he had an exceptional gift. He could read people's emotions, manipulate their minds. That was how he'd set up TLN and been elected chairman so young: he was still only thirty. He had intended to follow his father into the army, until he'd seen that true influence lay in television.

On the surface, he shared and promoted the aims of the Evangelical Right, passionate crusaders for strict, biblical patriarchy. Privately, though, he felt himself to be above them; cleverer, subtler, more intelligent. They were worker ants to help shape the world to his design. He could never be an electronic preacher like PGK because he didn't believe. The Bible was a useful tool to control the masses – not to mention extracting millions of dollars from them in sacramental contributions – but, secretly, Nathaniel's only God was himself. A cold, demanding force in his mind, driving him on.

His face was rarely seen on TLN. He preferred to work in the shadows, hedged around by mystery, smoked windows, and 'aides' like Gil who could cause his opponents to vanish. Nathaniel relished being feared. And if his operations slid from the legal to the illegal at times, he had no qualms. It was all in the service of a higher ideal.

How dare Eirian, in her youth and insolence, flaunt the power he'd thought was unique to him? She wasn't his equal yet, she was less than half his age, but that was all the more reason to deal with her now.

He couldn't just wade in, or send his wasp Gil to kill her; she was too clever for that. No, he must be careful, subtle.

Make her suffer. Pull her little world apart like a butterfly, leg by leg.

It would take time, maybe a year or three. Best to wait until she was on the very edge of adulthood for his plan to be most effective. In the meantime her influence would grow . . . but that would be even better. The higher she rose, the harder she'd come crashing down.

Replaying the interview, he looked into her feline eyes and despised her. But his fury was very cool, like ice-crystals shining in the void of his soul.

Destroying Eirian Rhys was going to be exquisite.

'Luke called it the One Truth,' Eirian told several million television viewers. 'I call it the One Lie. The denial of female sacredness has wrecked society. You don't even have to *believe* in the Goddess; she is the very energy of life. She doesn't send her "only begotten son" to be sacrificed because we are *all* her sons and daughters . . .'

Eirian didn't expect to reach everyone. Just enough people to make a difference.

Following her encounter with PGK, she'd flown to America again with her parents and appeared on a variety of programmes. She felt the Americans would happily keep her there for ever; after a few weeks of it she was quite glad to return to England. Her influence in the States was causing interest in the British media too, albeit in a lower key. Curiosity, rather than hysteria. Her parents let her give a handful of interviews – a couple of weekend supplements, a few Sunday discussion programmes – but again they called a halt as soon as school began. Eirian was content with that. No use in trying to do too much. In her own, more secular country, the need to speak out was less urgent. It would come, but not yet.

Her friends accepted her as being a bit different. In everyday life, Eirian was content. She had a handful of good friends: quiet Lisa, good-natured Tricia, Sam, Hugh and Peter. No boyfriend, although she and Peter had taken to studying together in the evenings. Her new friend Alastair came up from

Birmingham on the bus most weekends, and they all hung around together. Alastair was on a computer studies course, but he really wanted to be a theatre designer. He lived with his mother, was always broke, and rarely saw his father in Scotland. Eirian found him more complex and mysterious than Peter, rather tormented. He confided in her, and she liked that.

The following summer, when she was fifteen, Eirian went to America with Beth and Morgan a third time. The media loved her. Pagan groups wrote to say, 'Thank you for helping people to understand instead of dismissing us as cranks.' Television preachers denounced her, to no effect. There was panic in their eyes. Their followers were having doubts. Articles were written about this 'phenomenon', but Eirian kept repeating, 'I'm not the leader of a movement. All I ask is that people open their eyes and see life differently.'

When her few weeks of fame were over, she returned happily to school.

Eirian felt she was living her life on three levels. There was her everyday self, who worried over schoolwork, had fun with her parents and friends. There was her Goddess persona, which possessed her when she spoke of her beliefs. Then there was her nocturnal, lunar self, whom nobody knew.

Ictinike came to her when the moon was dark or horned, and always the night she felt liquid and aching on the crest of menstruation. He was never fully human; sometimes he was a beautiful young man with a serpent's tail, sometimes a male body with a leopard's head, or a wolf with the shaman's face behind a hairy mask. Or he'd be a hawk, a stag, a swan with long, trailing wings like bridal veils.

She felt herself slipping into a state between dream and reality, and then Ictinike came softly into her room, her bed. With hands, hair and feathers he turned her nerves to stars. His long tongue lapped at her rose-bud nipples, trailed hotly down her belly and between her parted thighs. She felt a hot, wet ache there. Just as it became unbearable, his long body flowed up over hers and she felt the rounded head of his phallus pushing between the folds of her vulva. The touch was electric.

She'd healed that organ, it couldn't harm her, it was hers. She groaned as he slid into her. Weightless, he made exquisite, animal love to her, every move devoted to her pleasure; never his own. Leading her through a star-scattered night towards something mystical, unbearably exciting. She was full of him, full of fire and life and pounding blood . . . and she reached the peak, hurtled out over a drop and fell in a sweet explosion of honey-gold ecstasy.

When she drifted to rest on the far side, Ictinike was gone. He never stayed long enough. As always she tried to hang on to him, only to wake with empty arms and a strangely painful emptiness inside.

She was fifteen, not ready to do this for real . . . but ready to dream about it. She thought the pleasure Ictinike gave her was harmless, but was it? Suddenly Eirian felt angry at him, because he made her want more than he could give. Made her crave, too young, a lover who was real, solid and alive.

Olivia had lived with her rage for so many years now that she knew no other way to feel. She was blind to everything but her holy anger against the minions of the Devil who'd conspired to ruin her life. Perhaps that was why they insisted she was mad. The medical staff never used that term, of course; it was always, 'clinically this' or 'an episode of that'. But her anger was righteous – so to be kept locked away from the very people who'd offended her was intolerable. That was why, driven to the limit, she had sometimes vented her fury physically on the other patients. And why she sometimes hurt herself. Frustration at the justified wrath of God being thwarted. Why couldn't they see that?

The first time the stranger visited her, Olivia was reluctant to listen. He was some kind of lay minister, apparently, who went around visiting prisons and hospitals. A do-gooder. His name was Joshua Andrews and he had untidy grey hair, small oval glasses, and the precise accent of a highly educated American.

Olivia invited him to her room and he sat on the end of the

bed, where her accursed daughter had sat, the one and only time she had deigned to visit. His tweed suit was pristine; she approved of that, at least. He was earnest, but she was aloof.

'Mrs Herne, you need help, more help than they can give you here,' he said. 'You need the Lord's help.'

'Do you think I don't know that?' she said stiffly. 'I have been a devout Christian since I was a child.'

'However, your faith has slipped, I suspect.'

'No.' But she went hot. Everything had changed the day the terrible Crone had made her destroy her son Luke. Her beliefs had become an armour to be clutched around herself in desperation.

'Mrs Herne, tell me about yourself. Nothing you say to me will go any further. I am here as a friend, a counsellor, a confessor or a brick wall; anything you wish. All I want is to help you.'

Something in his voice reached her. Studying him more closely, she was astonished at how smooth and clear his face was, for a man she had taken to be at least fifty. A strong, radiant face, and his eyes were extraordinary. Piercing, full of truth, as Luke's had been. For the first time in years she felt a thrill of hope.

It took Joshua several visits to win her full trust. She thought she'd disclosed very little, until he started telling her her own story. 'You were confused about your sexual feelings, you knew they couldn't be right, but you couldn't tell your parents. You worshipped your father but he was cold. Your mother would have said, "What nonsense. Go horse-riding, take a cold bath." They were too inhibited to tell the truth so you turned to the Bible and it was right there. We're all fallen and sinful. You were absolutely right to fight that evil and to purge your son with blows, every stripe a line of holy fire. It worked, you saved his soul! Poor Luke paid for his sanctity with his life – but you didn't kill him, Mrs Herne. Stop blaming yourself, here and now. *The child alone was responsible.* Luke died at the hands of his enemies, like Jesus, in order to save others. He's watching over you now.'

Olivia burst into tears. No one had ever expressed such a moving, profound truth to her before. She felt the dreadful burden of guilt falling away, her muddled memories coming clear. 'I didn't kill him,' she whispered. '*She* did.'

'That's right,' he said. 'Satan used her. She *let* Satan use her.'

Oh, what glory to be taken seriously! 'The Devil is cavorting right in the middle of my own family,' Olivia said fervently, clenching her fists. 'I've seen him, *seen* him. They invited the Devil among them with their lust! I know the Bible tells us to forgive, but even Jesus got angry sometimes – and they cannot be forgiven until they've been purged of this evil!'

'Dear Mrs Herne, you're so right. It's for God to judge them. You can only deliver them up to Him.'

She gazed at him, excited, inflamed. 'But how can I do holy work while I'm locked up in here? It's against God's will that I'm here, it's another of Satan's conspiracies against me!'

'But don't you see?' Joshua said softly, taking her hands. 'That's why I'm here. The Lord has called me to your aid. God sent me, Mrs Herne.'

'Yes. Oh, dear God, yes!'

'Let's pray together.'

The prayer and his eyes worked some hypnotic magic on her. She felt blessed and cleansed, ready to do anything for him. When they'd finished, she said impulsively, 'Call me Olivia.'

'And I am Joshua. Your friend.' She laughed in sheer gratitude, but he became stern, scaring her. 'I can get you out of here, Olivia, but only if you do as I say. Your anger is justified but it's working against you, because they interpret it as insanity. If we're going to persuade them to release you, first you must begin to co-operate; to make them think their treatments have worked. Can you do that?'

'Oh, yes. For you.' Her heart began to beat hard. 'Then I'll denounce my family. I'll make them face their own evil and beg for forgiveness, and I'll –'

'No,' Joshua broke in. 'That's not the way to win. You can't rush in and lay your cards on the table, Olivia; they'll expect that and arm themselves against it. You have to do what they don't expect.'

'What do you mean?'

He told her. Olivia put her hand to her mouth, her throat in such a spasm of revulsion she thought she was going to vomit. She said, 'I can't.'

'But you must. It's the only way you'll ever have your revenge.'

'Have you ever had sex?' asked Eirian.

She was in her bedroom with Peter, who at sixteen was a year older than her. They were studying together, as they often did, she sitting on her bed and Peter on her desk chair. He was tall, with thick brown hair and soft brown eyes, like his mother, Dee. He was attractive; she'd been aware of that for quite a while. He wore gold-rimmed glasses, which made him look gentle and intelligent, like her father. If anything he was too serious, but she liked him a lot.

Eirian had been asking chemistry questions from a text book, Peter answering. Then she asked the question, and he stopped and stared at her. 'What?'

'I said, have you ever had sex?'

'That question isn't in the book!'

'No,' said Eirian, 'but have you?'

He shrugged, off-hand. 'Yeah, 'course I have. Loads of times.'

'You liar,' she said flatly.

Peter went red. 'Well, I bet you haven't, either!' he said defensively.

'No, I haven't. So, do you want to try it?'

Peter gaped at her, his eyes circular. He pushed his glasses up his nose. 'What about your parents?'

'Oh, *they've* done it. They never stop.'

'I didn't mean that, I meant, what if they come in?'

Eirian grinned. 'I know what you meant. They won't, they respect my privacy.'

'It's not right. You're underage.'

'Only a few months. I'd never let a boy bully me into doing anything I didn't want, however old I was. I'll only do it if I want. And I want to try it with you, Pete. Don't you fancy me?'

'Oh, yes, I do, I really do,' he said quickly, looking panic-stricken.

'Well, you never try to kiss me or anything.'

'Only because I thought you just wanted to be friends! You scare me, Eirian, it would be a bit like making a pass at the Queen, umm . . .'

She frowned. 'I'm not that bad, am I?'

'No, I didn't mean –' He crossed his legs, Eirian realized with pleasure, to conceal the fact that he had an erection. 'God, no, I'd love to, but we can't! Not without a condom, anyway.'

'I've got some,' said Eirian. 'This sixth-form girl got them for me.'

His mouth fell open. 'Bloody hell.'

'Come on, then,' said Eirian. She lay down on her bed. There was classical music playing softly on her CD player, Rimsky-Korsakov; she preferred it to the rock music her parents liked.

Hesitant and trembling, Peter lay down beside her and kissed her awkwardly with closed lips. He tasted of coffee and pepper-mints. The kiss didn't make Eirian feel anything in particular, but Peter's breathing quickened and she felt a hardness in the front of his jeans pressing into her leg.

He pushed his hands under the black and grey striped top she was wearing and clumsily explored her breasts. It was nothing like the gentle touch of the shaman. Neither of them knew what they were doing. They kept most of their clothes on, just in case Beth did come upstairs. Eirian slipped off the knickers she was wearing under her long crushed cotton skirt, then she undid Peter's jeans and helped him, with difficulty, to roll the condom over the stiff shaft of his penis. It seemed small compared to the shaman's, though still a pleasing size and shape.

But she knew, as soon as he lay down on top of her, that

this would bear no comparison to her nocturnal ecstasies. Peter's weight on her pelvis was uncomfortable, the pressure at the entrance to her vagina blind and intrusive. She felt dry, unaroused. He was having difficulty entering her but she felt detached, couldn't be bothered to help him. He pushed so hard she feared the condom would break; the discomfort made her wince. Where was the thrilling lightness of the shaman's body on hers, the stars flaring, the sacred flight through the Goddess's eternal realm? This was leaden, awkward, and utterly disappointing.

The barrier gave and Peter was inside her. It hurt a bit, not much. He pushed deeper and began to thrust, four or five times. But just as Eirian began to feel a small flame of excitement, to think it wasn't so bad after all, he shuddered and stopped, resting his full weight on her. 'Sorry,' he said. 'I came.'

'Did you?' said Eirian, puzzled. 'You weren't gasping or anything. What did it feel like?'

'I dunno. Really nice.' He rolled off her, carefully taking the condom with him. Eirian felt empty, lonely and disillusioned.

She said, 'I'm meant to come too, you know.'

'I know, but I'm not sure what to do.' Eirian pulled his hand between her thighs but his touch was too rough. After a few moments she pushed him away and smoothed her skirt over her legs. 'Never mind.'

Peter looked desperately anxious. 'It wasn't much good, was it? I'm sorry, Eirian. Maybe it would be better if we tried another time. Mum says you have to practise to be any good at it. Can we do it again?'

'No, I don't think so. It was a mistake.'

'But – but we are still seeing each other, aren't we?'

'I didn't know we were.'

'But I thought – we spend so much time together – I want you to be my girlfriend, Eirian. I just didn't know how to say it. I love you. I'm really in love with you now!'

Oh, God, thought Eirian, what have I done? She felt indifferent. Suddenly she couldn't bear him near her, declaring dog-like devotion. 'I don't want to be anyone's girlfriend.'

'Sorry,' he sighed. 'I've messed everything up. But how could you do that, if you don't like me?'

'I was curious,' she said, 'and now I'm not. I like you, but I want to finish my homework. Alone.'

'Oh. Do you want me to go? Okay, I'll go home. If that's what you want.' Peter sounded deeply hurt, but she was unmoved. Perhaps if he'd argued she might have relented, but he didn't. It never occurred to her that she was being cruel. When he left, she lay back with her elbows behind her head, utterly numb. Is that all there is to sex? she thought. Won't I ever find the love and pleasure Ictinike gives me in real life?

She bit her lip, and felt a hot tear crawling down her cheek. She didn't know why she was crying.

Nathaniel watched the girls passing through the school gates in their black and white uniforms, like a scene from a more genteel time. The old town was so English, delightfully rural, with its glowing red buildings and chestnut trees shading the uneven pavements. He saw Eirian walking with a group of girls, just like any ordinary schoolgirl. The sight of her made him tingle with anticipation.

He had on a grey wig and a long tweed coat, middle aged and respectable. Posing as a journalist researching a piece about historic English towns for an American magazine, he'd gained access to the school earlier in the day. Having steamrollered the headmistress's natural caution with his powers of persuasion, he'd approached groups of girls, asking about the school, then slipping Eirian's name into the conversation to test their reaction. 'By the way,' said Nathaniel, 'one of your fellow pupils is quite well-known in the States. Eirian Rhys. Any of you know her?'

'Yeah, she's okay,' most of them said. 'Some people think she's stand-offish, but she's really nice if you get to know her. She'll always help people in trouble.'

But one girl had reacted with bristling hostility. She said nothing but she didn't have to; Nathaniel sensed it. He'd focused on her, his gaze delving into her and manipulating her will. And here she came now, glancing back to make sure no one was watching her. The big copper-haired girl.

'Are you going to put something about Eirian in your article?' she asked, thin-lipped.

'I'll let you into a secret.' His tone was confidential. 'The article is about her.'

The girl pulled a face. 'I suppose it's going to say how great she is.'

'That depends. A lot of people in the States think she's wonderful, but I want to know the truth. Even if it's not so good for her. That's why I don't want her to know. If you don't tell her you've spoken to me, I won't tell her either. Our little secret.'

He winked. She smiled. They understood each other. 'Oh, that's different. I'm Serena, by the way.'

'Well, Serena, can you tell me the truth about Eirian?'

Her mouth stretched in a cat-cruel smile. 'Oh, yes. I'll tell you everything you need to know.'

'Have you ever had sex?' Eirian asked.

'Depends what you mean,' said Alastair. He and Eirian were at a party at Dee's and Steve's house, for Hugh's fourteenth birthday. The house was full of teenagers, but she and Alastair had crept up to a semi-dark bedroom. Alastair was bored with the music and the behaviour of teenagers on one pint of cider. Eirian wanted to get away from Peter, who always seemed to be gazing reproachfully at her. 'Lots of times on my own, but I don't think that counts. I keep thinking about men, but I still daren't do anything. I'm too scared of feeling guilty, or catching something. How about you?'

'Hundred of times in my dreams,' said Eirian. 'And once for real. The dreams were better. Ever done it with a girl?'

'Once,' he said morosely. 'It wasn't much good.'

'Want to try it again? I won't get silly about wanting to marry you or anything.'

Alastair laughed. Light from a street-lamp washed into the bedroom and he looked very pretty in it, with his floppy fair

235

hair and grey eyes shaded by incredibly long eyelashes. 'Okay,' he said.

They hid on a pile of coats between the bed and the wall, in case anyone walked in. They were both slightly drunk. Eirian virtually ravished him, pulling off his clothes, caressing him until he was hard in her hands, rolling on the rubber sheath, then drawing him inside her. She was wet, aroused, determined not to be disappointed this time. Her own lust shook her. She felt such passion for Alastair's thin body that she wanted to devour him.

Scoring his back with her nails, she ground herself urgently on to him, feeling the heat of lust melting her . . . melting . . . until at last she dissolved into a fiery climax that burst out of her in loud, staccato gasps. But as she fell back, sated, Alastair pushed himself away from her and lay on his back, his erect penis outlined in the faint light from the landing. He was silent, staring at the ceiling. Eventually Eirian asked, 'Why have you stopped?'

'I'm sorry,' he said. 'I can't do it any more. It doesn't feel right.'

'Why not?' She frowned, worried. 'Was I too violent? Sorry, I got a bit carried away. But I enjoyed it, I want you to enjoy it too.'

'I can't.' He exhaled heavily, his erection wilting. It seemed a replay of her time with Peter, in reverse. 'Sorry. It's not your fault.'

Eirian stroked his arm. 'Is it because you just don't fancy women?'

'I don't know . . . I told you I like blokes . . .'

'Do you fancy Peter?'

'No.' Alastair sounded shocked. 'He's a boy. I like men. Especially older men, for some reason – but that doesn't mean I don't find you attractive. I don't know what it is. I just can't seem to let go.'

'How many times have I told you there's no need to feel guilty about sex?'

'I know, but . . .'

'Shut up,' she said. 'Relax.' She peeled the condom off, then took him in her mouth. The silky dome of skin tasted salty at first, then almost sweet, stiffening again between her lips

'Oh, God, that's nice,' he said, hands flopping above his head. She worked him with her tongue and her palm. Finally he came in her hand, the semen spilling on to his narrow abdomen. Then she felt forlorn again. *This seems so ordinary*, she thought, looking at the viscous little pools of fluid. *It's nothing at all, really. Ictinike never moans about fancying men or makes banal remarks like, 'That's nice.' Ictinike . . .*

He said something. Then, 'Eirian? You're miles away.'

'Sorry.'

'I just said, maybe I am bisexual after all. Do you think it's all right for us to be friends but sleep together sometimes?'

She laughed. She felt amused, resigned. 'Why not? It would be fun.' *Better than nothing, anyway. Experience.* She lay along his body and he put his slender arm round her.

'The person you did it with once,' he said, 'was it Peter?'

'Yes, why?'

'Because he's in love with you, the poor bastard. The guy's distraught. Hope he didn't see us sneaking up here together. Why are you avoiding him?'

'Claustrophobia,' said Eirian. 'At least I know you'll never fall in love with me.'

'I hope I don't. You'd eat me for breakfast.'

'Am I that bad?' She spoke half to herself. 'I don't mean to be cruel, but I don't want to be anyone's possession. I don't know what I want . . . oh, *shit*. When I'm in front of an audience, it's simple; the Goddess is there with me. But in between it's like she fucks off, saying, "Sorry, mate, you're on your own."'

The following night, lying in her own bed, Eirian began to dream. The bed became a big smooth rock on which she lay naked, spread-eagled. The horned moon shone. She sensed the wolf padding noiselessly around her, lean and dark and beautiful. She smelled his animal musk. His rough tongue moved

237

over her face, down the hollow of her throat to her breasts, making a shivery trail of pleasure around each nipple, deep into her navel and down her abdomen to the curls of hair between her legs. The tongue worked lower, into her warm cleft. The bud that nestled there lit up with a delicious red fire. She felt the fire spreading along her vulva and down the insides of her thighs, waking a serpent of light in her spine.

Then the wolf lay down along her body. His fur was dense silk, spicy and musky, and out of the fur between his hind-legs came a stiff prong of flesh. She felt the phallus probing between her secret lips, sliding deeper, gliding over nerve-endings until the intensity of sensation became unbearable. She must come, there was nowhere else to go. She flew through the universe on waves of light, arched backwards, her arms outflung. Her climax was as extreme as a knife-cut; the extremity of pleasure, not pain.

She saw the shaman's face above her. His feathered cloak enveloped her, a sheltering wing. As her head fell back she knew that this was the sacred union of the Goddess and Horned God; the ecstasy that gave birth to the universe.

She fought to hang on to him as the orgasm tingled away to nothing. She wrapped her arms round his hairy neck and he stayed for a little while. She cried into his fur, thinking, I'll never find this in real life. Peter, Alastair, no one will ever be this perfect . . .

A cry woke her. A cry that was not her own.

Strange noises disturbed Beth, just after dawn one March morning. She sat bolt upright in bed. Morgan stirred, stroked her thigh and went back to sleep, but Beth sat listening intently. Silence. Yet she was sure she'd heard Eirian's voice, moaning in distress. A dream, or was Eirian ill?

Beth got up and went to her daughter's room. She opened the door softly, so as not to wake her if she'd only imagined it. The light of morning was dim, but it was enough to illumin-ate clearly a shape lying on Eirian's bed.

Beth froze in disbelief. The shape was like a massive wolf

lying along the length of Eirian's body, black, hairy and feral. She cried aloud, couldn't help it. 'Eirian!'

The wolf's head whipped round and its eyes were human. Ferocious human eyes in the long, fanged mask.

Chapter Fourteen

For three heart-beats Beth saw the wolf, felt its presence filling the room; an aura of woodsmoke, rain-lashed soil, wild dark weather. Then it dissolved away, quite slowly, still looking at her.

Only then could Beth see Eirian under the bedcovers. She didn't seem distressed. Her hair was tangled, her arms flung loosely on the pillow. Beth entered the room warily and sat on the edge of the bed. One of the cats – white Cerridwen – came in and sat washing herself as if nothing had happened.

'Eirian,' Beth said carefully, stroking her daughter's forehead. 'I heard you cry out. When I came in I thought I saw . . . a kind of shadow on the bed. Maybe I was half-asleep. Did you see anything?'

Eirian sat up, her bowed head eloquent. 'I don't know what you're talking about, Mum.'

Beth curled her hand round the back of Eirian's head. 'Look at me. You don't fool me, madam; we've been through too much together.'

Eirian's green eyes were defiant and knowing. The look alarmed Beth more than the apparition. 'You don't share my visions any more, do you? Or you wouldn't have to ask.'

'That's only right, isn't it? How would you have any privacy, with your mother in your head all the time? But I know when *something's* going on. Had you seen it before?'

'Lots of times. For ages. It's nothing new, nothing to worry about.'

'Isn't it?' Beth's throat tightened. 'Is it always a wolf? Or is it sometimes more human, like those stained-glass things I made? Does it appear with horns, wings, what?'

'Stop interrogating me!' Eirian's defensiveness roused her worst fears. The image of the entity loomed up, attacking

Morgan and Randolph. No, that was a coy euphemism. *Raping*. To think of it with her daughter – Eirian's gaze was icy. 'Mum, it's nothing to do with you.'

Beth felt such a flash of fear and insight she could hardly breathe. 'Oh, isn't it?' she said softly. 'Right, this has gone on long enough. I'll sort it out if it kills me.'

'All right, what the hell is going on?' Beth demanded. She'd summoned Randolph and Rhianwen to the house and sat them at the kitchen table with Morgan, while she paced restlessly. They all looked uncomfortable. Eirian was still upstairs. 'I see some kind of ghost-creature in Eirian's room; she admits it's there but won't talk about it. Why do I get the feeling everyone knows about this thing except me?'

Like Eirian, they all looked guilty, but not shocked. Randolph said, 'Beth, we don't know any more than you do.'

'Don't you, Granddad? So what's this?' Beth put sheets of yellowing paper in front of him. 'Morgan's read it. I don't think Rhianwen ever has.'

Randolph read the letter, turning pale. A description of a fevered, sexual encounter with a demonic entity. Finally he said hoarsely, 'Where on earth did you find this?'

'Hidden in that vanity case of Gran's.'

'But I . . .' He shook his head. 'I never posted it. Beth, you must understand, I was feverish, hallucinating. When I read the letter through, I realized how mad it sounded. I meant to throw it away! My God, Heather must have found it in my kit when I came home. She never said anything!'

Rhianwen touched the letter. 'May I?' Reluctantly, he let her take it and she read it swiftly, frowning.

'Hallucinating, really?' said Beth. 'Because Morgan encountered it too, when he was nineteen and again a couple of years ago.'

'And I wasn't ill,' Morgan murmured. 'It was too similar to what you described to be a coincidence.'

Randolph's grey eyebrows drew down in concern. Rhianwen said, 'Why didn't you tell me, love?'

'What would've been the point?' said Morgan. 'Either you'd have thought I was nuts, or you'd have been off in the woods trying to find it for yourself!'

Rhianwen gave an uneasy laugh. 'Whatever, I've never seen it, Beth.'

'You obviously didn't hang around the Hellstone enough,' Beth said under her breath. 'Well, I'm worried sick this thing has a hold on Eirian.' She pointed at a stained-glass panel, propped on the window-sill above the sink. It showed a sinister, lupine figure. 'Can anyone explain why I keep making images of it? What is this thing, Granddad? Why is it haunting us?'

Randolph looked stricken. 'I have no idea.'

Eirian appeared in the doorway. Beth went on, 'Morgan, could the fact that it attached itself to you explain why Luke and my mother were so terrified of you?'

Morgan frowned. 'Were they?'

'It *was* terrifying,' Randolph put in. 'Not malevolent . . . *demanding*. Dangerous in that it was utterly self-interested, like a wild animal.'

'Come on, Beth, you know as much as we do,' said Morgan. 'You've always seen weird things!'

'Is that supposed to reassure me?' Beth exclaimed. 'It makes it worse! No one wants to talk about it – but maybe if there wasn't so much secrecy in this family, this would never have happened! We're all in it, we can't turn our backs any more. Help me find an answer!'

Morgan looked at his daughter in the doorway. 'Eirian, are you going to contribute to this discussion or just stand there glowering?'

Unsmiling, Eirian came in and leaned against a counter-top, at right angles to Beth. Her arms were folded, her hair hung in uncombed skeins. 'I hate you talking about me like this.'

'So talk about yourself,' said Morgan. 'That's much more entertaining.'

She remained silent. 'Your mother's right,' Randolph said heavily. 'How can we help each other if we keep secrets? Right, I'll go first. I often went up to the Hellstone in my youth and the more I went, the more I felt drawn there. It seemed utterly daft at the time to say the place was haunted, but . . . My friends never noticed anything. Only me. Finally, one time I was there alone, I had the eeriest impression of the stone turning to glass, and something dark moving under the surface, trying to reach me. I heard drumming and voices. I was so bloody scared I ran like hell and after that – I completely closed my mind to it.'

'Until you had that fever,' said Beth, indicating the letter.

'Exactly,' said Randolph. Eirian pounced on the letter; his attempt to stop her was half-hearted. 'It was only when my defences were completely down that the thing managed to reach me. But I still don't know what the devil it wanted. I rejected it.' He added self-mockingly, 'Things like that don't happen to rational men like me.'

Eirian waved the letter. 'I already knew what this would say, I saw it in a vision. Honestly, you all make me want to scream! Why didn't anyone tell *me* they'd seen it? I was waiting for you to tell me about those, Mum –' she pointed to the glass panel – 'but you didn't, so don't go on at me about secrecy! You still treat me like a child!'

'Well, forgive me for trying to protect you!' Beth exclaimed. 'Please tell us, love. No one's angry.'

Eirian shrugged, sighed deeply. 'All right.' Then an extraordinary story fell from her lips. A tribal shaman, castrated and crucified. A horde of animals, cruelly slaughtered in different times. Their souls melding into one restless, savage entity, seeking healing, finding it at last in Eirian. 'It was kind of fragmented before, but Dad coming home made it whole. Don't you see, we're the five points of the pentagram; our coming together enabled it to manifest! There's a place in Yosemite that's connected to the Hellstone, as if they're both the same place in the other-world. Its energy was imprinted in the stone, but it could only attach itself to people who were attuned to it. Like us. If it frightened or hurt Dad and Granddad, it was only trying to communicate with them. It was angry and in pain, it didn't know any better, but all it wanted was healing.

It even took me a long time to realize, so I can't blame you for not understanding. But in Yosemite, I healed it. I think, when it first fastened on Granddad, all along it was really searching and waiting for me. No one else had the power to help it.'

They took in what she'd said. No one disbelieved her. Rhianwen asked softly, 'So what does it want with you now?'

Eirian looked cagey. 'Nothing. It visits me, like a friendly wolf coming out of the forest to thank the witch who healed it. That's all.'

Beth remembered its ferocious eyes and shivered. 'I'm sorry,' she said firmly, 'but I don't think it's that simple. It's not a benign entity. Not evil, but fierce, maybe dangerous. It can't go on haunting you. You have to make it leave you alone.'

'I can't do that, Mum.'

Morgan said, 'Bethie, Eirian's always been more deeply in touch with the occult than us. We just splash about in the shallows. She's coped with stuff that would reduce most adults to screaming wrecks. She's not daft, she has wisdom. Give her some credit for that. I don't feel it's our enemy. I feel . . . how can I put it? Scared of it, but part of it.'

'There's something we could try,' said Rhianwen. 'A working, just the three of us, women's work . . .'

'What for?' said Eirian, exasperated.

'To communicate with the shaman and gently tell him to leave you alone.'

'I don't want him to leave me! He loves me. He's my familiar, if you like. And there's absolutely sod-all you can do about it, so can we drop it, please?'

Beth looked from Rhianwen to her grandfather to Morgan, but they all looked as helpless as she felt. Then Beth met her daughter's eyes: polished green diamonds, immovable. She saw a figure at Eirian's shoulder, faint as a reflection in clear glass. Feral eyes glowing through a wolf mask. And she felt the tension of the question that no one dared to ask.

'So what do we do?' Beth spoke briskly to mask the tremor

in her voice. 'Just say, fine, let's forget it, have breakfast and get on with everyday life like any normal family?'

'Yes,' Eirian said calmly, 'Exactly. What's the use of doing anything else?'

Morgan took Eirian to work with him, later that day. They sat on the edge of the quarry, watching the wildfowl down on the lake. Sometimes he couldn't believe they paid him to do what he loved so much.

'I know what the problem is,' he said. He lowered his binoculars and cradled them on his thighs. 'It was your secret and now it isn't.'

'That makes it sound petty,' Eirian retorted. She was still prickly. Morgan felt guilt-ridden. He'd closed his mind to the possibility of the entity haunting her, simply because he couldn't bear the thought of it . . . even touching her.

'I didn't say that. It's affected us all. At least be grateful we don't think you're barking mad.'

Eirian looked grimly amused. 'Is it true?' she asked. 'Did it do those things to you?'

'God, Eirian, I can't tell you about that. It's embarrassing.'

'Come off it, nothing embarrasses you!' she exclaimed. 'I'm sorry the entity scared you, though.'

'Doesn't matter,' said Morgan. 'It's you we're concerned about. If it . . . you know, did anything to you, you would tell us, wouldn't you?'

She turned her head and stared at him so hard he felt blood rising to his face. 'Do you mean something sexual? You can say it, Dad. I know the facts of life.'

'Give me a break!' Morgan gasped. 'I've never had a daughter before. I don't know what to say to teenage girls!'

'That's not what I've heard,' Eirian said cheekily. 'You're hilarious when you blush, Dad.'

'This is serious.'

'I know, but *please* stop worrying. I told you, he only manifests himself to me as an animal.'

'That's all?' he said. Eirian was an icon, so self-contained she left him at a loss.

'That's all. Now stop hogging the binoculars. Look, is that a heron?'

'Rhianwen?' Beth opened the back door of Blackthorn Cottage like a thief.

'Come in, love.' Rhianwen drew Beth into her kitchen and shut the door behind them. They gave each other a long tense look of mutual understanding. 'Where's Eirian?'

'Morgan took her to the nature reserve,' said Beth. 'I should be at work, but I can spare an hour.'

'Here or the Hellstone?'

'The Hellstone,' said Beth, swallowing hard.

'Right,' said Rhianwen. 'Randolph's out. No one needs to know what we're doing.'

Outside, the March air was mild, the trees still bare. As Beth and Rhianwen walked up through the woods, Beth said, 'This is my fault. Morgan told me about the entity over two years ago. I found Granddad's letter before that, I've been making those images even longer – but I never dared ask Eirian about it. I thought if I didn't, it would just go away!'

'I feel responsible too,' said Rhianwen. 'I've remembered, I *have* been aware of it. When Morgan first came home . . . I sensed it looking for her then.'

'So we've all felt it,' Beth said grimly. 'I want an answer. I want to make it leave her alone. Even if that means drawing it to me instead.'

On the Hellstone, she and Rhianwen sat cross-legged, facing each other. Joining hands they breathed together, calling up the Goddess's energy to protect them. They chanted themselves into a receptive trance. Then they asked the entity to show itself.

Beth half expected nothing to happen. But her power welled up as it only did when she was roused, and the entity answered. She felt the Hellstone turn icy. In her mind's eye it became translucent, its deep roots transmitting vibrations from other places, ancient times. Voices and shadows clamoured around her. Long-lost gods and goddesses, shamans and wise women, crushed by newer religions but never gone, only waiting to burst through the skin of reality.

The Horned God came storming through the wildwood. He filled her head with beating wings, glaring eyes, visions. 'Leave my daughter alone!' she cried. 'Take me instead!'

We need only her.

Beth clung to Rhianwen's hands, terrified yet transported. She knew what Morgan meant when he said he was scared of it but part of it. These were her pagan brothers and sisters, revealing the truth . . .

Eirian hadn't lied, except for this; Beth saw two figures writhing in the throes of love-making, one pale as the moon, the other all bronze and jet. Then a pair of fierce eyes seared into hers and she felt the savage power of his intent. *No one will keep us from her. She is ours. No one will harm her!*

'It's my place to protect her!' Beth responded, gathering her will. 'How dare you take that from me!'

Nothing is taken from you. You helped us, also. The energy of your copulation gave us strength, for it is the very energy of life. We thank you but your part is over, we need only her . . .

In frustration, Beth was forced to accept that she couldn't change things. The entity and Eirian were both too determined. Yet the fierce integrity of its thoughts reassured her to some extent. However wild this creature seemed, it had no ill intentions towards Eirian. It impressed its message upon her then whirled away, a madly dancing figure in a stampede of animals.

Rhianwen cried out. The visions ended abruptly. Beth opened her eyes to find Rhianwen pale and trembling, tears running down her cheeks. 'What is it, what did you see?' Beth seized her shoulders.

'Cats.' Rhianwen coughed, took deep breaths and managed to compose herself. 'I saw cats being burned as witches' familiars, because people believed cats came from the Devil. Stupid bloody superstitions! Beth, I could smell them burning . . .'

'It's over,' said Beth, holding her close. She'd never had to comfort Rhianwen like this before. 'It's all part of the entity. Animals unjustly killed. That was the part that attached itself to you. Hush, hush.'

After a few minutes, Rhianwen recovered herself and sat upright again, pushing her thick auburn hair off her shoulders. 'I'm all right. Help me close the ritual. It's not finished until we ground the energy and open the circle.'

'I can't make the entity leave Eirian,' Beth said wearily.

'I know. I saw that too. But we tried.' Rhianwen touched Beth's cheek. 'Love, there's more to the craft than causing "change in accordance with will". It's knowing when to let well alone, too.'

When Eirian came home with Morgan, she knew at once that something had happened. There was an atmosphere. Beth took her into the kitchen and Rhianwen was there. 'We did a working today,' Rhianwen began solemnly. 'Found out a few things.'

'How dare you, Gran!' Eirian exploded. It was her grandmother she was furious with, not Beth. Rhianwen who'd kept Morgan away for the first eleven years of her life. 'You had no right to interfere! You abandoned us, so how dare you try to run my life now?'

'Eirian!' cried Beth.

Rhianwen went ashen and spoke with apparent difficulty. 'I thought you'd forgiven me by now.'

'Why? I told you I never could.' Eirian was shocked at the anger she felt. She still needed to hurt Rhianwen, to show her that she could be cruel too.

'The working was for your own good.'

'Like you kept my parents apart, for their own good?'

'Stop it,' Beth said severely. 'How could we leave you to your own devices with a thing that as good as raped your dad and grandfather? What kind of mother wouldn't try to protect you?'

Eirian bit back her anger. Morgan was right, it was the embarrassment of being found out that enraged her – but that was only part of it. 'The times I've kept it away from you, or stopped it manifesting so you wouldn't be distressed!' Eirian said stiffly. 'I spent so much time and energy protecting you, and you didn't even know!'

'You were protecting *us*?' Beth seemed lost for words.

'You put us in an impossible situation, love,' Rhianwen said sharply. 'We're meant to be older and wiser than you, but you were born seeing and knowing things it took me years to learn! It's no fun being two steps behind you all the time. Have some pity on us for *trying* to restore the balance, at least.'

'If we *are* the five points of the pentagram,' Beth added, 'you should have trusted us.'

A pause. Eirian felt her anger fading. 'I'm sorry,' she said. 'What happened?'

Beth told her, Rhianwen adding details. 'You didn't tell us the truth, did you?' said Beth, gentle but disapproving. 'I have the impression you and this entity are . . . well, a lot closer than you made out.'

Caught out, Eirian turned hot. 'Mum, have you never had erotic dreams?'

'What?' Beth sounded astonished. 'Well, yes, doesn't everyone?'

'That's all they are,' Eirian said, meeting Beth's eyes. 'Dreams. The shaman isn't *physical*, he only exists in the same psychic plane as our minds! Can't I even dream about him?'

Beth breathed out heavily, exchanging looks with Rhianwen. Eirian had expected her mother to be horrified; instead she sounded accepting, almost ironic. 'Well, I certainly can't stop you dreaming. As long as he's doing nothing to hurt you!'

'Nothing. You should know that from your working. He loves me.'

Beth swore under her breath. Finally she said. 'All right, I give in – for now. I'd rather this wasn't happening, but what can I do? I won't go on about it.'

'Thanks,' said Eirian, relieved. 'But you won't tell Dad about the – the dreams, will you?'

Suddenly there was a small conspiracy that drew the three women uneasily closer. 'No,' Beth said softly, 'I won't tell him.'

Beth didn't see the entity again, but at certain times of the month she *smelled* it. It was a scent like icy rain on bare rock, of autumn and winter and dead bonfires. And on those days Eirian would seem withdrawn, lost in her secret thoughts.

Beth didn't like it, but she was forced to accept it. No harm – unless the dream-entity drew her away from real life. And Eirian was cutting out Peter, who'd once been so close to her. Now, while Eirian was out or working in her room, he often sat at Beth's kitchen table hunched miserably over a mug of coffee.

'I can't stop thinking about her,' Peter said, his head drooping, 'I thought she liked me.'

'She does, love.' Beth liked Dee's son a lot; he took after his mother, kind, caring and genuine. Nice-looking too. He had the potential to become a very attractive man.

'But she's been acting cold to me for months now. I ruined everything, telling her I love her. She says she doesn't want to go out with anyone.'

Secretly, Beth was glad of that. These days she had more understanding of her own mother's crazed reaction when Beth had got pregnant at fourteen. 'Well, she is keen to go to university. She wants to concentrate on her schoolwork.'

'But she hangs round with Alastair all the time!'

Beth smiled. 'Peter, Alastair is gay. She helped him break free from some evangelical group.'

Peter gave a cynical, *humph*. 'He seems to like Eirian an awful lot, for someone who's gay. I really love her, Beth. I don't know what to do.'

'Oh, love.' Beth placed a comforting hand on his shoulder. 'You've been friends a long time, haven't you? It's probably hard for her to think of you as a boyfriend instead. Maybe you should go out with some other friends, make her think you're having a great time without her.'

'Yeah,' Peter said despondently. He looked heartbroken.

'Don't tell her I said this,' Beth lowered her voice, 'but I think she's nuts. You are going to be fighting girls off very soon. Then she'll be sorry.'

Peter managed a smile. 'Thanks, Beth. You always make me feel better.'

'If it's any consolation, I don't understand her either. But I'm only her mother, what do I know?'

Eirian had grown more fond of Alastair than she dared admit. She could talk to him. She felt she couldn't talk to her family now they'd found out about Ictinike. He'd been her delicious secret and now he wasn't.

Not that she told Alastair this. She couldn't tell him that his love-making was surpassed by that of a ghost.

She and Alastair had sex about once a week. They always managed to find somewhere private; maybe at a party, if not Eirian's own bedroom. There was nothing particularly emotional between them; the experience was nice, but not transcendent. They were both experimenting. But as a friend, Eirian wouldn't have been without him for anything.

Then, two months before her sixteenth birthday, Alastair disappeared.

One weekend he simply didn't turn up. When she phoned him he was vague. 'Oh, had to do something for my mum. I'll see you next week.' But he lied. The next week she called again and there were more excuses.

'Those blokes from the church haven't got to you again, have they?' she asked.

'No! No, there's just things I need to do around here. I might go up to Scotland to see my dad. I'm sorry, Eirian. I'll call you.'

He didn't call. By the fourth weekend, she accepted that he was gone. That was when Eirian finally broke down and told her mother what was wrong. 'You do realize he's probably met someone, don't you?' said Beth, who was innocent of their sexual relationship. 'I'm sure you'll stay friends. You weren't hoping for anything else, were you?'

'No,' Eirian said, wiping her eyes. 'I'm not upset, I'm just pissed off. I don't know why I'm crying. I thought friends ought to show a bit more loyalty than this.'

'What, like you have to Peter?'

Beth's honesty was too much. Eirian was stung by guilt. 'That's not fair!'

Beth sighed. 'I didn't mean to get at you. But Peter would be the best friend you could hope for.'

'I don't need him,' she said, subduing her tears. 'I don't need anyone.'

'Love, don't say that.' Beth looked so distressed that Eirian had to turn away. She hadn't meant to hurt her mother, but somehow she couldn't say sorry.

That night, Ictinike made love to her with ferocious passion, as if relieved that Alastair was gone. He didn't want to share her; she read it in the green fire of his eyes. And while his passion seduced her to such liquid ecstasy that she thought she would drown, she found his jealous fervour terrifying.

On a warm Saturday afternoon a few weeks after Eirian's sixteenth birthday – with her exams over and the summer holidays approaching – Beth and Morgan were working in the garden. Eirian had gone to Lisa's house. Beth loved these times alone in Morgan's company. She thought that if only Eirian were still a child, life would be perfect.

Beth sat back on her heels from the flower bed she was planting and looked at Morgan, who was arranging boulders on a rockery. His torso and beautifully muscled arms, revealed by a sleeveless T-shirt, were sheened with sweat, hair plastered darkly to the back of his neck.

'You look hot,' she said, removing her gardening gloves.

'You're not so bad yourself,' he grinned.

Beth laughed. 'I'll get us some cold beer. We deserve a break.'

'Oh, thanks. You're a wonderful woman.'

Beth went inside, but as she reached the fridge, the doorbell rang. Sighing, she went down the hall and opened the door to a stranger, a slender woman of around fifty, quite tall, in a beige coat. Her hair was short and full of blonde highlights, her lips painted bright red.

'Hello,' Beth said warily, ready to give a polite refusal if she was selling something.

The woman smiled expectantly. Beth still didn't recognize her. But the way she stood, inclining forwards as if she were about to impart a vital message, had a familiarity that wrenched a nerve deep inside her. That and the big pale blue eyes, though she'd never seen them ringed with eye-shadow before . . .

'Hello, Bethia,' said the woman.

That well-bred, spiky voice! Beth's jaw dropped. 'Mum?' she gasped. She stood numbly in a rush of emotions: shock, dread, excitement. She had no idea how to react.

'Hello, dear. Sorry to turn up without warning, but may I come in?' Olivia sounded tense, but with none of her usual aggression.

'Of course.' Beth stood back helplessly, ushering her mother into the hallway. 'Erm . . . I don't know what to say. This is such a surprise. I thought you were . . .'

'Locked up in hospital,' said Olivia. 'You can say it.'

'Well, yes,' she said lamely.

Olivia smiled with tight red lips. Beth had never seen her wearing make-up in her life before; her religion had been purit-anical. That and her newly styled hair made her look sophist-icated, very different. 'Apparently I'm better. I've been discharged. Care in the community.'

'That's great news,' said Beth.

'Don't try to be polite. You look horrified.'

'No, no, it's just such a shock, I mean, a surprise to see you. Come in, I'll make some tea.'

'Thank you, dear. I don't mean to impose, but I need to talk to you. I do hope you don't mind.'

When had her mother ever been so self-effacing? 'Of course not, I'm glad to see you.' Bewildered, Beth took her coat and showed her to an armchair. The french window was open, sunlight drenching the beamed sitting room, birds singing loudly. The cats were flat out in a sunbeam, but they rose and left indignantly as Olivia entered.

Beth dashed into the kitchen, trembling. Morgan was still working on the rockery, showing no sign of coming indoors. How was he going to react? With shaking hands she made the tea – in a china teapot, not mugs – and tried to gather her thoughts. Olivia still had deep hooks in Beth's soul. It only took one sight of her mother, one tug of the hook, for all her self-confidence to unravel and the terrified child to surface. Beth felt cornered – and furious at herself for feeling like that.

No, I won't let this happen, she told herself firmly. I'm a grown woman! Last time I saw Mum it was a disaster. Goddess, please grant me the wisdom to handle it properly this time!

She took the tray into the sitting room and set it down on a coffee table. Beth had been gardening in an old, ankle-length Indian dress of dark dyes; holly, violet and umber. With her long raven hair she couldn't have looked more true to herself. But to her surprise, there was no glare of disapproval in Olivia's eyes.

'So, how are you?' Beth asked, pouring tea.

'I won't lie to you, Beth,' said Olivia, looking down at her hands. To her amazement, Beth saw that she was wearing pink nail-varnish. Whatever had happened to her? 'I feel rather fragile, actually.'

'You look marvellous. Your hair's really nice.'

'Oh, you know, I wanted to make a new start. The nurses said I needed a new image. But . . .'

'I suppose it must be a bit strange, readjusting to everyday life. How long have you been, erm . . .'

'Out? About a week.' Olivia breathed in and out, all controlled tension. 'I have this absolutely marvellous man to thank for helping me. His name's Joshua, he's a hospital visitor. He gave me so much help when no one else cared.'

'Mum, I cared,' Beth said in a low voice. 'I'm sorry I didn't come to see you again. But I couldn't see the use when we rowed all the time.'

'I'm not trying to make you feel bad, dear. I said some terrible things to you. I was to blame.'

This response astounded Beth. She'd rarely known her mother to be conciliatory. Her mouth opened in a silent gasp and the tea she was pouring spilled over the top of the cup and into the saucer.

Olivia tutted. 'Still clumsy, I see. Never mind.'

Beth laughed uneasily. 'Yes, I always had a knack for having accidents.' Like getting pregnant, she thought. The double meaning loomed painfully between them and Beth cleared her throat in embarrassment. 'Erm, anyway, tell me about Joshua.'

'Oh, Joshua.' Olivia's eyes were wistful. 'He was able to reach me when no one else could. He made me look at myself in a different way. He was so understanding.'

'He sounds wonderful.'

'He is.' Olivia gave an almost coquettish smile.

'So, where are you staying? With Dad, I take it?'

Olivia hesitated. 'No,' she confessed 'I'm in a bed-sit. It's only temporary.'

'But that's terrible.' Beth wasn't sure how to put her next question. 'Haven't you seen Dad? I mean, I'm sure he's willing for you to go home . . . isn't he?'

Olivia put down her tea cup. 'It's not possible,' she muttered painfully.

'Have you talked to him?'

'Yes, I've seen him, that's the trouble. Oh, Beth!' Olivia bowed her head and began to sob. At a loss, Beth rushed to the side of her chair and gave her a tissue.

'Mum, don't!' She put her arm round her mother's shoulders and for once Olivia didn't push her away. Everything her mother did took her aback. 'Dad can't stop you going home. He told me he'd have you back any time. What's wrong?'

'Your father would take me back, but I can't go!' Olivia went on weeping in distress. Her pain melted Beth. 'I can't explain. It's too horrible.'

'Is Dad ill? I don't see much of him, but the last time I spoke to him he seemed fine.'

'No, it's far worse than that! Go and see for yourself, I just can't describe it!'

'Okay, okay. Come on, Mum, it can't be that bad. You've still got me.'

Olivia dried her tears and leaned back. 'Have I, dear? You mean it's possible, after the way I treated you, that you can –' she swallowed hard – 'that you can forgive me?'

Beth was astounded. She nearly started crying too. She'd longed to hear her mother say these words but never dared to hope it would actually happen. 'If it's what you want. If you can accept the way I am.'

'It's difficult, but I want to try.' She went white, forcing the words out. 'I've changed.'

And she had, Beth could see that. The strident, unforgiving part of her personality was no more; had hospital done that for her, or the wondrous Joshua? Beth nearly hugged her, but didn't quite have the courage. Too soon. 'You know I live with Morgan, don't you? I call myself Mrs Rhys.'

Her mother gave a convulsive nod. A big effort.

'And you know that Granddad is married to Rhianwen now?'

Another agonized nod. 'He told me.'

'We're all really happy. If you want to share in that, I'd like nothing better. I only ever wanted you –' To love me, Beth thought, but couldn't say it. 'Wanted us to get on well. To forget the past.'

'That's what I want,' Olivia whispered, twisting the damp tissue. 'It's not easy, but please let me try.'

'Of course.' Impulsively Beth went on, 'Look, if you need somewhere to stay –'

A voice from the direction of the kitchen broke in. 'Hey, Bethie, what's happened to this cold beer?' Morgan called cheerfully. 'Fuck, I'm knackered. Any chance of you helping me peel off these sweaty clothes, madam? After all that work I deserve a rub down with a hot nymphomaniac.'

Beth cringed. Olivia's face went rigid. 'Um, that's Morgan.'

'So I gathered.'

'We were gardening,' Beth waffled, turning hot. 'Do you, erm, want to say hello?'

Olivia was deadly pale under her make-up, as if passing through some inner crisis. 'I suppose I must.'

Morgan called out again, his voice closer. 'Bethie, where are you?'

Beth shot to her feet, too late; Morgan appeared in the doorway before she could get him on his own to explain. The black T-shirt clung damply to him and his skin was satiny with perspiration, a few leaves caught in his untidy hair. He looked flushed and very, very sexy. The beautiful demon of the wildwood. 'It's my mum,' Beth said quickly.

Recognition dawned on Morgan's face. His smile froze and the teasing gleam of his eyes became the glitter of ice. Olivia stood up, her hands knotted together.

'Yeah, so I see.' He approached Olivia, grinning sardonically, his right hand held out in greeting. 'Mrs Herne, what a pleasant surprise. How are you?'

Olivia couldn't back off because the chair was behind her. But she drew herself up and glared at his mockingly outstretched hand until he let it fall. There was a silence. The tension between Morgan and Olivia was like white webbing, so thick Beth could have cut it. There was a spark of the old hatred in her mother's eyes. Beth thought, does she still see him as the Devil incarnate?

'She's been discharged from hospital,' Beth said. 'She came to say hello.'

Morgan turned to Beth. 'The doctors must have done some good, if she's learned a polite word.'

'Morgan!' Beth said warningly.

'I don't want to remain on bad terms with my daughter,' Olivia said, her tone dignified but raw. 'If I'm to speak to her, I suppose I must speak to you as well.'

'Don't strain yourself.'

Beth shook her head, her eyes pleading with him to be civil.

Morgan walked away and leaned against the doorframe, arms loosely folded, his eyes lowered. 'Well, I'm glad you're feeling better, Mrs Herne. I don't want Beth upset, that's all.'

'I haven't come to upset her. I have her best interests at heart.'

'So have I,' said Morgan, 'no matter what you think of me.' There was a pause, a spark passing between them like a vicious arc of electricity. Then, to Beth's relief, Olivia broke the tension.

'I'd better be going.' She gave Beth a piece of paper from her handbag. 'This is my address.'

'Look, Mum, if you're unhappy where you are, you can stay here.'

'No, I couldn't possibly impose.'

'How are you getting home?'

'I have a car.'

Beth was surprised. 'Oh. I didn't realize you were that organized.'

'Joshua is helping me.'

'Good. But we'll go and see Dad, try to sort this problem out, whatever it is.'

'It won't help,' said her mother, 'but thank you, anyway.' She gave Beth a dry kiss on the cheek. 'Goodbye, dear.' Morgan remained against the doorframe so Olivia had to squeeze past him, which she did with exaggerated care, as if to touch him would contaminate her. But when she was past, she said, 'Goodbye, Morgan.'

'Bye,' he said. Bast, Cerridwen and Eostre came stalking back in, tails aloft. Bast miaowed, for no apparent reason. From the front window, Beth watched her mother walking along the path towards a red Fiesta parked outside the front hedge. Reaching the car, Olivia leaned on its roof and bent over as if she were going to be sick. Beth watched anxiously. But after a few seconds, she composed herself, got into the car and drove off.

'Have you gone mad?' Morgan asked suddenly. 'Asking her to stay! Have you gone fucking crazy?'

'She's still my mother!' Beth was annoyed by his callous tone. 'She came to make peace. She's been in hospital for five years and now she's in some awful bed-sit; how could I not? Why did you have to be so rude to her? Can't you show some compassion?'

Morgan looked squarely at her, his green eyes calm but cynical. The look hurt her. 'Why should I? The only time you and I ever quarrel is when your mother's involved. Have you forgotten that the bitch condoned Luke kidnapping Eirian and nearly killing her? She was right there with those loonies, Beth, urging Luke on. You left home because you were terrified she'd kill Eirian, for Christ's sake!'

'She's changed. Give her a chance!'

'Oh, God, Beth.' Morgan rubbed the back of his neck. 'I know you want to believe it. Maybe you're right and I'm over-reacting. I don't want you to get hurt.' He came and hugged her, his heat and arousing scent enveloping her. 'All right, I'll give her a chance – only for your sake.'

As Eirian sat in the back of her parents' car, heading towards Birmingham, she was thinking about Alastair. She'd begun to see that she'd fooled herself, imagining that through having sex with him, she could magically change his sexuality. She'd tried to control him. And in her desperate search for the delicious completeness she found with Ictinike, she had used him.

If he dumped me, it was only what I deserved, she thought dully. But it still hurts.

She hated the way this overwhelming need for fulfilment was coming between her and her sense of purpose. It made her touchy and preoccupied. She was in two minds about going to America this summer. Although the compulsion was still there, she didn't feel like facing the cameras and the attention this time. She loathed the feeling of insecurity, of failing the Goddess. She felt that no one understood her, especially not her parents.

Since Olivia's visit the previous day – which Beth had

reported to Eirian later – there had been a certain tension between Beth and Morgan. The mild edginess of their conversation was the closest they ever came to quarrelling.

'I don't know what you expect to get out of this visit,' said Morgan, who was driving.

'Dad to take Mum back,' said Beth. 'It's in your interests, if you're so against her staying with us.'

'I wish you wouldn't get involved at all.'

'They're still my parents!'

'Great parents. What the hell does she want with you, after treating you like shit for all those years?'

'I don't know. Maybe my father can tell us. You will be diplomatic, won't you? You speak before you think sometimes, Morgan, and you draw blood.'

'Can't help being honest,' he said off-handedly. 'Hey, I'll behave! There's something strange about your father.'

'What?'

'I think he likes me. Doesn't he realize he's letting the side down?'

They drew up outside the redbrick Victorian house in King's Heath where Beth had spent her ordered, strict childhood. The sight of the house still gave her a *frisson* of dread. She rang the bell, and her father, Philip, answered. He was wearing grey flannels and a check shirt; he'd put on a little weight and there was grey in his light brown hair, but otherwise he was the same. The handsome, soft-mannered dentist, hiding behind shiny spectacles.

'Hello, Beth,' he said. He looked at Morgan and Eirian, plainly awkward in their presence although he'd been expecting them. 'Hello. Come in and sit down.'

He showed them into the sitting room, which still had the same faded gold brocade furniture and white-painted anaglypta on the walls. Memories rushed in with the familiarity of the room, smells of old paint and polish. Her father seemed on edge and kept clearing his throat.

'It's about Mum,' said Beth.

'Yes. Yes, I know.'

'It's good that she's been released, isn't it?'

'Yes, splendid, umm . . ,' Again Philip gave a nervous cough in the back of his throat.

'Something's upset her, though. She seems to think she can't come back here.'

'That's nonsense. She's welcome here and she knows it. She's still my wife. Ours hasn't been the best of marriages but I still have every respect for her. I wouldn't let her down.'

'So what's the problem, then?'

'It's difficult.' Philip glanced at Eirian and Morgan, who were sitting side by side, their expressions friendly but neutral. 'Not something one can really discuss . . . You'll know in a few minutes, anyway.'

There was a tense silence. Damn, Beth thought, I'll have to get him on his own before he'll open up. Then the door from the kitchen opened and a young man came in carrying a tea tray.

'I made tea, but does anyone prefer coffee?' said the young man, placing the tray on a low table. His accent was Scottish. He was about eighteen, slim and pretty with yellow hair . . .

Beth knew him. He was Eirian's friend, Alastair. Oh, bloody hell, she thought. Oh, shit!

'Er, this is Alastair,' said her father, turning red. 'My friend.'

'Yes,' Beth gasped. 'I mean, hello, Alastair . . .' Alastair had frozen and was staring at Eirian. Her expression was one of utter, wide-eyed astonishment. Morgan raised his eyebrows at Beth and she had a ghastly suspicion he was about to say something they'd all regret.

Philip appeared not to have noticed the looks. He said quietly, 'Alastair's the reason Olivia won't come home. She came to see me and he was here. I don't expect her to under-stand, of course, but I didn't think she'd be quite so upset. She can't accept it. But I'm damned if I'm going to be ashamed any more.'

'I see,' said Beth. 'Well, okay, great, um . . . oh, wow.'

At that moment, Eirian got to her feet, gave Alastair a glare that would have turned a gorgon to stone, and stalked out. The front door slammed.

'I'll go after her,' Morgan said, hurrying out. Through the net curtains, Beth saw them stop by the car, Morgan touching Eirian's arm, Eirian turning away.

Alastair said, 'Christ! I didn't know, Phil. Why didn't you tell me?'

'What?'

'That she was your granddaughter! Oh, fuck!' He shot into the kitchen, leaving Beth alone with her father.

'What's going on?' Philip asked, perplexed.

'Alastair's a friend of Eirian's. I think she was a bit shocked, that's all. So am I.'

'I didn't know!' Philip exclaimed. 'He never said anything! I had no idea you knew him! Oh, Lord.' He sank down into an armchair, his head on his hand.

'How did you meet him?'

'In the café near the surgery where I sometimes have lunch. He always seemed to be in there and we got talking. I've only known him a few weeks, but I feel I've known him for ever.'

'You know he's only eighteen, don't you? I don't think they've lowered the age of homosexual consent yet, have they?'

Her father's colour deepened. It had always nearly killed him to talk about personal matters. 'Beth, please try to understand. I've tried so hard. I've been celibate for years. You've no idea how lonely I've been. Then I met Alastair and I just couldn't bear it any more. Olivia will never understand, but I thought you were different. That's why I wanted you to meet him.'

'Dad, you know I don't want you to feel guilty or lonely. It's just – couldn't you have found someone closer to your own age?'

'Age doesn't seem to come into it.'

Beth wanted to touch him but she couldn't. The inhibitions of her childhood hadn't quite gone. 'Is he living here?'

'Only at weekends. But he knows he can move in, if he

262

wants. I don't think your mother would come back now even if I threw him out – and I'm not going to do that, even for her.'

'Right. Well, good for you.' Beth exhaled. She saw Eirian and Morgan coming back towards the house. 'Let's see if we can get Alastair and Eirian to talk to each other and sort this out. She claims he wasn't her boyfriend but she felt a lot for him, all the same.'

'Sorry,' said Alastair. He leaned against the fridge with his hands wedged in the pockets of his jeans. Eirian had shut the kitchen door, so her family wouldn't overhear. The room was cramped, the fittings outdated.

'It doesn't matter,' Eirian said. 'You're free to do what you want.'

'You're really mad at me, aren't you? Look, you always knew I was gay! It's not as if I didn't tell you. I told you I liked older men.'

'Yes, but not *that* old!'

'He's only fifty-six. That isn't old. He looks younger.'

'But he's my *grandfather*!'

'I didn't know who he was! He never talked about his family.'

'I'm not surprised. Try asking him why Mum didn't speak to him for eleven years. Or ask him about his son's fondness for children and animals.'

'What?' Alastair looked at her, uncomprehending. 'What son?'

'I'm not mad at you,' Eirian said coolly. She meant it, but she felt hollow. 'Do you really like him? Are you in love, or something?'

Alastair shrugged and looked down at his trainers, embarrassed. 'He's all right. He's quite well off.'

'You're just using him, aren't you?'

'No, it's not like that!'

Eirian's perception of Alastair had changed; his pretty face now seemed merely pinched and immature. She'd closed herself to him. But when he met her eyes, she caught a flash of light from the grey irises, a psychic impression that briefly skewed the whole world. The faintest glimpse of a figure like a white angel, hovering between them. It made no sense, but it felt chilling, weird, wrong.

'Why're you looking at me like that?' he said.

'Nothing. I'm not upset, it's none of my business, no hard feelings, and all that.'

'Can we still be friends?' Alastair said, looking sideways at her.

'We can,' Eirian said, 'but I don't suppose we will.'

Later, back at home, Eirian and Beth sat on a seat in the back garden, watching the violet dusk close in. The last crimson arc of the sun was slipping down behind the orchard, feathering the edges of their hair with red. With their arms linked around each other and their long hair mingling, they could have been taken for sisters.

The three cats padded around them in the rich, fading light. Beth was glad to have this moment of closeness with her daughter.

'I knew Alastair was gay. I knew he liked older men,' said Eirian. 'I'm just pissed off he didn't tell me he was seeing someone. Especially not Granddad Herne! It seems so weird.'

'I know, it must have been a dreadful shock, love.'

'He hasn't broken my heart or anything. I'll never let a boy do that.'

Beth squeezed her waist. 'I hope not. I know I've encouraged you to regard sex as sacred and natural, but it's still hard for me to accept that you're having sexual feelings. I made a real effort not to be the shocked mother when you told me about your dreams! But I understand. So if you do meet someone and you're thinking about having sex, you will tell me first, won't you?'

'No, of course I won't!' Eirian exclaimed. 'Are you mad?' Although she spoke tongue-in-cheek, Beth had a feeling she meant it. She'd kept her periods secret; she'd kept the entity secret . . .

'I thought I'd brought you up to tell me anything.'

'You have,' Eirian murmured. 'But some things are private.'

'Eirian, I talk to you the way I wish my mother had talked to me. I'd have done anything to be this close to her. The point is, I won't lecture you. I just want to be sure you know about . . .'

'Safe sex, yes, we did all that at school.'

'More than that. Olivia tried to make me believe sex was shameful and degrading, just some bestial thing men did to women. If she was trying to protect me, she went completely the wrong way about it. When you find the right person, like I did with your father, it's absolutely exquisite. I want it to be wonderful for you, with someone who really cares about you.'

'Mum, honestly,' Eirian sighed. 'I've got better things to do than wait around for some hypothetical perfect man! Even Dad's not perfect, you know!'

Exasperated, Beth said, 'Well, just make sure you find some-one who's bloody good in bed, all right?'

They had a fit of laughter, hugging each other. A few moments of supreme happiness. Then Eirian said softly, 'So what's going to happen about Olivia? Dad and I don't want her in the house.'

'I know.' As vividly as Beth had experienced Eirian's sweet-ness, she felt her dark intransigence now. 'Love, I won't ask Olivia to stay with us, for the simple reason that she was there when Luke abducted you and it might cause you bad memories. It wouldn't be fair on you. But I have to help her.'

'I'm not saying you shouldn't, but why?'

Beth rested her head on Eirian's. 'Because I want Olivia and me to be the mother and daughter we should have been, before it's too late.'

While Beth and Eirian talked in the garden, Morgan was cook-ing supper, enjoying a glass of wine and trying not to think about Olivia. His sister, ha; what a horrible thought. They couldn't have had less in common. And there was nothing he could do to make himself like the woman, not after her cruelty to Beth and Eirian and her hatred of Rhianwen.

The phone rang. He leaned over to answer it, stirring curry on the stove with his free hand.

'Hi, it's Suzanne. How are you doing?'

'Hello, mate. Don't ask.'

'Oh dear, what's wrong?'

'Oh, nothing really,' said Morgan. 'Just had a weirder weekend than usual. We're fine. How about you and Mark?'

'We're okay. Morgan, I know Eirian isn't sure about going to America this year –'

'That's right. So if we can persuade her not to, we are pretty damn keen to have her to ourselves this summer. I hope you're not going to tell me some producer is offering millions for her to appear.'

'Not exactly,' Suzanne said thinly. 'Morgan, you sound very pissed off. Have I called at a bad time?'

'No,' he sighed. 'Sorry, Sue. Go on, what were you going to say?'

'An editor from an American publishing house has been in touch with me. His name's Gabriel Jordan. Actually he's here in London; I've met him and he's a great bloke, really easy to get along with. He wants Eirian to write a book.'

'What?' Morgan put down the wooden spoon and fumbled for a notepad. 'Who is this guy?'

'Gabriel Jordan of Silver Dove Books, based in Baltimore. They publish a lot of theological and mystical stuff. He's desperate to meet Eirian.'

'Yeah, right.' He wrote the details down but he was sceptical. The memory of middle-aged Americans lusting after his daughter was distasteful. 'In his dreams.'

'Morgan, this is serious. He's already drawn up a draft contract, I've seen it. Two thousand on signature. Pounds, not dollars. He thinks Eirian has some really important things to say. They're a reputable publishers. But Gabriel can explain it all properly himself, so can I give him your number? Could be just the incentive you need to keep her at home.'

Chapter Fifteen

'J OSHUA!' As soon as he walked through the door of the cramped bed-sit, Olivia rushed to him, her hands clasping the sleeves of his tweed jacket. 'Thank the Lord you're here. I've been so desperate to see you. I went to my daughter's.'

'Quite an ordeal, eh? Tell me all.' He held her away from him and she regained her prim dignity. Her face was stiff, her voice low but raw with disgust as she described the visit.

'It was hateful. I could feel the presence of evil so strongly in that house! Joshua, must I go again? I don't think I can bear it.'

'Yes, you must,' he said, gentle but firm. 'You know that.'

'But I hate this.' She picked at the pink varnish on her nails, setting his teeth on edge. She dragged the talons through her bleached hair. 'This whorish disguise, it's so ungodly!'

'What makes you think you're godly, Olivia?' He spoke sternly and saw fear chase out her anger. 'You'll only please God by pleasing me. And I say cosmetics are essential for you to be convincing; only a truly changed Olivia would wear them.'

'Beth asked me to stay with her,' Olivia murmured. 'But I can't stay in that house, not with Morgan and his demon child there.' She began to tremble. 'There's something in the house with them, a malevolent spirit. It's the girl's familiar. I know how it sounds, but I'm telling the truth!'

Sensing she was close to a panic attack, he clasped her hands in prayer position. How interesting that she'd been aware of the thing! She had a touch of the power too, though she denied it. 'I believe you. That family is everything you say. You're right to be fearful. It's too much for you to face alone.'

She tried to lean into him but he held her away. He loathed her touch. 'Yes. I need your help very badly, Joshua.'

'You have it.' He was the reassuring mentor again. 'I wouldn't make you endure living there. Everything's arranged. I've rented a small cottage in Lullingford for you. You know the row of cottages between your daughter's house and the church? Right there. So you'll have your little retreat, but you'll be close enough to see plenty of your daughter.'

'Oh.' Olivia's shock gave way to excitement. He saw hatred hardening in her eyes, the rallying of her stubborn spirit. 'Oh, Joshua, thank you.'

'That's my girl. I know it's tough, but do everything my way and we'll win.' His voice became low and intimate. 'Now I have a little secret to share with you. And I mean *secret*. I'm going to look different from now on. If we meet any place but your cottage, don't call me Joshua. I'll be introduced to you as Gabriel Jordan and you'll make like we never met before. Got that?'

She looked blank, worried. 'Yes – yes – whatever you say!'

'Good girl. This is how I will appear to you from now on.'

Olivia stared in astonishment as he removed his gold-rimmed glasses, pulled off the tweed jacket and the grey wig. Transforming from eccentric do-gooder to his true self. When he shook down the mane of shining pale hair, Olivia gasped and took a step backwards. Her hands flew to her mouth. He laughed. 'It's all part of the plan. Our secret, Olivia.'

She fell to her knees. Literally fell, as if all the strength had gone out of her. 'Oh, dear God above!' she cried. 'You *are* an angel!'

Gabriel Jordan's voice on the telephone sounded familiar to Beth. He was friendly, humorous, very straight. As they tried to arrange a meeting, Beth found herself giving him their home address and saying, 'Why don't you come to us? That would be easiest.'

When she opened the door to him, she knew where she'd seen him before. The Hard Rock Café in New York. He was the friendly stranger who'd chatted to them in the bar, the one

Morgan had accused her of fancying. And he was attractive. Not overtly beautiful like Morgan, but very striking, with his long ice-blond hair tied back. He was slightly taller than Morgan, about six foot two, and all in white; jeans, shirt and a very expensive-looking suede jacket. He had handsome, strong features like a character actor, and a warm, intelligent expression. And his blue-green eyes were dazzling. Peacock eyes that seemed to focus inside her mind.

'Talk about weird coincidences,' Beth said, laughing. 'You won't remember, but we've met before.'

'I sure do,' he said. 'The Hard Rock Café, one sweltering afternoon about three years ago. It is so great to see you again, Mrs Rhys.'

'Call me Beth.' Eirian appeared at Beth's shoulder. 'Here's Eirian. She's grown up a lot since then.'

Gabriel's attention switched to Eirian. They locked eyes; he was business-like, but she seemed uncharacteristically shy. When he shook her hand the clasp lingered. Just American friendliness, Beth thought. 'I've watched your TV appearances with great interest,' he said.

'Hello, it's nice to meet you again.'

'I feel like we already know you,' said Beth. 'Would you like a drink?'

Gabriel didn't stand on ceremony. When Beth went to make coffee, he followed her and they ended up sitting at the kitchen table. Gabriel did most of the talking; he had an easy, enthusiastic manner. Morgan, however, was not his usual cheerful self. Their visitor probably read nothing into his cool manner, but Beth was aware of him appraising Gabriel.

'Here, look over the contract,' said Gabriel, pushing a sheaf of paper at Morgan. 'I believe in what Eirian stands for. It's very important for her to get her views across. She is such an exciting person; young but very mature for her age, extremely photogenic. It's not exploitation, its common good sense to play on that to get her philosophy across to millions. Eirian, have you ever tried writing?'

'Only at school. Essays, stories, poems.'

'She gets very good grades,' Beth put in.

'How d'you feel about writing a book?'

Eirian smiled uncertainly. 'I'd like to try. But I wouldn't know where to start.'

'That's where I come in. We'll work together. I'll guide you. It'll be all your own work – but when you need help, I'll give it. I've got leave to stay in England for as long as it takes to finish the book. That's how important my bosses think you are.'

'Oh.' Eirian and Beth looked at each other; Morgan studied the contract.

'We can draft most of it in your school vacation,' Gabriel went on, 'then refine it at weekends, as long as it doesn't interfere with your schoolwork. What do you think?'

His smile was warmly persuasive. Eirian, usually so cool, seemed energized, her face glowing. 'I'd love that, as long as Mum and Dad don't mind.'

'It's okay by me,' said Beth.

'It's your holiday, my dear.' Morgan looked at her, his dark eyebrows arched. 'If you'd rather work on the book than go to the States, it's up to you.'

She didn't hesitate. 'The book.'

Gabriel stayed talking for another hour or so. He made Beth and Eirian laugh but Morgan – quite out of character – was quiet and straight-faced. When Beth asked Gabriel to stay to dinner, he looked at his watch and said, 'It's a kind offer, ma'am, but I've imposed on you folk long enough and I have some calls to make to the States. I'll leave the contract for you to check over. Maybe I could come round, say, Saturday afternoon? Then we can start work for real.'

When they'd seen him out, Eirian ran up to her room – to gather her thoughts, Beth guessed. She turned to Morgan. 'Are you all right?' she said. 'It's not like you to be so quiet.'

Morgan folded his arms. 'You *do* fancy Gabriel, don't you?'

'He's an attractive man. That doesn't mean I want to go to bed with him.'

'Don't you?' Morgan said sourly.

Beth was devastated. 'How dare you!' she said furiously. 'What's got into you?'

He wrapped his arms round her, holding her fiercely. 'Beth, I'm sorry. I don't know why I said that.'

'How could you even think I'd look at someone else?'

'I'm sorry,' he said again. 'I don't know what it is, he just rubbed me up the wrong way. I don't mean to be jealous.'

'Why not?' Relenting, she stroked his cheek. 'It's endearing, knowing you can be as insecure as me.'

On Saturday, when Beth came home from a morning at her workshop, she found Morgan and Eirian unpacking boxes on the kitchen table. 'What's this?'

'I've bought Eirian a computer with a word-processing program,' said Morgan, 'so she can write her book.'

Beth was touched – and startled. 'That's thoughtful. Isn't it, love?'

'It's brilliant,' said Eirian, hooking her hair behind her ear as she studied the instruction book.

'Shouldn't take long to set up,' said Morgan. 'Trust me, I've done this before.'

'It's like the ones we use at school, anyway.'

'Oh, shall I leave you to it?'

'No, Dad, don't.' She pulled at his arm, grinning. Beth liked to see them teasing each other.

'Where are you going to put it?' Beth asked.

'In the corner of the kitchen,' said Morgan. 'Lots of room, nice and light. We don't use that little table anyway.'

'The logical place would be on the desk in her bedroom, wouldn't it?' Beth said without thinking.

Morgan gave her a meaningful, sideways look. 'No, she needs to be near the coffee-maker so she can overdose on caffeine and work all night. Eirian, can you fetch that pack of paper out of the car, please?'

Eirian put out her tongue at him and left the room. While she was gone, Morgan said, 'Look, we don't want her spending hours in her bedroom with a strange man, do we?'

Beth felt a smile pulling at her mouth. 'Honestly, you are funny.'

'Why, because I want to protect her from someone like me?'

'You said it. We've always let her take Sam, Hugh and Pete to her room.'

'Yes, because nothing goes on. They're her mates, like brothers. This is different.'

'You're right to be cautious. But Gabriel's a mature, professional adult, not a randy sixteen-year-old. I'm sure he's sincere. Not *everyone* is a rampant sex maniac, Morgan.'

He responded with a sarcastic grin. 'Takes one to know one.'

There was something about Gabriel.

Sitting with her chair pulled very close to his, so they could both use the keyboard, Eirian was alight with a weird excitement she'd never felt before. She remembered when she was small and she and Beth were living with the travellers, they'd spent Christmasses in a Scottish farmhouse. Suddenly they were no longer in the cramped caravan but in a big room where everything was golden; log fire, candles and Christmas lights, all glowing and magical. That was the feeling. Newness and innocence – although Eirian had never really been innocent. Perhaps that was her trouble.

His eyes were such an unusual colour. Ringed with dark blue, they went from azure to green in the centre, with a thin corona of gold around the pupil. Often when she met someone, Eirian would catch a flash of their inner soul, and know whether they were to be trusted. But Gabriel seemed to meet her halfway. The feeling was soothing, sparkling. He liked what he saw, that was obvious.

She had signed the contract. Despite Morgan's caution, neither he, Beth or Suzanne had found anything wrong with it. There would be money on signature, on delivery and on publication, followed by royalties. But Eirian couldn't care less about the money.

'Well, where d'you want to start?' he asked. She loved his accent.

Beth had made them a coffee, then left them alone in the kitchen. Eirian was aware of her parents in the house and hoped they wouldn't come in too often. Shyness had never been part of her nature, but in Gabriel's presence she felt self-conscious. Could he still see the entity haunting her?

'I want to write about the witch-hunts,' she began, 'and show how my experience with Luke wasn't so different. And how evangelists are as ignorant as ever about witchcraft. And how that preacher, PGK, tricked me. They're like flies, no matter how many fall there are always more –'

'Hold on, hold on,' he laughed. 'I think we should start with a little autobiography, don't you?'

Eirian winced. 'The ideas are important. Not me.'

'That's nonsense. You can't separate yourself from the concepts.' His voice seemed physically to caress her. Soothing, persuasive. 'You're what people want to read about. Come on, where you were born, your childhood . . .'

She felt embarrassed. 'No, I can't. I'd have to say things about my parents. It's private.'

He breathed out, raising his white-gold eyebrows at her. 'We can write stuff and delete it. It's not carved in stone. If you want to talk it over first, your secrets are safe with me.'

She didn't want to displease him. 'Well, I started having visions as soon as I was born. My memories of those go back much further than my memories of being a child.'

'Hey, that's fascinating!' said Gabriel, beginning to type. 'Go on.' The words flowed out of her mouth and scrolled across the screen.

As they worked, Eirian was thrillingly aware of his body next to hers. She liked everything about him. His milky-pale hair, his kindly, attractive face, his large hands and muscular frame. She liked the faint fragrance of deodorant, heated by his body. The way his white jeans and shirt clung to him. The pale skin of his throat and wrists. Everything.

The hours flew. Suddenly he was leaving. He put the printed-out sheets of their work into her hands and said, 'Tonight I want you to read through this and think about what changes you want to make. We'll do even greater things next time.'

School broke up. Every day for six days Gabriel came to the house and they sat close together at the computer, talking, whispering, laughing. Every day she became more aware of him and less aware of what she was talking about; her words flowed without effort and she felt enthused, but it was Gabriel's presence that enthused her. He reminded her of her father; he had a similar openness and charm, but unlike Morgan he was not always in a huddle with her mother.

Gabriel had come at just the right time. Just as the landscape of her life had seemed depressingly shallow, soured by Peter and Alastair, he'd walked in. Not an immature boy, but an intriguing, beautiful, many-layered adult. And he was an enigma: that intrigued her. Just as she'd begun to believe that everyone she ever met would be flawed and transparent, Gabriel appeared.

He gave her the rapt attention she'd never had from a mature man before. He listened. He was not merely interested but completely in tune with her.

As the week passed she grew increasingly frustrated that they were never left alone in the house; if Beth and Morgan were not there, Rhianwen was. Eirian grudgingly understood their reluctance to leave her alone with a near-stranger, but it was galling. Why can't they trust him? she thought. Why can't they treat me like an adult?

But does Gabriel see me as a woman, or just a child? she wondered one Friday afternoon as she sat beside him. Beth and Morgan were at work, Rhianwen and Randolph sitting in the garden. Eirian could hear their voices so she would know if they were about to come in.

She was feeling inspired, a thousand things to say. Gabriel had that effect. Sparking ideas off each other, they both tried to attack the keyboard at the same time and their fingers got tangled up. 'One at a time, now,' Gabriel said jokingly, lifting her hand away. But he didn't let her go. He looked at her fingers, then at her, his face suddenly serious. Eirian went hot. Then he leaned towards her and kissed her mouth.

His lips on hers were thrillingly warm, dry but satiny. Electricity tingled all the way from her lips to her groin and her heart stumbled. 'I'm sorry, Eirian,' he said, pulling back. 'I shouldn't have done that. I most definitely should not have done that.'

'It's all right,' she managed to say. She was going to add, I wanted you to, but her tongue wouldn't co-operate. She felt like a virgin; he probably assumed she was one. He tapped a few keys; there was an awkward silence. Then she asked, 'Have you got a wife or girlfriend at home?'

'No, Eirian, I haven't.'

'A boyfriend?' She spoke lightly but he frowned, a web of shadows lining his face.

'No, I am absolutely not homosexual.'

'It's all right, then, if you're not with someone else.'

His gaze was on the screen. 'It's not all right. I'm abusing the trust your parents have placed in me.'

'But –'

'I think we should concentrate on work now, don't you?'

Eirian gave in, feeling frustrated, confused, and somehow in the wrong. But as they sat with their thighs pressed together, fingers accidentally touching, the carnal tension between them was electric.

It's going well, Nathaniel reflected as he scrubbed himself under a hot shower in his hotel room. He could act any role, but with Eirian he hardly had to try.

She'd fallen for him already. Nathaniel hadn't expected it to be so easy. He was very aware of her sharp mind, her power, her dark female intelligence; aware also that the occult presence still lurked at her shoulder. He despised it. Most likely it had no real potency – but Eirian was more dangerous than she knew. He couldn't actually read her mind but he caught glimpses of her inner self as they worked and everything he saw disturbed him. Oh, he'd been right; her potential was lethal. TLN's takings had dipped every time she'd appeared, and hadn't fully recovered. So she'd already eroded his power base; Lord knew what would happen when she hit her stride.

But he had the advantage. Older and more experienced than her, he'd put barriers in place to prevent her seeing inside him. In fact he'd convinced her that his kindly, understanding shell was his real self. And there was nothing like first love for blunting her powers of perception.

He usually took God-fearing, passive women as his partners because, content to believe themselves mere vessels, they were no threat. The few who weren't compliant, he'd soon made them so. He even prided himself on pleasing such women, all the better to make them worship him. But the thought of having a witch like Eirian unsettled him deeply.

Drying himself on a thick white towel in front of the bedroom mirror, he reasoned with himself. There was no need actually to seduce her. To use psychological pressure, make her burn with virginal longing – that was enough for now.

The desire he felt for her, though, dismayed him. He'd meant it to be all feigned, the kissing and touching; instead he'd felt himself responding. Dangerous, that loss of control.

Has to stop. Be cold now, Nathaniel thought, watching his own pale form in the mirror, like a marble statue, his penis quiescent. Cold as ice. Cold as God.

'I have some good news,' said Olivia. She was immaculately turned-out, seeming elegant and vivacious. Morgan had answered the door to her and led her into the sitting room to join Beth. 'I'm renting a cottage in Lullingford. I moved in this morning.'

'Where?' said Beth, looking astonished.

'No. 3, Church Row. Virtually next door. So I can be near by without imposing on you, dear.'

Morgan was less than pleased. He'd endured Gabriel's presence in his house for a week, and now Olivia would be forever on the doorstep too. He muttered, 'Great,' under his breath, not quietly enough; Beth heard and glared at him.

'Mum, that's wonderful,' she said guardedly. 'But how can you afford it?'

'Your father's giving me money, of course, it's the least he can do. And Joshua's been so helpful.'

'When are we going to meet this amazing Joshua?'

'You might not, dear. He's so busy, helping people like me get back on their feet. He's a saint.'

'He sounds it. Mum, I'm really pleased.'

'Yeah, anything we can do to help,' Morgan said flatly.

'I won't inflict myself on *you*, don't worry,' Olivia retorted.

'Tea?' Beth broke in. 'Morgan's made the most divine chocolate cake, he's a wonderful cook.'

'I think it's called Devil's food cake,' Morgan said with a frigid grin.

Olivia turned her back on him. 'Let me make the tea, dear. I like to feel useful.'

When she'd gone into the kitchen, Beth and Morgan looked at each other. 'I know this is awkward, but please try to be civil to her,' Beth said with feeling.

He stroked her arm. 'Like I said, for your sake. D'you mind if I have a word with her alone? I want to straighten things out. You know, make peace.'

Beth gave a startled smile. 'I wish you would! Go on.'

Morgan went softly into the kitchen, closing the door behind him. Eirian and Gabriel were sitting out in the garden, talking – and Olivia was at the sink, staring out of the window at them. When she heard Morgan she jumped and turned round.

'What do you want?' The look on her face was accusing, challenging. This was not the woman who'd petitioned Beth contritely for understanding.

'Mrs Herne. Olivia – d'you mind if I call you that? We'd better find some way to get along with each other for Beth's sake.' Olivia said nothing, only pierced him with an incredulous blue stare. 'I'm willing to believe you've changed, that you were ill and now you're better, if it's what she wants.'

She gathered herself. 'I was not ill, have never been ill. My stay in hospital was all a misunderstanding. Are you really so arrogant as to believe that to have hated you, I must have been mad?'

'No, but I don't see why you still have to hate me. Beth will tell you, I'm quite nice really. Can't we forget the past? Look, I'm trying to apologize!' He remembered Olivia trying to destroy Eirian, and he had to force the words out. 'Whatever I've done to upset you, I'm sorry.'

Olivia went on staring, pressed back against the sink, as if she saw the Devil on his shoulder. Her lips parted, her breathing accelerated. 'You think you can put it all right by saying sorry? You don't take me in for a minute. You're still the same creature that ruined my daughter's life!'

Morgan was determined to reason with her. 'We've been incredibly happy for five years. We live in a beautiful house, our daughter goes to a good school and we all love each other. Beth's a highly successful artist. A lot of people would be glad to have their lives ruined like that.'

'You can't trick me by playing with words. You corrupted her.'

'I'm not trying to trick you.' He was finding it hard to stay patient. 'I introduced her to wonderful, loving sex; I don't call that corruption. But I know it shouldn't have happened when she was fourteen. I was wrong, I admit it.'

'It shouldn't have happened at all.' Harsh light boiled up in her eyes. 'There are worse sins than fornication. You are knowingly committing incest.'

'Most days. And twice on a Sunday.'

His flippancy seemed to make Olivia furious. 'You think it's funny? You're a devil from hell and you want to drag Beth there with you!'

'I love her. She chose to be with me, not some church-going twat in a grey suit. Maybe you should show a tiny bit of respect for her choice. Isn't Christianity about forgiveness? You should try it some time.'

Olivia gave a small, tight smile. 'But the Lord can only forgive the repentant. Until you repent and let go of my daughter, I won't give up battling for her soul. I'm not afraid of you.'

'Why would you need to be afraid of me?' he said, exasperated. 'You're the one Beth was terrified of as a child. I've seen

278

your idea of saving souls; beatings and threats of hell. I gave her love! And she kept coming back for more, all summer long. She used to cry her eyes out at the prospect of going home to you.'

Olivia turned white with fury. 'Liar. You and Rhianwen corrupted her.'

'And it was a lot of fun, sister dear,' Morgan said thinly. 'I deliberately introduced her to the pleasures you'd forbidden her because I wanted to take her away from you. Because you were ruining her life more effectively than I ever could.'

This admission out, Morgan knew he'd wrecked any hope of a truce. And he realized that Olivia had manipulated him into it.

'Well, now you've shown your true colours, you'll know why I couldn't accept your apology,' she said smugly. 'I will of course tolerate your presence for Beth's sake. But don't expect me to speak to you.'

'You don't love Beth. You just want to control her life. You're a fucking control freak.'

Her colour returned. Her eyes were very round and blue, not belligerent but eerily triumphant. 'Do you think your language shocks me? I know the real reason you're with Beth.'

'Yeah?'

Olivia said, 'You only stay with her because you want to fuck Eirian.'

Morgan was dumbstruck. He felt physically winded, as if she'd punched him in the diaphragm. While he stood speechless, Olivia briskly made a pot of tea as if nothing had happened. He daren't move; if he had, he might have tried to kill her.

Eventually he said, 'We lost a baby. That's real life, not your sick fantasies about God and the Devil.'

Olivia stuck a large, sharp knife into the cake he'd made and hacked it into slices. 'You should be glad the Lord would not permit a second abomination like Eirian to be born.'

'I'll tell Beth you said that, shall I? Where were you when she nearly broke her bloody heart?'

'Tell her what you like. We'll see whom she believes.' She

picked up the tray. Morgan went to the door and placed his hand on the handle, blocking her way.

'If you do anything to hurt Beth or Eirian, you two-faced bitch,' he said very softly, 'your feet won't touch the fucking ground.' He opened the door and Olivia stalked through with her head in the air.

In the sitting room, Beth looked up anxiously. 'Everything okay?'

Olivia replied before Morgan could say anything. 'Marvellous, darling. Morgan and I had a little talk, didn't we? He understands that I'm trying my very best to atone for all the mistakes I made in the past.'

Beth looked so relieved, he couldn't say a thing. Olivia had outmanoeuvred him. She was charm itself throughout tea, while Morgan sat in virtual silence.

Later, when she left, Beth waved her off through the window then turned to Morgan, all flushed with happiness. 'It's going to be okay. I'm so glad you talked to her. She's so different.'

'Beth,' he said helplessly. 'She isn't. The things she said to me – Bethie, she's conning you!'

'No.' Beth moved away from him, refusing to listen. 'Don't, Morgan, please. I want a relationship with my mother. I don't ask you to like her, but don't ruin it before we've even started!'

'God, Beth.' He was defeated. 'All right, I've said enough. But be careful, okay? I mean it.'

As soon as Olivia moved in, all Morgan's fears came true. She was round at their house every day, taking up Beth's time. She never asked anything of Morgan, but it was always, 'Beth, can you wire some plugs for me? I'm so hopeless with electrical things. Beth, I've a problem with my washing machine. Beth, my car's broken down, can you give me a lift? I'm terribly sorry to impose, but I'd be so grateful . . .'

Olivia even went to Woodbourne Hall during the day, asking Beth for little favours that took her away from her work. And Beth was so eager to win her mother's affection, she seemed incapable of saying no.

After a week of it, Morgan was exasperated. If he tried to point out the obvious – 'Beth, she's using you!' – Beth would only be wounded and say he didn't understand, how could he be so intolerant? Olivia seemed to be constantly in the house – or if she wasn't, Gabriel was. Morgan didn't know which of them he disliked more. But he couldn't say anything against Gabriel, either, or he'd have Eirian at his throat as well.

'I can't believe this is happening,' he told Steve, staring into a pint of bitter. They often met in the Green Man. 'Olivia snaps her finger and Beth runs. And I can't say a thing about it without hurting her, like it's me who's stirring the shit, not Olivia.'

'You know why Beth's so touchy, don't you?' said Steve. 'She's terrified you're right.'

'Yeah, I think she is. I can't tell her what Olivia said to me. She'd be devastated.'

'Beth's trouble is that she's too kind.' Steve shook his head. 'She wants to think the best of everyone. But she's not stupid, and she can be bloody tough when she needs to be.'

'With anyone except her mother.' Morgan sighed. 'God, I'd love a mother-in-law I could get on with, have a laugh and all that ... You know, I thought Eirian would freak, and that would make Beth come to her senses. But Eirian's too busy with her precious Gabriel to even notice Olivia's around. What would you do? If you were still with Beth instead of me?'

Steve grimaced. 'I'd be even more at sea than you are. But after seeing those fucking loonies in action, Luke, Katy, Olivia and the rest ... In the end, mate, I'd have to tell Beth, "It's her or me."'

'Christ,' Morgan said faintly.

Steve looked anxious. 'Forget I said that. For God's sake, don't split up with her! Not after everything you've been through. Beth's absolutely bloody devoted to you, you jammy sod.'

'But I feel as if I don't know her at the minute,' Morgan said grimly. 'Still, she won't get rid of me that easily. Olivia would love to see us split up. That is exactly what she wants.'

*

'We never get enough time alone,' Eirian complained after two weeks. 'There's always someone coming in or out. I can't concentrate.'

'If only there was some way you could come to my hotel,' said Gabriel, who'd told her he was staying in a luxurious new hotel on the edge of Lichfield. Her heart leapt forcefully. It drove her mad that he'd only kissed her that once; how could he be so cool? 'Don't get me wrong, my dear. I won't try to seduce you; you'd be perfectly safe with me.'

'Oh.'

'But we could work through the night, no interruptions.'

Eirian parted her lips. She could almost see the glow of candles in his blue-green eyes. What a delicious prospect. 'I can tell them I'm staying with Lisa,' she said too quickly.

'Will your friend mind covering for you?' She was glad he didn't say, '*telling lies*'.

'No, she'll do anything for me. My parents don't check up on me, anyway. They trust me.' They went on working and no more was said, but now the tension between them deepened into something dark, illicit and irresistible.

I've made her deceive her parents, thought Nathaniel. Now it's begun.

Eirian was aware that her parents were at odds about Olivia. They didn't shout at each other, but there was an atmosphere. Normally Eirian would have been upset by the situation, and she'd have done everything in her power to mend things, to make her grandmother Olivia leave them in peace.

But because of Gabriel, it all went over her head. She couldn't be bothered to think about anything but him. So she did something wholly out of character; she closed her mind and pretended it wasn't happening.

'Mum,' said Eirian, as Beth came in from work. 'Lisa's asked me to stay on Friday. Is that all right?'

'Yes, I suppose so,' said Beth, hardly even looking at her.

'One of us can give you a lift.' Lisa lived in another village about four miles away.

'No, it's all right, I'll get the bus,' Eirian said quickly. 'It stops right outside her house. No chance for strange men to get hold of me.'

Beth frowned at her. She was preoccupied, which made Eirian feel less guilty about lying. 'Don't even joke about it! Eirian, you're not upset by Grandma Olivia being around, are you? She's different now, she wants to lead a normal life. There's no need to avoid her.'

'I'm not! I just want to see my friend, okay?'

Nathaniel had lit the softest lamps in the room, placed his lap-top computer and a notebook on the desk. The huge double bed was crisply made up. The room was spacious, its soft beige and green décor neutral but pleasant and welcoming.

'Nice hotel, isn't it?' said Eirian. Her voice shook a little, he noticed. 'A bit like the ones we stayed at in America.' And most remarkably, he noticed that her shadowy familiar was not with her. Not a hint of it.

'Your country's getting more like mine every day.' He opened the mini-bar. 'Like a drink before we start? Coke, lemonade?'

'I'd prefer a vodka and tonic.' He raised his eyebrows but she said, 'It's okay, my parents don't mind me drinking occasionally.'

Nathaniel smiled. 'Well, never say I don't treat you like an adult. Let's celebrate.' He poured her drink, a whisky and ginger for himself, and they clinked glasses. 'To the book,' he said, and she smiled uncertainly. He went over to the desk, pulling up a second chair, but Eirian sat on the end of the bed. She was wearing tight jeans, a skimpy black top over a white T-shirt and a lot of pagan trinkets round her neck; pentagrams, stars, moons. Her hair was loose and shiny, gold strands glinting in the brown.

'Not ready to work yet?' he said.

'I'd like to talk first.'

'Sure. Let's take our boots off and relax.' She obeyed. He turned the chair, sat down and rested his bare feet on the bedcover. This was going well. He needed to relax her, make her feel the most desirable woman in the universe with soft words and kisses – then nobly keep his word not to seduce her. She'd be frustrated, maybe, but impressed by his self-restraint. His integrity, ha. 'What do you want to talk about?'

'I don't know. Anything but the book. You.'

'Oh, there's nothing to know about me.' He smiled. 'I'm a pretty dull guy.'

'I wouldn't say that.' She tilted her glass, watching the pearly streams of bubbles. 'It won't be the same when you go back to the States.'

'Well, we have a lot of work to do yet. And we work well together, don't we?'

An edgy pause. He sensed her growing tension. 'Only work?'

Nathaniel sighed. 'Eirian, I feel a lot for you. Things I shouldn't be feeling because you're so young.'

'I'm old enough to get married,' she retorted. 'Sorry, I didn't mean anything by that. I'm over the age of consent, that's all. I didn't mean anything by that, either. Oh, damn.'

'Hey, you're a terrific girl.' And the awful thing was that he meant it. He despised everything she stood for but, damn it, he loved her company.

'But?'

'But your demon's still there, Eirian. It's not helping you.'

Her head jerked up, eyes wide. She hadn't been expecting that. 'What demon?'

'Come on, I told you I saw it the first time we met. You know what I'm talking about, don't you?'

'Yes,' she whispered. She looked disconcerted. 'It's not evil! It just . . . needs me.'

'Sometimes these things attach themselves to people. They may not be truly malevolent, but they're not good, because they wear you down, sap your energy, like a too demanding friend. Have you met people like that, who suck out your love and give nothing back?'

He could see he'd touched a nerve. 'How do you know about it?'

'Eirian, I guess I'm what people call psychic. I see things, like you do. We're pretty alike, aren't we?'

She caught her breath. 'I've never met anyone like me before. Mum is a bit but she fights it. And Dad and Grandma, but they only get odd glimpses, you know? But I'm in there all the time. Sometimes I'd like to get out.'

'You're not on your own.' He leaned over and put his hand on hers. 'Am I the only one who's seen this creature?'

'No. My family know about it. I've told them not to worry, but they're not happy.'

'If you'd like to be free of it, I can help you. It's like giving up an addiction. You have to be ready to do it yourself.'

'I can't! Shit, I'm so confused.'

'Sure you are.' Nathaniel moved on to the bed beside her. 'Hey, come on. You're not alone now.'

He felt her trembling, yearning for closer contact. He slid his arms around her and felt her breasts pressing into his chest, the amber warmth of her hair spilling over his hands. Suddenly hungry for her mouth, Nathaniel kissed her. She gasped and shifted position, her arms clamping him to her body and her legs falling slightly apart. When her tongue touched his, he almost cried out.

Nathaniel felt blood gathering heavily in his groin, his penis straining uncomfortably against his jeans. He tried to pull back before he lost control.

'What's wrong?' Eirian said anxiously. 'Don't stop.' Her lips were moist, her eyes shining. She looked so young, so pretty.

'I didn't mean this to happen,' he said, trying to hold her away. 'Don't be in such a hurry to lose your virginity, Eirian. It's too precious for that.'

'Don't talk crap!' she said fiercely. She took his face between her hands and her mouth swooped on to his.

Then it was as if she took over his will. He was in control yet everything he did was what she wanted; she guided him with a gasp, a flicker of her eye, a movement of her hand. He helped her off with her jeans. When his hand found its way between her thighs to unhook the black body-top, she gasped aloud, and pushed against his palm. She was damp there. Her excitement shocked him. As the hooks came free he slid his hands under both top and T-shirt to find that she was wearing no bra. The weight of her breasts fell sweetly into his hands as she pulled her clothes over her head and undid her necklaces, throwing them impatiently aside. His own arousal became excruciating. Pushing his fingers under the thin cotton of her briefs he felt her springy hair and the delightful groove where her pelvis and thigh joined.

He'd expected Eirian to be nervous and inhibited, maybe pulling back when he touched her more intimately, but she seemed transported. He drew her briefs down over her feet, then his fingers slid into her secret place, a purse of musky nectar. She was soaking. The fearful trap of lips and muscles pulsed, sending a flicker of age-old fear through him. He hated this precisely because he loved and feared it. Yes, he was afraid.

'Are you sure?' he whispered into her neck. 'We could stop.'

'Are you mad?' she whispered back. She moved against his hand, her lean body arched, her breasts rising and falling with each breath. Then she pressed her hand to the bulge in his jeans, massaging him so sensuously he almost came. 'Get undressed, this isn't fair!'

As he obeyed, she rolled over on the bed and searched for something in her clothes on the floor. Nathaniel saw her through a honeyed veil of light. Stared at her curved buttocks and the dark pink cleft gleaming between them. She was a goddess and he was in thrall.

She rose again with a small packet between her thumb and forefinger. 'I brought some condoms in case you didn't,' she said. 'I'll put it on you.'

Again her brazenness took him aback. 'Do you know how?'

'Well . . . yes, a girl at school told me,' she said with a quick smile. She seemed to be mocking him. But as her hand folded round his hard member, he closed his eyes and forgot everything else. Instead of the sheath, though, he felt her lips and tongue folding like a flower round the head of his penis.

Nathaniel nearly passed out with pleasure. His limbs felt weightless. He had no strength, no will left. He was hers.

But she wouldn't let him go too far. The luscious pressure stopped and she rolled the sheath on to him. Murmuring in his ear, she writhed under him, easing him into position between her thighs. He felt her soft lips drawing him in.

Still convinced he was the first, he'd expected it to be hard to enter her, yet it was easy, each gentle thrust taking him deeper in. She laughed and moaned. 'That feels wonderful, so beautiful, Gabriel . . .' But he didn't expect a virgin to reach orgasm; he was beyond thinking of her pleasure at all, only wanted to empty himself in her and end this fire. He was close to climax but the condom deadened him so he didn't explode at once. Eirian was guiding him again, her thighs undulating around him, her hands moving over his back. She was flushed, her eyes glazed. God, she was in ecstasy!

As she controlled his rhythm to match hers he felt the surging of her blood in fugue against his own. They were climbing, leaping, falling together, lust fusing and convulsing, winding tight upon itself, then unravelling in wave after wave of agonizing release. He'd never had an orgasm like it.

For one second he touched her mind. She was one incandescent blaze of amazement and joy. Other fragments of insight rained into him too but he couldn't decipher them.

Then Nathaniel, lying drained inside her girlish body, felt a familiar disgust creeping upon him. Sick ashes of lust.

Why didn't I realize she wasn't a virgin? How in hell could I have missed that? I was arrogant, making that assumption. Careless. How dare she enjoy it so much? How dare she make *me* enjoy it? I should've known it would be this way. Why did I let her fool me?

He pulled carefully out of her, got up and disposed of the condom. Pulling on a towelling robe, he opened the curtains and the window. The air was cool and musty with exhaust fumes. The lights of Lichfield sparkled; headlights flashed past beyond the hotel car park.

He hadn't meant to make love to her. Not under her control.

Maybe much later, when she was fully under his influence. An act of power – not rape, nothing so unsubtle, but a flourish of dominance, pleasurable enough to leave her craving more. Like with the others.

Not this. Not a mutual, sensual act that dragged him somewhere he didn't want to go. He breathed in and out heavily. The other fragments he'd picked up from her mind came clear and he gripped the window-sill for a few moments in dread.

She'd killed Luke. He already knew that, but the cold, bloody vengeance with which she'd done it had never struck him until now. And there'd been another; a man who had harassed Eirian's mother had also died horribly. She could kill with her mind when threatened, like a scorpion lashing out. Christ. He had to be even more careful than he'd realized. Couldn't even begin to show his hand until he'd totally destroyed her mind. Okay, he told himself. Take it very, very easy.

As he stood there, trying to collect his thoughts, Eirian came and stood beside him. She'd put on his shirt, which was too big for her. A seductive elf. Witch. Lamia.

'Gabriel, why did you leave me?' she said anxiously. 'Did I do something wrong?'

'Of course not.'

She looked quizzically at his profile, then laughed in disbelief. 'You thought I was a virgin, didn't you?' He didn't reply. 'Is that why you're pissed off? Well, I wasn't, but I'm damned if I'm going to apologize for it.'

'You don't have to.'

Her voice hardened. 'Are you one of those bastards who fucks a woman once, then gets cold feet? Fear of intimacy. I've read about that. It's to do with your relationship with your mother.'

He'd thought nothing could shock him, but Eirian did. He watched her retreating towards the bathroom, long hair swinging against her indignant back, and he suddenly knew exactly how to handle her. Change of plan. But Nathaniel was nothing if not adaptable.

He went after her, put his arms round her from behind and kissed her cheek. 'You're dead right, I've always been afraid of intimacy. That was the best time I've ever had in my life, Eirian, and it scared me. Forgive me. I want you. I love you . . .'

He felt her breath run out in a soft, 'Oh!'

She turned and her eyes were crystal-bright with tears. 'I think I love you too. I've never said that to anyone except my parents. I never thought it would happen to me.'

'Why not?'

'Because I can be so hard sometimes. I thought I was fated to be on my own.'

'Not any more.' They smiled at each other, laughing in delicious mutual revelation. He pulled her back into the warm, rumpled bed.

Yes, yes, do everything her way, he thought. I'll never win by dominating her. Only by drowning her in pleasure. If she needs sex so badly, it's only fitting that lust should be her downfall, little scorpion witch.

Chapter Sixteen

J UST when Eirian had despaired of sex, along came Gabriel to prove her wrong. With him she felt everything she'd longed to feel. And he was real. No evanescent, nocturnal demon but a white angel of a man.

Over the next five weeks, Eirian 'stayed with Lisa' once or twice a week. There was subterfuge involved; Lisa had to be let in on the secret but Lisa's parents kept in the dark, otherwise they would have told Beth immediately. After a few hours' legitimate work on the book, Gabriel would leave Eirian as usual. Later, Eirian would go out with her friend – to the cinema, or swimming – but Gabriel would meet them afterwards, drop Lisa a few yards from her home, and take Eirian to the hotel. Meanwhile Lisa would tell her folks that Eirian had gone home. Then Eirian would return home the next day as if she'd taken the bus, leaving Beth and Morgan none the wiser. Lisa wasn't happy, but Eirian talked her round, making her feel involved. And some nights she really did stay with her friend, to make the deceit more convincing.

She knew she was using Lisa. But she didn't care, she was in heaven.

One day, while Beth was in her workshop, Gabriel appeared. She looked up from her bench and was astounded to see him behind the rows of Tiffany lamps, his face sheened by the coloured glow, his milk-blond hair floating around his shoulders in a draught.

'Hello, this is a surprise,' she said. 'Be with you in a minute. I'm just soldering a tricky bit.'

'Oh, don't let me interrupt. I heard how talented you are. I wanted to see for myself.' Gabriel moved around the stall, fingering lamps, lifting panels to the light. He looked as if he might drop or knock something to the floor; Beth was on edge.

'These are terrific. Wonder if I could take something of yours back to the States in one piece?' Then, in the same tone, 'I'm sorry Morgan doesn't like me.'

'So am I,' said Beth, startled. 'Morgan doesn't seem to like anyone at the moment.'

'He has a problem with your mother too. I don't understand, she seems a real nice lady.'

Beth exhaled through her teeth. 'It's a long story. She behaved badly in the past but she had mental problems. It's all behind her now. But for some reason Morgan is refusing to understand that I need a mother – and that she needs me.'

'Maybe he'll never understand.' Gabriel moved next to her, watching her work. He was very close. 'Maybe he's not the man you thought he was.' His shoulder touched hers. Beth's heart-rate rose; was he making a pass at her? 'I know you're concerned about Eirian. Something has attached itself to her, a kind of . . . entity, like a restless spirit. You're worried.'

Beth froze, hands hovering over her work. 'How did you know about that?'

'She told me. Well, I made her tell me because I sensed it. Sometimes I'm psychic.'

'Oh,' Beth breathed. 'Look, we're sure it's not harmful but . . .'

'You *hope* it isn't.' He moved out of her body space, but she still felt intimidated and oddly excited, the way Morgan had made her feel as a teenager. And, irrationally, she felt manipulated. 'It's no more evil than an animal, but it's doing her harm even if she doesn't realize it. It feeds on her strength.'

For some reason Beth pictured her mother. She couldn't speak. She felt darkness flapping around her as if the walls had been torn away, and Gabriel was the only light. 'Beth, I want to help,' he said softly. 'I can make it go away.'

'How?'

'Let me rephrase that. Eirian herself has to want it to leave. I can help her with that. She'll be free of it soon, that's guaranteed.'

Beth was so stunned she hardly knew what to say. 'That would be wonderful, it would be such a weight off my mind. What are you, really? A witch?'

In reply, Gabriel only smiled. His radiance bewitched her in a way that wasn't quite healthy. But the suspicion evaporated, and she couldn't pin it down. Too much else to occupy her, anyway. She was trying to ignore Morgan's antipathy to her mother, but secretly it tortured her. Couldn't he see that he was rejecting part of Beth herself?

'I'll see you later, Beth,' Gabriel said, looking seductively into her eyes as if he read her thoughts. 'Everything will get sorted out, don't you worry now.'

When he'd gone, Dee appeared round the end of the partition. 'Beth, that guy . . .'

'Gabriel,' Beth half smiled, wondering if Dee had the hots for him as well. 'What about him?'

Dee came to her work-bench, looking unusually serious. 'I don't know how to say this, but the other day when you weren't here, he turned up and started asking questions about you. Very personal questions.'

'He's just interested.' Beth didn't want to hear this. 'He's a friendly guy. He's helping Eirian write a book, he's bound to be curious about her family.'

Dee looked uneasy. 'I'm sure you're right. It's just that . . .'

'What?'

'It was almost as if he were trying to blacken your character in some way, turn me against you. Hinting that you and Morgan weren't very good parents, that you might be unfaithful to each other, or that your relationship was shaky – to see if I'd agree.'

Beth swallowed against a knot of ice in her throat. She couldn't believe it, any more than she could accept Morgan's warnings about Olivia. 'Did you?'

'No, of course not! I put him straight, believe me! Steve was here, he'll back me up. We were both very cool until Gabriel got the message he wasn't going to break us, then he left. But after he'd gone, it suddenly struck me how creepy it was. Almost as if he'd been trying to hypnotize us. He was so plausible, he probably takes some people in. Oh, Beth, I know how awful it sounds. Sorry, I didn't mean to upset you. Steve didn't want me to say anything, but I thought you should know. I hope I've got it all wrong. But if Gabriel *is* up to anything, we're on your side.'

'God, I don't know what to say.' Beth trusted Dee, and knew in her heart she wasn't lying – but her mind ejected the warning, all the same. She put her hand on Dee's arm and smiled. 'Thanks. But it must be a misunderstanding. Eirian thinks he's great, and she's the best judge of character I've ever known.'

'You must have had a lot of girlfriends,' said Eirian, lying contented in her lover's arms.

'Would it hurt you if I had?'

'Why should it? I don't expect you to have been a monk.'

'A few,' said Gabriel. 'No one I really felt close to, until I met you.'

'Oh, yeah,' she said, smiling.

'It's true. I was married once. She died.' There was no emotion in his voice.

'That's awful. I'm sorry.'

'She took an overdose of anti-depressants. She was a sick woman, no one could help her. I couldn't be close to her, she wouldn't let me. I've been cautious ever since.'

His apparent lack of feeling bothered her a little. He must be hiding it, because it hurt. She did that herself sometimes. 'What about your parents?'

'My father was in the army. Commander. Decorated in Korea and Vietnam. He was my hero, finest man on the planet.' Now there was real warmth in his voice.

'What about your mother?'

A pause, like a tract of emotion erased. 'She left us,' Gabriel said shortly. 'Went off with another man when I was twelve. How could anyone leave my father? Guess he was too good for her. I tell you, it killed him. He started drinking, finally died of a heart attack ten years ago. *She* killed him.'

The flash of raw pain she received from him shook her. 'Is she still alive?'

'Don't know, don't care. She tried to contact me once. I woulda been about thirteen. I told her to go to hell. Never heard from her again. She ceased to exist the day she left my dad.'

The unguarded spurt of pain over, he became hermetically sealed again. Eirian was aware that she didn't know Gabriel very well, even though they'd become so intimate. Now it struck her that his good nature was only one layer in; underneath he was opaque. Complex, enigmatic. And she felt his opaqueness was somehow flaking off and attaching itself to her. It was hard to think about anything beyond sex, Gabriel, and the sensual, immediate present. 'You don't like talking about the past any more than I do.'

'We're very alike, honey,' he said, kissing her. 'So, what about this guy who got there before me?'

'Oh, Peter,' Eirian sighed. 'It was so disappointing. Nothing like . . . my dreams. And then there was Alastair.'

'Alastair?' He sounded startled.

'Yes. More than one, less than three, okay?' Eirian felt a pang of regret at making the confession; she wasn't yet confident of Gabriel's affection. 'That was better, but still not what I wanted. And I knew from the beginning he was bisexual, so it wasn't really a surprise when he went off with – well, with this bloke. I thought it was always going to be like that. But the first time I made love with you . . . oh, Goddess!'

'I know. Same here.'

'I wonder what my parents would do if they found out?'

'My dear, they would want my balls on a skewer. And that would mean we didn't get the book finished, either. So we make sure they don't find out, okay?'

Alastair. Shoulda guessed, thought Nathaniel, alone in his room the following evening. I knew Alastair was friendly with Eirian, that's what made him the perfect boy to tempt the grandfather. And it worked, the pair of them slipped right into it, leaving

294

Olivia with nowhere to go, like I planned – nice touch of betrayal and family disruption – but the little bastard never told me he'd been sleeping with Eirian!

Hey, it's good. Imagine how she felt when she found out! And it made her more vulnerable to me. No wonder she fell so fast. Nathaniel laughed. Jesus, all the intricate plans I wove to bind the witch when all I had to do was screw the hell out of her!

Still, Alastair was something Eirian had kept secret from him. Nathaniel had learned that it was dangerous to make assumptions, like taking it for granted she was a virgin. Who knew what else she was hiding? The full strength of her power, for certain. He couldn't afford to be careless, or to imagine her infatuation was enough to undo her.

Sometimes, when she slept beside him, he sensed her haunting entity glaring at him from the darkness. His rival, his diametric opposite. But when Nathaniel stared it down it would back off, like a wolf recognizing its superior. Oh, you're so scary, he thought mockingly, but you daren't touch me. You know damn well you have no power in the real world.

Mid-August. The time was about right to move things on.

That evening, around midnight, he put on his Joshua disguise and drove a different hire car to Olivia's cottage. A precaution in case anyone saw his usual car. But it was dark; no one saw him.

Olivia was in a thick nightdress when she opened the door, her hair tousled. He'd got her out of bed but she was plainly thrilled to see him. She looked healthy, all aglow with confidence.

'Joshua – I mean Gabriel, at last! I never see you to talk to any more. I daren't say anything to you when you're at Beth's in case I give something away.'

'You're a wise woman,' he said gently. 'I know its hard but you're doing great.' He pulled off the grey wig and glasses. His hair tumbled down, a platinum veil. Olivia gazed raptly at him as he stroked her cheek and mouthed sickly lies. 'You're a heck of a woman and a heck of a soldier for the Lord.'

'It's going marvellously,' she said. 'I've got Beth running in circles to please me. She believes me, not Morgan! It's wonderful, it makes me feel . . .'

'Powerful?'

'Yes. Powerful again.' Her eyes glowed with righteous passion. 'If I could make that evil bastard leave it would be the happiest day of my life.'

'It's going to happen very soon. The Lord is pleased with you, Olivia.'

'Yes,' she said. 'God gives me the courage to withstand the evil. So do you.'

'Well, we're doing holy work, saving your family from Satan. Cruel to be kind, that's God's way. Now there's just a small thing I need you to do for me.'

'Name it,' she said confidently.

'I want you to ask a few questions about Eirian. Put a few doubts in their minds.'

'What questions?' He told her. She frowned. 'I can't say such awful things about you, Gabriel!'

'You don't have to. Just drop hints; their filthy minds will do the rest.'

She still looked suspicious. 'It won't be true, though, will it? You wouldn't *really* sleep with Eirian, would you? Tell me it's a bluff.'

He shook his head in disapprobation, his hands kneading her shoulders. 'Now, Olivia. You know me better than that. Of course I wouldn't sleep with your granddaughter.'

'Praise God,' she gasped, throwing herself against him. 'At least there is one being in the world too pure to stoop to that degrading filth! You're truly an angel.'

As Nathaniel held her away, he felt her heat through the thick flannel of her nightie. And he suspected that despite her virtuous protestations, the hypocritical bitch would have been happy to let him push her down and take her right there on the floor.

*

'Where did Eirian tell you she was going this evening?' Olivia asked casually, out of nowhere.

'Where she always goes on a Friday night,' said Beth. 'Lisa's.'

Olivia was sitting with Beth on the sofa, watching something inane on the television. This was the woman, Morgan observed, who once wouldn't allow a television in the house, claiming it was Satan's instrument! He'd curled up in an armchair with a wildlife magazine, trying to pretend she wasn't there. Good thing Eirian was at Lisa's house; she couldn't stand Olivia either, and made less effort to be polite to her than he did. So Olivia was driving their daughter away too.

'Are you *sure* your daughter is always where she says she is?' Olivia sounded gently concerned; Morgan shuddered, thinking, how come Beth doesn't notice the falseness in her voice?

'Of course, Mum,' said Beth. 'I trust her.'

'I trusted you, once.'

Beth folded her arms, looking quietly annoyed. 'Yes, well, I have an open relationship with Eirian. I trust her implicitly. I don't need to check up on her.'

'It's not for me to question Eirian's conduct, of course. That's your responsibility, Beth. But that man she's seeing . . .'

'Her editor,' Beth said sharply.

'Whatever.'

'What's that supposed to mean? He's a thoroughly decent, straightforward person.'

'I'm sure he is. But you know how impressionable teenage girls can be, Beth, from your own experience.' Olivia glanced at Morgan, who gave her a hostile, mocking grin in response. 'How easily led.'

'Are you suggesting my daughter would lie to me?'

'Of course not. But if she did, I can understand that you would prefer not to know.'

Beth's shoulders rose with tension. 'This is ridiculous. Okay, I'll prove she's at her friend's!'

She went to the phone, which was on a table by Morgan's chair. He caught her hand and said, 'Don't, Beth! We don't have to prove anything!' He sighed in exasperation as she shook him off and dialled.

'Hi, it's Eirian's mum. Can I speak to her please?' Her face fell. 'Oh. Oh, must be a mix up. She must be at Tricia's. Yes, thanks, 'bye.'

Beth put the receiver down very slowly, looking pale. 'Lucky you checked,' Olivia said smugly.

Morgan put his magazine down. 'Could she be at Tricia's?'

'I doubt it. I only said that so Lisa's mother didn't think I don't know where my daughter is.' Beth put her hand to her mouth. 'Oh, shit.'

Foreboding filled Morgan. He stood up and said grimly, 'Which hotel is Gabriel staying at?'

'Trusthouse – Posthouse – something in Lichfield,' said Beth. 'I wrote the number on the pad . . . here.' She passed him the notebook and he dialled.

'Is Gabriel Jordan in his room? No, I don't want to speak to him, I just need to know if he's in the hotel. Did he? Was there anyone with him? Did she have long brown hair, a long black and cream dress and a black mohair cardigan? Thank you.' Morgan turned to Beth. 'The receptionist said he came in a couple of hours ago and she hasn't seen him go out again. There was a young woman with him.'

'It might not be Eirian,' said Beth.

'What, wearing identical clothes to the ones she went out in?' All at once Morgan was coldly angry, in no mood to stop and think. 'Come on, we're going over there.'

'I'll get my coat,' said Olivia.

'Yes,' Morgan said thinly, 'and then you'll go straight home. You needn't think you're going to hang around gloating!'

'I have no wish to,' Olivia retorted. 'Like father, like daughter.'

He said sweetly, 'Just fuck off.'

'Morgan!' Beth exclaimed, but Olivia made a dignified exit, her face primly composed. She seemed pleased that he'd sworn at her, as if it proved a point.

*

Beth sat rigid in the passenger seat as Morgan drove to Lichfield. Tense and annoyed with each other, they didn't speak. Beth instinctively felt that this wasn't the right thing to do, but what was the alternative?

At the hotel they found out Gabriel's room number, 112. Up one floor in the lift, then along a quiet, carpeted corridor. 'Nice hotel,' Beth remarked.

'Yes, I'd hate to think he was shagging my daughter in a dump,' Morgan said grimly.

'Whatever happens, don't get mad.' She touched his arm but he was unresponsive. Morgan tapped sharply on the door of Room 112. It took a while for anyone to answer. Then Gabriel opened the door, wearing a white towelling robe. His long white hair was tangled and he looked flushed, bright-eyed.

Morgan gave a smile that could have cut glass. 'Is my daughter here?' Not waiting for an answer, he marched past Gabriel, who made no attempt to stop him. Beth followed.

Eirian was in bed, naked, the covers clutched over her breasts. One dim desk-lamp lit the room; in its rosy light, her dishevelled hair shone beautifully. When she saw Beth and Morgan, her face opened up with utter astonishment. Morgan suddenly seemed wrong-footed by embarrassment.

'I don't call this Lisa's, do you?' said Beth. She felt calmer than she'd expected. Shocked, but not really angry.

'Get dressed,' Morgan said heatedly. 'You're coming home.'

'How dare you!' Eirian gasped. Beth picked up a robe off the floor and gave it to her so she could get up and collect her clothes. Eirian glared at her, eyes spitting outrage. 'How dare you, Mum!'

'Just shut up and come home,' Beth said evenly. 'We can talk there.'

Gabriel stood in the middle of the room, elbows cupped in his hands. His face was grave and conciliatory. 'Mr and Mrs Rhys, I don't know how to begin to apologize. But I'm deeply in love with your daughter, I wouldn't treat her with disrespect for anything –'

Morgan, his eyes green lasers, responded by punching

Gabriel hard in the windpipe. Gabriel toppled backwards on to the bed, clutching his throat. He gagged, eyes streaming.

'Dad!' Eirian shrieked, rushing to her lover's side. For one horrible moment, Beth wondered if Morgan had fatally injured him. But he sat up, waving Eirian to go with her parents.

'If you ever go near my daughter again,' Morgan said in frigid menace, 'I will personally. Fucking. Kill you.'

Gabriel sat disconsolate on the bed while Beth helped Eirian to dress. Then they hurried her out of the room, down through the lobby and into the car.

All the way home, Eirian was silent. The atmosphere in the car was a solid block of ice. It wasn't until they arrived home and entered the kitchen that Eirian began to rage. 'How dare you, how bloody *dare* you humiliate me like that?' she shouted. 'Have you any idea how stupid I felt? Gabriel treated me like a woman! All you two can do is treat me like a child!'

'You're not an adult, you're barely sixteen –' Beth began reasonably, but Morgan spoke over her.

'He's at least twice your age. He had no right to be having sex with you. He's old enough to be your father!'

'He's the same age as you. So what?' Eirian snapped. 'Randolph's twenty years older than Rhianwen!'

'But they're old enough to look after themselves! There is no way you're seeing him again, book or no book.'

'You can't stop me, Dad!'

'Can't we? We might get him deported. I think he was using the book as an excuse to take advantage. I don't think there's going to be any book.'

'That's rubbish, of course there is!' Eirian flared. 'I signed the contract! We fell in love while we were working and I seduced him. It was my fault, okay? I wasn't a virgin, anyway, so what's the big deal?'

They stared at her. Beth began, 'Who did you . . .'

'For God's sake, only Peter.'

'Peter?'

'Forget it, it doesn't matter! The point is, Gabriel didn't take my "innocence" or some such crap. I grew up a long time ago. You brought me up to think how wonderful sex is, you're at it like sodding rabbits, then you go crazy when I dare to do it! Why can't I have a lover? What's Gabriel going to think of me when you come wading in and treating me like a naughty twelve-year-old?'

'I don't give a toss what he thinks,' Morgan said furiously. 'He had no business laying a finger on you. And if I see him again, I *will* kill him.'

Eirian gasped and retorted, 'You are such a fucking hypocrite, Dad! You were screwing Mum when she was fourteen! At least I'm over the age of consent! How dare you tell me how to behave when you weren't even around until I was eleven?'

Morgan went pale, drew a breath, and let it go. He said nothing but he looked devastated. Beth thought, what *can* we say? Trying to calm things down, she said, 'We don't want you making the same mistakes we made.'

'So why are you acting exactly like your own parents did, going crazy and forbidding us to see each other? What good did it do? At least I'm not careless enough to get myself pregnant!'

'Eirian, that's not fair!' Beth exclaimed. But everything her daughter said was the hard truth. 'We're trying to protect you. You shouldn't have lied to us, there was no need. Why couldn't you talk to me?'

'Why didn't you notice when my periods started?' Eirian's voice fell and she seemed close to tears. 'You don't notice anything. You and Dad both saw the entity – it was trying to reach me through you – but you were too busy fucking each other to stop and work out what it meant. Then when you finally do notice, years later when I've sorted everything out on my own, you go crazy about it! And then you wonder why I'm pissed off! Ever since Dad came back, you've been so wrapped up in each other you've had no time for me. Neither of you ever wanted me.'

'That is not true!' they said, almost in unison.

To Beth's dismay, tears began to flow down Eirian's face. 'I was just an accident. You wanted that baby you lost more than you ever wanted me! How can I compete with Auryn, who can

301

never grow up to piss you off, never be anything but this idealized angel? You wish you'd miscarried me instead, that would have made your life so much easier! I've always been on my own, always. At least Gabriel wants me. But the first time I find someone, all you can do is try to take it away from me.'

'Love, please, that isn't true.' Distraught, Beth went towards her but Eirian backed away.

'Isn't it? Where were you when I was so scared of the shaman I thought I was going to die? Oh, just go to fucking hell, both of you!

She ran out of the kitchen. They heard the drumming of her footsteps on the stairs, her bedroom door slamming. Morgan sat down heavily at the table, his forehead propped on his hands.

'Jesus wept,' he said. 'I had no idea this was going to be so difficult, or that I was going to make such a hash of it.'

'What?'

'Trying to be Eirian's father.'

Beth stood behind him and slid her arms down over his chest until her head rested on his shoulder. 'How do you think I feel?' She let out a huge sigh. She felt like death. 'I'll leave her for ten minutes to calm down, then take her some hot chocolate.'

'I still want to kill the bastard,' said Morgan. 'I always knew there was something suspicious about him. Why aren't you angrier, Beth?'

'Because Eirian's right, and you know it. Of course I don't want her to get hurt or pregnant – but really, has she done anything so terrible? It was the other stuff she said that worries me. I thought we were being loving parents; how did she get the impression we don't care about her?'

'Heat of the moment. I'm sure she doesn't mean it.'

'But we did neglect her sometimes.' Guilty memories crowded in. 'Why couldn't I see it at the time? I treated her like an adult too early, and now I'm trying to treat her like a child to compensate, and nothing is working.'

'And I get the world record for bare-faced hypocrisy.' Morgan rubbed his eyes then rested on his folded arms.

'Did the fact that you couldn't keep your hands off me when I was fourteen make you a nasty unlovable person?' said Beth. 'Maybe Gabriel really loves her.'

'But I wasn't old enough to be your father. I didn't act like a responsible adult because I wasn't one – but Gabriel is, supposedly. Anyway, I've never found him lovable.'

'Jealousy.'

'No, Beth. There's something about him.'

'Yes, Eirian's fallen for him and you can't take it! You don't like him, you can't get on with my mother – you know, I thought you were an easy-going, tolerant, happy person. Did I get that wrong?'

Morgan looked narrowly at her. 'No. It's just that the only two people in the world I can't stand seem to be forever in our house fucking up our lives.'

When they'd gone, Nathaniel fell back on to the bed, tears of pain turning to ones of laughter. Wonderful, he thought, his glee overriding the discomfort of his bruised throat. Perfect. Everything had gone precisely to plan.

But Morgan was going to pay for that blow.

Eirian accepted the mug of chocolate from Beth but she didn't feel like talking. Beth was all burgundy velvet, wild black hair, pale face and big dark eyes; the mother she knew and loved. But inside her shell of humiliation, Eirian felt only alienation, dull rage.

'Are you really pissed off?' asked Beth, sitting on the edge of her bed.

'Are you?' said Eirian.

'Yes,' said Beth. 'Not because you had sex but because you lied to us.'

'How did you find out?'

'I rang Lisa's to ask you something. I can't even remember what now. You had no right to use Lisa like that.'

'I know. Don't lecture me! I knew you'd be like this. I could kill Dad, how dare he act like that? I thought he'd be more understanding than you!'

Beth gave a short, sceptical laugh. 'He's angry with Gabriel, not with you.'

'Why? Does Dad want to screw me himself, or something?'

Beth gasped in shock. 'What on earth made you say a thing like that?'

Eirian hung her head. 'I've overheard Olivia whisper it really nastily to Dad, more than once. He says nothing.'

'Well, you must have misheard! You said some terrible things downstairs. Don't make it worse. It was a very impressive display of self-pity, Eirian, but it won't wash. You know damned well we love you.'

'Do you?' said Eirian, feeling nothing.

'Yes. I thought I was being loving, giving you the freedom I never had. Have I spoiled you, or made you feel I don't love you?'

'For God's sake, Mum, go and see a psychologist! I can't handle this.'

Beth crossed one knee over the other and tapped her foot in the air. 'We've had a talk. We've decided you can see Gabriel. We're going to sort this out like adults, all right?'

When Beth had gone, Eirian switched off her bedside light and lay staring into the darkness. She should still have been in Gabriel's arms now, not alone, feeling wretched. She swallowed tears. Then she felt the darkness moving, caught the scent of rain and smoke, saw the walls dissolve into the endless sweep of a prairie.

She felt an involuntary twitch of desire, but suppressed it. Her nocturnal lover Ictinike came slithering up over the foot of the bed like a serpent to lie alongside her, but for the first time she didn't want him. In her trance she shifted away, but he caught her with one arm and lay on top of her.

He'd never looked more beguilingly human. He was naked, unpainted, his skin like bronze. His hair was like a slide of black water, hanging to his hips. His gilded snake-eyes were beautiful. And he looked so young . . .

Ictinike never spoke, but the images that clamoured into her mind made his intention clear. *Gabriel is evil. We warned you, why*

*did you not take heed? Give him up. We want you to ourselves. You are
ours, not his. Ours. Ours . . .*

'No,' said Eirian. Somehow he passed through the bedcovers
to lie on her naked body, and she felt his phallus pushing at
her thighs, hard as oak. She flung the covers back and pushed
him off; he lay half on his back, the erection pulsing in the air,
an ebony tower. 'No. It's over. I don't want you any more.'

His face changed, features lengthening to become feral. As
he began to rise over her, she reached out to the bedside table
and grabbed a large pair of scissors. 'Would you rape me?' she
hissed. She opened the scissors, holding the thicker blade like
a knife as she gripped the phallus with her other hand. 'Because
I can undo the healing I gave you. Cut it off and stick it back
in your mouth. And I will, if you don't leave me alone!'

She was shaking violently. With an audible roar, Ictinike
rose off the bed and kept on rising, swelling, his body filling
the room. He was a huge stag, bellowing. His head was an
ugly melding of jackal and goat, his fangs long and wet, his
legs as thick as jointed tree trunks. He rose from all fours and
towered over her. Huge wings flapped from his shoulders. His
penis stabbed at the air and semen spattered down on her face.

Eirian screamed, muffling her face in the pillow. She'd never
been so terrified in her life.

We love you. You are ours!

'No!' she cried, rejecting him with all her will, with every
cell of her body. 'I don't want you, I hate you! I never want
to see you again!'

She felt a freezing wind blow over her. She held her breath.
She heard . . . silence.

When she dared to look up, Ictinike had gone. Not even the
merest psychic trace of him remained. It was as if he'd never
existed. She'd done it. Driven him away for good.

Eirian should have felt relieved. Instead she began to cry
bitterly. Went on crying until, near dawn, she fell asleep.

Chapter Seventeen

WHEN Beth opened the door to Gabriel, he was holding a huge bunch of white chrysanthemums. In his pristine white clothes, with his pearly hair and ivory skin, he looked pure, spotless, complete. Virginal.

'These are for you, Beth,' he said, pressing the bouquet into her hands. 'I'm so sorry about last night. I cannot tell you how much I regret the pain I must have caused. I've done Eirian a great wrong. However, I repeat; I love your daughter. I want to marry her.'

'Don't push your luck,' said Beth. 'She's in the kitchen.'

She followed him. Eirian, who was at the table drinking a coffee, went scarlet when Gabriel walked in. But she was very dignified. She got up, poured Gabriel a coffee, and sat down again without a word. Then Morgan came in from the garden, calm but icily hostile.

'I want to marry her,' Gabriel said again, when he'd uttered more apologies.

'Over my dead body,' said Morgan.

'Surely it's your daughter's decision.'

'Not until she's eighteen, it isn't.'

'I couldn't help falling in love with her.'

'You could help luring her to your hotel room and making her lie to us.'

'Stop it!' Eirian cried, leaping up. 'I'm not a piece of meat!' She ran out into the garden. Gabriel looked from Morgan to Beth.

'May I talk to her alone? You'll be able to see us through the window.'

Morgan said nothing. Beth felt the situation was so ludicrous, she couldn't bear it. 'Yes, of course, go on,' she said wearily.

Gabriel's peacock eyes fastened on hers, easing her worries in a way she didn't want. 'Beth, remember I told you that I could help with the entity that attached itself to her? Well, it's gone. Ask her.'

Stunned, she watched him walk out into the garden after her daughter.

'Of course I didn't think you looked foolish,' said Gabriel. 'Your parents' feelings are understandable.' He and Eirian stood by an apple tree, not touching. 'It was an abuse of my position to make love to you.'

'Whose side are you on?'

'I'm not taking sides. They can't help their anger. They love you – but so do I.'

'I hate them,' Eirian said bitterly. 'My father's being so unreasonable. He only turned up five years ago but now he doesn't want anyone else to have me. They won't let me grow up!'

'Everyone comes to realize that their parents are imperfect, maybe seriously flawed.' She met his eyes; Gabriel was so beautiful, pure and whole, while her mother and father contracted in her mind to two warped and selfish beings. Her heart swelled darkly; she caught her breath and it was almost a sob. 'Sooner or later, you have to break away. Maybe your time has come sooner than most.'

'What do you mean?' A fearful thrill.

'It's going to be hard to finish the book in this atmosphere. Impossible to meet and make love, with your parents watching us all the time. I think you deserve better than that.'

'Freedom to make my own decisions.'

'Yes. So come away with me, Eirian. I can take you where they'll never find you.'

'Where?' She was trembling with excitement. 'When?'

'We have to play it cool for a few days while I make the arrangements. Act contrite, do things their way, even if it means not seeing each other. Then we'll vanish. You'll need your passport, clothes, the disks for the book – hey, don't look so worried! Do you want time to think about it?'

'I'm not worried. I don't need time. Let's do it.'

*

Eirian could see no other solution. She was a good actress; it wasn't hard, over the next few days, to play the contrite model daughter. Gabriel stayed away, 'To prove I'm sincere,' he told the sceptical Morgan. Her parents forgave her, but she couldn't forgive them. Their professed love for her seemed a sham. All their failings stood like monstrous sculptures between her and them. They were blood-relations to Olivia and Luke after all; how could they be untainted?

As she lay awake, the night before she was due to run away, the absence of Ictinike was an aching silence around her. He didn't come again to say, 'Don't go.' Perhaps she'd destroyed him with rejection, as the Great Mother could. She visualized the Hellstone, but it was no longer a milky lens to the shaman's realm. There were no shadows, no past haunted by wise women, witch-hunters, gods and goddesses. The world was opaque, like Gabriel's eyes.

It would be good to leave everything behind. The convoluted betrayals of her grandparents, her parents' obsession with each other, the terror and the addictive pleasures Ictinike had inflicted on her . . . yes, leave it all and start again.

Her future lay with Gabriel.

Beth knew something was amiss the moment she woke up. It was before seven. Pulling on her dressing gown, she went into Eirian's room and found it empty, the bed smooth, a white envelope on the pillow.

'Dear Mum and Dad,' read the note inside, 'please don't get upset, don't go crazy and don't worry. I'm going to America with Gabriel. I don't know how long for. I didn't want to do it this way but I know you'd never have let me go otherwise and I have to be with him. Surely you can both understand that? I'll keep in touch. But please, please don't try to come after me, or call the police, or anything like that. This is my decision. If you try to force me to come home, I'll never forgive you. Talk to you soon, love, Eirian.'

Beth let out a cry, half muffled by her hand. Morgan came rushing in. 'Beth, what is it?'

She passed him the note. She saw her own anger and despair echoed in his face, but he didn't lose his temper. 'Christ,' he said under his breath. 'The bastard.' Then he held Beth's arms and said, 'Let's not panic. Are you all right?'

'What do you think?' Beth said with a humourless laugh. 'It's like Luke kidnapping her all over again – only this time she's gone of her own accord. I could kill her!'

'No. It's his fault.'

'Eirian has a mind of her own.'

'But what kind of man runs away with a teenager half his age?'

'For God's sake, don't let's start arguing about whose fault it is!' Beth said. 'How can she suddenly act the rebellious teen-ager, when I never gave her anything to rebel against?'

'Maybe that was the trouble.'

'So you're saying I spoiled her?'

'I didn't say that!' Morgan exclaimed. 'You said it! If you're guilty, so am I.' He sighed. 'We let her have her own way in everything. Then the first time we say no to her, she goes crazy.'

Beth leaned into his shoulder and he hugged her. 'What the hell are we going to do?'

'Let's think. They're probably at Heathrow or Gatwick by now . . .'

'Morgan, you know what she said. If we go after her, she's going to be furious.'

'Tough! She can't go! That bastard is not going to get away with this!'

'Listen to me, love,' Beth said firmly. 'It was her decision to go. If we try to bully her, she'll hate us for it. Think how she'd feel if the police waded in, arrested Gabriel and brought her back home! She'd never forgive us! Do you think I'm going to risk her vanishing and never speaking to me again? I know it's hard, but I think we should do nothing. Let her go. Wait for her to call. Then we'll be reasonable, not angry.'

'But maybe she wants us to get heavy, to prove we care!'

'We tried that. This is the result.'

He breathed out slowly. 'Okay, we'll do it your way. But it's not going to be easy.'

They went into the kitchen and drank tea. Beth was outwardly calm, but inside she was falling apart with anxiety. Morgan telephoned Suzanne, while Beth listened on the sitting-room extension. 'Hi, Sue. Just thought you should know that your so-called reputable editor has run off with our daughter.'

Suzanne sounded devastated as he told her the details. 'Oh, my God, Morgan, I don't know what to say. This is awful.'

'Are you really sure he is who he said he is?'

'Of course! I checked him out myself. Silver Dove Books is a reputable publisher and Gabriel Jordan is the senior editor. It was all above board. I met Gabriel myself, he seemed such a nice guy.'

'Unfortunately, Eirian seems to think he's too much of a nice guy. I don't care what his sodding credentials are, something about him doesn't ring true!'

'Oh, my God . . .' Suzanne hesitated. 'You don't think she's in any danger with him, do you?'

'I don't think so. But how do we know?'

'I'll get in touch with Jamie Baker,' she said quickly. 'He has contacts, he can find things out I can't. Have you got Gabriel's home address?'

'No, only the publisher. Baltimore. We're hoping Eirian will call and let us know where she is.'

'God, I hope so. I'm so sorry, I feel this is all my fault. If I find anything out, I'll call you straight back,' said Suzanne.

'Thanks, Sue. And it's not your fault. 'Bye.' Beth heard the line go dead. As she went back into the kitchen, Morgan said, 'Do you feel like going to work?'

'No, but I've got to. I have three thousand pounds' worth of panels and light fittings to deliver to a pub in Derby. I have to help fit them too. It'll take all day.'

'You'd better go, then,' he said, stroking her arm. 'I'll stay home in case the phone rings. At least it'll take your mind off things.'

'Thanks,' she said, giving him a hug. Beth went out, did her work on autopilot and returned at six. There had been no call. She and Morgan haunted the house, nerves frayed. Strangely, Olivia hadn't turned up; at nine o' clock Beth thought, I'll go round in a minute, make sure she's all right . . .

The telephone rang. She and Morgan both pounced on it but Beth won.

'Hello, Mum?' said Eirian's voice, clear but shaky. 'I'm in America. At Gabriel's house.'

Beth took a deep breath. 'How are you, love?'

'I'm fine. Just tired.'

'Come home, please. We won't be angry with you.'

'Why *would* you need to be angry with me?' Eirian said tautly. 'I'm sorry about the note, but I meant what I said.'

'I know. But there was no need for you to run away.'

'I didn't run away. I decided to leave.'

'Why? We didn't forbid you to see Gabriel. We said you could talk to him.'

'I don't need your permission to talk to him!' Eirian said heatedly. 'That's the whole point.'

'We're not putting any pressure on you. Come home when you're ready.'

A pause. Morgan took the receiver off Beth and said cheerfully, 'Hi, what are you up to?'

'Nothing much,' said Eirian. 'You should see Gabriel's house, it's huge! He's virtually got his own forest and river outside!'

'Lovely. And are you going to tell us where it is?'

'Maybe. Not yet.'

'We're not going to send in the SAS, dear.' Morgan's light tone was perfect. 'So what are you going to be doing, apart from the obvious?'

'Dad!' Eirian nearly laughed. 'We're going to finish the book. I don't know what I'll do after.'

'Your A-levels would be good. Have you got any money?'

'Gabriel's helping me out. There's no need to worry.'

'Why would I worry about a responsible adult like you?'

Morgan said sardonically. 'Funny, though. I thought you had too much pride to be a kept woman.'

'You don't know anything about it!' Eirian said indignantly. 'I have to go. I'll call tomorrow.'

Beth said, 'Eirian, wait!' but she'd put the phone down. Morgan slowly replaced the receiver and pushed his hand through his hair.

'At least we know she's all right,' he said.

'Do we?' said Beth. This was the closest she'd come to crying. She didn't want to break down.

'You're the one who thought Gabriel was wonderful!' Morgan said, not pleasantly. Beth bit her lip.

'I've changed my mind, all right? I was also the one who didn't want her appearing on telly in the first place, remember?'

'Yeah. Oh, hell.' Tears shone in his eyes. Then he reached for her and they hugged each other painfully tight. 'Bethie, you did absolutely the right thing going to work today. We've got to carry on as normal or we'll go crazy. I have a feeling she'll be home before the beginning of term.'

'Oh, Goddess, I hope you're right. Look, I'd better go and tell Mum what's happened.'

'Yeah, go on. Your mother's going to love it.'

Eirian was tired from the flight, but the first exploration of Gabriel's house and garden revitalized her. A chauffeur-driven limousine had brought them from Dulles Airport in Washington to Maryland, where the road cut through endless, forested hills. The heat was sweltering. Gabriel's house was in the middle of nowhere, on a long drive where each house was a mansion surrounded by acres of woodland.

The house itself was a huge chalet of dark wood amid unfamiliar trees and exotic feathery shrubs. Inside, the house was open-plan, with polished hardwood floors and unpainted brick walls on which violently coloured abstract paintings hung. Briefly, Eirian missed the cosiness of her own home. Gabriel gave her an hour to unpack, shower and change, then led her outside, touchingly eager to show her his domain.

The garden had lush wide lawns that edged into shadowy bowers of woodland. From the terrace, an avenue of banana trees – specially cultivated, he told her – led to a path that dropped steeply through a belt of greenery and came out on the wide bank of a creek. Eirian saw a private jetty with two powerboats moored under a boathouse. The creek itself looked wider than the Thames, though Gabriel insisted it was only a tributary off the Patuxent.

'It's so beautiful,' Eirian exclaimed, in heaven.

'Want to go for a boat trip?' he asked, smiling.

He helped her into the smaller boat, started the engine, and steered into the current. Eirian lost herself to the wind in her face, the sun, the steep forested banks on either side. Here and there stood a mansion in its own private forest. Otherwise it seemed a wilderness, no one else alive under the piercingly clear sky.

Eirian stood with her arm around Gabriel's waist as he steered the boat in a U-turn and headed home. He kissed her with cold spray on his mouth. The moment he'd moored the boat, they seized each other wordlessly and sank down on to the wet deck. As he pulled off her T-shirt she thrust her breasts into his hands, gasping with pleasure. His long, muscular thighs intersected with hers, squeezing. Her loins throbbed. His hands came gliding over her buttocks to push down her bikini bottom, while she undid his shorts and found his penis, already hard and swollen. Eirian held her breath. The prospect of the silken, purplish head inside her turned her to liquid gold. There was a quick struggle to shake the garments over their ankles. Then he was entering her, his legs scissored between hers, the smooth shaft gliding into her, their juices flowing thick and salty. It crossed her mind that they'd forgotten the usual protection, but she was too far gone to care.

The deck was hard at her back. Gabriel's hands felt wonderfully firm as they moulded her shoulders, breasts and buttocks. How urgent this was, yet infinite, slow as honey and so loving. They gasped and laughed, green and turquoise eyes meeting in rapture. Yes, Eirian thought, this is what my mother has with my father; I understand, I feel it, I'm not left out any longer . . .

He was an angel. A white halo of hair, body of gilded ivory. Behind her eyes all was flame, throbbing to a double heartbeat, winding tighter and tighter around two engorged plum-red nodes of urgency. Eirian cried out. This feeling was exquisite: approaching orgasm, knowing she couldn't stop. The soundless explosion, tipping her over the peak of a mountain to soar free, spiralling. And then the tingling pleasure of Gabriel's last deep thrusts, his face contorted with the same anguished bliss . . .

Nathaniel thought he would drown in her arms. She writhed under him as his semen burst into her, her climax so extreme it unnerved him. She was no innocent, passive victim, never had been. She was a temple whore, a priestess, a goddess. She was the primal devouring power he dreaded. But he couldn't fight her any more. She'd sucked him into the hot salty lake of her carnality and he wanted to stay there. To surrender to the honeyed fluids that bonded him to her.

He looked into her flushed face, so beautiful, and he thought, God help me, I feel love for her. This was not meant to happen. I love her.

He could feel himself melting into her beliefs, leaving behind the cold world of money and corruption for the seductive simplicity of nature. And he wasn't afraid, wasn't even disgusted at himself.

Nathaniel hugged her tighter so he didn't have to meet her eyes. The hot sun on his back was soporific. He couldn't think. His plans were in ruins. 'You'd better marry me, Eirian Rhys,' he whispered.

She said, 'Oh, don't spoil it. Just be my lover.'

'Who are those people?' Eirian asked later. They were sitting at a white wrought-iron table on the patio, drinking beers which a dour maid had brought. The garden glowed green, humming with insects.

'What people?'

'I keep seeing men around. Always in the distance, like they don't want me to see them.'

'They're my staff. Gardeners and so on.'

'I've never seen gardeners with suits and mobile phones before.'

'I have a few security guys. They're trained to be discreet when I have guests.'

'Oh,' said Eirian, reassured. 'I didn't know editors were so well-paid.'

Gabriel smiled but he seemed preoccupied. He'd been quiet since they returned from the boat trip. Like he'd been after the first time they made love. Eirian was puzzled. She was about to ask if anything was wrong when he glanced up past her shoulder, suddenly looking displeased. 'I have a visitor. Excuse me.' Eirian turned and saw, on the steps from the house to the patio, a black man in a colourful shirt, shorts and a single gold stud earring. He was good-looking but very thin, like a whip. For a moment Eirian received only that surface impression. Gabriel rose from his chair. 'Come in the house, Gil,' he said severely.

'Aren't you going to introduce me to your girlfriend?' said Gil. He started down the steps but Gabriel intercepted him. Gil's expression was mock-friendly, shrewd and cruel, and suddenly she caught a psychic flash from him. She recoiled..

'No, I'm not.' Gabriel steered Gil into the house. She saw them through the big smoky windows, arguing as they vanished into the interior. Eirian sipped her beer and waited.

'It's done,' said Gil, dropping a polaroid on the desk in Nathaniel's study. There was a picture of a man lying in a pool of blood, his dark suit hanging on his bloated body. Paul Gregory Keay, banished into obscurity and now gone for ever.

'You'll get your money,' Nathaniel said shortly. He met Gil's insolent eyes. 'How dare you come here without prior notice? Whoever let you through will be out of a job in fifteen minutes. Don't you ever try to approach her again!'

'Hey, I'm sorry, man!' said Gil, raising his hands palms outwards. 'I don't work without a contract. It's not a fuckin' hobby.'

'There will be no contract on her. Ever.'

'Sure.' Gil's full mouth bowed in a smile. He nodded knowingly. 'You've gone soft, boss. Don't tell me you've fallen in love with her, it's just too touching.'

Nathaniel felt himself tensing with irritation. 'I'm going to marry her.'

'You're what?'

'It's part of the plan. I made her fall in love with me; she'll do anything for me. You think you have a demanding job, Gilmour; let me tell you, *killing* your enemy is easy. But to seduce her, twist her against everything she believes in, humiliate her and still have her worshipping you at the end – that is true art.'

'Bullshit,' Gil said softly. 'She's got you all wrapped up in her web and you can't even see it. You're gonna give up all your high and mighty ambitions, just because you can't keep your hands off the little bitch. She's got you there, man.' Gil pressed his thumb on the air. 'Don't get mad at me, sir; I'm only trying to make you stop and think before it's too late.'

'When I need your advice, I'll shoot myself,' Nathaniel said menacingly. 'Now get the hell out.'

When Gil had gone, Nathaniel set fire to the polaroid in an ashtray and absently watched it burn. The blinds were drawn, the wood-panelled walls dark. His ears filled with the whoosh of the air conditioning, the chorus of crickets outside. He sat brooding, forcing himself to take a painfully objective look at his motives.

Gil was right, the bastard.

He remembered his surrender on the boat and felt sick at himself. Eirian had nearly tricked him with her witchy sexual power. God, she took me for a fool! Everything I ever fought against – and still I trip up and drop right down into her snake-pit!

He railed against himself. He wrestled with his own stupidity, the blind stupidity of all men. Beads of sweat dribbled down his back. Screaming silently he dashed his fists against his forehead, threw the ashtray across the room. It dented the wall and broke on the floor, scattering hot ash.

The fit was over. He sat shaking at the narrowness of his escape. I can't afford to love her. I don't love her. I nearly fell but no, she didn't get me, I saw the trap and pulled back just in time. Oh, God, she's dangerous. But by God, she won't win.

He thought bitterly of his mother, whose betrayal and desertion had killed his father. If even the sweetest woman in the world turned out to be a venal whore, there was no hope for the rest. What the hell was the point of marriage, if not to bind a woman to a man and prevent her ever escaping? It took heavy chains to stop them wandering off like cats on heat. Eirian was no different.

Nathaniel took the mush of sentimentality that she'd set festering in his soul, drew it up like snake venom, and spat it out. He was himself again. Cold, controlled, and right back on track.

Casually he strolled out on to the patio, kissed Eirian and sat down. 'Has that man gone?' she asked.

'Yes.'

'Does he work for you?'

'Just a business associate. Why?'

She said in a shaky rush, 'He kills people for money.'

Nathaniel felt a frisson of anxiety. He could blank himself against her, but not other people, and she wasn't fully under his influence yet. 'What makes you say that?'

'I told you, I sometimes see inside people, like you do. Couldn't you see it for yourself?'

He cleared his throat. 'Not always, sweetheart. But I trust your judgement. I'll have him checked out, okay? If there's a problem I'll get the police on to him. Don't worry, honey.'

Eirian relaxed. After a few minutes she said, 'Did you mean it, about getting married?'

317

'I never say anything I don't mean.' He took her hand. Easy, now he was in control again. 'I've never felt anything like this before.'

'Neither have I,' she said, colouring. 'No one's ever understood me like you do. But I'm scared to rush into things. I just want to be with you.'

'You will be, sweetheart,' he said warmly. 'You will be.'

Eight days went by. Beth functioned, trying to shut her ears to the concerned advice of Rhianwen, Randolph, Steve and Dee. The only person who did not make a fuss about the situation was Olivia. For some reason, Beth found that a relief. Her mother seemed too wrapped up in her own life to notice Eirian was gone; she turned every minor event, from a leaking tap to an argument with Philip, into a major crisis that she simply couldn't tackle without Beth's help.

Eirian phoned every evening to say she was well and having a wonderful time, still refusing to give an address or number. Hopeless pushing her; she'd only put the phone down. When Eirian missed two evenings, Beth was frantic. But Eirian rang at last, sounding shaky and artificially cheerful, to say sorry but she'd had sunstroke. She was fine again now.

When the call ended, Beth sat rigid, looking at Morgan. 'She's changed,' said Beth. 'She's not the daughter I know. It's like being in love has turned her brain to cotton wool. Gabriel's turned her into this shallow person I don't recognize. Are we ever going to get her back?'

'Yes,' Morgan said firmly. 'Come to bed. Early night. Your mother's wearing you out.'

They lay in bed holding each other. They'd both been too tense to make love since Eirian had gone. Sex meant so much to them that they hardly dared admit how serious this was. Olivia and Gabriel had forced this wedge between them, and drove it a little deeper every day.

'Mum's asked me to go shopping tomorrow,' said Beth. 'I don't know how I'll find time.'

'Why can't she do her own shopping?' Morgan exclaimed.

'She needs a lot of help to get back on her feet. It's not easy for her.'

He'd been grudgingly tolerant until now. Suddenly the relief of Eirian's phone call seemed to unleash the tension between them. 'She's using you, Beth! How can she do it at a time like this? She doesn't care about anyone but herself! Say no to her, for God's sake!'

'I like my mother to need me,' Beth said stubbornly. 'At least helping her stops me thinking about Eirian and feeling useless all the time.'

'She's using you,' he repeated. 'She's up to something.'

'Why are you intent on believing the worst? I've never known her be so nice to me!'

'She's nice to you but ignores your lover and daughter. Charming. Beth, I'm not angry at you for being kind-hearted, but if you'd heard the things she said to me –'

Beth was stiff in his arms. 'Why are you doing this?'

'Trying to make you listen,' he said quietly. 'You wouldn't listen about Gabriel, either.'

A pang went through her. Dee's warning haunted her, but she daren't tell Morgan. She said, 'Has it occurred to you that if you hadn't blown up about it, Eirian might not have run off with him? What are you going to do next, beat up poor Peter or the shaman?'

He raised his head. 'What do you mean, the shaman?'

Beth cursed her indiscretion. 'Nothing.'

'No, come on, what? She's been having sex with the entity too?'

'She said they were dreams, that's all.'

'Dreams?' he gasped. 'When I met it, it was no bloody dream! Christ, Beth, how could you not tell me?'

He was trembling with anger. 'Because I knew you'd be upset,' said Beth.

'Yes, and if you'd been there when it attacked me, you'd know why! Jesus!'

'Did you hear a word Eirian said?' Beth retorted. 'She psychically healed it. It became devoted to her. She started having erotic dreams about it. For heaven's sake, I wasn't thrilled about it either, but I've had to live with the idea. Rhianwen and I tried to stop it, but we couldn't.'

A long, fraught silence stretched out between them. Eventually Morgan whispered, 'I can't believe you didn't tell me.'

'It was her choice to stop, not ours. Apparently she's given it up for Gabriel. Morgan, no one's assaulted her or raped her! It's what she wants. Do you know what you're doing, going mad at the entity or at Gabriel? You're punishing Eirian for having sexual feelings. Which is exactly what Olivia did to me.'

'That's ridiculous. Don't ever compare me with that woman.' His long, lithe body, usually so compliant, felt taut with rejection against hers. 'I tried to make peace with her, Beth. I abased myself, I practically fucking grovelled. Her response was to suggest that I want to sleep with my daughter. That hurt, Beth. That is fucking sick. But that's your miraculously reformed mother.'

Tears stung her eyes. She couldn't answer. She hated him because believing him would have been even worse than thinking he could lie to her.

Morgan disengaged his body from hers. He turned away on to his side and went to sleep, leaving Beth to stare at the dark alone.

'You know, I'm a little worried about the tone of the book,' said Gabriel, out of the blue. They were sitting in the gazebo, an octagonal open-sided summer house that jutted out above the creek. A small wooden bridge led back to the tree-shaded lawn; below them, the overgrown bank dropped to the water's edge.

'How d'you mean?' Eirian was worried. She'd increasingly come to rely on Gabriel's professional judgement over the past few days.

'In sounding so convinced that your way is right and all the others are wrong, you put yourself in the exact same position as any other evangelist. You could be as self-deluded and open to ridicule as they are. How do you know you're right?'

'Because I've felt the Goddess,' she said simply. 'I've seen her, spoken to her.'

'But others have felt and spoken to their own gods. What's the difference?'

As Eirian rallied what should have been an effortless response, she suddenly felt her thoughts slipping out of her grasp. The feeling was horrible, confusing. Then, aghast at herself, she thought, Gabriel's right. I could be just as deluded as Luke and not even know it!

There had been delicious mornings spent making love, afternoons working outside in the meltingly warm shade, evenings on the boat. One long narcotic indulgence of sensual pleasure. Drinking wine, feeding each other with fresh crabmeat, laughing, stroking each other's egos. And it had blunted her. She was almost too lazy and happy to think about the book any more. Too much in love.

So when Gabriel dripped this icy doubt on her, it stung like acid. 'If you're too radical, too blind to counter-argument,' he went on gently, 'you're no better than your grandmother, Olivia. A fanatic.'

Eirian frowned. 'How do you know about Olivia?'

'You told me, honey.'

'Did I? Yes, of course I did. Sorry, it's too hot to think straight.'

'Well, these are some of the arguments you'll come up against: that there never was universal Goddess-worship. That the idea of the Goddess is no better than the idea of God. It's just female ego, isn't it, having its revenge against the male? Where would we be now, if we were still worshipping nature and despising technology? Nowhere. In a stew of fat old women producing endless streams of grubby children while the men sit on their asses staring into space 'cos they're too emasculated to do a damn thing. At least the Bible gave us a way to live. A way forward. What did women ever do or create?'

His words crawled right inside her. She saw ugly images, felt her convictions fragmenting. Shaking herself out of it, she said, 'You think that's what people will say?'

'They will, sweetheart.' This was the moment, though she didn't realize it until later, that the idyll shifted from dream to nightmare. Gabriel became the devil's advocate and she couldn't argue, because she adored him. He added, 'Come on, tell me I'm wrong.'

'I can't think. It's so hot.'

'Maybe the Devil's talkin' through you after all.' He mimicked PGK. 'Maybe you should admit it and repent and be cleansed.'

His eyes were intent, hypnotic. A ghastly tremor shook her. 'Gabriel, stop it!'

'It's not me talking. It's what they'll say. Your enemies are very strong. They won't let one very young woman talk 'em down. Who's right, who's wrong?'

The gazebo tilted. Eirian felt the blood rushing out of her head while Gabriel's voice whispered on.

Then he screamed.

The shock electrified her, making her heart lurch painfully. Shrinking back on the wooden bench-seat, her vision cleared and she saw Gabriel outside on the lawn, pointing at something on the gazebo floor. She looked down and saw a small, creamy-beige snake. 'Get rid of it!' he shrieked.

Eirian pulled her feet up on to the seat. 'Is it poisonous?' She wasn't afraid, only cautious.

'No, just get it away from me.'

Eirian picked up the snake and dropped it into the bushes beyond the gazebo. 'It's gone.'

Gabriel came back, visibly shaking. His face was as white as his hair. 'Thank you,' he said, putting heavy arms round her and sighing into her neck.

'You scared the hell out of me!' she exclaimed. 'I thought you weren't frightened of anything!'

'Only that one little group of critters. Snakes. Oh boy.'

She hugged him, laughing. For now he'd shown her an

imperfect, vulnerable side of himself, she felt she really knew him, and loved him even more. 'Sorry I scared you,' he went on. 'Eirian, you saved me. What would I do without you now?'

There was a rushing sound in her ears. She became aware that she was shivering violently despite the heat. 'Gabriel, can we go in? I don't feel well.'

The next twenty-four hours were a blur. Eirian was vaguely aware of lying in bed in a dark room, Gabriel beside her giving her cool drinks, helping her to the bathroom now and then, stroking her forehead. 'You got heatstroke, honey. My fault, shoulda known you weren't used to this weather.'

He seemed to be talking continuously as she lay there, nightmarish words that filtered through her delirium. Perhaps it was only her fevered conscience talking; surely Gabriel couldn't say such vile things? 'You were wrong about the Goddess. As deluded as Olivia and Luke. So it wasn't okay to kill Luke after all. If you'd let him live, Beth and Olivia wouldn't be so sad and twisted now. All your fault. But that's the only way you know, isn't it? If you don't like it, kill it. But that's not clever or grown-up. It's selfish and sordid. It's murder, Eirian. Murder. Murder.'

'You can't make me feel guilty about Luke!' she gasped.

'He wasn't the only one. What about that sad old gypsy guy whose only crime was to love your mother? You cursed him. Messed up his mind so he'd have a horrible accident. Poor Bernard.'

'How do you know about that?' Everything looked white and she was spinning, weightless.

'I know everything, honey. Read your mind like a book. Real horror story, isn't it?'

'Bernard didn't love my mother. He tried to rape her! He deserved to die. You can't make me feel guilty!'

'Okay,' the whispering voice said reasonably. 'Let's talk about your mother losing a baby, and calling him Auryn, poor little soul, and nearly breaking her heart over him.'

The pain that gripped her head seemed to spread right through her. She thrashed against the fever but it imprisoned her. 'What?'

'You killed him too, Eirian. Not miscarriage. Forcible abortion.'

'No!'

'With your power, you could make it look natural. You can heal and kill with your mind, you don't need weapons. You knew your mother was pregnant before she did, and you were jealous. You didn't want to share your parents with a brother; that's real understandable, honey. So you cursed him. Pushed him out of the womb, dried up her tubes so she'd never conceive again.'

She was screaming hoarsely, breath rasping through her throat. 'No. No!'

'Maybe you didn't do it consciously. Deny it all you want – but in your heart, you know you did it. Murdered Auryn. Caused your parents all that pain. That's your power, Eirian. Sad and ugly. Can you really go on using it, after what you did? Because you're not a bad person. You can repent.'

Gabriel's eyes burned into her like the sky. He was an avatar of God, not condemning her, only bringing her to see the error of her own ways. Eirian sobbed in her fever. Her whole life was an illusion. 'I didn't mean to kill him,' she cried in anguish. 'I didn't mean to!'

'Sure you didn't,' he said gently. 'Everything's not lost. Don't cry, honey.'

By the second morning, Eirian was more lucid. She sat up in bed, drank a cup of weak tea, and surveyed the ruins of herself. 'There's no point in finishing the book, I suppose,' she said dully. 'It's gone, I've got nothing to say. What shall I do now?' She thought about Auryn and an unbearable pain darted through her. 'I can't go home, I can't ever go home.'

'This is your home,' said Gabriel. 'Stay here, marry me.'

She wept on his broad shoulder. 'It all seemed so real.

324

The Goddess and everything. Now I realize it was all in my mind.'

'If I'd taken you out of a cult, they'd call it deprogramming.'

She stared at him. 'So when you agreed with all my beliefs, you were pretending?'

'Eirian, I didn't know how else to win your trust. Forgive me. But I do love you. That's real.'

'Fucking hell,' she said bitterly.

Gabriel was attentive and kind all that day and the next. They were never apart. He cosseted her like an invalid, and at night they made tender, emotional love. When she called Beth, Eirian convinced her mother that she was fine, she'd just had a touch of sunstroke. Beth sounded resigned but unhappy. Eirian had to blank her mind against the misery she'd caused her mother; she couldn't cope with it. I've never caused her anything else, Eirian thought. That's why I can't go back.

On the fourth night she felt like gossamer, wholly at the mercy of the wind. She belonged completely to Gabriel, his to kiss and heal and nurture. 'I love you,' he whispered over the chirp of insects and frogs outside their window. 'I'll help you. We'll be together and make wonderful love like this and be happy.'

'Yes,' said Eirian. Nothing else seemed to matter. This was all she had now.

'You really are a stupid little bitch,' he said in the same sweet tone, 'believing all that shit.'

For a moment she couldn't believe what he'd said. 'What, about the Goddess?'

'No, the shit about me loving you. Had you fooled, eh?'

Her heart froze. 'Stop it! This isn't funny.'

'It's not meant to be.' Gabriel rose over her, pinning her wrists on to the mattress. She had the sudden, hideous feeling that he'd sucked all her life-force into himself. She was a shell. 'You thought you'd got me but you're not even close, witch.'

'Don't.' She struggled, not making too much fuss in case it was all a joke. 'You're scaring me.'

'Be scared, you fucking whore. You think you can kill me

like you murdered Luke? No, your power could never touch mine. But even if you had any left, you wouldn't dare use it. Not after Auryn.'

He spoke the truth. She felt like water, strengthless. 'Gabriel!'

He slapped her. Not enough to bruise, just hard enough to shock her. 'Do you know who I am? Do you know what you've done? Of course not.'

'What's the matter with you? You're hurting me!' She was very frightened now. She fought to escape but he pressed her down brutally.

'Say, "I renounce the Goddess," and I'll stop.'

'I renounce the Goddess!'

He let her go and smiled lovingly at her. 'Easy, wasn't it?'

Eirian lay trembling and confused, rubbing at her sore wrists and cheek. 'Why have you changed?'

'I haven't changed. You have.' Eirian tried to sit up but he pulled her down again.

'Please stop this! What have I done wrong?'

'Been born.'

'Why?'

'I don't know, why were you born? You were an accident, no one wanted you.' His beautifully shaped mouth curved into a smile and he kissed her. 'Lesson over,' he said.

She stared at him, breathing hard in fear. 'What lesson?'

'You don't know what's real and what isn't. You don't know if I'm a nice guy or a bastard. You don't know if I love you or not. So how can you presume to tell other people what's real? I think you have some apologizing to do.'

'This is making no sense. What do you want?'

'If I told you, would you do it?'

'If I could, yes.'

'All right, sweetheart.' Gabriel's angelic eyes flooded her mind, as Luke's never had. Luke had never got inside her like this – but then, she'd never loved Luke. 'You are going to appear on coast-to-coast, prime-time television, like before. Only this time you are going to renounce all your pagan beliefs. Tell the world you were horribly wrong. Then you will announce that you've found God, repented and been born-again, courtesy of the loving ministrations of your friends at the True Light Network.'

She was paralysed. Finally she managed to swallow drily and say, 'That would be a lie.'

'So? It's what folk believe that matters. Some will say, "Those evangelists have gotten hold of her and brainwashed her." But the others, the ones who matter, will say, "Hallelujah, praise the Lord!"'

She swallowed again. Her throat felt solid. 'I don't know anyone at TLN.'

'Sure you do. You know someone very, very well.' He slid his fingers roughly into her vagina, hurting. 'I run the fuckin' joint. How can I maintain you in the lavish lifestyle you've been so enjoying, if folk don't start sending me their life-savings again?'

Eirian closed her eyes. Betrayal hit her like a wall but she felt too numb to cry. Couldn't think straight. Part of her still hoped Gabriel would announce it was a ghastly joke. But she knew it was real. Gabriel had taken her over, body and soul. And she couldn't fight back because she'd killed Auryn and that made her worthless.

As she lay there, Gabriel rolled on to her and forced his sudden erection inside her. She remained inert as he thrust roughly into her, his hands pressing on her wrists. He came quickly, grunting. This is rape, Eirian thought. But she stared past his shoulder, feeling nothing.

Now he smiled, his eyes dancing. 'Yes, Eirian, you've been well and truly fucked.'

In the morning, they had breakfast on the patio, served by the harassed-looking maid. The sun shone, the garden was exotically lush. But the beauty was soulless. Eirian sipped fresh orange juice and nibbled at pancakes with maple syrup, tasting nothing. She'd become a hollow-headed wax puppet.

'So, you're religious after all?' she said.

Gabriel threw his head back and laughed. He looked as

angelic as ever, but she could see the falseness of the mask now – only the mask, no deeper. 'No, no. There's no God up there, honey; no Goddess, either. All hogwash.'

'But you run a Christian channel.'

He leaned forward on the white metal table. 'I have strong beliefs but they're nothing to do with religion. I believe in power. Wealth. Control. Religion's the opiate of the masses, all right, or whatever the guy said. If the stupid jerks think they can save their souls by sending me money they can barely afford, they deserve to get ripped off. The point is, that's how you control 'em. Put the fear of God into them and the rest follows. Order and obedience.'

'Brainwashing.'

'So? Do you really think I want your kind of world, full of witches and queers and niggers?'

The words sounded unbelievably ugly on his perfect lips. But he was beginning to look ugly to Eirian now. He went on, 'I discovered I had this power over people very young. I can see inside and manipulate 'em. In theory I'm the chairman of the board of TLN; in practice I am God. I set it up, I got everyone obeying my every whim. How d'you think I got where I am so young? Never saw anyone else with the same power until I saw you. I knew how dangerous you were going to be.'

'Dangerous to what? A right-wing America with everyone, especially women, kept in their place by the Bible?'

'Everything under control. Yes.'

'How boring,' Eirian said coldly. 'I thought you were such an exciting person, Gabriel. But all you can think of to do with your power is something that predictable?' There was a flash of rage in his eyes. She knew his potential for violence now, but she no longer cared what she said. He could kill her; she wouldn't feel it.

'The simplest plans are the most effective,' he said. 'Life has to be controlled. You wanted anarchy. Woman are sexually unhinged. Their promiscuity would destroy society if we let it. You're as bad as the rest, Eirian. Open your legs for anyone, don't you? Women have to be controlled.'

'You told me your mother walked out,' Eirian said tonelessly. Not hard to analyse him, after all. 'You never forgave her, did you? The one thing mothers are not meant to do is abandon their young. She went from madonna to whore in one step, betrayed her hero-husband and adoring son. So now you hate all women for having that power to kill with rejection.'

'Quite the little psychologist, aren't you? You coulda had one hell of a career. Shame you won't even make it to university.'

'Did you never wonder if it was your father's fault she left?' Eirian went on. 'Your father was as cold as ice. That's why your mother left him. Cold and judgemental. Did he make you polish your boots and keep your closet like an army locker? You say you're an atheist. Is he your God instead? Lifelong battle to prove yourself to that demanding Father above, isn't it?'

'Shut the fuck up,' he said, soft but emphatic. He was trying hard not to show it but she'd riled him.

Eirian took a sip of coffee. The cup rattled against the saucer as she replaced it. 'You've controlled me. Is that what you wanted?'

'Of course. Coupla days, and you'll be ready to make your announcement. We'll get huge publicity. It'll be just wonderful.' And he was looking warmly at her as if he loved her again.

'No,' Eirian said quietly. 'I won't do it.'

Smiling, Gabriel dropped his napkin on his plate and walked off. The worried-looking maid appeared and began to clear the table. She was younger than Eirian had thought, but horribly pallid, as if life had worn her to nothing. When she spoke suddenly, it made Eirian jump. 'You'd better obey him. He'll make you do anything he damn well wants.'

'What business is it of yours?' Eirian gasped.

'Oh, none.' The woman gathered china on to the tray with bony, shaking hands. 'I'm only his wife.'

'No,' Eirian gasped. 'You're lying.'

The maid shrugged. Her tone was vitriolic. Eirian sat paralysed as another layer of illusion was sandpapered away. 'I had ideals once, just like you. I was a women's rights lawyer. But

I fell in love with him and now I can't string two thoughts together. I just watch him doing the same thing to women like you, who come here thinking they're so clever. And the God-awful thing is that I still love him. So will you. No one ever leaves him, except maybe in a hearse.'

Ten days after Eirian had gone, Morgan answered the telephone, expecting it to be her. Instead he heard a gruff American voice that he didn't recognize at first. 'Morgan? Hi, it's Jamie Baker, I'm calling from New York. Suzanne was in touch. I'm real sorry to hear about Eirian. Anyway, I had some people make enquiries about this Gabriel Jordan. Found out some stuff I don't think anyone is meant to know and it's not good news, my friend.'

Morgan sat down on the arm of a chair, the phone on his knee. He was alone; Beth was round at her mother's again. 'Okay, go on.'

'Silver Dove Books exists all right but they put out some very dubious publications. The theology's hard-line fundamentalist stuff. The books on witchcraft and other beliefs, if you actually read them, set out to ridicule the subject. Gabriel Jordan is a director, not a hands-on editor.'

'But he said his bosses sent him.'

'No, he *is* the boss. What Suzanne wouldn't know, 'cos of the convoluted ways these companies are set up, is that Silver Dove Books is owned by the same organization as the True Light Network.'

'But they're Bible-bashers! That PGK is the arsehole who tried to humiliate Eirian!'

'Yup. And he got his come-uppance, didn't he? TLN is run and controlled by one Nathaniel De Vries. No one knows him well but it seems his staff regard him as some kinda charismatic leader. They love him but they're scared shitless of him. He's an empire-builder and he's ruthless. Anyway, I've gathered enough evidence to be ninety-nine per cent certain that Gabriel Jordan and Nathaniel De Vries are the same person.'

'Christ. I knew he wasn't straight!'

'Well, I don't think he's doing anything illegal, but it seems he's misled you.'

'Why? What would he want with Eirian? He'd have no reason to think PGK's lapse was her fault . . . would he?' As the puzzle clicked horribly into place, Jamie voiced Morgan's thoughts.

'Whatever, Nathaniel wouldn't appreciate her speaking out against TLN's propaganda. Or reducing his network's takings by around twenty per cent. Maybe he decided to do something about it.'

'Oh, God,' Morgan whispered. 'Jamie, did you find out his home address?'

'No luck there. He's a multi-millionaire, he could have houses all over the States under false names. Silver Dove in Baltimore is just a mailing address. The only address I can give you for certain is the TLN studios in Atlanta.'

'Go ahead.' Morgan picked up a pen and notepad. When he'd taken the address, he said, 'Jamie, I really appreciate you taking the trouble to do this.'

'You're welcome, my friend. Your daughter's one special young lady, I hate to think of those bastards . . .' He trailed off. 'You want me to call the police?'

'No, not yet. Eirian might just vanish off the face of the earth if we do that. She thinks she's in love, she won't want to believe anything bad about Gabriel. Nathaniel.'

'So what do you want to do about it?'

'Beth and I will fly straight over there. I can't stand waiting around any longer, and neither can she.'

'Be careful,' Jamie said gravely. 'Be very careful.'

Chapter Eighteen

Olivia stood clutching the note, anger searing through her chest and head. Her rage was physical pain. Her head throbbed and she couldn't breathe.

She'd come home from the shop and found the note on her doormat. 'Dear Mum, I called round but you were out. This is to let you know that Morgan and I are flying to America to find Eirian. We're off to Heathrow tomorrow, flying to Atlanta early the next morning. Will you be okay on your own? Come round as soon as you can, Love, Beth.'

Olivia's fist pressed the note into a tight ball. Ever since Gabriel – she'd trained herself not to call him Joshua – had gone back to America, her life had been falling apart. With Gabriel around she'd felt safe, confident and worthy. But without him . . . Torture to think of him with Eirian, that unholy little slut. He'd sworn he would never touch her, so what was he doing with Eirian in his hotel room? 'Nothing was happening, Olivia, it was just a trap for her parents,' Gabriel reassured her afterwards. An angel couldn't tell lies – or could he?

Olivia no longer knew what to believe. In the end she decided to trust Gabriel, because he was all she had – and because even if he *had* touched Eirian, it was only to destroy her. She went to the telephone and dialled with unsteady hands. She had a secret number. When Gabriel answered, his soothing voice reached her across the Atlantic as if he were right by her shoulder.

'Gabriel, they're coming. I'm worried they've found something out about you.' She explained what the note had said but he reacted calmly.

'That's great. That's fine. You know what you have to do now, don't you?'

His voice made her feel better. 'Yes.'

'Call me again when you have some more news. It's happening, Olivia, this is your time. All your dreams are about to come true. You're gonna know I kept my promises.'

A spasm went through her. Her eyes blurred with tears. 'I already know. Oh, Luke. Gabriel, I mean.'

'God bless you, sister,' he said smoothly. 'You have holy work to do and souls to save. Go to it, Olivia. Improvise. And hey, enjoy yourself! You deserve it.'

The line went dead. As Olivia replaced the receiver she felt strange; panicky and excited yet detached. Trembling, she felt the Holy Spirit moving inside her, directing her fallen soul towards salvation.

The news about Gabriel left Beth in a state of shock. She'd spent days trying to convince herself that everything was fine, Eirian would soon come to her senses. Like watching a boulder teetering on a cliff-edge, telling herself, no, it won't fall. Now the truth had come crashing down.

Beth felt relieved at Morgan's decision to fly to Atlanta. Doing nothing had been unbearable.

'When Eirian rings, do we tell her what we found out?' asked Beth. She and Morgan were in the dining room, picking at a meal that neither of them really wanted.

'I don't see how we can,' said Morgan. 'What if Gabriel's listening on the extension, or she confronts him about it? He could turn nasty. No, we'll just act normal and hope to the Goddess we find her. Don't say anything to your mother either.'

'I agree with you.'

'Well, that makes a change.' Silence. The doorbell rang and Morgan pulled a face. 'Guess who.'

When Beth answered, Olivia was there looking dreadful; her hair was a mess, her face waxen. 'Oh, Beth, could I stay with you tonight? I don't feel well. I think I'm getting the 'flu.'

'Oh,' said Beth, concerned. 'Yes, of course. Come in.' Olivia went through to the sitting room, carrying an overnight bag.

'You've got your nightie and that, have you? Sit down. Have you had a meal?'

'I couldn't eat,' Olivia sighed, pressing a hand to her forehead. 'I feel shivery, my head's pounding.'

'Okay. I'll make you a hot-water bottle and a drink.' Morgan appeared in the doorway and stood gazing cynically at Olivia. 'When did you start feeling ill, Mum?'

'When I came back from the shop this afternoon.'

'As soon as she found the note,' Morgan said drily.

Olivia looked blank. 'What note?'

'Mum, we're going to America the day after tomorrow. To bring Eirian home.'

Olivia tipped her head back, blue eyes fixed on the ceiling, unblinking. She seemed in genuine distress. 'Oh, don't let me stop you going. Daughters will do this to their mothers, won't they, dear?'

Morgan said, 'Fuck,' under his breath and walked out. Beth followed him into the kitchen and switched on the kettle. 'Everything's sorted out,' he said. 'We drive to Heathrow tomorrow afternoon, spend the night in a hotel, and pick up the tickets at the airport first thing.'

'Yes, I know.'

'If she still thinks she's got the 'flu tomorrow, you'll have to find someone else to look after her.'

Beth bit her tongue to stop herself shouting at him.

While Beth was fussing over her mother, Eirian rang. She sounded more wooden and unlike herself than ever. Afterwards, Beth went back into the kitchen and had a solitary struggle not to break down. She won. Then Morgan came in, looking grim. 'I don't know what your mother's playing at. She hasn't said one word about Eirian. All she thinks about is herself.'

Beth had had enough. 'You've got something in common, then,' she snapped, taking her coat from a hook by the back door. 'You want someone else to look after her? You do it for a couple of hours!'

'What?' He looked horrified. 'Where are you going?'

'To the workshop,' she said, pulling on her boots. 'There's some work I need to finish.'

'Beth!' he cried, but she grabbed her van keys and walked out. She felt wretched; not because of the quarrel itself but because it seemed to spell the end of everything. If Morgan couldn't accept something as simple as her love for her mother, what hope was there?

The workshop was eerie at night, shadowy, deserted and chilly. Beth meant to finish a commission but found herself creating something unplanned instead. She worked automatically, concentrating but not thinking. When she finished it was as if she'd come out of a trance. She held up the panel to the light and saw a white figure on a red background; an angel on a sea of blood. A splinter of clear glass went from its feet to its chest, like a serpent or a horn. There were drops of dark crimson flowering from its tip.

The image filled Beth with foreboding. Glancing at her watch, she saw in dismay that four hours had passed. She tucked the panel under her arm and went home.

Being as detached and civil as he could, Morgan showed Olivia to the spare room, made sure she was comfortable, and left her to it. She did look genuinely unwell, it was true. But he was beyond having any kind feelings towards her.

At eleven he went to bed. Beth still wasn't home; he knew she forgot the time when she was working, so he was only slightly worried. He slept restlessly for a while. Then, to his relief, he felt Beth climbing into bed with him.

Hoping she'd stopped being angry, he slipped his arms around her, his penis stirring against her warm, bare thighs. 'Hello, babe,' he murmured, half asleep. 'I'm glad you're back.'

But the shape and the scent of her body were all wrong. Too angular, the hips too broad and bony. Wrong perfume, short hair. Waxy lips pressing against his cheek.

Horror flared through him. In a panic he pulled away and fumbled for the bedside light. Peachy light illuminated Olivia's face and bleached-blonde hair. She was wearing bright red lipstick which had smeared and her eyes were softly demented, a parody of seduction.

'What the fuck are you doing?' Morgan gasped.

'Beth's not here,' she said breathily. 'You want me, don't you?'

'Are you crazy?'

'Don't send me away, Morgan. I was so lonely in that cottage on my own.' Her hands came floating over his shoulders and chest. Morgan was so shocked he didn't know how to react. Only when her hand went drifting towards his groin did he grab her wrist and stop her. 'Jesus, Olivia! What the hell are you playing at? Stop it!'

'Don't pretend to be outraged,' she said softly. The lamplight softened her face and she looked pretty, her blonde fringe falling into her eyes. 'You want me, I've seen the way you look at me.'

To his dismay, he realized he had an erection. Bloody thing had a mind of its own. He was naked, so how the hell could he get out of bed? 'Don't be ridiculous. You're my sister.'

'So? That didn't stop you screwing my daughter. Why stop at your niece?'

Reaching for his dressing gown, which was on a chair just out of his reach, Morgan half fell out of bed and dragged the garment round himself. 'Look, just get out and go to your own room. We'll pretend this never happened.'

'You bastard!' she hissed. Then, to his consternation, her head drooped and she began to weep. 'Don't send me away, Morgan. I'm so lonely. I miss Philip and Luke so much, I don't know what to do.'

'Oh, shit,' said Morgan. It was impossible to hate her when she sat there looking so pathetic. 'Look, I'll make you some tea.' Seeing her discarded nightdress by the bed, he passed it to her. 'Put this back on.'

As he went out on to the landing, he heard a sound and saw Beth climbing the stairs towards him, the cats following her. Her hair and clothes sparkled with rain. 'Hi,' she sighed. 'Sorry I'm so late. Can we talk? I don't want us to go away not speaking to each other.'

'Nor me.' He put his arms round her. Her lips parted as she slid her hand under his robe to grasp his penis, which was still semi-erect. 'Oh, you are pleased to see me, after all! I wasn't sure you would be.' As Morgan searched for something to say, Beth looked more closely at him and frowned. 'What's that red stuff on your cheek? It looks like – ' She stopped. The sound of Olivia sobbing flowed out of the bedroom, loud and distinct. 'What's going on?'

Helpless, Morgan followed Beth as she entered the bedroom. Olivia was sitting up in bed, weeping. Her nightdress was on her lap, her shoulders hunched around her long breasts. Beth stopped in the doorway and stared; Morgan felt like dying. Olivia looked up, clutched the garment over herself and leapt out of bed.

'Oh, Beth!' she cried. Beth went white and the look she gave Morgan flayed him. 'I only came in because I felt so alone. I thought you were here but you weren't and he tried – he tried to have sex with me.'

'That's crap!' Morgan protested, quickly wiping the lipstick stain off his face. 'I was fast asleep and I woke up to find her climbing into bed beside me!'

Beth was as stiff as marble. Very matter-of-fact, she said, 'Go to bed, Mum. I'll bring you a drink.' She marched away along the landing, Morgan pursuing her.

'Look, Beth, I'm telling the truth. She got into bed with me with no kit on and said she felt lonely. I was so shocked I didn't know what to do. I told her to leave and she burst into tears. That's all.'

'You had a hard-on!' Beth flared.

They entered the kitchen. Beth switched on the light; Morgan sat down at the table and propped his head on his hands. 'Only because I thought she was you for about three seconds. It was an automatic reaction; it happens, you know? It doesn't mean I wanted to screw her!'

'That's what they all say.'

'You don't believe I tried, do you?'

'Oh, no, I'm willing to believe it happened like you said.

337

She got in and covered you with lipstick. What I can't accept is that you apparently enjoyed it!'

'No! Oh, bloody hell. Beth, calm down.'

'I'm very calm. I'm spitting ice cubes. How do you expect me to be when I come home and find my mother naked in my lover's bed?' Olivia came in, wrapped in a thick dressing gown and looking downcast. Morgan got up to leave but Beth snapped at him, 'Don't move!'

Olivia began to cry again. 'Beth, it's all my fault. I didn't know you weren't there. I needed some comfort. Morgan mis-understood – but it was my fault.'

Beth sat down suddenly, her hand to her mouth. 'I don't want to hear any more. One of you is lying to me. I don't want to hear it!'

'I'll go, then,' Olivia said, her face drawn. 'I'm not well. I'm so sorry to have caused all this trouble.' But as she stood up, she gave Morgan a brief, hard stare that Beth didn't notice. The look was knowing, calculating, and completely sane.

Morgan waited for her to go back upstairs then said, 'Can't you see what she's trying to do to us?'

'Morgan, she's ill! She got into bed with you in a confused state and you thought – what? "Oh, great, Beth'll never know?"'

'You're determined to blame me, not her, aren't you? Beth, nothing happened. Forgive me, please. Talk to me. I know you're upset.'

'I'm more than upset. I don't know what I feel. I feel . . . dead.' Morgan stood up and she looked up sharply. 'Where are you going?'

'Back to bed. I don't know what else to say to you.'

Morgan lay awake most of the night, but Beth didn't join him. The thought of Olivia – and his own treacherous excite-ment – made him feel sick. And the memory of Beth's anguish left him chilled to the bone by regret. He felt she'd been in the wrong before, but now he was. And there was no way to put it right.

Her fucking mother's always wanted to wreck everything between us. And she's done it. Taken our love and killed it, in the name of her God.

A wave of pain went through him but he let it go. I have to distance myself from all this, he decided. The only thing that matters now is finding Eirian.

In the morning, Beth found Olivia acutely ill. She was feverish, shivering and distressed. Every time Beth made to leave the bedroom, her mother seemed terrified and begged her not to go. And yet, Beth thought furiously, Morgan had the nerve to blame Mum for last night!

Morgan came in, his face impassive. Beth was infuriated by his ability to switch off. 'Beth, are you going to pack, or what? We have to go in a couple of hours.'

'I'm not going,' said Beth. 'Not with Mum like this.'

His dark eyebrows drew together. 'She's faking it. She's trying to control you.'

'Of course she isn't! Look at her! I don't think it's 'flu, I think she's having a breakdown.'

'Great timing.'

'No, maybe the hospital released her too soon. Mental illnesses are just as real as physical ones.'

'She's perfectly sane in her own twisted way. She wants to separate us and lessen the chances of us finding Eirian. And you're letting her get away with it.'

'But if you're wrong!'

He was calm but hostile. 'All right, suppose she really is ill. Surely your grandfather could look after her?' Even now, Morgan rarely called Randolph *my father*.

'She won't talk to him! I'm all she's got. She needs me.'

'Right. I'm not going to argue,' he said flatly. 'You're putting this scheming old bitch before Eirian? Fine. At least we know where we all stand. Well, I'm ready, I may as well go.'

And he walked out. Beth followed him, in anguish. 'How can you be so callous? Of course I want to come with you, I hate having to choose, but she's the only mother I've got. This is the first chance I've had to have a real relationship with her and all you want to do is ruin it!'

Unmoved, Morgan said, 'All I want to do at this moment is find Eirian.'

His coldness stabbed her. Wounded, Beth became cold in return. 'You'd better go, then.'

'When I come back with Eirian – *when*, not if – we'd better talk about what we're going to do.'

He means whether we should split up, she thought. Christ. A wave of sickening pain went through her but she swallowed it. 'Morgan, I hate this, but I can't help it. One moment you're in bed with her, the next you despise her again – can't you see, by rejecting my mother, how cruel you're being to me? I'm not sure I can forgive you.'

'If she'd been sincere, I wouldn't have said a word. I'm sorry. But at least I didn't put her before our daughter. Maybe I can't forgive you for that.' His face flickered with hopeless irony. He gave her a brief, dry kiss on the cheek. 'I'll phone. 'Bye.'

'Morgan,' she said quickly. A tear ran down her cheek. 'Have you got your passport? Don't forget your driving glasses either. Shit, I'm not very good at acting cool.'

'Me neither.' He looked down at the floor, shaking his dark head. Then he gripped her hand. 'Change your mind.'

'I can't. But please take care, come back quickly.'

He nodded. 'I will. I love you.' Unexpectedly he dragged Beth back to the door of her mother's room and gave her a long, passionate kiss in full view of Olivia. 'For Eirian's sake, come to your senses,' he whispered as he hugged her. Then he left quickly before they could stall or argue any more.

Beth went to a window on the landing and watched Morgan's car pulling away. She hugged herself, feeling churned up and bereft. However angry she felt, it was still unbearable to see him leaving without her.

From the guest room she heard her mother's plaintive voice. 'Beth? Beth, come and sit with me. I can't bear to be alone.'

*

Olivia refused to see a doctor, insisting she only needed Beth's care. Beth relented. Her mother was feverish, not at death's door. Beth gave her aspirin and herbal potions. By the afternoon, Olivia had recovered enough to get up and lie on the sofa.

When Eirian called that evening, Beth thought she sounded less like her real self than before. Beth didn't tell her Morgan was on his way, yet something in her voice must have alerted Eirian. 'Mum, are you all right?' Eirian asked.

'Yes. Your grandma Olivia's poorly, that's all.'

'I'm sorry,' said Eirian. 'I'm not sure I can call tomorrow. Gabriel's taking me somewhere.'

'Where?'

'Don't know. I'll call when I can. Take care, 'bye.'

Afterwards, Beth sat with her head in her hands, agonized. Then she did something she'd very rarely done in her life. She opened a bottle of vodka and began to get drunk. If her mother disapproved, tough. But Olivia, who was huddled under a blanket on the sofa, said, 'Aren't you going to pour me one, dear?'

Beth was astonished. 'You don't drink!'

'I can start, can't I?'

'Well, okay.' Beth poured a small measure and drowned it with tonic. Giving her mother the drink, she settled on the carpet, leaning back against the sofa arm, the vodka bottle at her elbow. Soon the alcohol began to envelop her, warming, numbing. Her mother's hand played on her hair.

'It's so nice to have you to myself,' said Olivia. 'I'm so glad you stayed with me.'

'I couldn't leave you.' Beth released a long, quiet sigh. Never in her life had she dreamed that she would sit drinking with her mother, that they'd talk to each other like equals. It was all she'd ever wanted.

Flashback to a scene many years ago. Olivia, mad-eyed with fury, dragging Luke up the stairs with quotes from the Bible, *'Now no chastening for the present seemeth to be joyous . . .'* and the muffled sound of blows and Luke's piteous cries. Olivia and her church cronies brutalizing Beth in an effort to exorcize Morgan's demonic baby from her womb . . .

A voice in Beth's head said, how can I sit with this woman, letting her stroke my hair? If Morgan's right . . . no, no. She deserves a chance to change.

The past few weeks had taught Beth that she had nothing in common with her mother. Now it seemed that their religious differences, far from driving them apart, had been their only passionate link. Beth could hardly bear to admit it, but the truth was that she didn't even like her mother very much. Loved her, yes, but didn't like her.

'I know Eirian can look after herself,' said Beth. 'She's a true witch. She's stronger than me, she was born to her power in a way I never was. Being a witch isn't about black magic or casting spells, Mum. It's about being proud to be female, not ashamed. Seeing your body and sexuality as sacred, not sinful. Taking responsibility for yourself instead of swallowing the dogma of some great holy man. It's about loving life.'

Olivia was silent, but at least she was listening. That was a first. Beth went on, 'Morgan doesn't mean to be hostile. He'll come round. When he gets home we'll start again and you'll see what he's really like. You don't begrudge us being happy, surely? I've always adored him, I couldn't live without him. I want us all to get on well and be a family.'

'But we don't need anyone else,' Olivia said soothingly. 'If he and the girl don't come back, never mind. What good is a man like Morgan, cruel and heartless? If he can sleep with his niece and his sister, why should he stop at his mother – or his daughter?'

The words slipped innocuously into Beth's mind then began to fizzle like acid. 'Mum, don't!'

'And what use is Eirian to you, anyway? She killed my Luke.'

'That's enough.'

'She killed her brother.' Beth thought her mother was confused and still meant Luke, until Olivia went on, 'Eirian didn't want you to have that baby, Beth. She was jealous. She's too selfish to share anything, so she made sure she didn't have to.'

The whole room seemed to throb in time with Beth's heart-beat. I didn't hear that, she thought, shaking her head in violent denial. She said quickly, 'I miscarried. It happens.' But memories rose, horribly poisoned by the insinuation; Eirian crying, *'How can I compete with Auryn? You wish you'd miscarried me instead!'* Surely she can't have willed me to lose him . . . can she? 'No, no, Eirian wouldn't do that!'

'How can you ever be sure?' Olivia's face was serene. 'So if they don't come back it's no loss. You still have me. You're mine, Beth. You were meant to be with me for eternity, my little gift from God.'

Beth poured another splash of vodka and drank it. The nearly neat spirit burned, bringing tears to her eyes. 'Mum, please stop. You're ill, you don't know what you're saying.'

Olivia smiled, raising her glass. 'Loosens the truth, doesn't it?' She giggled. 'The tongue, I mean.'

'You're drunk!' Beth couldn't bear to hear any more.

'So? You gave me vodka, of course I'm drunk. Oh, Beth, you were always such a touchy little girl, like a scared kitten. But such an angel. Your poor old mother doesn't know what she's saying. But you've been so lovely to me, I'm glad we've grown so very close. Aren't you?'

Later, as Beth lay in bed, the warmth of intoxication faded to leave her awash in sickening doubt. How could her mother have said such things? The bed was achingly empty. She'd forgotten how it felt to miss Morgan. His absence was tormenting. Beth dreamed she was fourteen again and pregnant, her mother standing over her with a strap in her hand and her eyes all mad anger. *'Satan works through that boy, you little whore! How could you?'*

Beth sat up in alarm, only to find she was alone. She felt stale and heavy-headed. She got up, drew back the curtain, and looked out.

The panel she'd made of the sinister angel was in the window. The lights on the village green lit the scarlet background, but the white glass of the figure itself was opaque. The image filled her whole field of vision, like a cathedral window.

It shimmered. It trembled, the soldered joints straining. Beth held her breath, petrified. Then it bellied towards her and burst, scattering slow-motion shards of glass all around her like a snowstorm. And through it exploded a dark shape, all serpentine limbs, clawed hands and wings, great horns on its head.

It bore her back on to the bed and impaled her on its long, rigid member. It was the Horn of Power. In a raging, itching frenzy of arousal she climaxed. A dark command pressed her mind into blackness. *Can't find Eirian. Help us!*

Beth woke up to find herself lying across the bed. She heard a wind whirling away from her, rattling dry leaves in its wake. Then silence.

As if sleepwalking, Beth got up and went into Eirian's empty room. She felt nightmare-ridden. Taking the Horn of Power from its hiding place under Eirian's bed, she sat on the carpet with the ivory shaft across her thighs. Her cats came and sat in a triangle around her: Bast, Cerridwen, Eostre. They were all that kept her sane. She imagined Morgan thrusting himself into Olivia, Eirian's stony gaze withering the life in her womb like the hag of death.

At dawn Beth went zombie-like back to her own room. The angel panel lay shattered on the carpet. A shard of it pierced her foot, but she didn't feel it.

The taxi brought Morgan into a car park with landscaped banks of flowers. The studio stood like a museum or temple, all ice-white marble with columns and sweeping steps. High on the apex of the portico was a white cross and blue neon lettering, TRUE LIGHT NETWORK. The towers of Atlanta gleamed beyond.

Morgan paid the driver, hefted his bag on to his shoulder and walked through the main doors, from baking heat to chilly air conditioning. He'd come straight from the airport. He was tired and needed a drink, but that could wait.

Inside, the foyer was no less impressive, with a pristine ice-rink floor and glossy marble columns. There were poster-sized

344

photographs along the walls, showing happy groups of people outside churches. A couple of television monitors were showing a TLN gospel programme.

He walked to the reception desk. The receptionist, a glamorous matron with dazzling teeth and a lacquered red bouffant, asked how she could help. 'I'd like to see Nathaniel De Vries, please.'

'I'm not sure he's here, sir. Do you have an appointment?'

'No. But I'm prepared to wait until he turns up or someone tells me where I can find him.'

His courteous, pointed tone brought a wary look to her eyes. 'Wait a moment, please, sir. Your name is?' He told her. She made a telephone call. 'Mr Morgan Rhys to see Mr De Vries; is he available?' A long pause. 'Oh, I see. Okay, great.' Her bright expression restored, she looked at Morgan. 'If you'll take a seat, Mr Rhys, someone will come down and take you to Mr De Vries's office.'

Surprised, Morgan sat down and waited for ten minutes. He saw security cameras high in the corners, turning this way and that like insect eyes. Finally a huge man with a fat neck and shaven head came towards him. He wore a dark-blue track suit. His smile looked like a Rottweiler's snarl on his fleshy face.

'Hi, I'm Moses. If you'd like to come this way, Mr Rhys . . .' As the man turned away, Morgan saw words emblazoned in white on the back of his track suit: JOGGING FOR JESUS. 'Mr De Vries will be only too pleased to receive you.'

Why had it been so easy? Morgan was led across the foyer and taken down one floor in the lift. They emerged in a basement, a well-lit office corridor with lino and white walls. The man led him to the end and took him through a kind of ante-room into a brightly-lit, windowless office. There was a desk, filing cabinets and a grey carpet, but it looked unoccupied. Decidedly not the boss's domain. A large television in one corner was showing TLN, with the sound turned down.

'Wait here, sir.' Morgan was ushered inside, then Moses stepped back into the ante-room and made to pull the door to

345

behind him. Morgan, in a rush of foreboding, did not want to be shut in alone. He grabbed the handle and held on.

'Don't shut it, I'm claustrophobic,' he said sharply. Moses faced him through the gap.

'Let it go, sir.' No pretence now. They struggled with the door. Morgan blocked it with his foot and Moses's glare became savage. 'I don't wanna do this. But even the Lord uses force sometimes!'

Moses released the door, causing Morgan to stagger backwards. Then Moses's rock-hard fist crunched into his chin and he collapsed into a black well of pain.

Red and purple flowers bloomed on the blackness and his ears rang. As the tide claimed him, he heard the door slam, locks and bolts clunking into place. Frustration, despair. Then oblivion.

'I thought you said your wife killed herself,' Eirian said dully. She and Gabriel were walking on the bank of the creek but she didn't consider trying to escape by swimming or stealing a boat. There seemed no point. He'd crawled inside her mind and put out the lights, and she hadn't even realized until it was too late.

'That was my first wife.'

'So this woman I thought was a maid is your second?'

He shrugged. 'In name only.'

'You've destroyed her. Like you destroyed the first one, and me.'

He smiled, shaking his head as if she were being very stupid. The golden weather and the radiance of his face and hair tormented her. 'She still adores me. And so do you. I guess even Beth does, and Olivia, of course. You're a lot like your grandmother, sweetheart. That evangelical fire must run in the family.'

'I'm nothing like her,' Eirian said thickly. 'How do you know so much about Olivia? Anyone would think it was you who got her out of hospital and inflicted her on my parents. Was it?'

He laughed softly. 'Oh, that's as likely as me having got to know Alastair and persuaded him to chat up your poor old gay granddad.' And he went on and on laughing, torturing her. She was aware of him as some monstrous white spider, spinning filaments in every corner of her life. Paranoia; was there anyone he *hadn't* infected? How, how could she not have known? 'All you have to do is make the announcement,' he said. 'Then everything will be fine.'

'I won't do it,' Eirian said stubbornly. It was all she had left, the last candle-flame of pride.

'You have to, honey,' he said, like a kindly doctor persuading her to undergo some unpleasant treatment. 'It's real easy. You sit on a sofa, the cameras roll and you tell America that you were wrong. You've seen the light. You've been born-again and you want to atone for all the confusion you've caused. Then you cry a little and praise the Lord. The viewers'll eat you up.'

'And afterwards?'

He shrugged. 'The world is yours. We'll be married, we'll have lots of kids and you can talk on TLN about how you escaped the evils of witchcraft and saw the light, by God's grace. Maybe you could have your own programme! Wow, you'd be bigger than PGK!'

She could hardly take in what he was saying. 'I thought you might have me killed by that Gil. Does he know you hate black people?'

'Sure, he knows. He's too scared of me and too well-paid to care. But honey, you got nothing to fear. I still love you.' He stroked her cheek. She couldn't stand it.

'Liar,' she said miserably, dropping her head to evade his touch. 'I know what you've done to me.' She knew, because she'd done it to others. To Luke and PGK . . . and to Auryn. Gabriel had plucked at the knots of her psyche and unravelled it. And she had no mental energy to fight back, no anger. Only self-loathing. She neither loved Gabriel nor hated him; nothing mattered any more. She felt suspended in a tank of murky water, seeing the world through grey glass walls while she slowly drowned.

'You can drag me in front of the cameras,' she said, 'but you can't make me say anything.'

He only smiled. 'I'll be there. I'll hold your hand.'

Gabriel had sex with her that night but she felt like his possession, not his lover. The next day he put her in a white, chauffeur-driven stretch limo with smoked windows. Numb, Eirian watched the lush hills sweeping past, the pumpkin fields, tobacco-drying sheds, red barns. Gabriel thinks he can keep me, she thought, a good little wife, a brood mare? No. I'll drown myself in the creek. I'd rather die than betray all I believed in. A hot tear rolled down her cheek. Good Mother, whether you exist or not, I can't betray you.

There was an airfield, a flight in a private jet, then another limousine to take them into Atlanta. Seething highways, the towers of the city standing square against the burning sky. Gabriel helped her out of the limo and she was dazzled by sunlight on gleaming marble. The shining edifice with its cross was all straight lines, all stone and light; nothing soft or shadowy, nothing feminine, or real, or kind.

Eirian was led across the palatial foyer, taken up in a lift and along corridors to a luxurious hospitality suite. A shiny blonde woman with a fixed smile and no apparent personality received her from Gabriel and sat her on one of the long soft couches. There was no one else there. Eirian was given coffee and sandwiches, and allowed to visit the toilet. When she came back, a big television was on in the corner, tuned not to TLN but to a news network. The words of the female announcer caught her attention.

'. . . And at ten after nine tonight we are carrying a live broadcast from the True Light Network, when Eirian Rhys, the young British woman who's been a prominent spokesperson for the pagan movement, will be making an important statement.' The announcer turned to her male companion. 'What do you think that could be about, Jeremy?'

'Well, I don't know,' said the beaming Jeremy, 'but TLN are promising quite a surprise and knowing Eirian Rhys, it's sure to be interesting, so tune in for that broadcast around nine. We'll be back with the weather after these messages . . .'

Eirian sat with her head in her hands. She felt too weak to move. Bastard, she thought. What are you, Gabriel? Why can't I defeat you like I defeated Luke? Because you made me love you? You drugged me with sex and lies. Took a proud witch and humiliated her.

But there was one, final humiliation she wouldn't allow. She looked around the room, wondering if there was some way to kill herself before the broadcast was due. But then Gabriel came in. He looked fresh in a white shirt and trousers but she felt travel-worn. He kissed her, laughing when she shied away.

'Let's run through what we're going to say, okay?' he said. 'I'll introduce myself and tell them you've got a special message. Then you say you made a big mistake. There's no Goddess. You didn't mean to mislead people but Satan was working through you. But now you've found the Lord – oh, come on, Eirian, you know the sort of bullshit people need to hear.'

'No,' she said. 'Never.'

'Fine,' Gabriel sighed. 'I had a feeling I'd have to do this.' Duly alarmed, she thought he was going to hit her. Instead he pulled her to her feet. 'Come along and say hi to your father.'

'What do you mean, my –'

He took her down in the lift to the basement. It was like a plain office building down here, with white walls and exposed water pipes. A big security guard in a blue track suit let them through a bare room, then opened an inner door to what appeared to be an office.

There, blinking in the fluorescent light, was Morgan.

Eirian put her hands to her mouth. A spurt of emotion reached through her numbness. Her father was sitting against a wall, handcuffed to a pipe. His jeans and T-shirt looked as if he'd been wearing them for two days. His thick dark hair was uncombed, his beautiful face unshaven and gaunt with tiredness.

As he looked up, she saw that the right side of his face was purple with bruising, his eye swollen.

Seeing Eirian, he came to life and got to his feet, the hand-cuff sliding up the pipe. Eirian tried to rush to him but Gabriel held her back. Then the security man, a thick-necked thug with a shaven head, went up to Morgan and stamped down on his left kneecap. In sick horror Eirian heard cartilege breaking, ligaments tearing. Morgan collapsed, gagging with pain. Eirian cried out. Then Gabriel let her go and she flew to her father.

Her resentment against Morgan was ash. He'd cared enough to come after her! All she felt for him now was love – and terror. Morgan's lips tried to form her name but only thin gasps came out. Eirian knelt helplessly beside him, stroking his shoulder and weeping with rage.

'You bastards!' she cried, but Gabriel and his henchman only grinned. That was when her soured love for Gabriel congealed to hatred. 'Dad, I'm sorry.'

'Not your fault, love,' he whispered. 'His real name's Nathaniel De Vries, he runs TLN.'

'I know, Dad,' she said. 'Too fucking late.'

'What happens now,' said Gabriel, 'is that you say exactly what I tell you on camera. Or your beloved daddy will die. Very slowly. Extremely painfully. We can torture him indefinitely, if you decide to be awkward.'

Eirian cringed. Now it was all over. She held her father's hands, resting her head on his as he slumped against the wall. She could sense his agony, the internal leakage of blood around the damaged joint. And pressure in his skull, concussion; he must have been knocked out at some stage. So her powers of perception weren't quite dead after all.

'I'm sorry,' he managed to say, between shudders of pain. 'I should've protected you from all this and I didn't.'

'Dad . . .'

'Eirian, don't give in to them.' He went heavy against her, passing out. She helped him down but he lay awkwardly, one arm twisted up by the handcuff. He was white. She saw an image of a blood clot forming on his brain . . . She thought, what if he dies, even if I do everything Gabriel says? He needs medical help . . . wait, what am I thinking? I don't know if I can still heal but I must try!

She laid her hands on him, one on his smashed knee, one on his head. With all that was left of her strength she projected healing fire into the injuries. No guarantee it would work, but still . . . She felt Morgan slipping away from her into a coma. Tears ran down her cheeks. 'Dad,' she said, but he didn't answer.

Trying to heal him had taken her last scrap of energy. When Gabriel came and pulled her away she was a rag doll in his hands. 'Time to go,' Gabriel said softly. No, she must think of him as Nathaniel now; the person she had called Gabriel didn't exist. The henchman relocked the door behind them. As she was pulled through the ante-room, she almost bumped into Gilmour, who was coming through the outer door. He, too, gave a cruel smile that stabbed coldly through her heart.

'Don't you know how much Nathaniel despises you?' she hissed.

'Not like he despises you, sugar,' Gil said impassively.

Eirian was so weak she could barely walk, let alone think. Nathaniel took her to the make-up room, where a cheerful southern belle, seemingly oblivious to her state, powdered her face and groomed her hair. They put her in a horrible flowery dress with a gold cross round her neck.

At six minutes past nine, Nathaniel ushered her into a studio and sat on the couch beside her. There was a small audience, shuffling and murmuring, and too many cameramen for them all to belong to TLN. 'What's going on?' she asked dully.

'Kind of a press conference.' Nathaniel spoke casually, as if this were all routine. 'We opened up to the main news networks so no one can accuse us of a fix.' If he was aware of the irony, he didn't show it.

At ten past, the floor manager cued them. A cheerful woman with stiff auburn hair and shiny red lips stepped forward with a microphone. 'Hi there, this is Amy Lee at True Light Network bringing you a very special item. We're always talking here about the need to take a long hard look at yourself, admit your mistakes and give yourself up to God's mercy. Lord knows, that ain't easy at the best of times! Even harder if, like the very special young lady who's with us tonight, you're famous for disagreeing with the Bible! So you'll appreciate how much courage it's taken for her to be here tonight but we are thrilled to welcome Miss Eirian Rhys with a vital message. Nathaniel?'

Nathaniel leaned forward, looking into the main camera. His voice was smooth, deep, seductive. 'Good evening. You may not know me but I'm Nathaniel De Vries, chairman of the board of TLN. I do the Lord's work off-camera but I'm making an exception tonight to talk to Eirian. She is one amazing lady. You see, I also work as a consultant for Silver Dove Books. All I set out to do was advise Eirian about a book she wanted to write – not to convert her. But in the process of advising her I was witness to the doubts that surfaced and to Eirian's very own Road to Damascus.' There were shouts of 'Praise the Lord!' from the staff on the set, but the journalists were silent. 'Eirian's here to tell you about it in her own words. So, Eirian, won't you tell us what happened to change your life?'

Eirian dragged her lower lip between her teeth. She couldn't do it. But Nathaniel's power netted her. She thought of her father and began to force the words out. 'I – I made mistakes. I deluded myself . . .'

Chapter Nineteen

'I don't suppose Morgan's rung you, has he?' Fraught with anxiety, Beth had come to see Rhianwen, leaving her mother at home. It was mid-evening, two days since Morgan had left.

Rhianwen frowned, looking worried. 'No, he hasn't, love.' They stood in the sitting room. Beth was too restless to sit down. Her grandfather was out.

'Oh. He called from Heathrow, said he'd ring as soon as he reached Atlanta, but he hasn't. I don't know whether something's wrong or he's just pissed off with me.'

'I'm sure he's okay,' said Rhianwen. 'He probably hasn't had the chance to reach a phone.'

'What if he can't find Eirian? I can't settle to anything. I'm worried sick about them – and Mum. Things she said last night . . .'

'What things?'

'It's too stupid to repeat. I'm trying to keep a stiff upper lip, but I've got such a bad feeling about all this.' Rhianwen put her arms around Beth and held her. Beth pressed her face into the fragrant, auburn hair, fighting tears. This was her true mother, this warm presence in her arms.

'If it's any consolation, I didn't pick up anything suspicious about Gabriel either.' Rhianwen stood back, holding Beth's hands. 'It's only when you think about him after . . . Feels like you were looking at him through gauze.' She frowned. 'You thought you were seeing a man but actually he was a white blur. His real face and character were hidden.'

Beth shuddered. 'Don't.'

'Love, we know Morgan can look after himself – and so can Eirian, we've seen enough evidence of that. You feel bad because you're stuck here. If you ask my opinion, Olivia's being very selfish to impose on you like this.'

'But if I don't help her, who will?'

'Her father and I would, if she'd let us. At least she's managed to forgive you, if not us. I suppose it's a start.'

'You don't think Morgan's right, do you? That Mum's faking it?'

'Honestly, I don't know,' Rhianwen said softly. 'I don't blame you for wanting to help her, or him for being suspicious. Maybe you're trying a bit too hard to win her approval, though . . .'

'I suppose so,' Beth said, shrugging. 'You think you've shaken off your childhood, then find you've just gone in a circle.'

'You don't have to feel helpless, you know. Use your craft, your inner power.'

'I can't even meditate with Mum there. I'm so conscious that she'd think I'm worshipping Satan.'

Rhianwen rolled her eyes. 'That's ridiculous. If you accept her, she should accept you too! I wish Eirian could forgive me like you've forgiven Olivia. She certainly knows how to punish people, does Eirian.'

'It's really hurt you, hasn't it?' Beth hadn't fully taken it in before.

'It's quite worn me down, at times. Bit scary to know that it wasn't in the heat of the moment and she might not forgive me for the rest of my life. I dare say I deserve everything I get for the way I treated you. Well, she's making me pay, all right. But I don't care, I just want her home safe with us.'

As soon as Beth went out, Olivia got up and made a phone call. Gabriel's voice was balm to her aching mind. Angelic avatar of her dead son.

'Perfect timing, Olivia. The doves have flown into the trap. They'll soon be gone and you'll have everything you dreamed of. I've kept my half of the bargain; now all you have to do is keep yours.'

A spasm went through her. 'I will, Luke. Sorry, Gabriel.'

His voice darkened, warm but commanding. 'Remember

you're doing this for God, Olivia. You must atone for your own sins, as well as theirs. That's the only way you'll all be saved.'

'I know, that's what the Lord revealed to me,' she whispered. 'I won't let you down.'

'You're God's bravest soldier. You will know His blessing. God go with you, sister.'

Olivia didn't try to keep Gabriel on the line. Everything had been said. She put down the phone and sat calmly, hands folded in prayer. Her time had come at last. The end of this ghastly phase, the beginning of a new life in God's grace. As soon as she had saved all the fallen souls in her family.

Gabriel hadn't hypnotized her, he'd empowered her; unleashed her desires, given her the courage to carry them through. The Holy Spirit was directing her now. Olivia rose and put on her coat and shoes, feeling excited but very controlled. Almost strangled by control.

She left Beth a note on the kitchen table, slipped a key into her pocket and slung her handbag on her shoulder. The bag was just large enough to conceal Beth's sharpest carving knife.

When Beth came back from Rhianwen's, her mother was nowhere to be found. She ran up and downstairs, calling out in anxiety, before she found the note. 'Beth, I am feeling so much better and I noticed we are very low on groceries so I've gone to the supermarket in Tamworth, the one that's open until nine. I shall be a couple of hours. Mother.'

'Stupid woman!' Beth exclaimed aloud. 'She's not well enough to go out, why didn't she wait for me?' She went into the front garden to check if her mother's red Fiesta was parked in front of her own cottage, but it had gone. The evening was sunny, but deepening towards sunset. Sighing in exasperation, Beth went back inside.

The phone trilled. Beth seized it, heart leaping. 'Hi, Beth, it's Dee. How are you? Any news?'

'Hello, dear.' Beth tried not to sound disappointed. Dee and

355

Steve knew the situation. 'I was hoping you were Morgan or Eirian. Neither of them has called.'

'I'm sorry. You sound rough.'

'I'm all right. Just on edge. Rhianwen is sure Morgan's okay. My mother's buggered off to town without telling me and she's still not well. Oh, God.'

'Look, you're not on your own, you know,' Dee said sternly. 'Steve and I will come round like a shot if you need us. Pete and Sam are really upset too. Just let us know.'

'Thank you,' said Beth. She was grateful but she'd had a lifelong compulsion to tackle crises on her own. The comfort of her friends might only make her break down. 'Erm, one thing I've been meaning to say. I'm terribly sorry I wouldn't listen when you tried to warn me about Gabriel.'

'It's all right, I understand.'

'You'll never know how sorry. Anyway, I'll call you if anything happens. Thanks, Dee, 'bye for now.'

She felt too restless to cook. She fed the cats and made herself a sandwich, which she ate in the kitchen while staring at the silent telephone. Darkness drew in. It was ten o'clock and her mother hadn't come back.

On impulse she rang her father. Alastair answered. 'No, Philip's out. Can I take a message?'

'I wondered, erm . . . if my mother had turned up there. She went out and I'm a bit worried.'

'No, she hasn't,' said Alastair. 'Are you all right, Beth? You sound upset.'

Beth exhaled. 'I may as well tell you. That American guy who was helping Eirian write a book, Gabriel? She's run off to America with him and I'm worried sick. We think he's tricked her . . . oh, never mind, it's a long story, but can you tell Dad?'

There was a long silence at the other end. Then Alastair said hesitantly. 'Beth, there's something I should tell you. I think I've met Gabriel.'

'What?'

'It was a few months ago. He approached me when I came

out of college one day; like he'd been following me. He persuaded me to hang around this café in King's Heath and chat Philip up. Never said who Philip was, only told me not to tell anyone I knew him, especially not Eirian. It all made sense at the time but over the past few days I realized he ... God, it sounds bloody ridiculous, but I feel like he hypnotized me. He's scary, he can make people do anything. I'm sorry, Beth. Oh, God, I'm really sorry.'

Alastair put the phone down. Beth stood there with the receiver in her hand. When she replaced it, she didn't try to call him back. She couldn't even think.

The electric lights seemed dim. Beth felt she couldn't see properly. Shadows moved around her. Ghosts of wounded animals, dragging themselves through her field of vision, whining and bellowing in heart-rending pain. And at their centre an upright figure in skins and feathers, horns sweeping up from a feral head, bony phallus pulsing in the air. *Eirian. Eirian. Help us find ...*

'Stop it!' Beth shrieked, leaping up. She rushed round the house, making sure all the doors were locked. Then she took the Horn from Eirian's room and brought it downstairs, taking Rhianwen's advice in desperation. She sat in the centre of the sitting-room carpet with the Horn across her lap, the three cats prowling around her; her guardians, her familiars. She visualized a sheath of light covering her, a shield through which nothing bad could touch her ... and she sat there, feeling connected to an endless line of shamans and witches who'd come under attack through the aeons.

Then the telephone rang.

About half past nine, Rhianwen answered a knock at the door and was stunned to find Olivia on her doorstep. 'Hello,' Rhianwen said guardedly.

Olivia seemed dignified but edgy. 'Is my father in?'

'No, he's on some village committee thing. They usually go down the Green Man after.'

'May I come in and wait?'

357

Rhianwen was surprised. Olivia normally refused to have anything to do with her, except to air a grievance. The last time they'd spoken at length – had a major row, in fact – was when Morgan had got Beth pregnant with Eirian. That long ago. 'Okay. Beth said you weren't well. How are you feeling?'

She expected a caustic remark in response, but Olivia only said, 'I've never felt better.' She walked into Rhianwen's sitting room, with its tasselled cushions and exotic paintings of goddesses, and perched on the edge of the sofa. She seemed wound-up, artificially calm. Her face was pallid and devoid of make-up, but her eyes were very bright.

'You look a bit pale,' said Rhianwen, trying to act normal. 'Any news of Morgan or Eirian?'

'No, none.' Her expression flickered; unreadable, but apparently not a look of deep concern.

Rhianwen sighed inwardly. She was trying not to worry, because it never achieved anything. 'Would you like a drink? Glass of wine, belladonna, aconite?'

Her attempt at a joke completely passed Olivia by. 'No, thank you. I'm driving. I'll just wait.'

Rhianwen sat in a chair opposite. 'Well, maybe we should take this chance to talk ... We haven't talked properly ... since Morgan was born, really. I'm so pleased you're getting on well with Beth now. It would be wonderful to bury the past, finally.'

'I'd like to bury it all,' Olivia said quietly.

'Good. After all, I'm your step-mother now; that's fairly amusing, isn't it?' Olivia did not look amused. Rhianwen cleared her throat. 'Look, I know I behaved badly in the past, trying to get Randolph away from your mother. I'm sorry. I'm not evil, I was in love and the same goes for Morgan when he met Beth. It's human nature, nothing to do with Satan. You know that in your heart, don't you?'

'But Satan is there, waiting to find chinks in human nature he can work through. Like lust.'

'What's so wrong with lust? If people would treat desire as natural and sacred it wouldn't cause so many problems! Oh,

I don't suppose we'll ever agree on this. But I thought Jesus had more to say about forgiveness than sex.'

In the past, Olivia had been outraged if Rhianwen dared to comment on Christianity, but this time she seemed unmoved. 'Forgiveness.' Olivia looked into space, her face long and solemn. 'I'm not pure enough to be forgiven. I've failed Jesus. Failed God.'

'Don't say that,' Rhianwen said gently. 'You don't really like yourself, do you? Why?'

'You could never understand.'

'Perhaps you were confused by the desires you felt as an adolescent, so you turned to the Church for answers. But the answers made you feel worse because they confirmed your fear that lust is sinful. So everything you hate and fear within yourself, you project on to Beth and Eirian. And everything you fear about men, you project on to Morgan.'

'So you think you know it all?' Olivia hissed with something of her old fire. 'You are so glib, the wise woman who thinks it's acceptable to steal other people's husbands, accceptable for her bastard son to ruin my daughter. What do you know?'

'Nothing, if you don't tell me. Tell me, Livvy.'

There was a long pause. Olivia's face worked as if she were reaching a decision. Finally she said, 'When I was fifteen, I saw the Devil. In our garden. I knew it was looking for me.'

Rhianwen caught her breath, trying not to react overtly. 'What exactly did you see?'

'A dark figure like a demon, seven feet tall. A great shadow. Like a man but half-animal, with hideous wings and horns. Obscene.' She shuddered and went on hoarsely, 'It did things to me.'

'What things?'

Olivia's eyes glittered with nascent hysteria. 'It . . . touched me. It made me feel . . . filthy desires I'd never felt before. It defiled me with its hands – only its hands, but what it did was obscene! It made me give myself up to my own revolting lust. It happened in the bushes in our garden but my mother and father never came out to help me! So I knew I was evil and

359

the Devil was real. And the only way I could fight it was to give myself to God!'

Oh, Goddess, Rhianwen thought, she's describing . . . 'Perhaps it wasn't the Devil at all.'

'Of course it was! You can't confuse me with your evil arguments.' She began to speak more rapidly, her walls of control fracturing. 'I know what happened. The Devil was out looking for servants. You succumbed and became a witch – oh, don't shake your head, I *know* – but I resisted and that's why I've been tormented ever since. Being saved meant dedicating my life and my children to God, fighting Satan with all my strength – and that's what I've done! I'll die fighting, because I'm still not pure enough to please God and I never will be until I give up my life to destroy the Devil and the Crone!'

'Livvy.' Rhianwen spoke very gently, hoping to calm her down. 'I wish you'd told me this years ago. I could have helped you. It might have spared us a lot of misunderstanding.'

'There's no misunderstanding. You seduced my whole family to Satan. That's all there is to know.'

'No,' said Rhianwen hopelessly.

'Beth thinks I've fallen too, but she's wrong.' Olivia's eyes were white-ringed, bright with psychosis. 'I have to save your souls!'

Rhianwen glanced at the telephone, thinking, I should phone Beth and suggest she gets in touch with the hospital. 'Olivia, let's look at things a different way. Suppose the creature you saw wasn't –' As she spoke, Rhianwen heard the garden gate and footsteps on the front path. Randolph, she thought with a sigh of relief. 'Your father's here. Sit quietly, I'll get you a drink.'

Rhianwen went into the kitchen, seeking a breathing space. Brandy with a few drops of a herbal remedy, that would help to calm Olivia down.

There was a sound behind her. She turned to find Olivia in the doorway with a big black-handled carving knife in her hand. Rhianwen didn't believe it was happening until Olivia lunged and stuck the point into her neck.

No pain. A cold burning, her stomach contracting with shock. She fell backwards to the floor and saw Olivia, her face weirdly serene, raising her arm for another blow. Suddenly Randolph was in the doorway, shouting, 'Olivia! No!'

Through a white rush of faintness, Rhianwen saw Olivia twist round and plunge the knife two-handed towards her father's abdomen. She saw a gout of blood, Randolph staggering back and catching his head with a hard thud on the corner of a dresser.

'Where were you when the Devil came, Dad?' Olivia screamed. 'You started all this! You! Satan!'

Beth was shaking as she answered the phone. The mantelpiece clock said ten fifteen. 'Hello?' Silence. 'Morgan?'

She heard a long, tremulous breath in the earpiece. Great, she thought despairingly, a heavy breather, that's all I need. Then Olivia's voice said, 'Hello, Beth.'

'Mum, thank goodness! Where on earth are you? Don't tell me your car's broken down.'

'No,' said the voice, calm and eerie. 'But I need you to come to me, Beth. I have to talk to you.' Her tone alarmed Beth. It was gentle, but not sane.

'Can't you come home and talk? I'm waiting for Morgan to call.'

'Morgan isn't going to call.' The words, although irrational, sent dread needling through Beth. 'Please come to me. I need you.'

'All right, I'm on my way. Are you still at the supermarket?'

'No, I'm at Woodbourne Hall. By the workshops.'

Beth was dumbfounded. 'What on earth are you doing there?'

'I . . . I don't know. I have to show you something. Please come, Beth. Quickly.'

'Okay, okay. Your car's on the drive outside the stable court-yard, is it? Just stay right there.'

Fevered, Beth grabbed a jacket and rushed out to her white van. She realized she had the Horn in her hand, as if she were unconsciously clinging to it for protection. She propped it against the passenger seat and drove off through the darkness. The journey was only twenty minutes along familiar country lanes. Hang on, she thought, to be using the phone Mum must be *inside* the workshops . . . but how did she get in?

Turning into the Hall drive, Beth speeded across the estate, rattling over sheep grids. As her van rounded the bend between the Hall and the stables, she saw her mother's red car in the headlights. She pulled up behind it, jumped out and rushed over – but there was no sign of her mother in or near the car.

Beth looked up and saw a dim electric light through the workshop windows. The old buildings looked haunted, deserted in darkness. Suddenly wary, she crossed the silent courtyard and found the main door ajar. She entered, walked past the first few stalls and round the corner into her own aisle. She saw no one but she could hear something. A scraping sound.

'Mum?' Beth called. 'Are you there?'

The sound burst into a crescendo of crashing glass. Beth's nerves jolted violently. Then her mother emerged from Beth's stall, at the far end of the aisle. Her expression was intent, but not mad.

'What are you doing?' Beth demanded, walking towards her. 'How did you get in here?'

'I took your spare key, of course,' Olivia said flatly. As Beth came closer she saw that Olivia had a shard of blood-red glass in her right hand. She held it like a dagger, the point pressed to her left wrist.

'Come on,' Beth said firmly, her hand held out. 'Let's go home. It's all right.' All her attention was on her mother. But as soon as she reached Olivia beside her stall, Beth stopped short in horror.

All her work lay in ruins. Tiffany lamps on which she'd spent painstaking hours, big commissioned windows, panels and ter-rariums – all was a glittering, multi-coloured shoal of smashed glass, heaped on the work-bench, the counters and the floor. Beth clamped her hand to her mouth. She wanted to scream but she couldn't even breathe. Tears sprang to her eyes.

'Why?' she gasped. 'Why did you do this?'

She looked round and Olivia's face was exactly as in the old days, when she'd quoted the Bible to justify a beating. Hard, self-righteous, unforgiving.

'Oh, shit,' whispered Beth, shaking so violently she thought she might pass out. She quickly mastered her distress. All that mattered was getting her mother to a doctor. 'Come on, I'm taking you home.'

'We'll go in my car,' said Olivia.

'No, I think we'll take the van.'

Olivia raised her hands, her left palm facing outwards as she dug the glass shard into her inner wrist. Beth saw the skin break, blood oozing from the shallow slit. 'We'll go in my car or I'll cut myself!'

'Don't! Okay, whatever you say,' Beth gasped, thinking, at least if she's driving she can't hurt herself. As they left, Beth didn't bother to turn out the lights or lock up. She'd have to explain to Harry in the morning. Oh, Christ.

Olivia seemed normal again as she turned the Fiesta round, pulled past Beth's van and drove towards the main gates. Beth sat tensely silent beside her. Presently Olivia said, 'You think I'm mad. I'm not.'

'I wish you'd tell me what's wrong, then.'

'Nothing's wrong. I have things to explain.'

'Go on. I'm listening.'

'The man who helped me to get out of hospital and the man Eirian ran away with; they are the same person. Joshua and Gabriel are the same person.'

Beth, strung taut as a harp string, didn't know how to react. 'Go on,' she said carefully. Olivia slowed down as they reached the gates, but turned right instead of left on to the road. 'Mum, you're going the wrong way.'

'Am I? Oh, well, we'll turn round somewhere.' A dark hedgerow flashed past on their left, the wall of Woodbourne Estate on their right, overhung by mature beeches. Olivia went on, 'You don't know who Gabriel really is, do you?'

Beth swallowed against a lump in her throat. Was her mother

363

suffering delusions – or did she really know something? 'An editor from an American publisher.'

'Yes,' Olivia said happily, 'but that publisher is owned by the people who own a television station called the True Light Network. And the person who runs both is Nathaniel De Vries. He also calls himself Joshua Andrews and Gabriel Jordan.'

Beth turned sick and dizzy. She thought of Alastair's confession. 'So your saintly Joshua was Gabriel all the time?' Olivia nodded. Her mouth stretched in a tight, triumphant smile. 'You knew. God Almighty, you knew! How?'

'Gabriel came to me long before he knew you. He doesn't love Eirian, he hates her. He wants to destroy her, just as Luke and I *should* have destroyed her. We weren't clever enough – but Gabriel is. He's a wise man, an angel. God sent him to me.'

Beth stared at her. 'Stop the car,' she said, but Olivia drove on along a thin lane that curved round the back of Woodbourne Hall's grounds. The right hand side of the road was shaded by the thick dark woodland of Morgan's nature reserve. Olivia swung the car into an open gateway, on to a track fit only for tractors.

'Where the hell are you going?' Beth cried, hanging on as the car bounced over the rough ground. 'Mum! Mum, stop.'

Eventually Olivia obeyed. They drew up in a curve of the track, trees looming grey and tangled all around them. The summer night was mild and clear. Olivia turned off the headlights and Beth was suddenly aware that she was in the middle of nowhere with a mad woman. There was a touch of radiance from a half-moon. Her mother took the shard of glass from the dashboard and toyed with it, pricking her palms.

'Gabriel made Eirian fall in love with him so he could take her away and break her evil soul in pieces,' Olivia said matter-of-factly. 'He saw the Devil in her. The Crone.'

Beth was struggling to hold on to her emotions. 'But how did he get to you?'

'Gabriel can find out anything. He's very powerful, you

know. He's everything Luke should have been, if he'd lived. Eirian might think she can destroy Gabriel too – but he's too strong. She's met her match. I am vindicated, Beth.'

'I thought you'd changed,' Beth said hoarsely. 'But you haven't, have you?'

Beth could barely see her mother's face in the gloom, but her tone was ferocious. 'It nearly made me sick, begging forgiveness from you and that demonic pervert you fornicate with! But Gabriel gave me the strength to do it because it was so important.'

'What was so important?'

'To help him destroy Eirian! To destroy all the demons: you, Morgan, Rhianwen, my father.'

'Oh, Goddess,' said Beth, tears of terror and betrayal stinging her eyes. 'I really believed you'd changed! I forgave you, and now you tell me it was all a sham, you were using me, secretly loathing me?' Olivia didn't reply, but Beth caught the glint of a tight, victorious smile, blue eyes ringed with white madness. 'Turn the car round and take me home. If I call the police, maybe they can contact the American police and find Eirian and Morgan before it's too late.'

'Morgan's dead by now,' Olivia said impassively. 'Gabriel says he walked straight into the trap.'

A wave of utter horror, grief, and denial torched Beth. It was all she could do not to scream. 'Take me to Rhianwen's! Let me drive!'

'Rhianwen is dead too.'

'Stop it, Mum. You're imagining things.'

Olivia gave a small, hard laugh. 'No, really. I was with her before I called you. I stabbed her.' She frowned. 'I stabbed my father too. Had to be done.' She pulled open her coat and Beth saw a dark streak down her pale dress: blood.

'You bitch,' said Beth, tears rolling down her cheeks. She tried to summon her strength, but it slipped away, as it always did in her mother's presence. 'You vile, heartless *bitch*! I trusted you, I loved you!'

'Don't think you can get round me with tears, Bethia Herne.

You called the Devil among us with your filthy lust.' Olivia put down the piece of glass and restarted the engine.

'What are you doing?'

'It's the only way, Beth. Gabriel revealed God's will so clearly. You're evil – but I gave birth to you, and I couldn't control you. So it's my fault too. There's only one way to atone for our sins. I must place us both in God's hands.'

'Mum, I don't know what you mean, I don't even want to know. Let's go home,' Beth was past arguing. All she wanted was to get away from her mother, to reach Rhianwen and a phone.

The car moved off. Olivia gripped the steering wheel and craned her neck as if looking for a place to turn round. Beth noticed that her mother's hands were shaking, taut. 'We'll be saved. Only way.'

'Put your lights on,' said Beth, but Olivia ignored her. 'I suppose you know it was Gabriel who got Alastair to seduce Dad?'

She saw from the stiffening of her mother's face that she hadn't known. 'No. That's a lie!'

'So how much of a friend is Gabriel to you?'

'Shut up. Stop trying to distract me!' To Beth's shock, Olivia jammed her foot on the accelerator and the car rocketed forward, lurching and bucking on the rough path. There was a clearing ahead, a mass of bushes and a warning sign. They went past too fast to read it, but Beth suddenly knew where they were.

'Stop!' Beth yelled. 'There's a quarry ahead of us!'

The track curved to the right, but Olivia kept going straight. Beth saw a gap in the bushes, a place where the protective fence had been removed. And Beth knew that her mother had planned this, brought her here to kill them both. Terror galvanized her. She struggled uselessly to undo her seat-belt.

Olivia's hands flew off the steering wheel to cover her face. She screamed. '*I can't do it!*'

And she slammed the brakes on.

Too late. The car skidded onwards over the rough grassy surface, cleared the edge of the drop and curved out through space. Beth endured the drop through darkness, her stomach looping up round her heart – then came the concrete smack of the car hitting the lake.

Water came gushing in through the open window and the car tilted. The water was icy, breath-stopping. Sheer panic focused Beth's instinct and dexterity. With two quick movements she undid both seatbelts, then dragged her mother out of the open window. Bubbling, suffocating chaos seethed around them. Then their heads broke the surface and they gasped greedily for air.

They floated in bitingly cold, black water. Walls of dark rock loomed all around the lake. The car was tipping, sinking. Beth struggled to draw her mother away from the vortex, but their progress was slow and she had to pause for breath, shuddering uncontrollably as she trod water.

'I have to die,' Olivia gasped, between coughs and splutters. 'Can't live with – what he's made me.'

'Save your breath!' Beth said fiercely. The summer air now felt like ice round her skull. The vortex sucked at them but she managed to keep both their heads above water. Beth struck out towards the shore. It was like dragging a sack of lead. Cold and shock exhausted her, but the thought of Rhianwen, lying stabbed and dying, filled her with panic.

'No, Beth. Must – must die!' Olivia clawed at Beth so she nearly went under. 'I thought I – hated you. I don't. Gabriel made me – made me do this! Please – forgive me!'

Beth tried to swim again but couldn't shift her mother at all now. She tipped her head back to keep her mouth clear of the water. 'Stop struggling! Is your foot caught?'

'Gabriel hates you. I don't.' Water ran into Olivia's mouth and she spat it out. 'I couldn't hate you like he did! He lied. Said he'd – never touch Eirian but –' Olivia's hands flailed, splashing them with chill gouts of water. Between wheezing breaths her speech became less coherent but she wouldn't stop. 'My daughter. Should've protected you. But I betrayed – betrayed you! Beth – Beth, I'm sorry. I forgive you. Forgive me.'

'Mum, not now!' Beth was sobbing with the effort of trying to shift her mother.

'Must be now. Last chance. Forgive me!'

'How can I?' said Beth through her teeth. 'You asked that before – and I – I forgave you. Unconditionally. Now you say – say you never meant it. Worked for Gabriel. Let all this happen – and you want – forgiving? Forget it!' Pushing her sopping hair back, she moved Olivia another few feet, but it was like dragging an anchor. She sensed a bulk under the water – the car, or something monstrous fighting for possession of her mother?

'No, Beth,' Olivia said faintly, teeth chattering with the cold. 'God will be my judge. Been a terrible mother. Bad wife, worst of mothers. Forgive me – before we die.'

'Shut up. Stop fighting me!' Beth cried thickly.

'No, stay with me. Forgive me. Come with me, daughter.' And Olivia pulled Beth right under the surface. Beth's head clamoured with the pressure of the water. Her consciousness changed; she sensed endless aeons of blackness passing them by. Became aware of Olivia's adversary surging beneath the black surface. In her altered state she knew it was the Crone, come to claim her due. The Crone would take them both . . . Death seemed peaceful, welcoming . . . They were sinking . . . Then a child's white face glared at Beth through the blackness, green eyes piercing. *Don't you dare die!*

The shock saved Beth. Survival instinct kicked in, made her release her mother and sent her striving back to the surface.

No sign of her mother. Panicking, choking, Beth reached out but her hands closed on chill water. Then Olivia's hand broke the surface and clasped her arm. Dragging her down again.

'No,' said Beth, flailing to keep her head in the air. Suddenly she could take no more; her anger and will-power surged and she rasped, 'You won't take me with you! Damn you!'

She plucked the hand off her arm and thrust it away. Oddly detached, she saw her mother's face sinking under the surface; white, resigned, tragic, like the dying Ophelia. The shadow-shape rose and fell in the depths, seeming to nudge Beth away even as it received her mother. The lake swallowed and was still.

Beth struck out towards the bank. She didn't look back. Reaching a rocky ledge, she dragged herself on to it, grazing her hands on scrubby bushes. She rested there on all fours, shuddering. Clouds obscured the moon and rain was pattering on to the foliage. The rain felt warm on her chilled skin. In a trance of physical and mental shock, she realized she had no idea which way to go. She must reach Rhianwen . . . but how would she ever find her way out of the nature reserve in darkness, lost and exhausted?

Morgan, Eirian, everyone taken from her . . . She heard Tom's prophetic voice, *'When you've lost everything,'* and now, finally, she knew what he meant.

Then she saw a small figure on the shale path ahead of her. It was a child with dark hair, a slim naked boy of five or six. He turned and looked at her. His face was angelic and knowing, with eyes as green as summer. Beth rose and staggered towards him, confused. 'Auryn?' she said.

As soon as he saw her following, he turned and went up the steep side of the quarry, along a path through the oak woods, leading her swift and sure to her destination. Beth was mesmerized.

Presently it seemed the white shape stopped and waited . . . She hurried, heart pounding, desperate to touch him . . . but as she drew close, her eyes focused and it was only her van that she could see. She was back at the workshops, shivering and bewildered, as if she'd lost a tract of time. Her keys were still in the pocket of her sodden jacket . . . but the ghost-child had vanished.

Beth ran into the workshop to use the telephone. 'Steve?' she said, her teeth chattering. 'I know it's late, but can you and Dee meet me at Rhianwen's house? Yes, now. I'll explain when I see you. I think my mother's hurt Rhianwen and Granddad.'

She put the phone down, choking on tears and coldness. As

she looked up she saw, in the aisle beside her stall, another ghost. An old man, with blue-veined hands and a bald skull. Tom. He was tutting over her ruined work as if she'd let him down. Beth let out a sob. 'I'm sorry, Tom.'

'S'only glass 'n' lead, gel,' he said gruffly. 'It's not *you*.'

He was inches from her. She reached out; his hand passed through hers. She felt something heavy, glanced down and found an undamaged piece lying on her palm; a candle-holder she'd made, like an up-turned harebell with long petals of blue glass. When she looked up again, she was alone.

With blurred eyes Beth hurried out, this time pausing to lock the door behind her.

Morgan hung in a strata of consciousness in which he couldn't see or move – and yet, strangely, could still hear. He was dimly aware of voices burbling on the television. A special live broadcast on TLN, a vital message from Eirian Rhys . . . Was he hearing it or dreaming it?

He found himself on a bleak, dark plain that spread to infinity. There was wet grass under his hands and knees, a thunderstorm splitting the black sky. Every whip of lightning was the pain from his own splintered knee. He was crawling in agony, desperate to reach someone or something . . . what?

He had no memories, no past or future. Rain and wind lashed him silently. The only sound was that of meaningless, electronic voices.

He realized he was moving towards a pale shallow rock that protruded from the earth. It was the Hellstone, the quintessence of all sacred stones, a clouded opal.

As he drew nearer he saw another shape coming towards him, mimicking his every move. A wolf, limping. In detail Morgan saw the heavy coat, black with rain, the long muzzle and glowing eyes, its shadow cast by lightning. It had terrible jaws, muscular legs bent double beneath it, broken wings trailing.

He was seeing his own reflection. Plain and stone were bisected by a mirror and he was dragging himself towards it, knowing that when he and his mirror-image touched they would cease to exist.

Ictinike. He recognized the entity that had haunted both him and his father. He knew its name. Knowledge stirred. It had touched Rhianwen and Beth and even Olivia in its desperate search . . .

And Eirian.

They mounted opposite sides of the rock and faced each other. The wolf-entity lowered its long head. Antagonism crackled between them through the lashing rain. This creature had violated him – but far worse, it had taken possession of Eirian. The paternal instinct to safeguard his daughter burned fierce. No one had the right to touch her, least of all this wild spirit . . .

But he had angered Ictinike in turn. He'd failed, turning away in fear instead of trying to understand. They stood eye to eye. *There is no turning away from us. You cannot reject the dark side of your own self. We have always been part of you.*

Morgan was no longer afraid. He finally accepted what he'd always known. He and the entity were separate but the same, existing in the real world and the virtual world, the eternal archetype of the diabolized Horned God.

Ictinike wanted more than healing from Eirian. He wanted recognition. For her to bring him into the light, as she'd brought the Goddess. For the world to remember that he represented not evil, not dominance, but the polarity of equals. Fecund nature, joyous sexuality, the antithesis of monotheism.

They strained towards each other but the unseen barrier kept them apart. Then Morgan looked up and thought he saw the gleam of leaf-green eyes, his lover's eyes . . .

A bolt of lightning struck him, simultaneously hitting his mirror-image and forming a brief, crackling arc between them. No pain. It felt warm, like Beth's hands. It joined them. As they moved forwards again, the stone beneath them glowed white.

When they met in the plane of the mirror, Morgan didn't touch the coldness of glass or oblivion. Instead he felt an icy nose pressed to his, a long tongue lolling out to lick his mouth, his face. They pressed shoulder to shoulder, resting long, furry heads across each other's backs.

Ictinike seemed diminished. Cast out by Eirian, he was only a fragment of himself, wounded like Morgan. The Horned God sundered from the Goddess.

If only I'd understood, Morgan told Ictinike in his mind. You were always with me, wild, dangerous, never malign. Others saw you in my eyes and were afraid, only because they refused to understand. You needed help – but I was too scared to help you. Who saw, who cared, except Eirian?

Since she rejected us, Ictinike answered, *we have wandered here in the timeless realm between worlds. Waiting for you.*

Perhaps they'd met here because Morgan was already dead.

They circled in the mirror, pushing against each other. They began to meld, two reflections sliding into one. It was like making love, weightless, in a dream. Morgan sank to the ground without pain, experiencing a breathless spasm like an orgasm. They had become a single entity.

He rose, his limbs strong again. Far across the plain he saw a single point of light, and knew it was Eirian. His must reach her before their enemies extinguished the light. Pointing his muzzle towards her, Morgan–Ictinike began to run across the storm-racked plain.

And all the time, the eerie television voices went on clamouring.

Eirian's voice, clear but hesitant. 'I – I made mistakes . . .'

Chapter Twenty

R EACHING Blackthorn Cottage, Beth leapt out of the van and ran up the path. She was numb with cold, her sodden clothes chafing her skin. She found the front door unlocked, the lights on. The first thing that caught her eye was a long splash of blood across the threshold of the kitchen and living room. Then she saw her grandfather sitting on the floor beside the sofa. It faced away from the door so all Beth could see of Rhianwen was her deep red hair hanging over the arm. Her grandfather looked ghastly-white.

Beth rushed to him. Rhianwen was lying down, her eyes closed, face colourless. Randolph was pressing a balled hand-kerchief to her collarbone, his free hand clasping hers. There was more blood on the rug around him. A selection of cats wandered worriedly around the room, tails swaying and fur on end.

'Beth, thank goodness!' her grandfather said as she dropped to her knees beside him. 'I've been worried sick about you.' His voice was level but thick with pain. 'Olivia . . . attacked us with a knife. Have you seen her? She cut the telephone wire so I couldn't call you to make sure you were safe –'

'I'm safe,' Beth whispered. 'What about Rhianwen?'

'It's not a deep wound but she lost some blood and passed out. I've stemmed the bleeding but she needs help.' A tear spilled down his handsome, lined face. 'Rhianwen, will you please keep your eyes open? How many times do I have to tell you?'

Rhianwen uttered a sigh and her eyelids flickered. 'I'm try-ing. I'm so dizzy and it hurts like buggery. Beth, thank the Goddess you're here.'

'Yes, I'm here, dear.' Beth clasped her hand. 'What about you, Granddad?'

'Got me in the thigh. Just a flesh wound, but like a fool I fell and hit my head. Out cold for a few minutes, and when I came round Olivia was gone and Rhianwen pouring blood. I assume Olivia thought she'd killed us. I couldn't contact anyone because I couldn't leave Rhianwen.'

'Steve and Dee are on their way. Shall I get them to call an ambulance?'

They both shook their heads. 'No, no, I'll be all right,' Rhianwen said hurriedly.

'We don't want anyone to know Olivia did this,' Randolph added. Even if his desire to protect his daughter was misplaced, Beth understood.

'Well, why don't we try healing Rhianwen?' Beth said intensely. 'I mean, *healing* her? Isn't it time we both stopped being scared of using our powers? I'll help you.' Beth remembered she had the Horn of Power in her van. The Wand of Rebirth . . . she'd seen it used to heal the sick, but it could also ease a sick person's passage into death. Beth shivered. No, better to rely on herself.

Randolph laid his hands on Rhianwen's chest and Beth placed her hands over his, feeling their bony strength. Her palms began to tingle, their heat transmuting to spiralling energy. She let the radiance flow out, trying to heal her grandfather as well as Rhianwen; willing their wounds to heal, channelling her life energy to sustain theirs. Beth was beginning to feel ill from exhaustion, but she couldn't stop yet.

Colour crept into Rhianwen's cheeks. 'Oh, that's better. I feel warmer now, and the pain's gone.'

Randolph said, 'I'll make some hot drinks. Plenty of sugar, for shock. I do believe I can stand up, at last.' As he did so, leaning on Beth's shoulder, he finally noticed the state she was in. 'My God, you're wet through! How did that happen?'

'I'll tell you later,' she said, eyes lowered. 'Granddad . . . Mum's dead. She tried to kill me, then she killed herself. Car went in a lake.'

Beth couldn't afford to succumb to tiredness or emotion. Leaving her grandfather to digest the news, she ran upstairs, stripped off and dried herself. Her hair smelled of rank quarry water but she towelled it and tied it back. Borrowing a russet Indian dress of Rhianwen's, she came hurrying down again to find Steve and Dee there, worried and bewildered.

They came to hug her, full of anxious questions, but Beth held them away. 'Tell me honestly,' she said, looking into Steve's grey eyes and Dee's lively brown ones. 'You never helped Gabriel, or told him anything that would hurt Eirian, did you?'

'No, we didn't,' Dee answered emphatically. 'He only tried it on that once, like I told you. He must have seen he was getting nowhere.'

Steve added, 'I always thought there was something weird about him. I was with Morgan on that one. Jesus, Beth, how could you ever think we'd betray you?'

Beth sighed with relief and a touch of shame. 'Forgive me. I had to be sure. I'm the one Gabriel took in, not you.' She hastily drank the hot chocolate Randolph had made for her. 'I need your help. Don't ask questions, just do as I say.' She asked Dee to prepare candles and incense while she rushed out to the van and fetched the Horn. The petalled candle-holder gleamed deep blue on the seat, mystical gift from Tom; she took that too. Back in the cottage she switched out the lights and the room glowed lusciously, misty with fragrant smoke. Desperation energized Beth. It seemed she could only access her deepest powers in extremity. Perhaps that's no bad thing, she thought. Perhaps it's time both Eirian and I accepted it.

'Form a circle,' she said. 'Follow me.'

To her surprise, Rhianwen sat up on the sofa. 'I'm going to help you. I feel much better.' Rhianwen and Randolph sat side by side while the other three knelt on the floor. Beth led the ritual. She set the Horn of Power upright in the blue glass flower; this seemed important. The flower was something she'd created, and it represented the Female as the Horn did the Male, and without each other they were incomplete.

Beth visualized a sacred, protective space, invoking the guardians of the east, south, west and north, while Dee and

Steve placed candles at the four corners. Steve lit frankincense in a large censer. The smoke blew around them in peppery clouds. Beth began to chant and the others joined in, calling on the Goddess. She let go of all her terror and pain, felt bathed in her friends' love. The room glowed deep reddish amber and it seemed softly to throb.

She leaned forward and caressed the Horn. Eirian was its guardian. It seemed the only link Beth had to her daughter. The bands of gold and the mystical carving imprinted her palms, seeming to move and whisper against her skin. She began to focus her energy through the Horn.

When she closed her eyes, she saw visions.

Gabriel or Nathaniel; white not for purity but for coldness as he plotted against Eirian, spying on her life; manipulating Alastair, using Olivia, fooling Beth. She saw him, whispering lies in Eirian's ear, seducing her, melting her . . . dissecting her with the most evil accusation of all. *You destroyed Auryn.*

That was what had broken Eirian. Beth saw everything. There was her daughter, her head drooping down, her eyes troubled and vague. Bereft of all her inner convictions. Beth quailed, desperately reaching out to her – but the image was gone.

She saw the wild, horned entity, wandering on some bleak waste land in an agony of loneliness, abandoned by Eirian . . . And she saw Morgan. He lay unconscious, as white as Rhianwen had been, his head tipped back and his hands curled limply. Unconscious or dead? Beth let out a single sob. No, she cried silently, don't leave me, I can't live without you! And she turned the protest into a single, fire-tipped arrow of rage. Goddess, *no*!

In her hands, the Horn blazed. She saw a curve of silver lightning spearing down to touch the entity, arcing between him and Morgan. With her will-power she united them, sending them the infinite energy of her love. The world trembled with silvery tension.

Then the tension broke in a surge of power. Beth felt the Horn rip through her palms, as if huge hands had seized it.

The pain was agonizing. Gold and ivory light imploded in her brain and she fell headlong on the carpet. When she opened her eyes, the candles were dancing wildly and her hands were burning with raw pain, but the stained-glass holder was empty. Beth glimpsed four astonished, concerned faces. She felt herself passing out, exhaustion claiming her at last. A child manifested in the centre of the circle; a boy with a sweet, intelligent face and age-old eyes. *'She didn't kill me, Mum. I couldn't live, I had to go.'*

Beth followed him down into the darkness.

'I deluded myself.' Eirian was struggling. 'I've been misled and I've –' She stopped. She was trying hard to spill out the lies Nathaniel demanded, for her father's sake. But she felt something alien materializing inside her mind. An odd dark pressure, voices calling her. It was too strong to ignore.

'You can do it,' Nathaniel prompted. 'Everyone here loves you.' But his fingertips dug painfully into her knee. A dire warning. Eirian hesitated, dizzy and confused. Superimposed on the bright, clinical studio she could see a dark landscape, lightning flashes, a wolfish figure loping towards her.

Nathaniel glanced at the announcer, Amy, who was listening intently to the director's instructions on her earpiece. She lifted her microphone and said brightly, 'Okay, we're going to a commercial break while Eirian prepares herself for this courageous statement, but we'll be right back so don't go away now!'

The journalists shuffled. Eirian felt burned by their eyes and by the cameras. Nathaniel leaned close and whispered, 'What the hell is wrong with you? You'd better do it. My men are watching this with your daddy, and I only have to twitch a finger for them to start breaking his bones one by one. Every second you hesitate – oh, one of his pretty eyes gone, maybe?'

'Please,' Eirian said weakly. 'I don't feel well. Give me a chance!'

And then the pressure burst like a drumskin inside her skull, and the wolf came tumbling through. Ictinike was inside her

. . . and so was Morgan! Their energy flooded her like a storm, a fiercely protective strength. Eirian had no time to question or resist it; instead she seized the energy by instinct, mastering its wild surge. The glass walls Nathaniel had built around her strained, trembled, exploded outwards. The murky water of lies went gushing out, a damburst. One cleansing rush and it was over. And the first thing she knew was that she had not killed Auryn. But that lie, that lie was the one thing she could never forgive.

Eirian became herself again. Until the searing clarity of this moment, she hadn't realized how far gone she'd been – but she hadn't lost her power. All Nathaniel had done was build false walls in her mind, but that wasn't the same as destroying her. The Goddess was still within her, shining, throbbing with anger. She could feel both Morgan's and Beth's passionate love driving her; the two halves of herself, god and goddess.

For once in her life, Eirian understood that she wasn't alone after all. There *were* others helping her – and, dear Goddess, she needed them.

By reflex she flung up mental shields to hide all this from Nathaniel. In the same moment, for the first time, she saw into his psyche. A pit. Not deep and complex as she'd expected, but shallow, stagnant. What she saw there made her shrink back in revulsion.

'Get a grip on yourself,' Nathaniel said irritably, oblivious to what had happened. 'Two minutes.'

'Okay,' said Eirian, taking a deep breath. 'I'm ready.'

Don't fear for us, said soundless voices in her mind. *Tell the truth*.

When the cue came, she was poised and fully in command of herself again. The announcer welcomed the audience back. Nathaniel's eyes leaned on her, the colour of icebergs.

Eirian gazed straight to camera, summoning her old charisma. 'As I was saying, I've been misled. I'm here today because my father is being held against his will in the basement of this building.' She heard gasps, but went on quickly, 'If anything happens to him now, the people who hurt him won't

378

get away with it. I've been coerced. Nathaniel De Vries, or whatever he calls himself, has spent several weeks trying to brainwash me into renouncing my beliefs. When that failed he resorted to threats.' She sensed Nathaniel's white-hot rage but didn't look at him. He couldn't make her stop. Even if TLN cut the broadcast, the news cameras would carry on. 'He's threatening to kill my father unless I sit here and pretend I've found God. And he wants this purely so that his viewers will start sending lots of money to TLN again. That's what it's all about. Profit. Mind control. Well, it hasn't worked. I stand by everything I've said.' She took the gold cross from round her neck and threw it away as she spoke. 'I'll never renounce the Goddess because I know who I am and what I believe. But who is Nathaniel? I think it's time he told us.'

Eirian met Nathaniel's gaze. His eyes were psychotic. She saw him mustering an eloquent rebuttal of all she'd said, but before he could speak she drove her will inside his mind. Not telling him what to say, only dissolving his self-restraint, as she'd done to PGK. 'Go on,' she whispered, her eyes lancing his. 'Tell them what's in your mind.'

To her dismay, he clamped his lips thinly shut. His only defence was silence. Eirian sensed the collectively held breath of everyone in the studio, the demanding electronic eyes of the cameras.

Then she felt a strange warmth in her left hand and glimpsed a streak of gold and ivory shimmering there, ghostly yet real. Eirian gasped. It was the Horn of Power. A gift from Beth, a reminder to use her inner magic. In a split second she knew what to do. Her will lashed out and the Horn became a snake, alive and writhing; a silver-white avatar of the Goddess, with golden eyes. It reared up on her palm, its scaly head swaying towards Nathaniel. He could see it – but no one else could. And she saw the breaking of phobic horror behind his eyes.

Eirian smiled encouragingly. She knew this was the one thing that would undo him. When he still hesitated, she made the snake hiss and lunge forward to poise its dripping fangs over his heart. Nathaniel pressed back against the couch, turning white. It wasn't that the terror changed his mind. Only that it kicked the last strut of his resistance away.

'What Eirian says is true,' he began in a rush. 'Sure, I threatened her father. Sure, I set out to ruin a little girl half my age and destroy her family. I conned her, seduced her, brainwashed her. Shoulda kept it simple and killed her.'

There were faint exclamations from the audience. He stopped, closing his eyes as if to blank his mind so there'd be nothing to confess. Eirian let the serpent touch his face with its flickering tongue; his eyes flew open and sweat bled from his upper lip. Illusion or not, it was real to him; his psyche was raw and open to hers. 'Tell them why,' she prompted.

For an anguished second he held back, grimly mesmerized by the snake. Then he burst out, 'C'mon, I had to do it. The witch was trying to ruin *me*. Oh, not just TLN's profits, though that's pretty damned important. I don't love God but I love your contributions, all you morons out there who think salvation can be bought.'

Indrawn breaths came from the studio staff. Again Nathaniel clenched his teeth, struggling. Goddess, he was tough! Eirian leaned on his mind. She was intensely aware of her own power, that she could quite easily blow his synapses apart. She didn't want to kill him, only to make him confess. Must be careful . . . *Come on, Nathaniel* . . . He tensed himself against her, battling the urge to admit his secrets, grimacing until corded muscles stood out in his neck. 'Your viewers are morons, are they?' Eirian said softly. 'You'd better explain.'

The silence was thick with tension. She wondered how the audience perceived them; Eirian quietly poised with her left hand palm-upwards on her knee, Nathaniel pallid and shaking for no apparent reason. Sweat sheened his face and trickled down. Suddenly his voice surged in a throaty staccato. 'Dollars mean influence; that's what counts, not your miserable little souls.'

'Influence over –'

'This whole damned society, you stupid whore? Women, blacks, pagans, liberals – they're anarchy. Without mind control, *all* of you are savages and fools. Life is chaos. I have to dominate it, any way I can.'

'*Any* way?' Eirian felt cold. 'Legal or illegal?'

He was trembling visibly now. Blue veins bulged in his temples. The serpent swayed on her hand as her will nudged at him. Gently now. Gently . . . He gasped, and out came the words, savage, incriminating, full of contempt. 'So what if I boost TLN's income with bribes from corrupt politicians, or help a few drug barons to launder their millions? If the dregs of society want to destroy themselves with crack and heroin, great. Helps get the country all neat and clean for the future. TLN gives to good causes too; we build Bible colleges and train even more evangelists to brainwash more suckers out of their hard-earned dollars. Maybe some of our charity slips into the hands of racist groups or redneck militias; so what? It's all in the same cause. I'm above the law, I *am* the law. One little witch won't be allowed to undermine all my hard work.'

'How will you stop me?' she said quickly.

'My guys in the basement, I pay 'em to kill bitches like you. Scum who piss me off, like PGK. Anyone who gets in my way.'

There were gasps. Nathaniel put his clenched hands to his head, as if in despair. Then he went on viciously to camera, 'What're you bitching about? You think those right-wing religious leaders are any better than me? Some are sincere believers, some may be fuckin' saints, but we all want the same thing: control. And we'll get it, but they'll be my puppets, in the new America, 'cos I have a power they can't touch.'

'Did it never occur to you to use this wonderful power for good?' Eirian spoke icily, but felt a sudden spasm in her throat.

Nathaniel gave a cynical laugh. 'What the hell is "good", honey? The Evangelical Right and the Fundamentalists think they're doing God's will on Earth; their opponents think they're one shade pinker than Hitler. "Good" is what you believe in. To that end, the Bible's one heck of a tool and the financial rewards just a symptom of success. Divine approval, even. You won't stop us, bitch. Never.'

He slumped back, panting, sweat and tears running down

the white creases of his face. His strength was gone, but she still felt the hatred flowing from him. The snake turned stiff and lifeless in her palm; the Horn faded and vanished. Her hands were empty, her heart coldly overflowing. She could keep his mind pinned down now without effort, but her victory tasted of wormwood.

'*You* are a symptom, Nathaniel,' Eirian said intensely. 'I wish you were the cause but you aren't. I hear it on the news every day. The human race is in danger of losing all the progress we've made. Religious groups are trying to close the separation between Church and state as the millennium approaches. The Pope installs bishops who are against women's rights, let alone women priests; the anti-feminist lobby in the States is rising. It's not politically correct to criticize other religions or cultures, so Western countries play down their own women's rights rather than offend religious states. Western "intellectuals" won't even take a stand against female genital mutilation. We'll all be turned into brutes, men and women alike, if we don't open our eyes and fight back. All you've done, Nathaniel, is feed on that sickness. So go on, tell them the inside story. I've said enough.'

Further confessions of fraud and corruption began to pour from Nathaniel's helpless mouth, but Eirian couldn't listen any more. Her eyes and her throat ached. As he spoke, she stood up and walked down the side of the studio between the wall and the tiered seats. The audience were deathly quiet, the studio staff dumbstruck as their angelic boss spilled out the sick truth to millions. People glanced at her as she passed, but no one tried to stop her.

At the rear door she stopped and looked back. But Nathaniel was ashen. He knew it was the end of his world.

She began to open the double door, meaning to slip out and find Morgan. That was when a hand closed on her arm, and a burly figure whispered, 'Eirian!'

In the basement, Morgan–Ictinike crouched in the shadows in the shape of a wolf. He saw his human body lying inert. He saw two figures silhouetted against the television screen, ne big and bull-necked, one neat and slender. He heard Eirian's voice, then Nathaniel's, pouring out his ugly confession.

'Jesus!' hissed the slim one, horrified. 'Jesus, I don't believe this!'

'Gil, what are we gonna do?' said Moses.

'I'm gettin' out. Our lord and master's blown it! After that performance, do you wanna be here when the police arrive?'

Moses pointed at Morgan's body. 'What about him?'

'Kill him, so he can't identify us,' said Gil. He reached inside his jacket and brought out a hand-gun.

Morgan–Ictinike watched the two men closing in on Morgan's helpless body. It must be protected. Roaring, the wolf-entity came surging out of the shadows. He swelled in size as he came, horns springing from his temples, fangs lengthening, claws unsheathed like clashing daggers.

The two men turned and screamed. Snarling, ruthless, unfettered, the entity leapt and Moses flailed backwards in terror, cracking his skull on the edge of a desk as he fell. Gil fled, flinging doors open as he went. Lying panting on Moses's stomach, Morgan–Ictinike sensed a haemorrhage inside the skull, a vein leaking clouds of blood to bathe the brain ... If Moses recovered, no one would believe what he'd seen.

Abruptly Morgan found himself in his own body again, lying beside the unconscious guard. He felt an agonizing pain in his left wrist, a throbbing ache in his injured knee and a dull headache. For a few moments he didn't know where he was. He was free, but the handcuff was still attached to the pipe, the circle of metal broken open; how the hell had he done that? No wonder his wrist was killing him. He heard footsteps dwindling rapidly along a basement corridor, the faint click of wolf claws fading ... He saw the open door and the bright TV screen.

A male newsreader was talking intently. 'A shocking on-screen confession of murder, drug involvement, corruption and other illegal activities has just been made by Nathaniel De Vries, the chairman of the True Light Network. We're hoping to return to that live broadcast where De Vries is rumoured to have left the building, evading the police officers who are waiting to question him.'

Morgan got painfully to his feet. He found he could walk, with effort. He had a sickening memory of his kneecap being dislocated . . . then remembered that Eirian had healed him. Without her, he probably wouldn't be walking at all. And without Ictinike . . . he'd be dead.

Dizzy, Morgan grabbed his leather jacket and bag, quickly checking his documents. At least they hadn't stolen anything. Then he began to make his way along the corridor outside, searching for a way out.

Nathaniel heard the words falling from his mouth as if they were coming from someone else. He watched himself in full, horrified consciousness, but he couldn't stop.

The terrible snake reared in front of him, bringing him out in a silver-cold sweat of terror. Its fangs and its mindless eyes horrified him. Behind it, Eirian sat serenely, her eyes agleam with age-old power. He hated her bitterly but he was impotent. How had she conjured the serpent to undo him?

She got up and left before he finished, but Nathaniel was in such a state of anxiety he barely felt any relief. He was compelled to go on until all his vile secrets were spilled. Perversely, it felt almost good to gloat, telling people what fools he'd made of them. But the moment he'd finished speaking, he sat in full knowledge of what he'd revealed. The police would be on their way already. He must escape them – and Eirian. God alone knew what else she might do to him. The serpent could be waiting . . . anywhere. Must run, hide.

In panic, Nathaniel tore off his mike and scrambled over the back of the couch. None of his staff or technicians tried to apprehend him. They only stared – Amy, Aaron and others, with their sugary smiles wiped away – as he staggered backstage over a tangle of electrical cables and made for the outer doors. His brain was a haze of fear. He could hear journalists shouting after him, a rising clamour of voices. Maybe the exits were covered already – but he knew a way out. He ran half-way along a deserted corridor and slipped into the men's toilets. Climbing through a window, he dropped softly into the service road that led to the back of the studio canteen. It was ill-lit, no one about. As he raced across the narrow road to a land-scaped bank of shrubs on the far side, a police vehicle with lights flashing came cruising around the corner of the building, a hundred yards away. Nathaniel flung himself down in the bushes until it had passed. Dry earth clung to his face and clothes. The car drew up in a loading bay, blocking the doors to the kitchens, as if they thought he might come out that way. He saw a cop get out and shine a torch behind the trash cans. Nathaniel gave a grimace of contempt, then he was up and running through the foliage. Where the shrubs ended, he slipped into an alley between two old office buildings. He felt hunted, the image of Eirian and the snake burning into his mind.

His brain worked furiously as her bewitchment faded. How the hell did I get into this? Running like a rat! I shoulda stayed, denied everything. I need my lawyers . . . and a place to hide while I call them.

'Eirian, hey, it's all right!' said the man who'd grabbed her. He was middle aged, rotund and black, with a shiny bald head rimmed by grey hair. He wore thick glasses. 'It's me, Jamie Baker.'

She recognized him. 'Oh, Jamie,' she said in relief at seeing a face she knew. He ushered her through the doors to the corridor outside. 'Help me find my father, please.'

'Sure, come on.'

A journalist came rushing out of the door behind them. 'Miss Rhys! I need to ask a few questions –'

Jamie turned and said gruffly, 'Will you leave the lady the hell alone?' The man fell back, disgruntled. With a hand on her back, Jamie hurried her along the corridor. Although Eirian knew she could have dealt with it herself, she was glad of his protective presence.

'What are you doing here?'

'Suzanne called, told me you'd run off with that Nathaniel and your parents were going crazy. So I found some stuff out about him.' Jamie shook his head gravely. 'Guess you know it all by now. That's why your dad came after you. I was real worried so I flew down to watch out for you.'

Eirian couldn't speak. His concern moved her unbearably, and all she could think of was how much trouble she'd caused her family.

As they reached the foyer, where a knot of police officers and journalists were gathering, the lift doors hissed open and Morgan came out. He looked as if he'd been sleeping rough and he was limping badly, but when he saw Eirian his tired face lit up. She raced across the marble floor and threw herself on him. They hugged fervently. Eirian started to cry. 'Dad, I was so scared you were dead when you came to me with Ictinike. You saved me. But I thought you were dead.'

'No, I just look like I am,' he said into her hair. 'You saved yourself; we only helped you.' Jamie was keeping the reporters at bay around them. 'All I want to do now is go to the airport, phone Beth, and fly home. Have you got your passport?'

Eirian hesitated. 'It's in my jacket, up in the make-up room.'

Jamie said, 'I'll make sure you get it, honey. But it's not that simple; the police are gonna want to talk to you both.'

'Oh, shit,' said Morgan. 'Yeah, they would. Nothing's ever straightforward.'

Jamie patted their arms reassuringly. 'Don't worry about a thing. You're gonna be too late to get a flight tonight. I'll get you to hospital for a check-up and book you a hotel so you can get a good night's sleep. You can talk to the police tomorrow. With luck they'll let you folks go home tomorrow night; I'll sort out your tickets.'

'Thanks,' Morgan sighed. 'We really appreciate this.'

'Thank you, Jamie,' Eirian said faintly. 'I'm sorry to have been such a nuisance.'

'A nuisance?' Jamie chuckled. 'When you got that bastard

to confess to all his crimes on air? Hey, how the hell d'you do that?'

Eirian shrugged. She felt hurt, angry and cold, but she was beginning to shed the skin. 'He did it to himself. They always do.'

Everything went as Jamie said. About seven in the morning, Morgan tried to ring Beth from the hotel. Eirian was still fast asleep in the other bed. He felt infinitely better for a night's sleep and he was desperate to talk to Beth – if only to begin the process of abject apology. With distance – and the nearness of death – he could see how heartless he must have appeared to her. God, what the hell does it matter what I feel about Olivia, as long as Beth's happy? But she wasn't happy, that's the whole point. And I was only mad at her because I couldn't make her see it . . .

It would be mid-day in England. A woman answered, but it wasn't Beth's voice. 'It's Morgan,' he said. 'Who's that?'

'It's Dee. I'm here looking after Beth.'

He was alarmed. 'Why, what's wrong?'

'Everything's all right,' Dee said hurriedly, 'but Beth's had a bad time. She's sound asleep and I don't want to wake her. Steve's here too. Are you all right? Beth's been frantic!'

'Yes, we're fine. I've got Eirian with me. Dee, tell me what happened.'

'Olivia,' Dee began hesitantly. 'Olivia had a – well, a car accident. She's dead.'

'Oh, Christ,' Morgan gasped. 'How?'

'Apparently she meant to kill herself. She tried to take Beth with her, but Beth got out. Morgan, I've got some other news, it's not good but it's nothing to worry about now. Before she died, Olivia went a bit crazy. I'm afraid she turned up at your parents' cottage and wounded them with a knife.'

'She *what?*'

'Morgan, they're all right, they're resting. They're going to be fine. I'm terribly sorry you had to hear this from me.'

'That's okay, Dee. Thanks for being straight.'

'Well, Beth can tell you the full story. I'm so glad Eirian's all right. Any message for Beth, when she wakes up?'

'Tell her we love her,' he said heavily. 'And we're coming home.'

On the flight home, Morgan had a centre seat, Eirian the one nearest the aisle. The window seat was empty. Several hours spent answering police questions about Nathaniel De Vries had worn them both out. Eirian was pale and preoccupied, especially since he'd told her about Olivia.

'Olivia was working for Nathaniel,' Eirian had said quietly. 'I should have known. We should have protected Mum. *Mum nearly died because of me.*'

Now Morgan wished she would be angry, upset, anything rather than silent. An hour into the flight, she got up wordlessly and went to the loo. When she came back, she looked whiter than ever.

'Aren't you feeling well, love?' Morgan asked, concerned.

'Stomach ache,' she said. 'My period's started.'

'Oh. Is it painful?'

'Not too bad. I'm relieved, more than anything.' She exhaled, biting her lip. 'We had unprotected sex a few times. Don't lecture me, I know it was stupid. If you're worried about the other thing, Gabriel told me he'd had HIV tests and they were clear. I believe him, even if he lied about everything else, because it's just the sort of thing he'd be paranoid about.'

'Oh, Eirian. Right, imagine I've delivered the standard lecture and we'll leave it at that, okay?' Eirian smiled. Morgan breathed a quiet sigh of relief with her. 'Do you want to sit in the window seat?'

'Okay. Don't get up.' As Eirian squeezed past him, her denim-encased bottom swaying past his nose, he wished he were not continually being made aware that she was no longer a child.

She settled herself in the seat, then leaned into him and rested her head on his shoulder. Morgan put his arm round her. 'Dad,' she said, 'you know how I said I was never going to make a mistake?'

'Ooh, I bet you're sorry you said that.'

'I really thought he loved me.'

'I know,' he said gently, 'But we love you, your mum and me. And Rhianwen and Randolph. And Sam and Peter and –'

'All right. Nathaniel completely screwed my head up so I couldn't see anything straight, couldn't even believe you loved me. I'll never trust anyone else.'

'You will, but give it time. Don't try to grow up too fast.'

'You want me to stay a child for ever.'

'No. Just until you're about thirty-five, that'll do.' Eirian laughed; that pleased him. 'I'm sorry I acted the heavy-handed father. It's not that I don't want anyone else to have you. It was because I always felt uneasy about Gabriel, Nathaniel, whatever. I'm not going to say I told you so, but I wish I'd trusted my instincts. With Olivia too.'

'She was poisoning us,' Eirian said, very low. 'I heard her say things which I know aren't true.'

'Things?'

'I overheard her accusing you of wanting to screw all your female relatives, including me.'

Morgan gasped in shock. 'For God's sake!' He struggled for a moment with hopeless fury. 'Malicious bloody hag. It's one thing Olivia saying it to me, but for you to hear it – I suppose she *wanted* you to hear it. God, I feel terrible. I'd like to strangle her. Christ . . .'

'Dad, it's all right. I worked out what she was up to.'

He calmed down. 'Well, I'm sorry to disappoint you, Eirian. I think you're gorgeous but the only person I'm interested in making love to is your mum.' He grimaced. 'If she'll forgive me.'

'She'd better,' Eirian said fiercely, intertwining her arm with his. 'It took Nathaniel to make me realize where I really belong. Don't split up with her, Dad. I couldn't stand it. I'm so sorry. I love you.'

*

389

Nathaniel jogged softly along an alley, collecting his disordered thoughts. The witch mind-fucked me for about ten minutes, he told himself, not for ever. I'll clear my name – there's no evidence against me – and then I'll destroy her. Hey, plenty of sickos out there will think I'm a goddamned hero!

He'd spent the day holed up in some rooms used by a drug-dealer he knew. He hadn't washed or eaten, but it didn't occur to him that his sanity might be slipping away. Now, the following night, he was heading for Gil's apartment – one of the assassin's many bolt-holes. Gil, despite his wealth, seemed to feel safer in the shittiest areas of town.

Nathaniel's mind was awash with grievances against the mother who'd abandoned him, the employees who'd let him down and most of all against Eirian, who'd seduced him in every possible way then turned round and injected him with her venom.

At least she'd go home and find her mother dead, ha. Unless Olivia had fucked up too.

The brick walls were high and forbidding, garlanded with grime and rusting fire escapes. The alley between them was a deep narrow chasm, with burst garbage bags strewing their mouldering contents across his path. It stank. His aesthetic senses were revolted. What the hell was he doing here, a million miles from the jewelled beauty of his Maryland estate?

Then a piece of shadow took shape and stepped out in his path.

'I've been waiting for you,' said Gil's voice, sharp as a snake's fang. 'You stupid bastard. You ruined everything. You ruined us all, for the sake of screwing that little bitch!'

Nathaniel began to say, 'No!' just as he saw the crack of fire, heard the shot. The word came out as a bark of shock. He reeled back on to gritty concrete, his head whirling and blood pouring from a coldly aching hole in his ribs. The pain washed in slowly. Gil was an expert, he meant it to be slow.

Staring up at the grimy glow of the sky, Nathaniel saw a silhouette blot out the light. Half goat, half ragged demon, it rose over him – like the creature he'd seen haunting Eirian but overblown, hideous, terrible. It leapt clear over him and bore Gil to the ground. Through a nightmarish glaze of unreality, Nathaniel watched the beast making long gouges through Gil's face, shredding his designer clothes and drawing out his intestines in long, bubbling loops. Then it turned on Nathaniel.

He saw long horny claws clashing like scythes, a monstrous mouth full of fangs, horns on its head that writhed like snakes. Its long head swayed above him. He was petrified, numb. Its claws tore away his trousers. Then he felt its phallus, hard as bone, thrusting painfully into his rectum. It tore him, perforating his bowel. The fanged jaws gaped open, dripping red saliva on to his face from a lascivious tongue. Nathaniel screamed, went on screaming until the jaws closed on his throat. Images danced in his mind. *His ancestors marching across the land with guns and Bibles . . . a shaman of a heathen tribe nailed to an X-shaped cross . . . darkness subjugated by light . . . darkness undying, rising again like night, like winter, like the hag of death . . . Voices whispering, join us, share the suffering your kind inflicted on us . . .*

It took Nathaniel a long time to die. He lay with his blood oozing out into a warm pool around him. The warmth cooled quickly and he began to shiver. His teeth chattered. He heard police sirens a long way off but no one came to help him.

Eyes watched him. The six sorrowful green eyes of the triple Goddess: Eirian and Beth and Rhianwen. And the glowing orbs of the Horned God, the wolf, Morgan.

Nathaniel drifted. He remembered Eirian's rare smile, her luxuriant brown hair, her sweetness. Her body undulating around him, her breasts against his ribs and his penis embedded deliciously in her hot female core. I love you, she said. I've never felt like this about anyone. I never thought I could. Eirian in the boat, melting beneath him in orgasm. Both dissolving into each other in the sun's heat like honey into wine.

He remembered how close he'd come to forgetting himself.

She'd given him so much. Trust, love, time; all the things she couldn't afford to give. She would have given him everything. A chance to leave his bitter life-hating self behind. Redemption.

He could have drowned in her love. Been happy with her. At peace for the first time in his life, for the rest of his life. Instead he'd hardened his heart and kicked it all back in her face. And thought himself such a genius.

He could have been warm in her arms now, instead of dying here in this alley among the stinking garbage, the dead rats and the cockroaches.

Bleeding. So cold. Fading now.

Alone.

His lips formed her name as he died. 'Eirian . . .'

Eirian's eyes flew open. The cabin was dark, passengers dozing or watching the film. But Morgan was awake and he saw his daughter jerk out of sleep in wide-eyed, stiff horror. 'What is it?' he said gently.

'Gabriel's dead,' she whispered. 'I felt him die. He was sorry, at the end. He said my name.'

Eirian began to weep, soundlessly, her head hidden in his chest. Morgan held her tight. He had no reason to disbelieve her. When she finally finished, she seemed tranquil; a woman, not a girl. He stroked her hair and kissed her stained cheeks. She was never again going to doubt that he loved her.

Eventually they both slept, hand-in-hand. Morgan stirred at some stage and clearly saw, in the aisle seat next to him, a dark-haired boy of about five. The child stared at him with apple-green eyes; it was like looking at an image of himself at that age. But when he woke properly, the seat was empty.

Walking out of the customs hall into the main concourse of Terminal 3 early the next morning, Morgan and Eirian were both tired. His car was in the airport car park, at great expense, and he wasn't looking forward to the drive home. Idly glancing over the crowds of people waiting behind the tape for the arrivals, Morgan saw a man with long, fair hair who looked a lot like Steve. Wait . . . it *was* Steve. And there was Dee beside him, hair like dark fire . . . and Beth, tall and slender in black velvet, eyes and lips dark as wine against her white face.

He nudged Eirian. 'Look who's here.'

Beth had seen them. Light came to her eyes and she waved, dancing along behind the crowd until it thinned out and they could reach each other. But as she came closer her smile set to a grimace of anger. Rushing to them, Beth seized Eirian's shoulders and said savagely, 'Don't you *ever* do that to me again!'

Shocked, Eirian burst into tears. Then their arms went round each other and they embraced fiercely. Beth reached for Morgan and they all clutched one another, laughing, crying. Beth kept kissing them both in turn, not knowing which one to favour. 'Morgan, I've been such a fool, please forgive me,' Beth said, sobbing. 'You were right about Olivia and I was wrong.'

'I didn't want you to find out like this,' he said softly.

'But if anything had happened to Rhianwen and Granddad, I couldn't have lived with myself!'

'But they're all right, aren't they?' She nodded. He held her to him. 'And so are you, thank the Goddess. Let's not think about what nearly happened.'

'What's all this?' Beth said, stroking his bruised face. 'Why are you limping?'

'TLN hospitality,' said Morgan. 'I'll live. We'll talk later, eh? Let's get a coffee before we go home. Hey, we weren't expecting a welcoming committee!'

'I couldn't wait to see you,' said Beth. 'We came in Dee's car. Steve or I can drive yours back, save you driving.'

'From what Dee said, you should be in bed, madam,' Morgan said, mock-severe.

Beth smiled shakily. 'That's the best offer I've had all day.'

At Blackthorn Cottage that afternoon, Rhianwen greeted Morgan, Eirian and Beth with hugs and expressions of pro-found relief. Steve and Dee discreetly left them to it. Morgan was shocked to see how pale his mother looked, but she and Randolph were recovering. He was suddenly overwhelmed by the horror of how it would have been if he'd come home and found that Olivia had succeeded in killing his parents. The

393

feeling was so devastating that he had to go and sit on his own in the kitchen.

Randolph came in and sat across the table from him. In a quiet voice, he told Morgan exactly what had happened. When he'd finished, they looked at each other. 'Well, over the past five years you've progressed from calling me Dr Cross to calling me Randolph. Is there any chance you might refer to me as Father before I expire of old age?'

Morgan laughed tiredly. 'Yes. You don't have to ask. Life's too short, isn't it, Dad?' Tentatively, he clasped his father's hand across the table. This felt somehow embarrassing yet very, very good. 'I'm sorry about Olivia.'

Randolph breathed out, his face grim. 'I never expected to outlive Heather, let alone our daughter. Now I have to live with knowing I failed Livvy in some way and I can never put it right.'

'You didn't force-feed her religion. She did that to herself. You've still got me and Beth. We need you.'

When they went back to the living room, Rhianwen was on the sofa between Beth and Eirian. They were talking softly, but as the men came in, Rhianwen looked up and said, 'I've something to tell you about Olivia. Just before she attacked us, she told me she once saw a being that sounded exactly like the entity. It manifested itself to her when she was fifteen. She thought it was the Devil. I don't think I could have said anything to persuade her otherwise. So when she spent her life fighting Satan, in her own mind she was fighting something real.'

'My God, not Livvy too,' said Randolph. 'Wish I'd never been near the Hellstone and drawn the damned thing to us.'

Beth turned even paler, her face like porcelain against her ebony hair. Her eyes were smudged with tiredness, but she looked exquisite to Morgan, unutterably precious. The thought that he'd nearly lost her, too, was agonizing. He wanted to get her home and tell her, show her how he felt. 'Do you think,' she said, 'that Mum's religious obsession was all caused by the entity? If she hadn't seen it . . .'

'Her obsession started long before that,' Randolph put in.

'Other way round, Mum,' said Eirian. 'Her rigid viewpoint gave her no capacity to understand that the entity might *not* be evil. She saw in it what she wanted to see. Vindication.'

'But she suffered.' Rhianwen sounded sad. 'Olivia never seemed able to be happy. I only hope, in the end, she found some kind of peace.'

'The idea was to punish you for eleven years. The length of my life before I met my father.' Eirian had followed Rhianwen into the kitchen and slipped her arms round her waist. 'But I can't, Gran.'

'Since when have you had a change of heart?' said Rhianwen, returning the embrace.

'Since I found out what it's like to make a horrendous mistake while being absolutely convinced I was doing the right thing.'

Rhianwen was so moved and elated she could have cried, but she kept her voice light. 'Well, that's a two-edged apology, if ever I heard one. Still, I can't tell you how glad I am to hear it, love.'

'I wanted to hurt you,' Eirian said frankly. 'If you hadn't *cared* that I wouldn't forgive you, I could never have taken it back. But you did care, so I can. I always loved you, Gran. I mean, people can only really hurt you if you love them, can't they?'

'Quite. Exactly. Well, now we're in the same boat for behaving badly, you might find out what it's like to have your nose rubbed in it. But not by me.'

'How's the knee?' asked Beth, lying in bed with Morgan. It was mid-afternoon. They'd had lunch with Rhianwen and Randolph and arrived home about three. Eirian had gone to her room for a rest. Although it wasn't easy to let her out of their sight at present, Beth and Morgan were happy to spend some time alone.

'Eirian's a miracle-worker,' he said. 'It's just a bit stiff.'

'And your knee,' said Beth, groping him. They laughed.

She'd never seen anything more beautiful than his bruised, tired face and sleepy green eyes. She held him, inexpressibly grateful for his presence, his wholeness. 'Oh, God, I really thought I'd lost you. We're so lucky.'

'Wasn't luck, Bethie,' he said thoughtfully. 'You did something to help us, didn't you?'

She hadn't told him about that yet. 'What?'

'I felt so strongly that you were with us. I felt your warmth, I'd know it anywhere. You gave us your energy. I'm sure we would never have escaped without you.'

Beth was so moved she could hardly reply. 'Well, we tried.' She told him about the working, how she'd collapsed afterwards, been taken home and woken the next day by Dee telling her that he and Eirian were on their way. 'Then the police came. They found my mother's car in the quarry, her body a few hours later. I told them I last saw her at the workshop in a disturbed state, but she drove off by herself.'

'Why?'

'Same reason Granddad won't tell the police she attacked him. I don't ever want people to know my own mother tried to kill me.' Beth released a long sigh. 'I had to identify the body. Strange, I felt nothing.'

'I'm sure that's not true.'

'You tried to warn me about her and I wouldn't listen. I can't even ask you to forgive me.'

'No, Beth, I'm the one who should apologize. I behaved appallingly. I should've been more understanding, but all I could feel from her was this calculating malevolence. I can't believe what she did! How could she go to such lengths to hurt her own daughter? God, if I'd lost you –' They clung together, hands and hair and limbs entangled. The luxurious relief of being together was warming to lust. Morgan entered her, pushing gently into her moist inner sanctum. He was home.

'But I'm not hurt,' Beth said darkly, moving against him. 'When she died – once I'd got over the shock – all I felt was relief. The Olivia I wanted to love was an idealized mother, not the real woman. I was trying to make her into someone she wasn't . . . and it's such a relief not to have to try any more! When she smashed my work, she was destroying everything I am; that's how much she hated me. Well, she smashed anything I felt for her too. The horrible thing is that at the very last moment, she realized that maybe she loved me after all. She started saying she got it all wrong, it was Gabriel who hated me, not her, and she should have protected me. Too late. I couldn't forgive her, couldn't . . .'

'Hush, babe, hush,'

'But to think that, if not for Gabriel, she might have really changed!'

'Don't,' he said tenderly. 'You're only tormenting yourself.'

'All that work,' Beth gasped as his hands moved over her. 'I've got to start again from scratch.'

'You can do it.'

'Yes. It was only glass and lead she ruined. Not us.'

Physical sensation took over from speech. They made love as if they'd been apart for twelve years, not four days. Beth was still weeping a few minutes later as they took each other thrusting and gasping through the fire of orgasm. A healing outflow of fluids; salty, musky, milk-white.

As they lay deliciously drained afterwards, Bast slipped into the room and climbed on to the bedcovers, pressing her furry body between theirs. She purred loudly as Beth stroked her thick slate-blue coat. Her eyes were round, glowing, full of meaning.

'I wonder how long this lady will be with us?' said Beth. 'She's twenty. Which means you and I have known each other twenty years, give or take a gap.'

'So we have. Wow, we'll get to know each other yet.' Morgan's fingers met hers in Bast's fur. 'A couple of Mum's cats are well into their twenties. Llew and Anki. Could kip for England.'

'Bast's not just a cat. She's been my best friend.'

'She's a goddess, actually.' Morgan smiled. 'She graces us with her presence.'

Beth began to laugh. 'I can't believe what you did when we went to see Rhianwen this afternoon.'

'What?'

'Hugged your father.'

'I know.' Morgan smiled. 'I think he was as shocked as I was.'

'Concentrates the mind, doesn't it, knowing someone nearly died? Makes all the resentments and arguments seem futile.'

'The last time your mother saw us together,' said Morgan, 'we were kissing, not arguing. And that's why I kissed you in front of her. To show her the truth, that there was nothing she could do in all her warped jealousy to destroy us.'

'Maybe that was why she killed herself,' said Beth.

Later that evening, Beth experienced the luxury of having her daughter all to herself. They leaned on the window-sill in Eirian's room, watching the sunset drenching the garden with rosy-amber light. Their arms were round each other; Eirian was as tall as Beth now. Beth loved the feel of her daughter's warm body against hers, the silky hair against her face as they told each other their stories. Eirian didn't cry.

'You were right, I was wrong,' she said bitterly. 'Mum, I'm sorry. I couldn't see the pain I was causing you. I've been so stupid.'

'No, you were taken in by a subtle criminal who fooled us all.'

'I was bound to make enemies,' Eirian said pensively. 'But I don't regret my appearances, I'd do it all again. It'll start in England soon, the evangelical broadcasting. I can't let them do it without putting the Goddess's side! Otherwise I'll be letting bastards like Luke and Gabriel win –'

'Eirian, please,' Beth said chidingly. 'You've barely been home half a day.'

'Sorry, I'll shut up. Anyway, I thought I was too clever to be taken in by someone like Gabriel; at least he taught me I'm not.'

'Didn't get away with it, though, did he? I'd give anything to have seen that broadcast!'

Beth was smiling, but Eirian remained grave. 'A real victory would have been him changing and coming over to our side. Took death to change him . . .' Her voice fell. 'But I didn't cause his death, Mum, not this time. Not that I regret Luke, but there are better ways.'

'Yes,' said Beth, 'but some people deserve harsh judgement.'

'I took no pleasure in destroying Gabriel. I thought I loved him. I don't any more. But it still hurts.'

'I know. I know. You tried to grow up too soon. I've been there, done that.'

'Got the T-shirt,' Eirian added morosely. 'I'll never trust a man again.'

'You will. But there's nothing wrong with being careful.'

'I trust you and Dad. I didn't mean the vile things I said to you! Gabriel completely warped my perceptions, and I couldn't see it until it was over.'

'He warped ours too,' said Beth.

'But some of my delusions were all mine,' Eirian confessed, 'like thinking I was alone and didn't need you. Without your strength and Dad's, I couldn't have defeated him. I need you. I love you.'

Beth held her close, thinking, I wish it hadn't taken a broken heart to make you realize it. 'And Rhianwen?'

'Of course I love her! I was an arrogant little sod, refusing to forgive her for the past. I told her today. Whatever Rhianwen did wrong, she never made a mistake that nearly got us all killed.'

Beth leaned on the window-sill. 'Well, I'm the one who welcomed my mother into the house. Not your dad, and not you.'

'But you did it out of love, like you do everything,' said Eirian. They were silent for a while, caressing each other. When Eirian spoke again her voice was barely audible. 'Mum . . . I didn't make you lose the baby. Yes, I was jealous. But I never ill-wished him. I would have loved him.'

They looked into each other's eyes. There was no need to explain, they both knew. But Beth had come so close to swallowing Olivia's poison . . . and to have believed any of it would have pushed Beth over the brink of annihilation. Yes, it would have been worse than death. —

'I haven't really lost him,' said Beth. 'I often see him.' Eirian bit the corner of her mouth as if to stop it souring with tears. Beth changed the subject. 'What will you do about your book?'

'Oh, that. Stick it in a drawer. Maybe I'll fetch it out again in ten years' time and rewrite it; maybe not. But I'm not going to be a martyr about the advance money; I'm going to use it to help me through university. I want to do psychology, or whatever will make me best able to help people.'

Beth hugged her. Another affectionate pause, then Beth said, 'Eirian, I've done something awful. When I used the Horn of Power in the working to help you, it vanished.'

Eirian frowned. 'But Mum . . . You did help! I felt you! The Horn, the snake! But I don't understand . . .' She turned away and knelt down, reaching under her bed. When she came up, she had the Horn of Power in her hand. 'It's still here. It was the first thing I checked when I got home!'

'Oh,' Beth said weakly. She didn't know whether to laugh or scream. 'Oh, my God. How did it – did I just imagine I was using it, or what?'

Eirian stood stroking the long ivory spike. It seemed to light her face from below, making her look eldritch. 'Sometimes I'm angry with the Goddess for making me grow up too soon,' she said broodingly. 'But I can't go back to childhood. It's too late. Loss of innocence, or something. I still have to go on working for the Goddess. I won't let this stop me.'

Beth said with feeling, 'I know, and we want to help you. But give it a rest until you're older, eh?'

'Yes,' Eirian said softly. 'Until I'm older.'

Envoi

AFTER the funeral, Beth, Morgan and Eirian went with Randolph and Rhianwen to the quarry to say a final farewell to Olivia. They asked Steve, Dee and their sons to join them there.

Philip came too, alone. He explained awkwardly that Alastair had left him and gone to live in Edinburgh. He seemed resigned. Beth hadn't the heart to tell her father how Nathaniel had manufactured the relationship. That would be one blow too many. But she vowed to visit him often, so he wouldn't feel abandoned.

How to say goodbye to the intransigent spirit of Olivia who, when they'd tried to love her, had fought them every step of the way?

They stood on the bank amid trees and bushes, the grey quarry walls enclosing them and the lake lying as still as iron. There were no tears and no words of ritual, pagan or otherwise. They simply threw flowers on the water. Yet Beth felt a change of energy, from the darkness of the drowning to a sombre peace.

There had been a call from America a few days ago. Nathaniel De Vries had been shot dead by one of his own hitmen, who had then, apparently, turned the gun on himself. Eirian had shown no emotion at the news. She'd already known, even though she *couldn't* have known. And she had the strength, Beth saw, to close the episode and move on.

Beth glanced at her companions; Randolph and Philip standing side by side in dark overcoats, their gloved hands folded reverently in front. Steve and Dee, such dear friends. Rhianwen, who'd set Beth on this strange path so many years ago, her face strong and serene amid the henna-red waves of hair. Eirian, who'd learned to forgive as well as to punish.

And Morgan. She sensed how badly shaken up he'd been, jolted out of his youthful illusion that his charm made him somehow invulnerable. But Beth would take pleasure in healing him.

Beth had become stronger in the past few days. It felt wonderful to be sure of her family and friends, to receive back the love she gave so freely. She was finally certain, from the firmness of Morgan's arms around her, that even this beautiful wild god who had her in thrall could alight on the earth and stay for good. She felt released by Olivia's death to make the most of her power instead of skirting around it. To tame the fire and become a true witch.

She and Eirian and Rhianwen would work together now. Healers.

Beth looked at Steve's and Dee's boys. Sam, an ordinary but considerate lad, no longer tainted by Luke – thanks to Eirian. Hugh and Peter, two kind-natured, attractive youths. Beth didn't feel deprived at having no son of her own . . . only at losing part of Morgan, a child of his exquisite sensuality who would have been even more beautiful and completely, sweetly hers . . . as if there could ever be another Morgan.

She tried not to cry. She looked up at the clouded sky, thinking, why did you have to leave us?

The high walls echoed as a flight of ducks came flapping down to churn the lake surface. The flowers were swirled and tossed. Beth hugged Eirian and Morgan closer to her. Then she saw . . .

On the lip of the lake, a tall slim child with dark hair and Morgan's eyes. Auryn. A grey cat like Bast wound briefly round his legs and vanished, but the boy remained. Whether he was really there – as Ictinike had been real to Eirian – or a conjuration of Beth's intense longing, she didn't care. He would always be with her, a beautiful spirit more perfect than he could ever have been in the flesh . . . but she would still have swapped that for life with all its imperfection.

Auryn spoke. *'What are you crying for, Mum? I've been waiting for the right time to come to you again. It's not that I've left you. It's only that I haven't arrived yet.'*

Beth became aware that Morgan and Eirian were both staring at her, wide-eyed. Morgan said faintly, 'Beth, did you see . . . or hear . . . what I think I did?'

'Oh, my God,' said Beth, starting to laugh. 'We thought there could only be one like Eirian? Hey, and I'm two days late. Now we know the Great Mother has a sense of humour. Oh, my God. Oh, well . . .'

'You should have gone out with me,' said Peter, 'not that flash American bastard. I would never have treated you like that.'

He and Eirian were sitting on her bed. She'd asked Peter to come round a few days later, so she could explain what had happened – and apologize, as she'd already apologized humbly to Lisa.

'I know, I behaved like a complete shit,' Eirian said quietly. 'I'm sorry, Pete. Can you forgive me?'

'Maybe,' he said. 'If you don't do it ever again.' But his brown eyes were shining and he looked thrilled. With his soft chestnut hair and sensitive face he was going to be very hand-some as he grew older.

They went on talking. It was growing dark but her parents showed no sign of coming upstairs to suggest Peter left. He and Eirian lay down side by side to talk. They moved closer and cuddled. Soon cuddling became an intimate exploration of each other's bodies.

Their love-making wasn't clumsy or brief this time; it was relaxed and sensual, at least until the mutual urgency of the climax. Peter made such an effort to hold back and please her, she couldn't help feeling tender towards him. How good it felt to be with someone kind, uncomplicated, transparent.

'I can't help being inexperienced,' he said afterwards, lying in her arms. 'You're the only person I've done it with, I don't want anyone else. Teach me. I can get better.'

'I know,' Eirian said, smiling. 'You already have.'

'I still love you. I always will.'

'Pete . . .' She breathed out slowly. 'I'm really fond of you, I want to see you, but I can't promise anything. When I go to university I'll meet other people and . . .'

'I don't care.' He looked hard into her eyes and she saw strength of character there that she hadn't given him credit for. Embryonic, but growing. 'You'll fall in love with me eventually, even if it takes ten years.'

Tired and satiated, Eirian fell asleep and entered the otherworld of visions. She was still on the bed but unaware of Peter's presence. The bed became the Hellstone, and it turned from granite to glass; a lens through which the Goddess displayed hidden worlds to Eirian, her warrior.

Eirian heard the throbbing of a primal drumbeat. A weird blue glow surrounded her and she felt her heart fluttering in excitement, her spirit rising, floating. Ictinike leaned over her. His long bronze body was naked, except for a fall of feathers at his loins. He had long wings trailing from his shoulders, feathers in his long black hair. His face was young, masculine and beautiful, his eyes two pale gold moons.

'You've come back to me,' she whispered, holding out her arms. 'Yes, I want you. But everything will be different now. You won't control me any more. You'll never frighten me or my family again. We are equals. Goddess and god.'

Yes. I am your lover, your guardian, as you are mine.

Ictinike leaned down and kissed her. A light kiss that lingered deliciously and faded. And oh . . . *oh Goddess* . . . it seemed that even Gabriel was part of him now, peacock eyes gleaming behind the gold. But that was as it should be. Ictinike had assimilated the part of Nathaniel-Gabriel that was capable of transformation; the part of his soul that had felt, after all, some secret tenderness for Eirian.

'We transformed each other,' she said out loud, talking to herself. 'I gave Ictinike healing and peace of mind, I taught him gentleness. He gives me passion and loyalty. For ever. Yes. We need each other, the perfect balance, Horned God and Goddess . . .'

'Eirian?' said Peter. 'You're talking in your sleep.'

She opened her eyes and found Peter watching her with a mixture of affection and bewilderment, as if wondering what on earth she really was.

'If you want me,' she said, 'I hope you don't mind sharing me.'